An
Explanation
of the
Birds

An Explanation of the Birds

ANTÓNIO LOBO ANTUNES

*Translated from the Portuguese
by Richard Zenith*

Grove Press
New York

Grove Press
841 Broadway
New York, NY 10003

Published simultaneously in Canada
Printed in the United States of America

The translator thanks the National Endowment for the Arts for
supporting the translation of this book.

Library of Congress Cataloging-in-Publication Data

Antunes, António Lobo, 1942–
[Explicação dos pássaros.   English]
An explanation of the birds / António Lobo Antunes ; translated
from the Portuguese by Richard Zenith. — 1st American ed.
p.   cm.
Translation of: Explicação dos pássaros.
ISBN 0-8021-1339-7
I. Title.
PQ9263.N77E9713   1991
889.3'42—dc20   91-4471
ISBN 0-8021-3420-3 (pbk.)

Manufactured in the United States of America
Designed by Irving Perkins Associates

First Paperback Edition

An
Explanation
of the
Birds

THURSDAY

ONE OF THESE DAYS I'll beach right here, devoured by fish like a dead whale," he told me on the street in front of the clinic while looking at the neighborhood's sad and faded buildings, the unlit neon signs like monograms on a napkin, the glittery remnants of season's greetings in the windows, and a single dog, this January morning, nosing through the remains of a demolished row house: dust, rubble, wood scraps, and soulless shards of tile. He'd walked from the road where the streetcars ran, smelling the crates of fruit outside the groceries with the foggy, voracious appetite of a sea gull, like when he was a kid on the way home from school and would sniff the acid aroma of the pharmacies or the scabby brown darkness of a tavern where a blind man, mug in hand, would glare at him with the intimidating eyes of

3

a politician on a poster, and he thought, One of these days it'll be me they bring to the clinic, they'll push the brass handle on the storm door ("Don't you bother, we'll get it for you") and make me wait in the lobby full of leather chairs with huge gold upholstery tacks (chairs for death vigils, I note), and a table with corkscrew legs, drapes as heavy as judicial eructations, with the invisible guests at my funeral murmuring gravely in the corners, while they consult in low tones with the dusty maids who probably use feather dusters to clean themselves each day, and pull packets of old letters from the drawers of their stomachs and sewing boxes from the closets of their bowels. The scrawny switchboard operator, squatting behind a counter like an owl in its hole, was drawing impassioned hearts on a pad of paper: she must have gone out to the movies a couple of times with the same nearsighted bookkeeper who lives in a rented room in a godforsaken neighborhood and is taking a correspondence course in English, spending every night bent over a notebook of cartoon figures (*my uncle, my dog*) next to an empty coffee cup. He stated his mother's name while the operator, her tongue hanging out, perfected an enormous heart, identical to the label on the metal polish his grandmother used to use: a battalion of gray-uniformed maids would rub vigorously at the door handles downstairs: "Keep your hands still, young man, or I'll tell your sisters." They smelled of blue-and-white soap, yellowed sugar, and day-old bread, and at night their servicemen cousins, with lanky farmer's or shepherd's fingers, would feel up their breasts at the gate to the yard.

"Third room on the right," the owl informed him, while sketching a cupid's arrow and smiling a languid postcard smile: the bookkeeper's ears must have been burning as he beheld a suddenly impossible sum. He walked through a kind of pantry where two nurses were cooing, their backs to a cupboard, like a couple of pigeons perched on an eave: one of them was eating a sweet roll, catching the crumbs with a cupped hand, and the sun from the window gave their starched overdresses the smooth whiteness of chalk. He crossed paths with a middle-aged man who was studying a flask of urine held at eye level as if it were a dead scorpion. The hospital odors of alcohol and fear and hope advanced and receded in the corridor as in a sleeping stretch of sea, littered with the floating debris of the patients' low groans, which were drowned out by the sorrowing sighs of their families: I don't want anyone to visit here when my time comes: I'll shoo them away with my eyebrows so that at least I won't have to see their disgustingly contrite amiability, their excessive solicitude, their eyes tinged yellow from fear of death. I'll lie here alone, my nose toward the ceiling, slowly emptying out myself: my name, where I was born, my age, my gray-haired children supplying information in the corridor.

"Hi Mom," he said, thinking, Holy Jesus how skinny you've gotten, when he saw the tendons in her neck, her pale forehead, the veins popping out of her arms, the sticky sweat on her nose, her green irises riveted in the pillow like the round heads of nails, peering at him. Her wedding band danced on its finger: Which one of us will take it out of here and place it in the porcelain dish overflowing with necklaces, earrings, and rings that sits on the dresser in your bedroom, below the mirror? I don't have a black tie for the funeral, just the gray knitted one from a Christmas way back, when I still wore a sport coat and took myself seriously, writing interminably boring essays that no one would read, bristling with high-flown concepts, confused theories, absurd approximations. The editor's invisible finger touched him on the arm:

"We might be able to use a little something from these studies of yours."

"How are you feeling?" he asked in a defeated voice, staring at his mother and thinking, Now the tears are on the other side of your eyes, falling in your head and down your throat, burning like stiff brandy.

"Doesn't she look better?" someone at his left suddenly asked, and he saw, seated in the only chair in the room, jammed between the bed and the window, a distant cousin with a book open in her lap: I'll bet you're the only one in the family who's willing to keep a dying person company. The ugly faded buildings of northwest Lisbon filled the window: Will you still be around when my time comes?

"She has more color," I corroborated, "her cheeks look fuller." And to myself, ashamed: Forgive me, Mother. When I was little and I got the flu you'd bring Dad's old Philips radio to my room, and in the torpor induced by my fever I'd listen to the record request shows: Hit Parade of the Century, When the Telephone Rings, Listeners' Choice. He thinks, How brown your hair was, how decisive your gestures. You would never let any harm come to us.

"The boys?" asked my mother from the infinite distance of six feet. There were rusty oxygen bottles on the headboard, an inhaler next to the sink, and a bunch of flowers in a cut-glass vase centered on a doily.

"They're fine, Mother, just fine."

"Whenever I pick them up from school, they ask about you." And he was sure that his mother had perceived the pause, the hesitation, the lie. They would scramble into the car like puppies, pushing at each other to be the first to kiss him. The school secretary smiled at them with her chubby mole cheeks while a tall redhead in the boutique next door tapped a thin bottle of perfume with long red fingernails: My God what a hard-on you give me.

"Where do you want to eat lunch?"

"At The Red Pony."

"At the café."

But the redhead came to the door and immediately his tenderness was dissolved by his animal desire for that porcelain face, for the tight skirt that imprisoned the fan of thick

6

flesh between her legs. Across the years the schoolmate that had sat next to him whispered:

"That's what they want, Rui—you grab on to the mattress, grit your teeth, and it's back and forth, back and forth, got it?, until the pictures on the wall start tilting."

"They must be huge by now," affirmed his cousin from the depths of her chair as she pulled a piece of knitting from a plastic bag. His mother's breathing became a strained, barely audible whistle. Her bony bluish fingers wandered over the blanket with an arachnid's slow gait.

"This afternoon I'm going to Tomar, Mother, for the conference. I'll be back on Sunday around dinnertime. Now don't go falling in love with that sly doctor from India while I'm gone—I don't want any sacred cows in the family."

That was about as funny as a piece of pink shit—you can't even tell a decent joke, he reproached himself. Your humor's as heavy as the drops of lead in the bathtubs of insomnia, as corny as stories from grade B magazines: I've got to go through my old joke books. The distant cousin carefully positioned the balls of yarn on her lap:

"Indian people are so gentle and friendly. Did you notice his mustache, Fernanda?"

"An elevated number of pulmonary metastases," the doctor announced, "and a monstrous hemorrhage in the pleura." (It sounded as if he were referring to the tonsillitis of an Eskimo that none of them knew.) "You should prepare yourselves for the worst."

He held up X rays, produced analyses, and furnished grandiose explanations. The perfection of the knot in his necktie pisses me off no end: I'd like to crumple his shirt and take care of his collar with a good swift yank: my mother's dying and this fucker couldn't care less.

From out of the pillow the green eyes stared at me mercilessly:

"Has your manual been published?" she managed to wheeze out.

A cart loaded with bandages jolted along in the hallway, so that the chrome-lidded jars full of the soft silence of gauze rattled like milk bottles. From the next room came a rhythmic moaning, a kind of rippled grunt, a woman's rising and falling protest: "Cover my mouth or else I'll scream." He answered crossly:

"Not yet, Mother, there are all kinds of problems at the printers, the galleys were a mess," thinking, The cynical critics, irritated at their own impotence, will do everything they can to screw me with the minuscule, dry, anonymous, photoless reviews they write for the afternoon tabloids. When I start doddering they'll consider me a trailblazer, they'll interview me, write dissertations about me, and insert me in their boring graveyard anthologies. He took a step forward and patted his mother's hand: porous, bloodless, light and hard like the hollow roots of grapevines.

"People no longer care about history or poetry," sighed the cousin from behind her knitting needles, busily producing a horrid sweater with a motley diamond pattern that no one would ever wear ("Thanks a million but I don't need one right now, I'll bet Francisco would adore it"). "All they want to read is cheap novels full of scandal, profanity, and sex—the more the better."

The smell of hospitals, he thought, makes my head spin. I get a weird pain all over: when they operated on my back I saw my own pus in a pail and felt like puking out my guts right then and there, face down on the table. While they poked around in his mother's body, the surgeon talked to his assistant, and he noticed that their boots were made of the same material as the donkey suit worn by two circus performers. A girl with a sequined skirt and a parasol was balancing on a high wire, lit by a purple-and-yellow spotlight. In the empty aisles, the tall red-mouthed clown tried out the saxophone.

"Where's Dad?" he asked, and for a long time the words hung before his lips like the notes of a scale.

The progenitor, in tails, with penciled eyelashes, walked up to the microphone gesturing like a master of ceremonies. A bluish cone of light followed him:

"No introduction is necessary," he announced through the static on the loudspeaker while smoothing the remaining hairs over his baldness: "He's a Portuguese performer!"

"Lots of work at the office," his mother explained. "He should be here soon."

"His secretary's already phoned three times," clarified the cousin. "She sent those flowers wrapped in cellophane with a pink ribbon."

The cut-glass vase loomed suddenly larger: his father pulled back a fraying curtain, and he and his sisters, dressed as Tartars, ran out in a whirl of leaps and somersaults.

"Shut up," his father ordered, "I'm trying to read the paper."

Your stern baldness and tight face, the smell of cologne and American tobacco in your clothes, and, later on, the periodic business trips that took me years to understand: Mom locked in her room, lying in bed ("It's just a headache, go ahead and eat, I'll be right there"), her visits to the psychiatrist, yoga classes, health food, card parties, gymnastics. And my mute eyes looking at you from behind, asking, Why don't you come home earlier?

"Maybe he'll show up soon," his mother sighed, "always maybe, wherever he goes."

The sickness had rounded the edges of her voice, making it sweet and soft, delicate like a seashell's chanting: Mozart, *la mer ou l'echo de vos rêves:* an ad for some brand or another of French record players, seen in a magazine at the dentist's. He stepped over to the window and looked out: an aproned woman was plucking a chicken in the street (the animal's head, hanging down, swung to the rhythmless rhythm of her plucks) while two dogs, planted on their hind legs, watched from a distance with controlled craving. The buildings drifted aimless and ugly in the fog: shitty city, why don't I cut out while there's still time?

"Lunchtime!" sang a cheerful creature with metal tray in hand: chicken soup, boiled fish with turnip greens, a pear, and a glass of water protected by an upside-down saucer. His sisters disappeared in a backward somersault and his father tested the microphone with a fingernail:

"Food for sick people," he proclaimed to an audience of distant cousins knitting in a semicircle of wooden stands. "Careful, Fernanda, I wouldn't try it if I were you. Ladies and gentlemen, we ask that you maintain strict silence during this dangerous meal."

The cheerful creature began cranking up the head of the bed, like the blue-uniformed stagehands that stretch out the trampoline for the jumping act. The starched bow of her apron bounced stiffly on her bottom like the wings of a trapped butterfly.

"Now who's going to be a good patient and gobble up her whole lunch?" she asked in the obnoxiously animated voice of a kindergarten teacher. "Nice hot soup, a yummy piece of fish, a sugar-sweet pear, a capsule to start with, and a pill for afterward—you're all set, aren't you?"

"Alley-oop," his father yelled with a triumphant flourish of the hand.

"Your sisters called too," his mother said while carefully removing the pale white, comma-shaped fish bones. "What with all the people who've promised to visit tonight, the room's going to look like an association hall on New Year's Eve. It'll be just grand."

An orchestra of feeble relatives wearing silver-striped jackets played a slow bolero next to the washbasin, with the impassive or mildly bored air of bar musicians. By the dim light of the bedside lamp, whose fluted shade was dotted with stains, the nurses and doctors and dour uncles talked in low voices and ate croquettes off toothpick spears, their pale, moonlike faces floating in and out of view. The Indian doctor and the knitting cousin danced with a timid caution worthy of termites when the dining room table's taken away for a gloomy evening of sad cellos.

"Shut up," his father repeated, "I'm trying to read the paper."

His mother smiled unexpectedly: childhood slowly slid across her mouth, like water over a slanting board:

"Don't worry," she said, "they take good care of me here."

He'd leave the house carrying a suitcase covered with foreign hotel stickers and you'd be left by yourself—a diminutive figure on the edge of an enormous bed—reading thick and incomprehensible books in English, novels, war stories, a man and woman unabashedly kissing on the cover. He'd come back after three or four days with a suntan and the vestige of a strange light in his alienated eyes. I'd watch him shave in the morning, fascinated by the flashing razor. He'd be wearing only his pajama bottoms, he used Azevichex, the Hair Cream for Successful Men, and he'd tilt his head back to gargle in earnest against cavities, bad breath, and periodontal disease: when I grow up I'm going to order everyone to shut up so I can read the paper. The dogs outside the clinic were sniffing in the fog at the chicken feathers, some spilled blood, and a mound of repulsive, gelatinous poultry guts. My mother would mark her place in the book with a streetcar ticket and turn off the light, and I was certain that her eyes stayed open in the darkness, brilliant and unmoving like the dead eyes of portraits. A phone began to whine on the small table next to him.

"Hello," answered the cousin, grabbing the receiver like an elephant its bunch of carrots. "Yes. That's right. No, she had a pretty good night, the doctor will be by in a while to visit her. I'll let you know if there's any change."

His father, his father's vague guilt, his father's forever

11

preoccupied mind, the girlfriend of whom he knew nothing but her voice, rough and raspy, as if an alcohol burner were in permanent contact with her throat. Once a month his father took him to a restaurant near his office, and they had lunch together with hardly a word, eating in an oppressive silence that could be touched, and that grew. His bald head leaning over his plate shined like a coffeepot. His elastic cheeks puffed in and out as he chewed, and I'd remember the faraway days of my childhood when we went to the farm (the shifting shadow of trees on the ground, the dry smell of leaves, and the soil) and a younger man, slim and happy, whose laughs rolled across the afternoon calm, would trot toward the house with me riding piggyback. He thinks, Let's roll the film backward and take it from the top.

The cousin covers the receiver with her hand:

"Do you want to talk to your husband?"

The fish knife trembles without answering. I grab the phone:

"Hi Dad."

The syllables arrive from the other end with the distinct precision of stiletto-engraved landscapes on sheets of bronze:

"How is she?"

The young man, slim and happy, gave way to an aging and overweight individual who constantly patted what hair he had left against his temples:

"She's better, Dad, don't worry."

Perched on your shoulders I almost touched the chestnut branches with my head, wrapped in light like one of the saints, and the eternity of a photograph immobilized the smile that today, years later, stares out from my bedroom mirror, mocking me with its bitter frown: how I've grown, my God, how my hair too has begun falling out: I try to figure out my father's age at that time (were you younger than I am today?), but my equations are scrambled by the voice that comes through the plastic pinholes:

12

"I hear you're going out of town for a few days."

He could distinguish the sound of the office typewriters, employees bent over desks, the secretary's deodorant transforming the cubicles, walls, and hallways into a gigantic warm and depilated armpit: so did you already pork her, Dad?

"What?" his father asks.

"Nothing. I was saying that I'm leaving for Tomar right away. One of those conferences on the nineteenth century."

My sister told me that you have another house with other children, other paintings, another television, another backgammon table, another jar of Azevichex Hair Cream for Successful Men, another newspaper. "Writing's a waste of time," you'd said, "except for those who win Nobel Prizes: I'd go for a degree if I were you."

The voice of the bald individual hesitated before answering:

"Jesus, it's impossible to hear anything over these phones."

"I said I'm leaving right away for Tomar."

"Hmmm," his father grunted skeptically.

And he imagined the dark eyes behind his father's glasses, seeing but not believing: I had to lie to you, I always had to lie, because you couldn't accept that I wasn't like you, that I scribbled verses, that I preferred to be a teacher earning slave wages at a school way the hell out of town instead of wearing a suit and tie and working for your company like everybody else in the family. Sometimes it consoled me to imagine that the young and happy man who played with me at the farm would have understood: we'd go to the stone wall with the broken bottles on top and gaze in fascination at the neighbor's monkey on a leash attached to its shelter, at the fig tree stretching across the well, and at the lavender tranquillity of late afternoon, reaching way beyond our family's garden statues and faded canvas chairs scattered around the yard. Wild peacocks raised anguished cries in the distance.

"They're afraid of the night," his father explained, "they're afraid they might dream."

13

He thinks, The man who carried me piggyback might have understood; of course he'd have understood: anyone who knows peacocks would understand a poet, even a bad one, from a mile away. He thinks, Christ there's so much I'd like to say and can't. He thinks, To be born without guts is one hell of a handicap.

"When are you getting back?" his father asks as if twisting a needle in an infected wound.

"I think on Sunday," he answers.

And he changes his answer—hating himself for it (See how afraid I am of you? I'd never be able to direct a firm)—into a categorical assertion:

"Definitely on Sunday."

Sunday was synonymous with nothing to do, the playroom in a mess, his bored body dragging itself along the wall. His mother playing cards in the living room with her girlfriends, bracelets jangling, earrings glinting, lipsticked mouths chattering like parakeets about children, maids, and their husbands' jobs. Mom. And now she was dying in the autumn of Lisbon, in a hospital room, facing a trayful of fish bones, which the cousin finally set next to the vase of flowers before sinking back into her knitting, oblivious.

"Leave your phone number just in case," his father orders. "You never know, we might suddenly need to get a hold of you."

The cardplaying friends erupt in a chorus of laughter, tilting back in the red velvet chairs: a group of white faces, he thinks, around the cadaver of the short clown, whose enormous shoes—comic and pathetic—point toward the tattered circus tent. A donkey formed by two uncles canters around the ring, braying and shaking its bright pink mane. The farm manager, wearing a phony mustache and a plastic tiger skin, shows off the ballpoint-etched tattoo on his right arm, and while the crowd roars with thundering applause, he lifts the bed with his dying mother, thin and light as an autumn sparrow.

"Of course, Dad," he promises. "I'll leave it with the receptionist."

His father hangs up without a word, and he stands there holding a mute phone, like a seashell without a sea. The impatient voice of the switchboard operator asks, "Did you want to make a call?" and he stares at the receiver in surprise, startled by the talking cricket inside it that asks questions with such bossiness: the bookkeeper, if she manages to catch him, is going to have to put up with an awful lot.

"No thanks, I'm all through," he stammers quickly, setting down the receiver (*cling* sings a wilted bell) and again looking in the mirror at his aging face, eyeglasses, thinning hair that's chronically oily no matter how much he shampoos, the young wrinkles furrowing their way into his thirty-year-old cheeks and forehead: in a couple more years I can hang it up. He thinks of old men in bathing suits at the beach, each with flaccid tits and a sagging gut, propped on a skinny pair of hairless legs, trotting toward the water in arthritic glee; he thinks of old men who go to expensive restaurants, escorted by young girls to whom they whisper sweet nothings over the sirloin; he thinks of the blonde he saw last month driving his father's car as if she owned it and how his outraged blood started pounding in his temples: he's set her up in a nice apartment and here I am with two rooms in a run-down neighborhood, four tenants per floor, the garbage cans forever tipped over out front, stray dogs, Gypsies, mud, ugly clothes hanging from the windows and making the mornings sad, books and newspapers everywhere, grimy ashtrays, the smell of fried food in the kitchen: fuck. He sits on his mother's bed and caresses her foot through the sheet, her thin bones, her toes, her protruding ankles. Mom. The patient's eyes, blurred by a kind of inner fog, observe him from near and far simultaneously, like the caged animals at the zoo. Dabs of pinkish foam swell and subside at the corners of her mouth. He thinks, How distant the afternoons of canasta, how unex-

15

pectedly shrunken your face, how fragile and thin your trembling neck.

"I'm going now, Mother."

We never had time for one another, did we? And now it's too late, stupidly late, so we look at each other absently, as strangers, full of superfluous hands without pockets to moor them, searching in our empty heads for the words of tenderness that we never learned, for the signs of affection that embarrass us, for the closeness that frightens us. A truck completely filled the hospital room window in the decrepit morning, and the driver's face, neutral and impervious, practically pressed against the yellowed curtains, against the mirrors' glassy skin, against the impersonal off-white furniture, against the buzzer hanging above the bed in a braided despair. The blonde he'd seen driving his father's car crossed high above the ring with rod in hand, balancing on a taut wire: "Watch out, Dolores, I wouldn't try it if I were you." Small clouds of chalk rained down after each pirouette of her golden slippers.

"See you on Sunday, Mom," he said, and thought, It's never today, it's always next Sunday, next Friday, next Tuesday, next month, next year, and we scrupulously avoid facing each other, because we're all afraid, afraid of what we feel, afraid of saying I love you. The truck vanished, replaced by the same depressing scene as before: the chipped facades of melancholy buildings, the dreary balconies, the sky's swollen pallor, the flapping sign of a barbershop, Gomes's Salon. The cousin followed him out to the corridor.

"The doctor gives her a week at the most."

"The heart attack affected the entire organ," the Indian specialist in the center of the ring announced to the family clapping and whistling in the stands.

He extracted a bleeding, roundish mass from his pocket and held it up, turning it around for all to see.

"Would the distinguished audience please be so kind as to observe."

The donkey suit with the two uncles scampered in to sniff the heart, but the doctor kicked them away with his gigantic hobo shoes. His short, baggy trousers left his red-striped socks completely exposed. Enormously long fake hairs poked out of his legs. The ambulance man who'd brought his mother to the clinic hawked balloons in the stands. A nurse charged past brandishing a syringe, so that he and his cousin had to dart to one side of the dark hallway, flattening their palms against the wall. Splotches of pale sunlight danced here and there on the ceiling.

"One week at the most," repeated the cousin. "See how she's wasting away by the minute?"

"This heart's no good," the Indian yelled like a swindler at a fair during a lull in the audience's laughter over the donkey, which lay on its back and kicked the air. "Do you want to see what a good heart looks like? Then take a look at mine, ladies and gentlemen."

From under his shirt he pulled out a crumpled felt ball that expanded and contracted, expanded and contracted, powered by some mechanism or other. "If any of the distinguished members of the audience would like to touch it, then feel free to enter the ring." And at that moment, a figure dressed in burlap stumbled out from behind a curtain, snatched the ball, and skipped away on his scrawny legs, vanishing through a small door.

Death, he thought. I'd always pictured it as an angel. Or a blond-haired woman. Or an ancient man with a scythe.

"I'll leave the phone number with the receptionist in case anything comes up," he said to his cousin, who looked at him with speckled orbs, harsh and tarnished. "I have to reach Tomar by lunchtime." He pressed his ear against the door-jamb and heard nothing: she's probably fallen into a fright-

17

ened sleep, light like a squirrel's, surrounded by worthless magazines for patients. A week at the most. The walls of the corridor glared at him: Get out of here! "Dr. Oliveira Nunes, Dr. Oliveira Nunes," called a voice behind him. In the pantry area, the nurse with the sweet roll was now seated on a revolving stool, painting her nails and blowing through pursed lips on the ones that were done.

A maid dressed in brown was bent over a buffer, pushing it like a hand mower: how stupid to die in the morning, during coffee with milk and the somnolent tidying up of the house, when the universe is reduced to the innocuous size of an empty coffee cup, how awful to stop breathing before the twelve o'clock whistle, time's Cape of Good Hope, when people shake their rugs from the balconies and the street vendors weigh fish and fruit with broad gestures of spectacular honesty in Lisbon's damp autumn. He left a note ("This is where I'll be should you need to get in touch") with the skinny switchboard operator, pushed open the storm door, whose hinges creaked like a stiff knee, and walked out onto the gray street under a zinc-gray sky. In the barbershop the flashing metal was multiplied in the mirrors, as scissors flew across heads while opening and closing their long sharp beaks. He tried to spot his mother's window and found a row of identical sills, peeling paint, slanting blinds, pigeonless rooftops, and a black chimney that coughed: I hope she can at least die at home, in the big double bed I loved to lie in when I had the flu as a kid, trying to make my small body coincide with the cavity left by my father's, while you stood next to the dresser, adding up numbers in a black notebook. From time to time the embers in the fireplace would shudder, emitting orangish vibrations. The pictures in the living room, framed in carved wood, depicted landscapes, river bends, trees, and churches in the distance. You've come a long way from the green cloth of the canasta table, from the porcelain dogs and the round portraits of your children hung from a kind of tree made of silver, a long way from the maids, the basset hounds, and the painting of St. John the Baptist in the dining room. The nurse who'd been eating the sweet roll was blowing on her nails while leaning against the desk in his father's office. The nauseating smell of medicine was contaminating the food. Slowly he began to climb the hill toward the road with the streetcars: I parked illegally, half on the sidewalk, I hope to God I didn't get ticketed. The morning's sadness trickled down the faces and clothes of pedestrians, the traffic glided noiselessly at his side like a huge, soft, segmented animal: first to the apartment to pick up Marilia and then the endless highway to Tomar, bumper-to-bumper trucks, buses, motorcycles, and crossing dogs: two or three hours in the car with her, what on earth will I talk about? "I'm taking you with me to Tomar to tell you I don't like you anymore." They always imagine there's another woman: "There's absolutely no one else, I want to be on my own for a few months, think things over, then we'll see, try to understand." And her hard, unmoving, rigid profile reproaching me in silence for four years of frustrated hopes: so easy to begin and so hard to end. And then the long, drawn-out phone calls, the accusations, the pleas, the shouting, and, of course, the eternal prophetic blackmail: "It's not your fault if anything happens to me." He reached the top of the hill, where there was a newsstand manned by a filthy creature on crutches whose shirt advertised a soccer team, whose left hand had no fingers and whose one-legged hopping made him look like a lame grasshopper. A dignified gentleman was leafing through one of the stand's porno magazines, lingering over the centerfold color shot, and he remembered his sisters, serious and well-married knitters, following their mother's pattern (same kind of friends, same interests, card games, holidays in the Algarve, children): he peered over the dignified man's shoulder, Jesus, what a huge pair of tits, and then he thought, Wonder what they're like in bed with their husbands. Probably they just wait in resignation as the hubbies take off

19

their watches, empty their pockets, slowly undress, fold their slacks along the crease, lay the slacks over the chair, stretch out on their backs, and fret about the firm's financial woes: at least I always know when you want to make love, Marilia, I feel your heavy breathing on my neck, I sense your body's anxiety in my blood, I see the liquid agony of your eyes, "Turn off the light": hazy forms that get all jumbled up in the blue darkness, a waving arm, an elbow, the trembling of your feet, I'm in you like a Parker in its case, "Now now faster faster do it that's it come now come with me God that was good." He thinks, But is that enough? He thinks, After classes I never feel like going home, climbing the stairs, turning the key in the door, standing on the threshold of the kitchen watching you stir something in a pot, "Hi, honey," same old furniture, same old knickknacks, the television turned on with the sound off, and some asshole with sea bass eyes silently haranguing inside it. Should I call it quits or should I stay, what should I do, where would I go, will I be happier by myself, can I ever be happy with this constant gnawing that goes on inside, this kind of cardiac colitis, this visceral anguish? I turn up the volume, Portugal's joining the Common Market, I turn it back down, the book spines annoy me, the buffet annoys me, the cloth dolls annoy me, the oversoft sofa annoys me. I go to the window to peek at the serenity outside, the still cars under the streetlights, the lunar skin of the buildings opposite. How do others manage to swallow the pill, do the couples I know really feel satisfied, are they able to brush their teeth every morning on the strength of a hope—what are we supposed to do when there's nothing left to learn, discover, or invent. "We had four wonderful years, but I'm sorry, I think it's time we split up," and your face, pot still in hand, mouth wide open with shock, then wrinkled with doubt and disbelief. "You must have been drinking," she says, "I didn't touch a drop," I say. "At any rate let's discuss it later because I'm not in the mood right now," she says. "I'm being perfectly serious," I say, my voice trembling, "You're a serious asshole," she yells from the kitchen while adjusting the flame on the stove, and the wall tiles amplify her words, shattering them into a thousand sharp pieces and recomposing them in an intricate mosaic of rage. I plop down on the sofa and think, How dismal this living room is, how depressing the reproduction from Picasso's pink period, how ugly your small writing desk. The dignified gentleman folds shut the magazine and sets it back on the newsstand counter, behind which an eight- or nine-year-old girl is chewing on a ham sandwich while sizing me up with her gigantic pupils, dark and unmoving. He thinks, It's going to rain, the humidity in the air is a sure sign of rain, the buildings in Lisbon will become even more faded, even more pallid, even uglier, older, and sadder. He finds the car (Thank God, no ticket) between a motorcycle and a green-windowed American sedan from the fifties with a little man wearing a hat inside—I'll bet he has a bracelet, a chain, five rings on his fingers, and a photograph of his wife and two kids—"Think Of Us"—on the dashboard, I'll bet he's waiting for his lover who's getting her hair peroxided at the beauty parlor two blocks up on the left. The little man with the hat was busy adjusting the knobs on the car radio, a muffled gush of music, static, and distorted voices emerged from inside. You opened the door on the driver's side and sat down behind the wheel, What a fucking uncomfortable seat, and now to the apartment to pick up Marília, the suitcases, your complete lack of desire to have her along, the hotel in Tomar, the new and old faces, the hassle of arriving, the revolting five-and-a-half-foot length at your side, leaning against the sleeping rock of your kidneys. He went down the steep part of Carvalhão Street with his foot on the brake (Something's wrong with this jalopy, one of these days I'll ram right into a wall and be through with all this crap, all my insecurities, my classes, my essays, the sneering of the bastard critics), turned at a neon sign just after the police station, where a toylike soldier

21

guarded the entrance with a machine gun, and headed toward Azedo Gneco Street through a monotonous geometry of roads with five-and-ten stores and old dairies reeking of musty receipt books and moldy cheese. Some kids were playing ball on the asphalt in front of his building. An elderly woman with a church missal and an overweight dog went into the bakery for her eucharistic crisp toast. The sky was clearing on the other side of the river, behind clouds of soot: the turds of Barreiro's smokestacks, he thought, Hooray for industrial Portugal. From a certain friend's house one could see all the way to the wharf and the warehouses on the opposite shore, and in the evening, while the others were discussing literature, politics, and music, awash in cheap brandy and nauseating French cigarettes without filters, I'd lean over the windowsill and look at the slate-colored sky: that was the first year we lived together and I lusted so much after your body that I'd stand still in the living room just to look at you, dazed by your gestures, your smile, the slight curve of your shoulders. I must have written your name a million times with my index finger on the windows of that winter, and the letters would drip down the panes as if slowly crying a long-legged species of tears. He turned off the motor and thought, This neighborhood's in my bones for good, I doubt I'd be able to live away from these dreary blocks, from this sad prison of unequally identical façades, built on the modest scale of a scene portraying melancholy resignation. His father, dressed up as a tour guide, beard unshaven and shoes unpolished, pointed to the apartment with a hurried finger, with a craning cluster of myopically smiling Japanese following his gesture:

"He lived here for four years before separating from his second wife at age thirty-three. There were no children and no scenes. The neighbors weren't aware of any change, and the concierge only found out a week later. The woman took the clothes she was wearing and a toothbrush, rented an apartment in São Sebastião, and quit teaching. She apparently intends to immigrate to Angola—Communism made her brain go soft."

"That was quick," remarked Marilia. There was an open suitcase on top of the bed (The same one you had when I first met you, how little things change), and her torso disappeared into the clothes closet on whose mirrored door hung ties and belts I never used: only flannel shirts, jeans, and a fur-lined jacket, the uniform of the Left: my father's rich, which gives more weight to my proletarian option. A light, sweet smell wafted out of the drawers, because your perfume permeates everything, even your absence when I remember you. Sometimes I'll be talking to a student, and the smell hits me so strongly that I look for your hand on my arm or I glance around but you're not there, I can't find you, and then, little by little, you begin to draw away from inside me and I stop stumbling into your perfume, I stop remembering your wrinkles while I'm working, I stop missing you while eating alone in the cafeteria. My mother began dealing out the canasta cards, turned her head to me, and said:

"We've never approved of your relationship with her."

"So how is she?" Marilia asked while straightening out a pile of shirts. "I didn't expect you back so soon."

My mother refused to meet you and you replied with a haughty frown, "I don't need those fucking fascists." But when I'd go there for Christmas and birthdays you'd let out with wisecracks as soon as I got back: "You're nothing but a bourgeois ding-a-ling, a disgusting conservative, I'm going to complain to the Party." One night you locked yourself in the bathroom crying, I spied through the keyhole and saw you wiping your swollen eyelids with toilet paper: I felt so much like hugging you, I love you, I love you, I love you, like making love right then and there, standing on the tile floor, talking to you about why life had to be so complex.

"The clinic says she's only got a week," he answered. "Of course, a week for a doctor is maybe three days."

"I never thought it would end this way," swore his mother while serving her friends tea from Grandma's silver pot. "I imagined something less unpleasant, more civilized, something different, where I wouldn't be subjected to these repulsive nurses with dirty fingernails and this black doctor who could pass for Mahalia Jackson's husband."

"All he needs is a top hat," snickered my oldest sister. "All together now, let's sing a spiritual."

"Grab the sweaters you want out of the drawer," says Marilia. "Me and your sweaters have never understood each other—I always manage to pick out the ones you don't feel like wearing."

"She had absolutely no sense of color," charges the cousin from the clinic while dressing his deceased mother, like a giant cloth doll, in a black-and-lettuce-colored skirt. "Poor thing, her father was a national guardsman, bad taste must have run in the family."

The first things I noticed at your parents' house (it seemed like we had to take the bus to the end of the world) were the brightly colored walls and the profusion of doilies, glass fairies, and bronze Sancho Panzas instead of books, and the ratty little yard that the cats clawed like a blanket. I felt completely out of place, Marilia, sitting in that chair covered with a crocheted slipcover and talking to your father over a glass of port wine, while you and your mother set the table: a lace tablecloth, shiny utensils, small dishes with almonds and bonbons. The national guardsman's huge hands fumbled nervously with his shirt buttons. "Dinner's on": soup, a roast, instant pudding that shook like a laughing double chin, your little brother looking at me suspiciously out of the corner of his eye, the cast-iron porch light as we were leaving, "Good night, thanks very much," again the bus, now empty and heading back toward town, and below us the still and silent river, dotted with the lights of boats like eyes.

"We're going to get to Tomar awfully late," he said. So on

Sundays I'd go to her parents' house, they were simple people, no pretensions, nice enough to me, we studied together on the stone steps of the dinky backyard. You'd be wearing a floral-patterned dress that hugged your thighs, we could see your mother through the frosted panes of the kitchen door wrestling with the frying pans beneath the round electric clock whose noiseless hands hastened on twilight, your father would appear in the window wearing slippers and a robe, "Are you eggheads coming in or not?" He'd been a streetcar switchman in his youth, his own father had worked the land, and now his important daughter was getting her doctorate, teaching rich kids at the university, and helping out with the household expenses, she'd open her wallet, and "Here, take this." And yet, he thought, you were unmistakably from their stock, I never came across feet as big as yours, with skin all cracked and wide, flat toenails: feet like a water bird's at the other end of the mattress, or like kicking spurs if I was on top of you, "Go on love that's right love go go what soft skin you have, what a beautiful cock."

"Get your shaving gear and we're all set," Marilia said.

"Marriage between people of different social classes is a guaranteed fiasco," pronounced his sister while cleaning her youngest boy's mouth with a Mickey Mouse bib.

Yes but five years ago I was a starry-eyed idealist, a bit ingenuous, I'd come out of my marriage to Tucha feeling pretty badly burned, and I grabbed on to the Revolution, he thought in the bathroom as he dumped objects into a plastic bag: razor, shaving cream, toothbrush, the comb with a cavity that I've had for God knows how long, the shampoo that at least makes my bald spot shine. His face, worried and serious, loomed in the mirror. His godmother, dressed like women whose poodles go to obedience school, gravely shakes her long earrings and directs the audience's attention to a velvet-framed picture:

"Believe it or not he was a beautiful baby."

25

Her husband, wearing evening clothes, appeared behind her and squeezed a rubber bulb inside his plaid trousers, making two jets of water gush from his eyes:

"Who could have guessed he'd commit suicide like that?"

The face in the mirror forced a smile as wilted as a dried flower. He ran discouraged fingers through his incipient baldness. He thinks, Start fresh at age thirty-three and do what? He had a friend who'd said he could sleep on the couch ("Sorry, but what with the kids that's the best we can offer") for a few weeks, and then what? His students, rented rooms, an occasional movie, emptiness.

"There's always hope," yelled his father, dressed in tails and a derby hat, pulling a stream of coins from the noses of the children in the first row.

"Are we leaving today or next year?" asked Marilia from the bedroom.

He thinks, You don't have the slightest inkling of what's in store for you. Or maybe you won't care, people are so unpredictable. When Tucha told me that she wanted to split up, we were in the living room holding hands and watching a play on TV, a bearded old man opened his mouth to recite his line but instead of his voice I heard yours, peaceful, polite, and smooth: "I'd like you to move out by the end of the month."

In the mirror his features bulged from terror, then calmed: don't be so bourgeois, maybe the divorce will give you time to write the paper on Sidonio Pais that you've been planning for ages.

"I feel nothing for you except maybe friendship," Tucha says, "and when you feel nothing, psshhhhhh."

She dropped his hand and lit a cigarette.

He thinks, And now what?

"The boy's problem," his smiling mother says while marking the score on a pad, "is that he never learned how to get girls to like him."

26

He got up to turn off the TV (the image shrank and shrank until it was a luminous point that vanished into the screen) and began to pace back and forth between the sofa and the buffet. He thinks, I can't understand it, I'll never be able to understand it, you don't just tell someone after all this time to go to hell, you're treating me like dirt, like a piece of shit you sweep out of the house. He felt a huge hatred welling up inside, You're crazy if you think I'll let you take the kids. He thinks, You little bitch, I'll bet you've been plotting this with your friends for months, whispering, hinting, phoning up some lawyer friend to get advice for this conspiracy of busybody women, because you'd never have the guts to do it on your own. With his forearm he swept all the objects off an Empire buffet, sending framed photos and dishes crashing to the floor:

"What the fuck is this all about?" he demanded.

He closed the plastic bag and returned to the bedroom. Marilia was sitting on the bed. She'd already closed the suitcase and was watching the rosary of bubbles emanating from the glass tube in the aquarium, where a translucent fish was quivering like a leaf.

"It must have a fever," she said.

"That fish has always looked to me like it has sinus trouble," he said while jamming the plastic bag into the suitcase. "Toss a tetracycline capsule in the water every six hours."

The elevator—the kind with folding metal doors—arrived teetering like a skiff. At the bottom of the vertical chrome plate of black buttons there was a red one marked *Alarm*: whenever he entered that precarious diving bell he always felt a mad urge to press it and hear what he imagined would be the terrifying sound of a fire truck siren, enough to bury the whole building under the debris of its howls. The fat, disheveled concierge would emerge from her cubicle, armed with the aggressive broom reserved for special occasions. He dragged the luggage into the elevator, closed the doors, and pressed for the ground floor: the coffin jolted their squeezed bodies down to the street.

"Did you fill up the tank?" she asked.

"Don't make ridiculous scenes," Tucha said while emptying an ashtray into the trash. "And don't go smashing up the furniture, I don't think the neighbors would appreciate it."

"With the way you act, what did you expect?" asked his youngest sister, wearing a turban and puffy pants as she walked barefoot on a mat of broken glass. A nephew, his navel exposed, played the drum.

His mother moved her pale white wrists over the hospital bed sheet:

"Poor boy," she murmured, "he never had any direction in life."

"Yes, I filled it up," he informed her, irritated, "and I checked the tires, the oil, and the water in the battery, I had the wheels aligned and balanced, and I got on the radio to ask every motorist in the country to do likewise. Now if your highness would grant me the pleasure of your company, then we might just arrive intact." He thinks, Why do I get so upset, why the fuck do I get upset with people over such piddly crap? Without any warning or control this wave of fury rises up in me, my testicles swell, gases churn around in my intestines, a strange tingling begins in my fingers, and for no reason at all I start shouting.

"All bark and no bite," says Tucha, as if distorted by one of those wavy carnival mirrors, her voice mixed in with cries and laughter. "If you don't leave, then I'm leaving," she calmly adds while rolling a joint. Her shapely legs are crossed in their usual position, and her drooping eyelids cast half-moon shadows on her cheeks. He thinks, You're so beautiful. He thinks, What are my parents going to say about all this?

He slammed shut the car trunk (it was always hard to get the key in, you'd think there was some kind of resistance that

28

was fighting to the death from inside), and the façades of Azedo Gneco Street, gray beneath the gray sky, looked utterly neutral, blind, uninhabited. Middle-aged housewives scurried along the sidewalks dragging grocery-filled rickshaws, which bounced up and down over the uneven stones. An old and unshaven, staggering-drunk Gypsy tried in vain to climb into his decrepit mule-drawn cart. He thinks, This is life? Tucha remarried (A guy with glasses, kind of dorky, what in God's name did she see in him?), he saw his kids every other weekend, he'd ring the bell downstairs and then wait, his hand gripping his cigarette lighter nervously, and suddenly the two boys were hugging his legs, "Hi Dad, can we go to the zoo, Dad, can we go to the circus, Dad?" and that excruciatingly sad, almost liquid look in the giraffes' eyes. They'd eat ice cream and peanuts, buy balloons, get bored with the seals, and then, at seven o'clock, the buzzer, the door that opened with a kind of mechanical belch, the boys running off, already forgetting him, and he'd feel so abandoned that he'd almost—goddammit—start crying.

"For a weekday there's a lot of traffic on the highway," Marilia said while hunting for chewing gum in her purse.

"His problem was that he never really believed in anything, he never had any religion," pronounced his godfather, wearing priestly vestments and blessing the coffin. A group of dwarf clowns, masquerading as mourning women, sobbed loudly in a corner, waving large red handkerchiefs. "This, my dear brothers and sisters in Christ, is how those who don't believe in anything end up," he concluded, his arms extended, to the sound of crashing cymbals.

Marilia threw the gum wrapper out the triangular car window and began chewing noisily. They left Lisbon, preceded by a long line of army trucks crammed with soldiers, their faces pointy and restless like birds'. He thinks, I don't have the slightest desire to go to this conference, the nineteenth century can go fuck itself. He thinks, You have no idea what kind of farewell speech I'm going to spring on you tomorrow or the next day, the beautiful and histrionic phrases, the pauses full of subtle underlying meanings, the rehearsed gestures, and you standing there among the suitcases in the hotel room with your mouth open, staring at me.

"You're crazy if you have any ideas about me splitting up with you," he told Tucha while kicking the broken dishes under the table. "And if you think you're fed up with me then I'll give you something to be fed up about, you little cunt."

"Supper's on," announced Marilia's mother, poking her head out the kitchen window like a clock's cuckoo. The sun congealed in greenish layers over the leaves of the trees, from the nearby cemetery came the heavy fragrance of begonias and corpses, and the national guardsman cleared his throat, making the walls shake. Whereas Tucha's father never coughed at all, he wore a vest and slaved away at the office day after day, breathing the dust of old tomes and drinking piss-colored whiskey from a bottle with a fancy label. Her mother played canasta with his mother, she suffered from some kind of heart disease that made her constantly nod her head yes, and it seems that when she was young she ran off for a few months with a Navy officer cousin named Tomás. Now she was a helpless, almost poignant old lady who wore lots of jewels and dropped cards from her fingers with a clumsiness that wouldn't interest the most desperate lieutenant.

I'm smoking too much, he thinks, lighting up his third cigarette of the trip as isolated houses, telegraph poles, and an occasional biker slipped past the sides of the hood like water cut by a prow. The slumbering fields of autumn unfolded unimpressively into little round hills that resembled bald skulls: Azedo Gneco Street fell far behind them with its books, pictures, posters on the wall, and forever running toilet.

"He never believed in anything, he never really believed in anything," repeated his godfather, mounted on the fake donkey, his tears falling in dark furrows down his painted face.

The nineteenth century, he thought, who gives a damn about the nineteenth century? A half-dozen half-baked sexagenarians, some horrendously ugly girls, one or two distracted foreigners financed by the university, and a few fusty women capable of lecturing to a class drunk with sleep on the landing of the Liberals at Mindelo in 1832 for twelve straight evenings.

"Another cigarette?" Marilia says, surprised. "Just look at the color of your fingers."

The Indian doctor held an X ray of the thorax against the window. "Lung cancer," he diagnosed. "I'll bet it's spine-cell. A little more time wasting away and you can kiss her goodbye. Then your mother's room will be disinfected and the bed vacant—ready for you."

Or Saturday nights, Tucha, when we'd drive along the river in the old Peugeot my father gave me, the geometric shapes of the warehouses looming enormous in the dark, the car doors shaking and rattling like the carts in the Haunted House as they weave past skeletons and scary masks, and my nuts would start aching, I felt like taking you to the beach at Guincho and pulling over on the shoulder, where you can hear the ocean and the wind pelts the windows with furious fistfuls of sand, I felt like hugging you in the darkness that smelled of car upholstery, burned rubber, and cold cigarette stubs as the waves crashed onto the rocks below, I felt like going wherever there was no light, to deserted parking lots or the lanes of Carcavelos with its shadowy cottages, groping for your breasts with my hands, the joint between your thighs, the flavorless saliva of your mouth, and then Tucha, "Let's go dancing," and I'd follow her without really wanting to, into a noisy basement with blinking lights, full of diffuse people squatting on low stools in front of bowls of popcorn. He thinks, Did I get married because I loved you or because everyone was getting married at the time, my sisters, my cousins, my friends, all with wedding pictures showing them raising glasses before long tables overflowing with food? He thinks, Did I get married because of your body's dizzying odor, because of the way you glance from the corner of your eye, because of your indifferent, inert arms? He thinks, Did I get married because of a deluded notion that I'd have power over myself if over nothing else, power to eat what I wanted for dinner, to go to bed when I wanted, to owe no frigging explanations to anyone? He thinks, Twenty years old—did I want to wear a wedding ring, pick out my own suits, be a grown-up, go to my parents' place for dinner with you holding my arm, alienated and silent?

"I never cared for him much," Tucha explained, while putting out the joint in the ashtray. "He had no patience for anything but books, books, books."

"His family was a pain in the ass," reported his first girlfriend, dressed as a trapeze artist and applying chalk dust to her hands. The coliseum net cast a diagonal shadow across her face. "I couldn't stand any of them."

What could I do, I had no other family to offer but my father with his aloof dignity, my mother playing cards in the smoke-filled sitting room, my sisters and their conclusive and depressing cackles, the honey-colored stillness of the apartment in summer, the furniture shrouded with dusty bed sheets. The house, the garden, Mass at St. Isabel's, São Domingos Street devastated by the sun: that was where I realized that I had died, he thinks, that I could no longer pretend I was still alive. The first death was at a dinner party on my birthday where everyone at the table—Tucha included—was disguised as a Bulgarian tightrope walker, the whole troupe laughing and shouting, recoiling from me with their strange accents against a clamorous background of clarinets and drums. Marilia stopped chewing, lowered the car window, tossed out her gum with a flick of the wrist, shifted her buttocks in the seat, and said:

"Can't we stop and get some coffee?"

32

A roadside dive, a dilapidated counter, a few tables and chairs, jars of penny candy, and a tubby man lost in the immeasurable breadth of the afternoon, shooing away flies with a filthy rag. Behind a straw curtain, an old woman was bent over a large plastic bowl, peeling potatoes. A meek, yellowish dog with wax-clogged eyes stood before the door, delicately extending one of its front paws like a pinky when a teacup is picked up. The tubby man sidled over, limping.

"Two cups of coffee," I ordered.

He thinks, Is the old lady his mother? His sister? His wife? Probably his wife: at night they grumble and push each other in a narrow bed that's coming apart, twisted and warped from endless battles, rancorous insomnias, and abrupt embraces on the lumpy mattress. The man placed two saucers, two spoons, and two packs of sugar on the counter, and bore down on a chrome lever. The dog, persecuted by a stubborn wasp, vanished in the afternoon, and he thought, When you bought a coffee maker and brought it to my place, Marilia, I realized for the second time, That's it, I'm screwed, How can I escape you? And then came the suitcases, an unfamiliar toothbrush appeared next to mine in the bathroom, and the clothesline filled up with strange shirts and slacks.

"So where do you want me to go?" he asked Tucha.

"Indecision," affirmed the psychologist, dressed as a lion tamer with a chair in his right hand and a whip in his left, "is one of his fundamental character traits. If you ask him whether he wants to live or die, he'll spend hours pacing back and forth, hands in his pockets, without knowing what to answer. Let's try it."

He cracked the whip on the ground, took two steps toward a colored platform on top of which I was shrinking and cowering, demanded in echoing cries, "Do you want to live? Do you want to die?" stepped back with his arms open before the proof of my silence, raised an eyebrow to the persuaded audience, and concluded:

33

"There you have it."

"Two coffees," said the tubby man setting the cups onto the saucers. A huge impassive silence spread from the dive to the landscape outside, clouded by the thick humidity of autumn, from which the trees struggled to free themselves, like thin fingers from a splotch of mud. The sky, hanging low, seemed to consist of the wind's very fabric.

"We sent him to the psychologist for an aptitude test," disclosed his mother as she put on the eyeglasses hanging around her neck and examined the score, "and he described my son's personality to a tee. A remarkable doctor. I was told he studied in Switzerland. The schools we have here are dreadful."

They drank their coffee while looking out the door at Santarém, shimmering unfocused in the distance, refracted by multiple layers of vapor. In the glass and wood cabinet hanging on the wall lay stacks of old chocolates, with fly-specked wrappers. Marilia's citified eyes looked around in search of streets.

"Can we go now? This place depresses me."

Once or twice a week, I wasn't sure how often, she went to the psychiatrist for long and mysterious conclaves. I met the guy once: a nondescript sort, effeminate, nearsighted, with a portfolio under his arm and a shabby overcoat. What did she talk to him about? About her childhood in Olivais, about her first boyfriends at college, clumsy and insensitive, about me? And what could that hunchbacked asshole understand about me? He thinks, His portfolio probably contains her case history, my case history, the dull, difficult, depressing story of our relationship. He thinks, Case History #326, re Marilia So-and-So and Husband Such-and-Such, in which we've been unabashedly stripped naked with the aid of technical terms and empty formulas, clichés that can't portray us. He planned to sneak up on the psychiatrist from behind and shake out his secrets, which he imagined would jingle like a piggy bank (there'd be the afternoon when I hauled off and slapped you, there'd be your orgasms carefully labeled, numbered, and filed in chronological order, or in order of intensity, or by some other frighteningly obscure criterion), but before he could get his feet going the psychiatrist had climbed onto a crowded streetcar and disappeared.

"How much is it?" he asked the limper.

A tiny male infant, barefoot and diaperless, toddled in: the space between his mouth and nose was glassed over with snot. His dirty, clumpy hair grew in all directions, like the prickles on a bush. An uncle, dressed as a magician, threw off his cape and pointed his wand at the boy, to the general laughter of the audience:

"And now, ladies and gentlemen, I'll turn this frail creature into a high school teacher."

"Hi there, colleague," he said to the kid, and the limper glared at him in astonishment.

He made sure Tucha was watching before he administered an additional kick to a chair, which fell on its side, mortally wounded, whinnying like a downed horse:

"You're crazy if you have any ideas about separating me from my kids."

Marilia waited for him inside the car, unwrapping yet another tasteless stick of that gum that seemed to be her main source of nourishment. The car, parked all alone, resembled a sleeping toad.

"You can see them whenever you want," Tucha said. One of the children had woken up and was crying at the end of the hallway tunnel of shadows.

"Typical behavior pattern of weak personalities," explained the psychologist as he showed the hieroglyphic test results. "Strange alternation between infantile supplication and trivial aggression, resulting in a harmless but dull temperament."

"A total bore," sighed the oldest sister, who was playing

cards with their mother. Her eyebrows, painted on top, looked like they were taking off from her forehead's airfield of facial powder.

"Did you pay for the coffees with colored beads?" Marilia asked. "I had the impression that guy wouldn't know what real money looks like."

You have a sour side that I've never understood, he thought as he sat down next to her in the car, under the transparent green-menthol shadow of a small tree with a flat top whose name he didn't know, a sharpness that suddenly makes you serious, biting, almost savage, distilling poison like one of those big spiders that hid in the bougainvillea in my parents' garden and that I'd kill by throwing stones from a distance, afraid of their dark sorcery. The barefoot child, now planted in front of the car, observed them with the fixed and ardent gaze of a calf. Up ahead a road-repairing machine belched out smoke among vats of tar, and exhaled water from somewhere or other. The smooth gray sky fused with the gray ground like a featureless face glued to its own reflection. Perhaps your sourness comes from never having been happy, he thought, from your parents, from your broken marriage, your lack of money, despair over not doing what you really wanted. Far away, beyond some hills, the long whistle of a train blew.

"And if we say to hell with the conference?" he asked all of a sudden.

Milling around wearing typewritten name-tags, listening to erudite papers, growing solemnly weary, dying of boredom during the never-ending speeches at the farewell dinner, enduring the photographer hopping around the table and clicking unexpectedly. He distinctly heard train wheels rolling on their tracks, and a lone bird's two-note song. The dashboard clock had read eleven-twenty ever since he smashed into a truck at a stoplight: the static time of a day long ago, when I'd only recently separated and found you merely irritating, Marilia, and slept in a rented room near the Prazeres Cemetery—

I'd open the window at night, and the cypresses, straight and stiff, would lean toward my bed, wrapped in the halo of dead air from below.

"He could have stayed at our house," said his youngest sister, pulling at her skirt to cover her thighs. "We have a spare room where we could have put the kids. Carlos told him that on the phone but you know how my brother is: he never took much interest in the family, and ever since he went Communist he likes to feel sorry for himself. He apparently found a cheap room somewhere or other."

"What?" Marilia said, startled. "Skip the conference?"

"Let's talk this over calmly," he suggested to Tucha. "This is all a lot of twaddle, and unless another man has entered the picture I can see no reason for us to separate. Because of a whim? Because you're fed up? Well, join the club, I'm fed up too, but I think we ought to have a little consideration for the kids. Pedro's problematic, I'm afraid he would really suffer."

The pimply eighteen- or nineteen-year-old boy in charge of the stage lights leaned over from a balcony:

"I don't remember my father. He split from my mother ages ago, I heard he took up with a girl he met at work and died a short while later, in some country inn north of Lisbon. Maybe my brother remembers the story better, but you'll have to go to Canada to talk with him: he works for a computer firm there. I don't know his address, we never write."

"Have you thought about what a colossal bore it's going to be?" I said quickly. "Think if we changed the program and spent the weekend at a quiet place with no obligations, no people, no small talk. Hell, let's do it, seriously, four days. There are some decent country inns we've never tried out."

The asphalt machine chugged like a sick locomotive, spitting out orange sparks from between its wheels. A human figure, perched on top and bobbing up and down, commanded the frenzy of flames. The old woman went out behind the building, overturned a bucket into a ditch, and walked back inside with small and stooping, arthritic steps. The bare-bottomed child continued to observe them keenly with his glowing calf eyes. The sky's uniform grayness was breaking down into a confusion of clouds.

"Azedo Gneco Street," yawned his mother while putting away the decks in the drawer of the card table. "Who'd ever think of living on Azedo Gneco Street?"

Carlos signaled with his hand for the driver to wait a minute, and he put his sunglasses in the breast pocket of his jacket:

"In spite of our diametrically opposed ideas [in his mouth the word *diametrically* seemed to blink, underlined in red], I never argued with my brother-in-law. He was basically a good-hearted soul that the socialists took advantage of. I told him more than once that he could stay at our house, but he always refused. I assume no responsibility for what happened."

"Talk?" laughed Tucha. "I've made my decision, there's nothing to talk about."

"Smells funny to me," Marilia said. "A honeymoon four years after the fact—what the hell bit you?"

He thinks, When I was little the road repairmen would give us big waves with their hats, leaning against Biblical picks, and we'd flatten our noses against the back window, watching them disappear in a swirl of dust. He thinks, At that time I still had no thoughts of joining the Party, I served at Mass before school in the deserted church, and Donald Duck was my favorite animal. He thinks, The doubts came later, my selfishness and fear of being trapped and of dreaming came later. Sign here: and immediately I was seized by the fear of betraying my parents and of breaking with the idiotically swank set, and I couldn't join, I'd make up stupid excuses and console myself with a farfetched Stalinism. My bearded and myopic friends, arrogantly dogmatic, eventually stopped coming around to fill my ashtrays with butts and my heart with the glorious achievements of Socialism's Homeland, and Tucha, relieved, began to feel free to invite her dumb coworkers and opinionless friends to come over and be howled at by the Jefferson Airplane.

"He did have a few good points," said the second-oldest sister, who was single and taught Beginning Music to high school students (cymbals, triangles, and other assorted noise-makers banging together in a joyous pandemonium). "He liked Chopin, for instance. We'd have lunch together on Tuesdays and I'd hum him a Polonaise over dessert." (Their heads close together, her ugly face singing in a jam-packed restaurant. Those who were standing up waiting for a table would lean over to listen, amused. You were easy to please and not at all pretentious, he thought: how is it you couldn't find a husband?).

The roiling clouds acquired a cardboard consistency: soon it would begin to rain. Looking more closely he made out another house (half demolished?) in the distance, a gate, the remains of a stone fence.

"I'm sick to death of the nineteenth century, that's all," I said. "And we never go out, we're always tucked away like moles in Lisbon, in that hole of an apartment, stuffed with books, our cold knees pressing against the coils of the heater. Let's go to the ocean."

"Pedro will be all right with me," said Tucha with her back turned, cleaning the stereo needle with a special little brush. "What gets him upset are the arguments we're always having."

"Who around here argues?" I said. "I never raise my voice. I admit I got a little out of hand just now, but it's over, so let's forget it."

"Aggressive-submissive, aggressive-submissive, aggressive-submissive," the psychologist pronounced, metronomically moving his index finger. "Women detest men who are too predictable, they want a coefficient of surprise, and what surprises does this type of personality hold? None."

"All together now," his father-turned-master-of-cere-monies yelled to the family-turned-audience. The tails of his jacket fluttered behind him. "Repeat with me on the count of three. The sentence is: Anyone could have guessed his next screwup."

"It's not a question of Pedro being all right," I asserted. "Of course he'll be all right. But at his age it's important to see his parents together."

"If my husband didn't spend much time at home, it's be-cause the poor man was overworked," his mother explained with a sad smile, seated on her end of the sofa, next to the fireplace. "You know how business is. But he made sure our children got a good education: he'd phone up every other day."

"He died in Aveiro, that's all I know," the young man in charge of the lights called out, his hands cupping both sides of his mouth. "My mother remarried, with a friend they had in common; they went to live in Switzerland, and my grand-parents on her side took care of us. She's living in Lausanne now, just her and a dog. She sometimes sends a box of filled chocolates, which I pass on to the diabetic porter who's al-ways dying for sweets."

"The ocean?" Marilia said. "Every single morning I face Azedo Gneco Street with its rotten smell of garbage cans hidden behind cars and forgotten by the trash men."

"Hello?" said the microscopically authoritarian voice of his father. "What grade did he get in Math?"

"You're wasting your time," Tucha remarked, "I'm not interested in hearing your arguments."

"If he gets a D in Geography," the microscopic voice or-dered, "then no movie for three straight Sundays."

He thinks, Where were you when you phoned us, Dad? Hamburg, Paris, London, or some other large and unknown city, in the rain? Were you in a hotel room, holding onto a glass of whiskey and sitting next to a fur-coated girl who looked like a movie star on a bubble gum wrapper? He thinks, You were happy, are happy, what more do you want? One twilight, when I was little, we were at the farm and a flock of birds rose up from the chestnut tree by the well and flew toward the patch of forest, blued by the oncoming evening. Their wings flapped with the sound of windblown leaves, tiny and thin, innumerable leaves, dictionary leaves. I was holding your hand and said, "Explain the birds to me." Just like that, "Explain the birds to me": an embarrassing request for a businessman. But you smiled and said that their bones were made of foam from the beach, that they fed on crumbs of wind, and that when they died they floated in the air on their backs, their eyes closed like old ladies receiving Communion. To think that five or six years later what mattered to you were my Geography and Math grades made my head spin from the absurdity, the almost laughable impossibility, as if the Indian doctor had suddenly turned to me and declared out of the blue, "You've got cancer."

"I heard about a nice inn on the lagoon at Aveiro," I said. "Why don't we check it out?"

Gray sky, gray earth, the rain that kept stalling and would no doubt keep stalling, to judge from the earth's difficult, almost asthmatic breathing. The Santarém Valley resembled overlapping cotton curtains that gently waved in the midday cold. The bare-bottomed kid toddled back toward the building with his mouth hanging open. Inside, the limping man was probably washing their cups in the stone sink by the dim, depressing, watercolor light of a small high window.

"In Lausanne, just her and a dog," the young man on lights repeated. His indistinct face seemed to be smiling at the idea of an old, gray-haired woman with newspapers in her arms and a white dog on a leash.

"I knew from day one that the marriage would flop," said Tucha's father, while counting up the unsold tickets inside a kind of sentry box, next to the trailers and the circus tent.

"They were both unstable, fragile, a bit different. Sooner or later they were bound to break up."

"He liked Chopin," said the musical sister. "He'd go to St. Rock's Church to hear the Gulbenkian Choir, he'd sit in the rear and look in awe at the high walls from which the voices seemed to emanate. He and I are kind of the two black sheep of the family."

"Aveiro," Marilia said, "why not Aveiro? You've got something up your sleeve and I want to see how it turns out: even when the film's lousy, I always stay till the end."

He thinks, At the hospital I left the phone number of the hotel at Tomar, so if anything comes up they won't be able to get a hold of me, all they'll get is a confusion of conferee names amidst conference clamor. He thinks, Mom wouldn't do this to me on the weekend, she's been concerned about the elegance of feelings ever since her other beauties started waning. He thinks, The cancer fund never got a dime out of me—I avoided the earnest and benevolent well-dressed girls who accosted me on street corners with the slots of their metal cans. I avoided them because in my opinion it's the Government that etc. etc., which is a great way to get rid of what's concretely horrifying, dumping it in the hands of an indefinite entity.

"A lot can happen in three days," I said to Marilia without conviction, as if lying to a child. "And we need to rest some, talk some."

The obstetrician married to my other sister lit his pipe: his gelatinous fingers had the thickness and texture of octopus tentacles:

"Perhaps his mother's illness was an influencing factor, though I doubt it: he'd been acting weird for months."

"I never stopped loving you," he shouted at Tucha while he punched uselessly at an antique wooden chest. (We bought it in Sintra.) "And for your information I'm not going to give in just like that." He put the car in gear and hopped back onto

42

the highway. The solitary roadside dive shrank behind them, irreparably lost, next to the pointless aquarium shadow of its one tree. Best thing is to head for Coimbra, he thought, and if we get hungry, we can stop at one of those small-town diners with paper tablecloths on painted-metal tables, and the nineteenth century can go to hell with its mustached grandees and its rinky-dink revolutions. They passed the asphalting machine, which trembled like a boiling pot. The workmen were patching the road with black pellets that percolated under the tires. Dark bits of gravel bounced like hail against the car's mudguards. Randomly bunched shrubs flailed like desperate castaways, and the city on the right withdrew, closed in on itself, a mystery.

"Get him a Physics tutor if necessary," the microscopic voice commanded. "I don't want my son to end up a good-for-nothing."

"He never understood the Second Law of Thermodynamics," revealed an elderly man with a high-school textbook open in front of him and a ship in a bottle on his bookshelf. "Maybe he was better in the Humanities, I don't know, but he was a total disaster in the pure sciences."

One way or another I have to tell you that I'm leaving, he thought, and it's easier to do it far away from Azedo Gneco Street, away from the home we set up together, from the constant phone calls from your Party comrades, and from the numbing, caustic, castrating environment of objects I know too well. I've got Friday, Saturday, and Sunday to work up my courage in the unfamiliar room of an inn, watching the lagoon waters slowly slip toward the sea. My brother-in-law the executive shot some film there: sea gulls and boats on a blue morning—the projector click-clacked in the dark and we sat there with the silent and solemn attention of spectators watching the Last Judgment from a theater box. My sister, standing on a balcony, highly embarrassed and out of focus, waved timidly at the camera.

"If there's no changing your mind, then all right, I'm leaving," he said to Tucha. "At least help me pack my suitcase."

"She's weird," yelled the young man running the lights. "She lived for a few months with a Russian antique dealer and twelve Dalmatians."

The Indian doctor carefully removed the thick rubber gloves he'd used for the autopsy:

"Nothing except for gallstones. If not for suicide, his internal organs would have had another thirty or forty trouble-free years."

"Aveiro," Marilia said while foraging in her purse for more chewing gum. (Her profile pained him like a deep regret.) "At least I'll find out what the devil you're up to."

He thinks, Am I that obvious? Does everyone see straight through to my hesitations, my uneasiness, my doubts, the tide of bitterness that gnaws inside like an acid some nights and keeps me from writing my dissertation on Sidonio Pais, driving me to the window instead, to observe the dark, domestic, familiar night, the neighborhood dogs sniffing garbage cans, the huge street-cleaning trucks with their rotating lights? He thinks, I should vote conservative, wear a tie, work for my father, and visit Estoril's bars with foreign investors who would get smashed and puke up their dinners on our driver's subservient uniform, while our equally drunk escorts, their mouths caked with lipstick, would trip in their overly high heels. He thinks, Maybe I should have been an economist, married rich, and managed a bank, phoning long distance to demand good Math grades from my children, threatening them with movieless Sundays, with not going to parties, dances, or friends' houses.

The obstetrician brother-in-law, smiling, waved an enormous pair of cardboard forceps over the cadaver menacingly:

"We will now extract all that sadness."

"He was moody and short-tempered; he'd leave the table in

the middle of lunch," his mother reported while painting her little fingernail brown. "Not at all like his sisters."

"Communist," confided the priest in a low voice, afraid he might be overheard. "Such a disgrace, and from a family so upright, so Catholic. When he was a student, he surreptitiously passed around leaflets and wrote propaganda on the walls, and he nearly got arrested."

"If his father wasn't so important," said a man in a raincoat trying to hide behind his raised arm, "he'd have been put in the pen."

Tucha worked the lever that lowered the stereo needle onto a record and sat back down: a screaming voice made the living room shake. "Why should I help you pack your suitcase?" she said. "You know where all your clothes and books are. You do it."

"You want to know why Aveiro?" he asked Marilia. "There are dozens of sea gulls around the inn, among the rushes, on the muddy banks, in the lagoon itself, and on the anchored barges. When I was little my father explained the birds to me, their nests, their habits, the way they fly. Don't give me that look, we were both different then. If you'd known him then, you'd understand."

He'd taken her to his parents' for dinner, and through it all—during the cocktails, the meal, the conversation afterward in the living room, and the farewells in the foyer—he'd felt, on the one hand, their hostile etiquette, shocked by his girlfriend's poncho and clogs and extreme-leftist garb; and, on the other hand, her proletarian rage as a national guardsman's daughter, stubbornly exaggerated in the coarseness of her manners and in her use of toothpicks. He thinks, Why was it so necessary to scandalize my parents, hurting them and me in the process? At heart I'm bourgeois (I wish I knew what the hell the word means), I married a bourgeois girl and there are things I'll never be able to change in myself: a certain way

45

of looking at things, a reticence about expressing feelings, a concern for the proper handling of utensils, my taste in clothes, a subconsciously censored vocabulary.

"He wasn't a bad guy and he made a good cover for us," said a bearded, T-shirted hulk surrounded by vehemently red posters depicting men with raised fists standing in front of the outlines of smoking factories. "With a rich shit like that among us the police never dreamed we were a cell group. But then he began to take himself seriously, pretended to be a Marxist, and started running around with illegal pamphlets under his arm, so that we finally had to tell him to cool it."

"What I want to know," said his father's voice on the telephone, "is if it's your fault or the tutor's. One more D and I'll pull you straight out of that school."

He thinks, Ho Chi Minh, Mao, Che Guevara, Lenin, Trotsky the traitor playing up to the ruling classes, instead of Geography, Math, and French. Impassioned meetings clouded by cigarettes, the certainty of an imminent and definitive redemption. He thinks, They were all older than me, my family served mammon, they never asked my opinion, did they take me at all seriously? He thinks, There was no one I could talk to: Tucha would start yawning the minute I brought up the achievements of the proletariat, my sisters—their fingers intertwined with their fiancés'—would sink into the sofas, exposing their legs that melted with desire; my mother had a friend who quit coming to play cards, a red-headed widow with children my age, she was tall and thin and clinked with bracelets, it was rumored that she and my father were seeing each other, that he'd take her on trips abroad, introducing her as his wife.

"The only thing to discuss," Tucha said, "is how much child support you're going to pay. My lawyer drafted a proposal. I'll go get it."

"Birds?" Marilia said, "What did you two understand about birds?"

46

They continued toward Coimbra on the highway full of big trucks huffing and puffing up inclines bordered by ugly, drought-stunted trees beneath the pale morning sky: it wasn't going to rain, it would never rain again on the earth, the sea would give way to deep and dusty craters, like the craters we imagine on the moon, where the stony silence of a perpetual night hovers. Coimbra struck him as a trivial, prolix town, with signs and arrows indicating Lisbon, Leiria, Aveiro, Oporto, Figueira da Foz, and other places he couldn't remember: a lone traffic cop on a kind of throne frantically waved around his arms. They stopped to eat in a café populated by gray-haired men who were joined in pairs like butterflies born of caterpillars in cardboard boxes, playing checkers before empty coffee cups. Through the window he could see the attendant at the neighboring gas station wiping his hands on a filthy rag or extracting change from a cowhide pouch hung from his shoulder. The buildings on the hill behind the station formed a mishmash, like domino pieces haphazardly scattered. My stomach ached slightly, as if it suffered from a mild case of nostalgia: hunger, he thought, it must be hunger. Or I'm getting old. Or I'm sick like a carriage horse retired from service. "The birds," explained his father leaning against the well on the farm, "die very slowly, without knowing why and without even noticing, and one day they wake up with their mouths open, floating on their backs in the wind."

"As a boy he was no problem," said his mother, carefully examining the polish on her nails. "Courteous and happy, and he didn't cry a lot. It was after he grew up that he got difficult. Particularly after he got involved in politics."

"He never belonged to the Party, he lacked a militant spirit," declared the hulking bearded T-shirt. "Too selfish, too bourgeois, too scared. He lacked guts, nerve, backbone, conviction, the fighting spirit. He passed out pamphlets and hung up posters to appease his guilty conscience, that was about it. A true Communist, comrades, doesn't commit suicide."

The Mondego River was a canal in the sand, a timid thread that barely cut a passage through the muddy grasses: blackened stone walls uselessly contained its nonexistent water. The gas station attendant was squatting down to check a motorcycle's tires. The jowls of one of the gray-haired checker players turned purple as he suddenly broke out coughing.

"The cadaver was easily identifiable," announced the obstetrician, pointing to the gigantic cardboard coffin with four make-believe candles on the corners. "That turd-colored thin hair, that blue-and-maroon sweater, and those humongous crumpled shoes were him. There was no need to examine the gloves and the red suspenders. Dead, on his back and with his mouth hanging open, like a bird among the birds, unable to fly."

His father hoisted him up again, piggyback (his head almost touched the chestnut trees), and headed toward the house. His mother was waiting for them, smiling and seated in the living room with a novel on her knees. "My two men," she said, and there wasn't one wrinkle, not one shadow, not one hidden sorrow in her clear gaze. The sparrows had already absconded into the woods. His sisters, whose bottoms were still nice and firm, discussed boyfriends in their room.

"He couldn't master polynomials," lamented the Math teacher, "and when a student can't master polynomials, then what can you do?"

"In spite of everything, we tried to work with him," justified the T-shirt to a silent audience, "because some true revolutionaries have come from his class. We gave him some little jobs to do, we let him attend meetings, and toward the end of the course we elected him head of the publications section, but instead of focusing on the working class and the manuals he wrote verses, vacillated, and dragged his feet. If Fidel had been one of his kind, Batista would still be in power. And the worst thing, comrades, is that he fell in love with an aristocratic airhead."

"My proposal is for five hundred a month," Tucha said. (The Eric Burdon record reached the end.) "Your parents can help you out."

"There's not a doubt in my mind that you're plotting something," Marilia affirmed across her toast. "Whenever you get crazy ideas you always wear that silly smirk that irritates the hell out of me."

Making no comment, he got the bill from an incredibly tall and affected waiter who bent toward the tables like a graceful reed, searching our faces with soft canine eyes. He thinks, Were we ever really in love, impassioned? He looks at her harsh, inquisitorial profile, her wide-palmed hands with their stubby fingers, her disproportionately large chest, and he thinks, What kept us together for four years? It began after I broke up with Tucha: I felt lonely, abandoned, worthless, the walls of my rented room pressed in against me; you taught Semiotics at the university; we went to the movies together a few times. I liked your hard-boiled way of dealing with life, your unbending pragmatism, the smell of your body in the cinema darkness; we talked about one thing and another; you kept your cigarettes in a case made of wicker; one Sunday I visited you at home, I met your parents. "A friend from the university" is how you introduced me. Then one day it just happened, we kissed each other in the car after a conference; I'll never forget your eyes staring straight into mine; you didn't believe me, you thought I was still hopelessly stuck on Tucha and in a way, goddammit, you were right. He thinks, Did I go for you because you belonged to the Party, because you'd been in jail, because you represented my redemption, my vengeance against the fear that immobilized me, my attempt to assuage a guilty conscience by marrying someone from the exploited class? Then the apartment turned up: "A hundred fifty a month isn't bad, we could split the rent, you'd live there with me, I'd go fetch my kids on Sundays." And the smell of your body pursued me, you wouldn't let me touch your chest, "Hands off hands off hands off," and finally, after a long fight, I pulled down your stockings, removed your skirt, ripped (did I rip?) your panties on the divan that was too narrow, banged my elbow on the ground, a sort of electric current ran through me up to my shoulder, I grabbed onto it howling; and you, "What happened, Did you break something?" "I think I broke my arm, help me, Marilia, help me." Your parents had gone out, there was no one else home, the setting sun crept across the bedroom floorboards, filtered by the polka-dotted curtains, you brought cotton, rubbing alcohol, a worried wrinkle on your forehead, "Let me see it, bend it back and forth, oh this is nothing," half-dressed, half-naked, your toes pressed flat on the floor, your open shirt revealing your pink bra, me stretched out on the mattress, my eyes closed, and suddenly a weight at my right side, your mouth against my ear, "Put it in." I unlocked the door for you and started the motor. Maybe the Mondego fills up in winter, maybe the dark stones are covered by a muddy current that flows this way and that toward the sea. The monkshood-colored buildings looked at us unmercifully, and the brown sky stretched on without limits, like the wings of a nun's coif.

"My lawyer says five hundred dollars is nothing," Tucha argued while rubbing a spot on her slacks with the sleeve of her sweater. "With your old man's money I could demand a lot more."

"Birds," Marilia said, "birds and featherbrained ideas. I want to see what this is going to lead to."

Once more the drab highway north with its steady stream of trucks, cars, tractors, and slow and insistent, trembling scooters. Something in the rear—a loose part, the flares, the toolbox in the trunk—jumped around making an incessant, nerve-grating sound.

"We never approved of his second marriage," said the oldest sister while beating egg whites in the kitchen, "but he was a big boy, of legal age, so what could we do to stop him? Carlos, the dear, went over to talk with him and came back all worried. I remember him saying clear as day, 'Either I'm completely mistaken or your brother's going to end up in a bad way.' And at my parents' it was an absolute disgrace, what with that ill-bred girl insulting everyone in sight."

"He liked Chopin," put forth the music teacher in a sigh as she opened the piano. "I'm going to play you his favorite Nocturne."

"I don't give a damn whether you marry or not," said his father, standing in his office and ignoring the ringing telephone. "As far as I'm concerned, you stopped existing on the day you began meddling in politics."

He thinks, You already had a lot of white hair, Dad, your back slumped, your suit hung slack around your chest, you'd no longer have been capable of carrying me piggyback. He thinks, I'll bet that you forgot about the birds, that you never gave them another thought.

"Of one thing you can be dead certain," added his father, staring at him with a look of defeated hatred, with a trembling, yellow, estranged look, "you're not going to get a thin dime out of me."

Modern paintings on the walls, a shelf of legal codes, the sofa where his mother's friend probably stretched out and spread her legs, dressed in black stockings and a fur coat. He thinks, Would you still be up to it, would you still have the strength?

"Just you wait and see how much you like the lagoon," I said. "A few days of peace and quiet will make you feel like a new woman."

Politics, he thinks: once when I ended up at the police station for scribbling slogans on buildings you came to pick me up, and from then on I never caused you any more problems. They nudged me out of the cell group, explaining that they needed me in the reserves, when in fact they wanted nothing to do with a rich man's son. You argued in earnest

51

with a minuscule and pompous man wearing a dingy tie while I, droopy-eyed, watched you beneath a shadeless light bulb in a tiny room with a desk and a chair and air that was heavy with a thick and greasy silence made of absent shouts.

"I beg your pardon, sir," droned the minuscule man, "but it's not our fault you had to come down here. Your boy, no doubt influenced by others, was running around writing graffiti against the government."

His father answered him in a low voice, saying something that he couldn't make out, and the microbe immediately threw open his arms, sympathetic and understanding:

"These small fry aren't much of a threat, but we have to nip the problem in the bud—don't you see?—before it has a chance to develop. As for the big fish, we've got their every move covered. At any rate, we felt it was our duty to forewarn you, a pillar of the regime, one of our leading industrialists. The general director is well aware of the nation's debt to you, but please impress on your son the risks he's incurring." (The dwarf became serious, comically serious and aggressive.) "Indulgence has its limits, sir, we can't keep closing our eyes indefinitely."

He thinks, That over there must be the interrogation chamber, where they knock people around—what did they extort from my father? Referrals, contacts, business deals, a discreet check from a Swiss bank? My father, pale with shame, listened to the paramecium's dumb speech while nervously looking for the ashtray that wasn't there; he held his cigarette upright in order to keep miles of precarious ashes from falling, and I'll bet the other jerk noticed this and my father's anxiety and got sadistic pleasure from my old man's embarrassment.

"Is there an ashtray around?" my father finally asked in a submissive tone, humbly pointing to the butt with his chin.

The microbe triumphantly cracked an enormous smile (Asshole, he thought), displaying all his rotten teeth:

52

"I'm sorry, sir, I hadn't noticed. Smoking's not allowed in the police station."

His father, with a palm cupped under the ashen tip, waited until a second policeman—hunchbacked and meticulous—knocked on the door, asked permission to enter, and set a dented metal saucer on the table. I'd never seen him so ashamed: grayish wrinkles covered his cheeks and the twisted knot of his necktie began to come undone. The exultant inspector exhorted him with friendly slaps on the back, suddenly buddy-buddy and protective:

"I know what a pain in the neck this is for you, and you can't imagine how sorry we are. At any rate, your boy seems to be repentant, which is the important thing. But to be on the safe side we're going to keep his record on file."

His father searched in his pockets for a fresh cigarette, expressing his gratitude with the unprecedented subservience of a subordinate ("I can assure you, Inspector, that this won't happen again") while pushing him toward the exit, past gray desks where gray men wearily typed documents, past narrow and dark corridors, past closed offices with red and green lights over the doors—the lairs of police chiefs secretly plotting to slaughter the Communists. The minuscule man trotted behind them, finally vanishing ("Good day, sir. You be careful, young man") into some office or another. His varnished nails gleamed in the dim light, and we were suddenly back outside, in the city, where the chauffeur was leaning against the hood with his cap removed and a sports paper in his hand, and the November sun was falling across the houses, rooftops, trees, and the neutral faces of pedestrians. He thinks, It was then and there that I died, Dad, that you considered me dead because of what I made you suffer, because you had to bow down to a nobody, a poor sap with a sixth-grade education and clothes from a crummy shop with pasty-looking mannequins in the window, a sap just like one of your office clerks

53

that you never even look at. The chauffeur closed your door respectfully and seated himself behind the wheel. "Where to, sir?" "Drop me off at the airport fast and then take my son home." I took a bath, sat down to lunch; no one asked me anything; my mother took pills for her headache, and my sister the musician—her glasses glued to the staves—butchered Debussy in the living room. You never let me really rebel, never let me go all the way with my indignation: your authoritarian, overbearing shadow castratingly protected me, and that's when I decided on Liberal Arts, to become a professor, to stay out of the business, to stop wearing a tie, to teach structuralism, literary theory, French poetry, or other equally useless inanities. He might have liked to work in the union, but the Left didn't trust him, whereas the Right hated him for being a traitor, and both were justified in their reservations, their wariness, their criticisms. He thinks, What I am after all, what I want after all—having had a bourgeois wife, then a Communist one—is a bizarre combination of conservative with frustrated adventurer, ultimately and pathetically powerless.

"All right, I'll come down to four hundred dollars and every other Sunday," Tucha said while squatting down, hunting for another record in a gigantic pile, "but don't expect me to give another inch. You can deposit the money at the bank and ring the bell three times for me to send down the boys. Pedro knows perfectly well how to work the elevator buttons, he inherited your knack for mechanical things."

How gorgeous your body looked with your bottom almost touching the ground. God, how your ass cheeks gave me a hard-on: to hug you from behind, press my penis against your back, breathe your hair's confused, changing perfume. The crease between your thighs, the shape of your mouth, the grape-colored hue of your eyes. And I love it when you go to bed with your makeup still on; I'll miss your mascara on the sheet, I'll miss grazing on the clear, firm skin of your tummy, I'll miss the whitish scars left from your pregnancies.

"Here's your son, sir, Now make sure he's careful about the friends he hangs out with."

Mickey-mouse conspiracies in the student lounge, whispered conversations among friends who shut up as soon as I came close. They never let me witness any more than innocent and trivial student shenanigans: "Maybe one day, pal, but first you have to pass various tests, we have to take precautions, you know, play it cool, make sure everything stays under control, get it?, what with the fuzz always breathing down our necks, we have to be extra careful." A half-dozen cagey faces, slaps on the back, the sun was setting beyond the woods, and all together the birds shook loose like strange fruits from the chestnut tree by the well, gliding for an instant in the wind as if lost, then breaking into flight toward the night, his classmates skipped off to class in their faded raincoats, they looked for empty places in the rows of benches, like robins in the branches of fig trees. "Now I want your son to keep straight as an arrow—no more monkey business." "My two dear men," my mother said, smiling—I wasn't even big enough to touch my feet on the floor when sitting on the sofas, I couldn't see what was on the tables, on the bookshelves, on the buffets, couldn't see the bibelots, pictures, silver boxes, tureens, and the plates sitting upright in wooden tripods; he found a seat in the back—the professor had already begun class, King John VI; he pulled a pad out of his pocket to take notes, "Maybe one day you'll be able to join the Party and fight seriously for the working class, making up for your bourgeois roots," the young arms of my father hoisted me onto his lap, his sweet cologne entered my nostrils, he pointed to the blue woods with his finger, his head leaned into mine, "Show what you can do for us, distribute these pamphlets in the university," and he said, "I'm going to explain the birds to you."

"Aveiro, what a bizarre idea, Aveiro," objected Marilia, looking at the pines, the eucalyptus trees, the anonymous villages, and the convex sky weighing heavy with rain that still hadn't fallen and that, according to the newspapers, probably never would. He thinks, The comments your comrades at the Party must have made when you told them you were going to live with me, the recriminations, warnings, ridicule, "You're going to give us up for a rich kid, an aristocratic piece of shit, a closet exploiter!" And yet I had no money, I'd practically broken off with my family; our fortune consisted of the aquarium in the bedroom and the transparent fish slithering over the pebbles at the bottom; I wanted to wipe out the sad memory of my life with Tucha, start out fresh and be happy, if possible.

"Hopeless with polynomials and a disaster with square roots," declared the Math teacher, wearing a false mustache with twisted ends and raising a cardboard dumbbell with *20 Tons* written in white chalk. "For someone whose father was a business administrator, he had a complete and total block against numbers like I'd never seen."

The gym coach, dressed in white, emerged from behind the trampoline, flexing his muscles athletically. A round, red nose, held in place by an elastic band around his ears, added a clownish touch:

"Terrible on the parallel bars, terrible with the jump rope, mediocre in handball," he offered in a grating monotone. "He'd just sit there, quiet, skinny, almost rachitic, watching the others."

Two fellows with helmets were talking next to a motorcycle outside the town of Estarreja. He stopped, lowered the car window, stuck his head out, and asked:

"How do we get to the lagoon?"

The words they spoke were wrapped in humidity—a sluggish, thick, and sticky steam. February, he thought, who says I have to decide my life in February? Who says I should go back to rented rooms in winter, fifty cents extra if I want a bath, no visitors, no TV, having to save on heat, on water, on the very air I breathe? Who says I should change my life at age thirty-three? How stupid.

Tucha straightened a picture on the wall and stepped back to see how it looked:

"In spite of all this fighting I'd like to remain your friend. If you want to, that is. We do have two children in common, after all."

"The children, poor dears," said his mother, serving tea to her guests, immovable as wax figures, perfectly erect on the sitting room couches. "It wasn't their fault they were born into the world. I never separated from my husband even though he gave me plenty of good reasons to."

"His body could hardly be made out," Carlos clarified, "eaten up by the birds, by the sludge in the lagoon, by the time it took for him to be found. The Inspector told me it's not easy to spot a corpse in the midst of the rushes, and then too, the sea gulls play tricks, they pretend to be ignorant, not to understand, not to smell. The sea gulls, the albatrosses, the ducks, all that strange marine fauna."

One of the fellows abandoned the motorcycle and approached the car. Up close he looked older and somewhat burned out, his cheeks with dark furrows and his hands red and swollen with chilblains and calluses:

"Go straight on as far as Murtosa and then just follow the signs that say *Inn* as if it were a city. To cross over from Aveiro you'll have to use the boat."

"Just like that you can blow off your career, the conference, your dissertation on Sidonio Pais, your doctorate—what the devil's gotten into you?" Marilia asked. "It's as if life suddenly lost all meaning for you."

"The hell with staying friends," he answered, "you can stick friendship right up your ass."

And purple with rage he yelled:

"So who are you getting ready to romp around with, bitch?"

57

"Don't expect this much out of me," warned his father, indicating the tip of his pinky. "All I needed was for my son to go batty and start plotting against the government. Politics is too serious a matter for kids."

"Well, I'm giving you a post as lecturer," said the old mustached man, installed beneath the confused engraving of a battle scene wherein men with brandished swords (Spaniards?) massacred one another in a joyful fury. "No one's much interested in the First Republic and you can make a valuable contribution. I was intrigued by the psychosocial aspect of your study on the root causes behind the overthrow of the monarchy, although some of your theories strike me as debatable or fanciful." ("The birds when they die," his father explained, "float in the wind on their backs.") "A little less Freud and more objectivity wouldn't do you any harm. Though in this respect Oliveira Martins wasn't much different from you."

At that time I wore Gramsci-style glasses, was fat, pimply, and still had all my hair—a halo of blubbery swirls surrounded my cheeks—but my father was rich, Tucha, and I was a fairly indulgent husband: within a few months of the wedding you were forever going out by yourself, you'd spend long hours away from home, you constantly had work-related meetings at night, you did secretarial work for an unidentified friend of your father's in some sort of container business, you sold insurance to make extra money for clothes, shoes, skiing in the mountains during Carnival, weekend group trips (*group*?) to the Algarve. Somewhere along the line there was a married man, a good bit older than you, whose name I never found out—were there other older men, other intrigues going on during our relationship? The oily morning impregnated Marilia's gestures with its sad heaviness:

"Just like that it's off to the lagoon at Aveiro. Sometimes I have to wonder why I put up with you."

Black caprices, raging melancholies, anxieties whose color

58

matched that of the clouds gathering over the ocean, pillows on pillows, replete with double chins, with taffeta. The annoying voice of the minuscule man giving him amiable slaps on his bottom in front of the two plainclothesmen guarding the doorway. Long and heavy tears hung from the melancholy of the pines, transparent; what in God's name ever possessed me to hook up with a bourgeois?; the gray-haired woman who was walking her dog in a foreign city park removed her sunglasses and smiled: her eyes were swallowed up in a pile of wrinkles:

"I don't have a clear recollection of my first husband," she hesitated, "twenty years have gone by and little by little we begin to forget people. I remember that he didn't want to separate, he went into a tantrum, shattered the chinaware, woke up the neighbors—you know, the rage of the impotent, the pathetic anger of the insecure. Then he lived for a while with a colleague, one of those pitiful Communists who wear red ponchos and clacking clogs, and then he killed himself, he turned up in the mud among the rotten reeds of Aveiro, surrounded by birds. He was supposed to go to some conference or other but he never made it, in fact he was always bailing out of his commitments. Sexually I've never seen such a washout, he couldn't get it up, he'd get all frustrated, apologize, cry. I don't know why you're so interested in him, nobody else is."

"Six pounds and thirteen ounces at birth and some difficulty in getting him to breast-feed," the doddering pediatrician read from his file. (There was no one in the waiting room.) "The usual childhood diseases, had all his vaccinations, got circumcised when he was eight."

He slowly lifted his eyes from the page:

"That's done, as you probably know, when the foreskin doesn't separate from the head of the penis."

"We're almost at Aveiro, Marilia, look at all the inn signs," *Inn, Inn, Inn, Inn,* arrows pointing into the morning fog, the smell of stagnant water, the sensation of beach nearby, and I still haven't thought of what to tell you, I can't find the words to explain what I do and don't feel, my longing to run away again, to turn my back, to leave, staying in this crappy country, making the rounds of the same old cinemas, the bars, the bearded and verbosely artistic friends who mumble over solitary beers about things they'll never do. I don't love you anymore (did I ever?), I want to live alone for a while (have I ever wanted anything else?), I need to feel that I'm my own man, understand?, that there are no strings tugging at my arms and legs (don't worry, I'll find some new ones before long), my kids are growing up and I need more time for them (how many weekends has it been since I've seen them?), "We're almost in Aveiro," and I forgot the smell of your hair, the shape of your chest, the oozing, saplike way your thighs become moist. When our relatives visited, my father would set up the screen at one end of the living room, get out the projector, turn off the lights: a trembling white rectangle appeared on the screen, red crosses and lines vibrated and vanished, cigarette smoke would wind into slow swirls in the cone of light that passed over our heads, and then the sea full of albatrosses, the crooked line of foam, the sawdust-colored beach stretching on and on, and once more the albatrosses gathering in the film's square of thick blue, their tapered bodies, their pale open beaks, their wings like flattened feather dusters, tens, hundreds, thousands of birds whose caws, cries, and childlike whining you could feel if not hear, birds perched on rocks, challenging or fighting each other, puffing out their chests, fierce, impassioned, happy, calling and teasing and chasing one another—my father only filmed birds and the guests threw out learned and asinine comments, lit up cigars, added ice to their whiskey glasses, the microscopic voice of the telephone abruptly hardened, aghast, and adamant:

"Liberal Arts? All you can do with that is become a high school teacher for peanuts. Have a little sense, young man,

Economics or Law. Liberal Arts—that's ludicrous. Do you know anyone with a Liberal Arts degree who heads up a big business?"

"He refuses to work for us," reported his father's friend, a bifocaled individual who directed the London office and was going through a huge dossier with a red pencil. "He shows absolutely no interest in what's his or will eventually be his. His brothers-in-law are robbing him blind and like an idiot the guy thinks of nothing but King Afonso Henriques and King Pedro IV, stupid old fossils no one gives a damn about; he spends entire days consulting manuscripts in libraries. I can't for the life of me figure out where he got such weird interests."

"Liberal Arts?" his mother asked, wrinkling her forehead. "What's that?"

She shuffled the cards with a prestidigitational agility, briskly dealt them around the green cloth to the cardplayers, and now you have cancer, you're pale, emaciated, dying, the unemployed cousin knits while watching your solitary agony; the phone will probably ring over the weekend in the hotel room where I won't be, my youngest sister sobbing, "Dad just left, it would be a good idea if you came back," but I went to Aveiro, Sis, to explain—how selfish—the birds to myself, the gulls that I'm beginning to make out in the distance, behind the pine trees, flying in circular paths or in long rising ellipses; I went to Aveiro and you can all go to hell, you and your family bullshit, your trite family deaths as far away as the farmhouse when I was little and my father sat me in his lap to tell me about the birds under the big chestnut tree; everyone and everything can go to hell except for the smell of the stagnant water I'm arriving at now, the weeping willows, the grasses, the nameless trees. "I just hope the bed's not too soft," says Marilia. "I can't sleep in soft beds, even my dreams sink away." She's already resigned, already humble, already prepared for the security of a long-lasting truce. This woman

61

likes me, he thought with surprise while passing a tractor, This woman—how amazing—sincerely likes me; more fog, more pine trees, not a house in sight, only earth and water, both flat and gray, nearing and commingling, reflecting each other like facing mirrors—"Which is the real one, young man?, Tell me without touching which one's real and which one's false," ordered the Geography teacher—dark men pedaling along the highway shoulders, where to?, their wide and inflated backs hunched over the handlebars; "Liberal Arts," repeated his forehead-wrinkling mother, "what in the world is that?" How do the birds sleep? he wondered while fishing in his pockets for his cigarettes; My God, how much there was in my childhood that never got explained, darkness, the sun, rain, people's laughter, and at that moment an isolated building appeared on the edge of the water where some small rotted boats were anchored in the sludge, two or three cars with foreign license plates (French? English? German?) parked next to its door; we took the bags out of the car—as usual the trunk refused to open, refused to close, he had to bear down on the hood with all his weight before finally hearing the tranquilizing click. "There we go," Marilia was standing next to the sand and contemplating the river that slid without a wrinkle toward seas they could only presume, for they were wrapped all around by fog and trees and silence in the suddenly enormous morning without a window of blue; he grabbed the suitcase, a large bag, and a small one, she took the shiny black bag that looks like what bow-tied doctors tote around in Westerns ("Where's the sheriff that got shot?"), that she used for her toilet articles ("Over there, Dr. McGraw," stretched out on the shattered saloon mirror), and they walked without talking, one in front of the other, toward the inn, the glass entrance doors, *English Spoken*, insignias of tourist organizations around the door's lock, hundreds of sea gulls gliding in silence over the borderless bay, as if lightly perched on an unreflecting metallic film; there was a woman with glasses at the counter on the right, writing in some sort of accounts journal, the keys were hanging on a board behind her, and farther back there was a miniature waterfall lavishly decorated with flowers; a tall, skinny bellboy wearing a waist-coat and patent leather shoes was climbing some stairs in the rear. "We need a room until Sunday," I said, and the woman with glasses nonchalantly continued her additions and sub-tractions, the sea gulls outside began quivering gently, almost imperceptibly; "A room until Sunday," he repeated energet-ically while dropping the suitcase and the larger bag, plop, plop, sounding like dead bodies hitting the floor tiles; some posters advertised Espinho, Armação de Pera, and other sights, there was the obligatory Barcelos rooster on a shelf, a pottery ashtray with an unextinguished cigarette butt; the nearsighted woman—chin still down, eyes fixed on her notebook—handed us a registration card. "Do you have a pen?" I asked Marilia, who was stepping from poster to poster with ironic curiosity. What a shit of a country we've got, she expressed with her frowns before the paper land-scapes, What a truly shitty country we live in. As always, when you're mad or bewildered at me your vexation becomes cosmic, he thought, expanding in concentric circles until it encompasses the entire universe in a single wave of bitterness. I like Espinho, I like Armação de Pera, I like Barcelos, I like our apartment in Lisbon on Sundays when my head's not stuffed up, Benfica won at soccer, it's summer, and my back isn't killing me; I like being here and with you at times; somewhere a branch brushed its ancient and dried-out tufts against a window and the sound grated in my ears like the teacher's chalk at school. I slid back the registration card, and the woman with glasses blindly extended her arm, without so much as glancing at me, snapped a key off the board with the astonishing precision of surgical pincers, handed it to me, and lifted her head—and I found myself facing her huge, di-optrically magnified eyes, a pair of repellent insects with an infinite number of eyelash legs; the sea gulls took flight in unison, traced an ascending semicircle in the fog, and resettled further on down the bay. I began to individualize them, counting one two three four five six seven eight, and had almost reached nineteen when you called me, "Rui," there were still so many gulls to count in my head, so many gulls on that somber morning saturated with damp cold; our baggage was carted down the hall by another waistcoat with patent leather shoes, but this one much older, his face all fissured, having that humbled animal look of rustics and the wide bony torso of a mule (They probably pay him less than the others), down the hall over a worn-out runner, past rooms with metal numbers, past tacky watercolors on the walls, past a brown-uniformed maid dragging a vacuum cleaner whose long pouch hung like an elephant's trunk. "Here it is," the rustic said while fighting with a lock as recalcitrant as the car trunk's: a narrow entryway with the prices posted on a framed card, a dark compartment in which only the gleaming towel rack could be distinguished (Tiny bars of soap, he thought, I hate the tiny soaps wrapped in slick paper with flowers that are invariably found in hotel bathrooms), two beds with floral-patterned spreads, the room service buzzer on one of the headboards, a dresser with a mirror, and the three of us on the other side, identical but left-handed, mutually regarding each other with a serious air. I never could get used to growing up, he thought, how absurd it all is; it was great when my father took care of everything, he'd choose the vacation spot, he'd pay the tips, he'd get the car fixed, one after another he'd smooth out life's little tragedies with miraculous ease, "Your Math teacher will pass you on the condition that you stop screwing off in class," "You've got a dentist appointment this week," "Present yourself to Colonel Barroso at the General Staff office day after tomorrow and he'll straighten everything out in a jiffy." His father, his father's friends, his father's stratagems, his father's power, his father's money, and here he was reduced to working out the cost in his head to see if there would be enough in his account to cover the check he was going to write for three nights' lodging; the rustic pulled aside the curtain to reveal the Vouga River and there it was again, the peaceful film of water, like a breeze running over the grass—his mother talked with her friends about problems with maids; "Explain the birds to me, Dad"—he put a crumpled twenty-escudo bill in the bellhop's hand, the door closed, they were alone, and he felt the same panic as on the afternoon when he made love for the first time: he'd asked his oldest brother-in-law everything, "Which way do the legs go? . . . and the arms? . . . then what do I do?", the woman lay in the bed smiling, the sheet pulled up to her neck, "Come over here, sonny, a kid brings good luck and God knows I need it," she belonged to the pathetic class of people entangled in unbelievable misfortunes, the suicide of her husband, the death of her son, a few months in a sanatorium, "See this scar on my ribs? That's from when I had a pneumothorax." He finally sat on the mattress, running his fingers through her hair and feeling like a responsible grown-up, "You should get married again and try to be happy"—her armpits had a penetrating and disgusting odor (garlic?), her tongue ran down his chest, lingering over his navel, groin, and testicles as he lay stretched flat on the sheets with his eyes closed, twitching from a pleasure he'd never known, wave after wave that made his skin swell—and he thinks, I'm going to take care of you, make you turn a new leaf, as soon as I graduate from high school I'll find a job and a place to live, there are lots of places, I'd rather live in Estrela or a neighborhood where you can see the river; you'll put on your imitation leopard-skin coat and we'll go to the movies on Saturdays, to romantic dramas at the Odeon, MODEL COUPLE, SON OF INDUSTRIALIST AND REFORMED PROSTITUTE, RECEIVED BY THE POPE—her tongue slowly moves up and down his penis until her lips finally close over it, a drop of goo leaks out, his shaft turns red, How fucking hard I'm getting, I'm going to come, what are you going to do (spit? swallow? spit? swallow? spit? swallow?) with what I'm about to dump out?; and almost immediately, "That'll be five dollars; that didn't cost much, did it?" She hadn't even removed her black bra with an embroidered rose in the middle, even the son was probably a lie, he went down the stairs feeling the kind of disillusion with the world that he imagined led people to jump off bridges, he walked up to the lookout at São Pedro de Alcântara, kicking the litter in his path and meditating on how to get even with the universe, he grabbed onto the cold iron parapet, Goddam Lisbon, he thought, goddam rotten city, so many houses and so many streets full of bastards and shitheads, he had leaned his forehead against the panes to observe the river and the movement of the birds, while behind him the mirror on the wall of their hotel room was no doubt reflecting his sagging, muscleless, thirty-year-old back. They arranged their clothes in the drawers without speaking, he brushed his teeth to get rid of the tobacco taste in his mouth, here I am again with shaving cream running down my chin, and these wrinkles, and these dark circles, and the receding hairline of a seventy-year-old; you pulled down your slacks and panties, Marilia, and sat on the toilet to urinate the scale of a harp with your elbows on your knees and your chin in your palms, and I was disgusted by your complete lack of decorum: you could have waited until I'd left the bathroom to do that, to wipe yourself, as usual taking too much toilet paper, an interminable length torn with a furious snap from the holder, daughter of proletarians and a confirmed Communist but as wasteful as they come, the amount of toothpaste you slather on your brush, for instance, water in the bathtub filled to overflowing, the pilot light eternally lit on the boiler like a votive candle; and your underpants back up, then your pantyhose, your slacks (you have to shake your haunches like a turkey in order to fit), your short hair combed any old way with your fingers, your nonexistent makeup, your oversized sweater hanging on you like flesh on the bones of people who've lost weight. Tucha would take hours to get herself ready, she'd pencil her eyes with a precise hand and put shadow on her eyelids with a tiny brush, but from my present, somewhat removed vantage point, my boredom is equal, my desire for solitude identical, my longing for silence the same, I want to be simultaneously left in peace and not left in peace, loved and not loved, called and forgotten; Tucha repositioned the photograph of the four of us on the dresser and asked in a friendly conversational tone:

"Now that everything's been decided, exactly what day are you moving out?"

Two old foreign couples were eating lunch at two separate tables in the empty restaurant whose windows looked out onto the lagoon. A skinny waiter was pushing a two-story cart of desserts and cheeses, and after they'd sat down across from each other, as if for a game of chess, one of the old foreigners smiled at them. The water outside, the color of smelted lead, seemed to be flowing backward and slowly dragging its count-less birds with it. A large boat with a yellowish sail and a crew of three hazy men passed by the terrace. An invisible dog barked. A red-jacketed waiter wearily picked up the menus (with a cord down the middle; for what?).

"Aveiro," Marilia said, as if announcing a last stop. "Time for the big scene."

"As far as I could tell they were ordinary guests just like any others," the woman wearing glasses at the front desk affirmed, blinking her gigantic eyes. "I don't distinguish be-tween clients."

The consommé was a store-bought kind (Forever con-demned, from birth until death, to eating packaged soup, he noted with resignation), the fried eggs runnier than those of his parents' maid, who finally got married when she was pushing fifty ("It was like she was one of the family," gloated his mother), wedding a cross-eyed policeman; and I was godfather to their baby boy, a booby who came around every Christmas in a checkered jacket, with greedy hopes for a few bucks, "Merry Christmas, Godfather," and he, silently, Go to hell, you little mongoloid, and the godson would stare at him relentlessly like a hungry pup, his timid feet poking at the fringe of the rug; the tasteless meat seemed an agglomerate of grease surrounded by potatoes and wilted plants, the English tourists (they had English newspapers lying next to their plates) uttered educated throat gurgles from one table to the other, through the open door of the kitchen a diligent broom could be seen sweeping the tile floor, I leaned back in the chair and ordered two coffees. "Most birds," his father explained, "except for parrots, parakeets, and such, live a very short life, if they don't die at birth; some migrate in the winter to warmer climates, while those that aren't up to the journey stop along the way, and risk being devoured by owls if they tarry too long and are caught trying to escape into the woods at night." She led me up the garden path no doubt about it, he thought at the São Pedro de Alcântara lookout, gazing at the rooftops, the labyrinth of streets and the sky's pale blue with a melancholy beyond words, up the garden path, and gullible me believed every word of the hairy little bitch, who didn't even take off her underwear, "Come in my mouth, sweet little thing. How salty your dinghy's goo is." "No thanks," he said abruptly, "I don't want any pastry, and no fruit either," he filliped the little pouch of sugar, tore one of the corners, and dumped the contents into the brown liquid; "Only girls and homos study Liberal Arts," observed Carlos. "Your mother said she'll pay for you to study journalism in Brussels if you want. Belgian chicks have amazing bodies, you'd have a great time." "By the end of the month at the latest," allowed Tucha. "There's absolutely no reason to keep dragging this thing out," and he stood up, paced back and forth in the living room, stopped in front of the bookcase, where photographs of smiling babies and adults leaned against the spines:

"For the sake of the kids," he argued. "The only thing I'm concerned about is the kids."

"My grandsons are profoundly traumatized," his mother said, her hair under the dryer, as the kneeling pedicurist massaged her feet, scoured her bunions, and painted her toenails. "They wetted their beds until age thirteen, and what housemaid will put up with that nowadays?"

"An utterly normal infant," concluded the pediatrician while handing the file to the nurse, "at least during all the time he was my patient. He must be what, thirty-three or thirty-four by now?"

"I consulted a psychologist," Tucha said, "and he assured me that the ideal solution for the children is to live alone with me and without arguments, without friction, without the constant nit-picking that goes on between us two."

The feeding bottles, the diapers, and most of all the pregnancies, your huge belly bouncing on top of swollen legs—you looked like a plastic goose with a string; the ridiculous natural childbirth exercises, twenty potbellied women down on the floor and breathing rhythmically as their husbands held their hands (It seemed as if our arms were leashes attached to bizarre and repugnant animals); waking up in the middle of the night to feel your face stretched into a kind of beached whale's torso, gently panting against the foam ripples of the embroidered pillowcases, the new and unfamiliar smell of your skin, the strange fish inside you, all rolled up, your intestines, your wan smile in the clinic—"Are you happy, dear?"—your white hands, your deflated stomach. He thinks, How is it that things have changed so much? How can there be this coldness, this distance, this sudden gap between us? Maybe it's because we were too young, too naive; maybe it's because time and our lies and our mistakes have no compassion and so won't forgive us the slightest slipup, the slightest miscalculation, the slightest oversight: where in our life together did I go wrong?

"We can always try," he insisted. "Nothing's irreparable."

They finished drinking the coffee and returned to their room. The moored boats were tarnishing like ancient hair, the birds flitted across the lake, on the opposite shore a few charcoal-drawn smokestacks stuck out above the mist that formed a gray-stumped swirl over the lonely inn. He sat on the mattress to take off his shoes (a sketch of a green boat in a raffia frame hung over the bed) and stretched out on his back while Marilia brushed her teeth in the bathroom (what an obsession, she was forever brushing her teeth, producing that horrible noise of enamel being scrubbed—when she woke up, after meals, and before turning in). It had been different with her, slow and calm, without much passion, but on the other hand he could talk about things that interested him and got him excited, like the Party, and he felt understood, accepted, they exchanged opinions about films, books, the university, their vague and grandiose ambitions, their vehement dreams of revamping the methodology for teaching History; one night they stayed up talking later than usual, his eyes hurt from the cigarette smoke, a dark blue clarity began sweeping the sky; "Why don't you bring your clothes here tomorrow," he suggested in the middle of a discussion about Michelet or Toynbee; "Those are cockatoos," his father said, "those are kites, there you have eagles, and those with the long bills are ibises"—the two of them would go to the zoo to look at the birds up close, at their ferocious crystal retinas, the claws on their feet, the way their feathers were arranged on their wings, the old birds, the young ones, the fuzz on their breasts; the crows walked like us over the cement floor littered with excrement, husks, and peels; the storks reminded him of one of his father's friends who lifted his knees way up when he walked; he felt sorry for the ostriches, whose feet seemed pinched by tight shoes; his father said, "Each sound they make means something different, we humans are the ones who haven't evolved enough to understand certain languages, certain movements of the head, the patterns in which birds fly." Marilia extracted a trashy-looking book from her bag and sat down on her mattress to read with the same resigned air worn by the wives who knit in parked cars next to soccer stadiums; the springs creaked in protest whenever one of them shifted on their pillows; his youngest sister, with swollen eyelids and dressed in black, opened the car door and said:

"I refuse to talk to the press, you reporters distort everything."

"No, no, and no!" Tucha said hotly. "It's time you learned to accept things as they are. Relationships die."

He thinks, That's not your own thought, you heard it from someone else, from the shrink, from a friend, a lover, during one of those endless phone calls when you shut yourself up in the bedroom to confide inanities into the receiver. He thinks, I hate you, I'm going to do everything I can to turn the kids against you, I'll slowly, subtly inject them with venom, drop by drop, Sunday after Sunday. "Your mother doesn't want to live with me." "Your mother doesn't want you to have a father." "Your mother wants to replace me with someone else." I'll stand in the shadows of the house at night, armed with a crowbar, and I'll break open the head of anyone who enters; at eleven o'clock some creep pulls up in his car, walks to the door, and rings the bell while I softly tap the bar against my thigh. "If you want to talk to the woman of the house then talk to her husband first, pal," and the guy backs off, nervous, stumbling. "I must have the wrong house—what's the number?" And with a feeble smile of disguised defeat, "Oh right, I wanted fifty-six and this is number fifty-four, sorry." I take a couple of steps forward, inwardly amused, outwardly surly, "That may be, but at any rate your face rings a bell, come here into the light so I can get a closer look." "I got the number wrong, that's all, I've got to get going, I'm in a big hurry," the

71

fellow whimpers; and I think, You little turd, I'm going to bang your balls in, your pea-sized balls; his forehead is a mass of panicky wrinkles by then, he sidles over to where his car's parked, tries to insert the key without me noticing, to slip away, disappear, flee; I grab him by the tie and observe his strangled expression; "What do you want from me what do you want from me what do you want from me?" he moans in terror; "Just what the fuck do *you* want?" I correct, flattening him against the hood and pushing his ribs in with my knee; Marilia puts her book on the nightstand and lies sideways on her bed, which is separated from his by an unsightly throw rug, she closes her eyes; but I know that you're waiting for me to talk, that you think I'm brewing something, that your worried eyes are spying me from behind your closed lids, that you think I'm acting strange, anxious, unhappy; I pick up the phone and give the operator the number of the clinic—what a bitch to have to die in northwest Lisbon, Jesus—"Room seventeen, please." "One moment," answers the voice of the impassioned owl, some clicking, clacking, static. "Hello," says the cousin. "It's me," he says. "How's my mother?" "All right," the cousin replies after a pause. "Do you want to talk to her?" "No," he says, "I just want to know how she's doing." "Don't worry," the cousin says with forced cheeriness, "just have a good time with King Dinis and we'll manage okay here." "Did my father show up?" he asks and there's another, shorter silence. "He called from the airport, he's on his way to Scotland, but your sisters came and if you want me to give them a message . . ." I hang up abruptly. I look at the ceiling plaster, the straw lamp, the slowly darkening lagoon. What will the gulls do now? Hold me in your lap and explain to me how the birds go to sleep, the night will swallow the boats and the birds, the smokestacks of Aveiro, the lights that shimmer indecisively in the distance. "Well?" Marilia says, groping for her cigarettes on the nightstand; she lights one at the filter end, tosses it aside, and tries another. What does my mother matter to you? What in truth does she matter to me? She blows a smoke ring. "Well what?" he says.

"He disappeared on Sunday and the woman paid; she took their car and left the inn the next day," clarified a thin man in shirt sleeves, speaking from an office full of file cabinets. "They probably had a fight, couples are unpredictable, we never know what they're going to do. I walked down the aisle one time and swore never again."

Tucha helped him carry his suitcases to the elevator and gave him a peck on the cheek:

"So long," she said with zero emotion. And yet your lips, your fragrance, and the closeness of your body stung my eyelids with a strange acid. Tears? he wonders, mortified. You mean I'm going to break out crying on the doormat like an abandoned baby? He pulled the elevator door shut, pressed the button to take him down, and something indefinable changed in my life. He stared for a while at the building and then drew away from it in small steps, lugging his bags along with him.

"Don't you want to tell me how she's doing?" Marilia asked.

"One, two, three, or a million tutors—however many it takes to keep this nincompoop from failing his courses," his father stood in the living room and bellowed at his mother, who listened from her chair, looking down and clicking her knitting needles in flawless time. (He couldn't see me because I was in the doorway and he had his back turned, next to the sofas that needed reupholstering.) "Only an imbecile like him could fail at Math, even a retard could learn what they teach there."

"He's determined to pursue Liberal Arts," his mother revealed. "Last week he told me that he wants to study History. I was flabbergasted."

73

His father banged his fist on the art nouveau bar, making the bottles and glasses jump:

"Liberal Arts? History?" (He spoke the words slowly, surprised to no end.) "Are you sure the lunatic we're talking about is really my son?"

At the street corner, flanked by suitcases, he tried unsuccessfully to get a cab. Tears ran down along his nose and formed a puddle in the hollow of his chin, a few drops overflowing and dampening his shirt. And yet, he thought now, I didn't love her, I couldn't really have loved her; they had nothing in common except the same decadent origins and the same forever drifting adolescence: like two kids in a room full of toys and not the least notion of what to do with themselves or with their meaningless plans. Had he become an adult since then? An adult on the inside, responsible and determined, with the strength to face the stupid absurdity of day-to-day living?

"Those who can't find a meaning for life no matter how hard they try," spouted the psychologist while using a pencil to draw precise circles on a piece of paper, "are always potential suicides. Sooner or later the emptiness of their daily existence plunges them into an anxiety not unlike what trapped laboratory rats experience, and the next thing you know it's pills, gas, the rope, a bullet, sulfuric acid, the ninth floor, a knife, electricity, a bridge, pesticide, kerosene, the ocean. Their imagination, ladies and gentlemen, literally has no limits."

"History, how could he?" roared his father as he lifted his glass of whiskey to eye level and refilled it from a cut-glass bottle that sat with a dozen others on an antique backgammon table. "I'll give you some History, dear wife. A worthless idiot who doesn't understand the first thing about life, a bum, a fuck-up, a baby—the ingrate has no right. Economics, Engineering, or Law and he'd be all set. History, think of it.

74

History, so he can be a simpleton without the least notion of what a logarithm is."

Light entered via the living room verandas, silverishly and surreally filtering through the bougainvillea and wild roses of the garden, and their bodies, the furniture, the pictures on the walls, and the bric-a-brac that littered the house became imponderable, suspended in the scintillating glow, as if helium vapor had filled their veins. His mother's hair had the mysterious angelic texture of fairies, her dress rippled slowly, wafted by an inexplicable breeze. I began climbing the steps to my room without touching the runner, and something spongy and stretchy made me fly, as it were.

"After we separated," declared the sunglassed woman walking her dog in a foreign city, "I hardly ever saw him again. The divorce was by proxy; he was in Strasbourg on a study grant."

The lagoon disappeared completely, transformed into a deep and shoreless lake dotted by a few asymmetrical lights, devoid of any brilliance. There wasn't a bird or a boat to be seen, and even their own movements became invisible in the dark.

"They've probably stopped serving dinner," murmured the bodiless voice of Marilia, reduced to the orange-colored arabesques of her lit cigarette and the dark blob of her head. "They've probably closed the dining room and all gone to watch TV in that horrendous lobby that looks like it came out of a nursing home, with chairs for invalids pulled up in front of the screen. We'll find the whole crew there, you'll see: the icy receptionist, the two guys in waistcoats, and the chambermaid who's going to make our beds tomorrow, without any stains on the sheets to report to the others."

She spoke slowly, without anger or resentment, but I'd completely stopped listening to her: I found myself on my father's lap, under the chestnut tree by the well, on an ancient afternoon that had never completely died in him (Inside the house his mother watched them, smiling, with a book across her lap), listening to the explanation of the birds. So absorbed that even the noise of the water outside their window, the sound of the TV commercials, and the coughing of the English guests in the hallway had ceased to exist, giving way to an infinitely vast clearing inhabited by nothing but the hoarse cries of gulls.

FRIDAY

Witness Alice F., manager of the inn at Aveiro and resident of same. She took the oath and under questioning testified: That on Tuesday, February 10, between 4 and 6 P.M., she was at her habitual place of work, explaining the bill to an elderly English couple and watching as their luggage was hauled to their rental car, when a male child, son of the cook and approximately twelve years of age, burst into the lobby, extremely agitated, bumping into the English woman with his dirty elbow, and shouting to the deponent, "Missis Alice, come look what's out there." When the deponent severely reprimanded him for his lack of good manners and for his total and complete disrespect for the tourist industry, consubstantiated in this case in the person of the geriatric British woman, whose conduct was scrupulously restrained (as is customary in her native Isles) within the parameters of the most perfect decorum, the boy hurled down a white-painted metal rack full of lovely illustrated postcards of interesting spots in our beautiful country such as Monsaraz and yelled with rabid fury, "Stop lecturing, you silly biddy, there's a dead man out there in the middle of the sand." In spite of her incredulity—she being well aware of the fertility of infant imaginations, which modern means of communication have morbidly exploited—the deponent hastened the departure of the foreign couple, waving them off with a smile from the front steps, and as soon as the vehicle had jerked out of sight down the road bordered by pine trees and shrubs withering from drought, she found the boy, and in an admonishing tone—after first commenting, "Is this what they teach you kids in school?"—she asked, "What ever possessed you to act like that in a private establishment?" To which he answered, in between obscenities the deponent wouldn't dream of repeating and which she attributes to the progressive dissolution of social mores set off by the lamentable revolutionary period we lately had the misfortune to suffer, that there was a man's body about two hundred yards west of the inn, semidevoured by the sea gulls' uncontrollable gluttony, and that its dimensions, clothes, and eyeglasses corresponded to those of a guest who had arrived on the previous Thursday, with his wife, with whom he would walk on the shore of the lagoon, having long conversations whose content was in no wise known to the deponent. Notwithstanding her legitimate doubts as to the veracity of the information received, in order to alleviate her conscience the deponent proceeded to the place indicated, where birds from the Vouga River were flying overhead in a swarm that intrigued her, for it was unusual to find so many birds and hear so much cawing on a morning with neither rain nor threat of rain, just a gray, sticky, and humid fog drowning the town in its canvas of stationary tears; and there among the reeds, stomach upward, arms open, and face beyond recognition, apparently pecked away by bird beaks, she found the guest Rui S., identified on page two of these proceedings. The deponent was immediately certain that the corpse belonged to said Rui S., not only because of the facts recorded above in the present testimony, but also because one of the cadaver's eyes was still intact, large and round, staring with the expression of agonizing distress or of submissive resignation with which he usually looked at her, even to ask for the key to the room. The sea gulls expressed their annoyance at her intrusion by breaking out in a chorus of ferocious screeching and by beating their wings in a commotion that so frightened her she hurried back to the inn to telephone the police and inform them of the occurrence, after first awarding the boy a pack of anise candies and two illustrated postcards of Viana do Castelo, *partial view*. Questioned about what she knew of the deceased, she claimed to have met him for the first time on the aforementioned Thursday, shortly before two o'clock, when he arrived at the inn with a woman presumed to be his wife and requested a room for the weekend in a needlessly rude manner, thus prompting the deponent to hand over the registration card and the key in silence, depriving them of the usual warm welcome accorded to her clients without distinction of race, nationality, or social class. She added that he appeared at the reception desk three or four times a day and that he seemed nervous and worried. On one occasion he asked her to place a call to a clinic in Lisbon, but he didn't talk for more than two or three minutes. Questioned about the woman in his company, the deponent answered that she was about the same age as the deceased, had a simultaneously hostile and neglected appearance, and had left by herself the day before the body was discovered, having first paid the bill with a check not as yet verified for sufficient funds. She generally wore a poncho, predominantly red in color, blue jeans, and black clogs. She was characterized (in the deponent's opinion) by the ironic sidelong glances she gave to the pictures and prints of attractive regional scenes that hung on the inn's walls, pictures chosen by the deponent both to beautify the premises and to cheer the idle moments of her clientele. With respect to the motives for the suicide, assuming that such a hypothesis be confirmed by the data thus far compiled and the medical examiner's report, the deponent affirmed complete ignorance, notwithstanding the obvious anxiety of the victim and the strange behavior of people in our day and age. The deponent wished furthermore to call attention to the frantic commotion of the sea gulls, mallards, and other smaller birds whose names, common or scientific, are unknown to her; said creatures all demonstrated an absolutely singular behavior, such as she had never seen—to wit, on the one hand protecting the cadaver and on the other hand tearing it to pieces, reducing it to confused shreds of blood and clothing, thereby greatly hindering the removal of the body, an operation made all the more difficult by the birds' fury, which was unleashed against anyone who tried to approach the corpse, so that ultimately it took shotguns and fire-truck hoses to disperse them. The deponent was so agitated by the incident that she suffered an attack of fever in the night and dreamed of birdmen with human faces and bleeding black claws whirling around her, calling out with appeals even sadder than church hymns, and trying to peck her thighs and chest. Even after the deceased was transferred by ambulance to Oporto (How could one forget the stretcher covered with a blanket, the newspaper cameras, and the paunchy, meek man who seemed to command the whole operation with his hands in his pockets and a match in his mouth like a construction foreman), the birds stayed for several more days, never once leaving the spot where the departed had lain, tracing bizarre, disturbing ellipses in the grass until things gradually returned to normal with the arrival of the first rains: the sea gulls went back to the water, the ducks emigrated south, the serenity of winter calmed the eucalyptus and pine trees, the boats resumed their habitual routes, the strange dreams ceased, the deponent canceled her appointment with the Aveiro psychologist she was counting on to alleviate her nights of fevered sweating, her fears and nightmares of winged men; the large dark clouds of March mingled and separated, and the sadness of a swampy peace consisting of the smooth, uneventful passing of the months took hold in her blood, in the fabric of her person, like a form of death, the certainty that her old age would be spent behind the front desk of an inn, giving keys and receiving keys, do you understand, until the day that, I mean, giving keys and receiving keys, giving keys and receiving keys, giving keys and receiving keys, giving keys and receiving keys, writing up bills, writing up bills, writing up bills, making out receipts, paying the personnel, the suppliers, the landlord, carrying the picture of my late husband in a locket around my neck, watching television standing up, behind the guests, going to bed alone, taking baths alone, eating alone, do you see what I'm saying, until the day when at last. And that was all she said. Read, ratified, and signed.

HE WOKE UP EARLY because he'd slept in the bed next to the window without remembering to lower the blinds and draw the curtains, and he had the sensation that the sheets were drifting in the mist of the lagoon, among heavy, low clouds born of the water's turbid thickness. He got up, went to the bathroom, urinated without turning on the light, returned to his bed, and crawled under the covers: my head hurts, my back hurts, my legs hurt, the heat must have been running all night. A dingy light, like a patient potter, slowly modeled the outlines of things, and I began to make out your face squeezed against the pillow, an eye, your open mouth, your cheeks' parenthetical wrinkles, the still blurry shape of your body. The clothes draped over the chairs oscillated to the rhythm of

81

a mysterious breathing, the walls slowly swelled and contracted: the barking of my temples in the pillow makes the world
throb. He thought of smoking a cigarette or reading a book
but preferred to sit on the mattress and watch the morning
advance across the floor inch by inch, revealing the wood's
imperfections, the rug's fringes, the furniture's bowed and
splintering legs: every day begins with this physical discomfort, this strange birth of things familiar, your distorted face
that still sleeps. On Azedo Gneco Street blurry figures rum-
maged through the garbage cans, a municipal truck moved
down the street slowly, spouting jets of water from above its
wheels, and the Tagus could be felt panting far away, beyond
all the buildings.

"Is this where you live?" asked his youngest sister from the
doormat, poking her curious chin into the foyer: the mannequin that served as an umbrella stand, the wooden wagon
wheel leaning against the wall, and the pseudo-oriental print
with a long-tailed bird fluttering on a branch suddenly struck
me as trite, ugly, and ridiculous. "Aren't you going to ask
me in?"

The woman turned her face away and its contorted features
disappeared, replaced by a ball of dark, sleep-tangled hair,
identical to a ball of yarn full of loose ends. He thinks, How
many weeks since I last felt like making love to you? He
thinks, Everything's become so predictable between us—our
foreplay, the taste of our saliva, our unsatisfying orgasms, our
bodies' way of separating, slow and indifferent, like cells
when they divide. Her body was now gaining substance under
the sheet; the bureau mirror emerged from the shadows and
reflected a closet, pictures, a strip of ceiling.

"So many books," remarked his sister, looking around at
the minute living room, at the photos glued onto pieces of
cardboard and propped against the book spines, at the park
bench clawing the rug with its iron paws, at posters of the
Party, old postcards, tin toys on a table. Tucha would die if

she saw this: forbid her from filling up her house with china-ware and she'd start gasping for breath.

He thinks, You're taking note of everything that's tacky, filing it in your head so you can tell it to your friends, amidst derisive laughter: "I wish you could see how my brother lives; if the Communists win the elections, they'll make us all put a wagon wheel inside our front doors and fill up our houses with the foul smell of books." And Carlos, in an easy chair, solemn and serious, entrenched behind a genuine silk tie: "I have one in the factory who's a model employee." He thinks, Exactly the way my mother talks about well-trained dogs that don't go wee-wee on the carpet.

"Social Democracy, Socialism, Communism," his father said in annoyed commiseration, "don't you see that it's all part of the same plot to destroy us? I don't want to hear that you're conspiring against the government, it's the same as if you said you were going to kill me outright. And as for that impertinent police rookie, I'll talk to the chief and get his wagon fixed good."

Sitting up, with his hands buried under the covers, he watched blinkingly as the morning rose over the lagoon like a gigantic loaf of baking bread, the first sea gulls already perching on the water's smooth surface, its color that of an eyelid's underside: do they sleep that way, drifting wherever the current takes them, or do they hide in the sand, in the reeds of the shore that are gradually emerging from the fog, straight and thin like strands of hair? He considered lowering the blind to keep out the light, to return to the egg tranquillity of night, to transform the room into an island accomplice of darkness, to go back to sleep: his body floating, his dead eyes drifting, his heart at last in peace, just like an anchored boat. Quick steps approached in the hallway, broke in his ears, and went away toward nothing: the large-eyed woman from the front desk? The emaciated bellhop? His rustic colleague? His sister scrutinized his apartment, bending forward as if visiting a museum, her lips pursed in polite disapproval: an indescribable hovel, clothes strewn about, things littering the floor, papers in disarray, I couldn't possibly live here. Going around with her he realized painfully the mess everything was in, the hair in the bathtub drain, the stains on the couch, the silky film of dust, the broken venetian blind in the window.

"How did you find out where I lived?" he asked. "The phone's not in my name, and I didn't give my address to anyone at the university."

In the morning a female voice from the phone company's wake-up service mixed in with the dull neighborhood noises four stories down, hoisting him out of the fishless, seaweed aquarium of his dreams: a neutral, immaterial, precise woman announced the time without a trace of emotion, pushing him to the bathroom, where the razor blade shone on his cheeks like the moon on the sea. The plumber who'd come the day before to fix the sink had left rubble, bits of brick, and mud from his shoes on the tile floor, so he went to the kitchen, full of dirty dishes, in search of a dustpan and broom to dump the debris into the orange plastic trash can that you never remembered to set out on the landing no matter how often I reminded you. I never understood your negligence, your disinterest in the apartment, your total apathy before overflowing ashtrays, the ashes on your tablecloths, and the newspapers stacked up on the bed. On Fridays a cleaning woman of your breed would run an oblivious and innocuous cloth over the accumulated filth, steal some sugar, break a few glasses, and leave after lunching on my tuna fish without so much as a second thought. From the other side of the wall came the sounds of eating utensils, voices, and the muffled music of a radio, while the hopeless morning of Lisbon leaned wearily against the panes.

"You forget how small the world is," his sister answered, frowning as she examined a poster of Lenin's peremptory, orientalish face. Her nose screwed into a sarcastic grimace, "Someone from your wife's family?"

The number of sea gulls increased; a triangular flock of ducks arrived from the direction of the town, describing a vast semicircle in the mist; the dawn wind rustled the leaves. A truck rode past on the highway, resounding with the complaint of exhausted shock absorbers. If I were little, he thought, I'd fog up the window with my breath and write my name with my finger, or I'd imagine a pirate ship going up the lagoon, with a black flag on the highest mast and mean-looking men spying from the gunwale. If I were little, I'd ask if I could use some of my dad's hair cream after my bath; I'd eat dinner in my pajamas and be sent to eat in the kitchen if I held my knife and fork wrong, put my elbows on the table, or splattered the soup. If I were little, I'd be the son of the important industrialist, and the teacher who told me to name the rivers of Mozambique would be more worried about my ignorance than I was. He thinks, The grades they gave me were for him not for me; the school couldn't afford to dishonor the regime by charging the undersecretary of state's son with being a loafer or a dummy; the principal himself would greet me with ceremony; the attendants made sure my schoolmates never hit me; if I felt like yelling *son of a bitch* during recess, the monitors applauded enthusiastically, and the vice-principal's wife, who taught Drawing, melted with effusive respect: "So little and already so precocious."

"Lisbon's a small world," his sister repeated, "and you live in an honest-to-goodness pigsty." Her eyes squinted in disdain, she ran her finger across a shelf and wiped the dirt off on her coat: "I hope you have enough sense never to invite Mom and Dad here."

Maybe I should never have invited myself there, he thinks, while the brunette ball of yarn rolls around on the pillow, mumbling garbled words; an arm emerges from the sheets, teeters on the edge of the mattress, and falls limply until its gently bending, stubby-nailed fingers touch the carpet. He wonders, Would there be long red fingernails at the conference in Tomar, women carefully perfumed, carefully dressed, giving knowing glances while revealing the pubic plantations underneath their skirts? Maybe I should have gone back home after I separated, started dating the daughter of one of my mother's friends, proposed marriage, and started over, instead of choosing the national guardsman's heiress because she'd read more about Godard than I had. Tucha's laughing away at this very moment with her boyfriend, he thought, in one of those bars where people resemble mechanical dolls driven by the motor of their indecision, until at the end of the night they unite in hazy and haphazard sexual embraces: "If you saw what he found to replace me, if you saw the gal he hangs out with now!" Maybe if I'd worked in the firm and ignored Godard I'd be happy; I could be content with bridge, expensive suits, the secretary's nice bottom, the tureens of the East India Company, a foreign bank account. More sea gulls had arrived at the lagoon and another kind of equally white bird whose name he didn't know. A tangerine hue, similar to a bloodstain, spread across the morning as the clouds slipped quietly southward. He looked at the sleeping body aloofly and thought, You'd read more books than me, that's what conquered me; you talked to me about writers, painters, and film directors that I never dreamed existed; you expounded on them as your square-fingered hands opened and closed like underwater plants. He thinks, Your concerns were so different from Tucha's, from my parents', from my friends': May of '68, Vietnam, Black Power, Marshall McLuhan, explosive and distant matters.

"He didn't even know the films of Dreiser," said a slovenly woman in her forties while scratching her head with a red pencil. Her unpolished shoes rubbed against each other as if attracted by a restless magnet. "I spent four years putting up with a man who fell asleep at the Gulbenkian's film series."

"A pigsty," insisted his sister, "an honest-to-goodness pigsty, full of posters against God and family." She lit her cigarette with a porcelain-encased lighter and smiled: "They had a silly collection of tin figures, carts, plows, and such."

His father stepped out from behind her, raising his arms and looming enormous, dressed as the gorilla that frightens visitors to the Haunted House at the amusement park: his voice, simultaneously smothered and reverberating, seemed to rise out of a pail full of cotton scraps:

"What a cockamamy marriage."

"One of my father-in-law's cherished dreams," Carlos said, "was that Rui would work for us, but the guy didn't have the slightest knack for business. Come to think of it, he didn't have much of a knack for anything."

"And when I say Dreiser," continued the slovenly woman, licking her finger to clean a spot of dirt off her stocking, "I mean Marguerite Duras, Andy Warhol, experimental cinema, the classics of the twenties, avant-garde art, etc. Abstract expressionism, for example, was never more than a confused notion in his mind. I think my attraction to him was based on a misperception, an illusion of a certain innocence, a certain naiveté that in fact he didn't have: the mildew of the bourgeoisie had rotted his thinking; he didn't amount to more than a decadent milksop. Read the draft of his dissertation on the Sidonio Pais Administration (she held up a stack of typed pages, frayed and full of corrections) and you'll understand what I'm getting at."

The tangerine hue filled the whole window, the landscape outside became bright and distinct, almost without shadows (the trees' shadows, the clouds' shadows, the water's shadow that shifted and bore the color of raw egg white), the objects in the room acquired the unmysterious depth of daytime, nothing had moved during the night, and your body—triggered by an inner mechanism—began the long, onerous task of waking up: moans, snores, sighs, legs stretching and contracting, head restless, the sheets at high tide. Out in the hall the English geriatrics turned the key in their door lock, excruciatingly, inside my head, as if ferreting for my nerves with a knife; the old woman bubbled a sentence in her smooth fish language, her husband coughed. Friday's here, he thought while turning on the shower in the tiny bathroom and watching the jet of water descending from the ceiling like a cluster of glass filaments that burst open, smashed against the bathtub enamel, headed lazily toward the drain, and gradually fogged up the mirror, the light, and the ceramic of the bidet on which he sat, looking down at his bare feet on the rubber mat and thinking, I'll bet that right now you're reaching out your hand toward the nightstand in search of a stick of strawberry gum, that you're staring around at the room with the swollen, stupefied eyes you have when you've just waken up, that you're beginning to surface from your long-winded dreams of class struggle, of which I sometimes hear a few isolated, incomprehensible words, filtered through your bridgework. When we were first together, he thought, you'd serve me breakfast in bed—"Do you want coffee or tea?"—with your hair combed and dressed in a bathrobe, smiling, you'd kiss my neck, eat the toast crumbs on my chest, you'd stick your hand under the covers and slide it down to my hips, you'd assess my penis and make a funny face, momentarily forgetting Marx, Visconti, concrete poetry, and the fierce and historic fight for women's liberation: how many months since your soft, warm tongue ran over my ribs, how many months since your head went down on my pubis, how many months since I entered inside you, all at once, led on by the impatient, impassioned impulse of my groin? He tested the water with the back of his hand, hesitated, stepped under the shower with a shiver, and began to soap his face, ears, armpits, navel. At their apartment on Azedo Gneco Street the shower leaked from a hole in its pipe, spraying the towels and flooding the floor: there was always a list of things that needed fixing, doorknobs that didn't turn, broken faucets, leaky pipes, a short in the heater that lay idle in the corner like a stringless guitar; there was always a makeshift uncertainty in the air, the atmosphere of a waiting room at a railway station or at a rural airport, the only difference being that instead of enamel spittoons in the corners there were books, rolls of posters, and a heroic radio that had long ceased working.

"I can just imagine the sort of hole he lives in," Tucha said to her friends while drinking a piña colada through a straw, her cheeks sucked in. "The other day I ran across his girlfriend, a horrid little troll who acts like a man." She laughed. "She probably is."

"This is absurd," said his sister, pushing the elevator button. "Don't be so stupid. Ask Mom and Dad for a room at their place. Sooner or later you'll come to your senses and realize how ridiculous you're being." Her head disappeared, shaking a silent no as she descended behind the rusty harmonium doors.

The shower water got cold and I stepped out of the tub and wrapped myself in a towel, my teeth rattling. A cockroach ran between the wall and the floor tiles, cautiously testing what lay ahead with its sensitive antennae. My phosphorescent, ghostlike features shimmered in the beads of steam on the mirror: an Our Lady of the hairy legs, he thought, a transvestite Our Lady surrounded by the cackles of choristers. And yet no matter what you may think, Sis, I had some good times at Azedo Gneco Street—reading *Le Monde* on Sundays when it was raining outside, feeling at home with Marilia, having a brandy, drinking some tea—good times with almost no chinks, I swear, just the slight shadow of a vague, inexplicable melancholy, that incurable ulcer of sadness in the background. Later the anxiety began growing and with it my uneasiness, my fear, my body flailing around in the bed sheets of life, feeling out of place. Why? he wondered while drying his ears, neck, and nape, Why do I always drag this sort of burdensome tail behind me? He wiped a section of mirror with his elbow, quickly combed his hair (Now that I'm thinner I look like Schubert), returned to the room, and got dressed in the clothes he'd worn the day before as you watched in a stupor, half asleep: What country are you traveling in? What strange lands are you returning from?

"I'm going out," he said. "I'm going to walk around a bit, I'll come back at nine with breakfast."

The Japanese watch resting on the nightstand next to the book read seven-thirty, and its worried little mechanism made him think of a panic-stricken heart (my own?) tirelessly galloping toward death.

"A good fellow and not a bad instructor," esteemed the white-haired professor beneath the battle scene engraving as he played with a paper knife whose blade was inscribed with the words *Made in Hong Kong*. "He was working on an unusual dissertation, a bit farfetched perhaps, but I always appreciated his adolescent originality."

"There's nothing else I can tell you, that's all I remember, I was too little to understand certain things," said a man's faraway voice on the phone. "Besides, I've been in Canada for eight years now, without once returning to Portugal, so the memories fade away, you know how it is. I remember the look in his eye, his smile, going with him to the zoo and the circus, and that's about all. Yes, I remember his smile and our excitement on Sundays when he'd ring the doorbell from down below: we were allowed to go down the elevator on our own."

The woman with the dog put her sunglasses back on:

"Poor guy," she said, "it's a pity when someone ends it that way, don't you think?"

He descended the stairs (passing by the hideous cascade that bristled with flowers, the front desk, the key board, the wire rack of illustrated postcards), pushed on the glass door, and walked out onto the gravel patio, the soles of his shoes groaning in protest against the hard little stones. His face smarted from the early morning cold, and he felt his nose and mouth harden and his tongue, with no saliva, shrivel up against his gums. He thinks, Flat water, flat sky, hundreds of birds, the pine trees shivering in the mist, sheathed in the sugar clouds. There was no one in sight, the English geriatrics had vanished, and the inn looked two-dimensional, insignificant, unbeautiful. He began walking distractedly toward the town, his feet digging furrows into the sand as a dog howled in the distance, its barks unmercifully tearing through the tissue paper silence. He thinks, In spite of everything, Sis, I had some okay moments at Azedo Gneco Street, until I began to feel—as I always end up feeling—like a person without a place, an exile both in- and outside me, divested of country and moorings, despairingly free. He thinks, I've got to go back to a rented room (the usual drab furniture, the wardrobe with a curtain instead of a door, suitcase under the bed, and an unpleasant, fastidious, intransigent landlord) and go it alone until I figure out where and what broke, because something, you see, must have gone kaput. A flock of sparrows hopped among the reeds on the shore, the heavy, moldy lagoon smelled like an unwashed armpit: something along the way went kaput, life took an abrupt ninety-degree turn, and here I am more lost than ever. He thinks, Good thing I didn't have any kids with Marilia, good thing there's nothing left behind. Smoke rose in slow motion from the smokestacks of Aveiro, its dim black swirls dissolving in the zibeline clouds, and the houses' blurry outlines could just barely be made out. His sister, out of focus and highly embarrassed, wearing a sleeveless summer dress and propping her chubbiness against the veranda, waved good-bye in the film in front of this same blue water, now the color of brick. Tucha nagged him for years to buy a camera ("Because of the kids if for no other reason"), but the idea of faces frozen in a time that got progressively older had made him shudder since childhood; he hated to squint through a little lens and see someone smiling on the other side; and so he refused: "I like to see the family in the present, Tucha," getting wrinkled, hunching forward, older and older, hobbling toward death. But the truth is you were afraid that your grandchildren would notice your receding hairline and your big gut, and that they'd laugh at you or ignore you, encased in a frame as in a coffin, buried in a wicker chest, at the back of a drawer, or in a pitch-black nook in the attic, until all the useless old clutter was finally tossed into cardboard boxes and into the bilge of a garbage truck. He thinks, My mother's probably waking up right now, unless. He thinks, Fuck it. He thinks, Better go back to the inn and call Lisbon to find out the story, but he felt no emotion as he remembered her, not even a shadow of nostalgia if he imagined, for example, the family gathered together in the clinic, the exasperated calls to his father (Luanda, Toronto, New York), the relatives arriving in small groups, solemn and ceremonious.

"I want to be buried in the grand piano," his grandmother burst out, along with a string of shocking obscenities, as she lay in her deathbed with a rag around her head. I was just a kid and I stared at her in horror from the doorway: is this what the end is like? The IV balloons, the doctor's circumspect visits, my grandmother quiet, still, sleeping, and then unexpectedly, without any warning, her hoary mouth would open into a huge cavern, three or four spongy teeth would appear among the dark gums, and the alarming, inevitable, tremendous yell would issue forth:

"I want to be put in the piano, you little whores."

"A pigsty," assured his sister, sucking on a throat lozenge that enhanced her sentences with an herbal scent, "an unbelievable pigsty."

"I wouldn't call it a big funeral but it was decent enough," his father, still wearing the false beard from his last act, affirmed as his moistened finger swiftly counted through the stacks of money taken in at the ticket booth. (The waves rose and fell on the beach, which was still invisible in the darkness, producing a lazy, heavy, insistent sound. Rows of lights shimmered.) "As for the grand piano, she never even owned one. She had an upright that she gave to some charity when she got it into her head to unload everything."

And he remembered a black, glass-footed piece of furniture, with a pair of empty candlesticks over the keys and a fringed shawl covering the lid, pressed against the wall of a gloomy living room replete with buffets and portraits of bearded men, and he remembered the afternoon when his dry, determined, imperious grandmother hobbled across the rugs with her cane and single-handedly began to sell off cabinets and dishes to stupefied auctioneers; he remembered the moving men in blue jeans lugging the chests down the stairs, and then the piano, floor by floor until they reached the street, clinking displaced B-flats like goutish groans, and the old lady stood on the doormat impassively observing the departure of that strange box of notes, which was finally hoisted onto a ramshackle truck that jolted off to some cellar or other. Her daughters came by the next day, took issue, yelled, laid down the law, called up psychiatrists ("I'm afraid, Doctor, that my mother's not quite right upstairs"), called up lawyers ("She's selling all the furniture, what can we do to stop her?"). They would insult each other in the living room, red-faced or livid, full of nervous tics, shaking with indignation and spouting accusations and recriminations as his grandmother listened, chin propped on cane, an ironic smile slanting across her countless wrinkles, victorious in an empty house where the loud ticking of the clocks had become oppressive, until the dinner she pitched forward in the middle of soup, and we put her in bed with spinach leaves still stuck to her nose and chin, her neck gleaming with grease and her left eyebrow cut, the blood slowly beginning to clot. And every time she came out of her coma, deformed by delirium and rage, she'd scream:

"I want to be put in the piano, you little whores." And she'd wave her arms, grabbing for her daughters in the empty room.

There's a piano in the sand, he thought as he beheld a black and almost geometric thicket behind a bundle of reeds, a piano in the sand circled by gulls and other ocean birds, and his straggly-haired grandmother, wrapped in the wedding dress she had kept in a chest, tapped her arthritic fingers over the caries-riddled keys, stumbling through a children's lullaby. The low-blowing breeze made the tulle of her veil flutter. There was a dead cat in the sand, nearly covered over by the shore's stubble. A cloud of huge flies, blue-winged and red-bodied, buzzed around it. The anchored boats lazily shifted their haunches. He stood for a moment, empty-eyed, looking at the rotted animal, then turned and went back to the inn.

———————

WITNESS VITOR P., single, twenty-nine years old, bellhop and waiter at the inn of Aveiro and resident of same. He took the oath and under questioning testified: That on Tuesday, February 10, a little after 6 P.M., as nearly as he could remember, he was informed by the manager, Alice F., identified on page thirty of these proceedings, that the body of a former occupant of room number seven, Rui S., had been found near the inn, that the corpse, both flesh and clothing, had been largely devoured by local birds, which naturally caused him great shock and revulsion, all the more so since the aforementioned Rui S. was a particularly affable and polite individual, who never got impatient over tardy or delinquent service. The deponent appreciated his invariable amiability, which stood in marked contrast to the obvious hostility and ill will of the woman in his company, presumably his wife, who, in the deponent's opinion, combined a monumental lack of taste in clothing with an insolent manner of addressing inn employees, who were dedicated to the best possible treatment of their clientele in a country as preoccupied with the rules of etiquette and civic education as ours is. As soon as he received notice of the body's discovery, he went to the employee lounge to ingest a tranquilizer (two Valiums) because of what felt like a skipping heartbeat, washed his face with cold water to regain courage and fortitude, and proceeded to the place indicated by the aforementioned Alice F., where he found her as well as the English couple from room number six, the cook, the cook's assistant, the chambermaid, and two men who apparently belonged to a truck loaded with wood and parked on the shoulder, all waiting for the imminent arrival of the authorities, represented in this case by a pair of national guardsmen from the neighboring township, who got around on bicycles, pedaling up the inclines with manifest shortness of breath, encumbered by the butts of their prehistoric rifles and the other useless accouterments of their uniforms. The deponent noted that the onlookers—who formed a wall made up of diverse faces, arms, legs, and hands, like the singularly still bodies of a Mexican mural or one of those paintings full of people that you find on public buildings at election time—stood at a respectful distance from the deceased, not daring to get close on account of the sea gulls that hovered over the body, screeching frightfully, their eyes transformed into circular bits of glass, roundly protruding in a strange mixture of hate and tenderness. Naturally terrified by the attitude of the birds, which had been shy and friendly until then, always peaceful in the lagoon, always meek and quiet between the inn and the town, he returned to said inn (it still hadn't rained and the plants in the flower beds were slowly withering like the brittle skin of old people) and occupied the vacant switchboard, situated in a tiny cubicle behind the front desk, with a calendar displaying a bathing-suited girl hanging from a nail, the cap and gold-striped coat of the nonexistent doorman, and assorted out-of-date phone directories piled up on the floor; he found the address of the deceased on the registration card, inserted the green peg into the hole for long distance calls, dialed the number, and waited. A sharp, disagreeable, bony female voice answered, and the deponent immediately recognized it as belonging to the deceased's presumed wife; he considered hanging up without saying anything but finally said "Hello?" in a hesitant whisper, already sorry he'd thought to call. What the fuck put the idea into my head? The voice on the other end asked "Who's calling?" two or three times, answered by his stubborn silence, before he finally answered, in a reticent tone, syllable by syllable, "I'm calling from the inn at Aveiro to notify you that your husband's dead." There followed a pause whose length the deponent is unable to estimate, after which the female party asked "Really?" in a distracted and neutral voice that surprised him, for it gave him the sensation, if you know what I mean, sir, that she had her mind on something else. "He died, his body was found outside among the reeds and the sea gulls," the deponent clarified, and again a pause, and again the voice answering, "Really?" with the same indifference as the first time, hollow and distant, cold and apathetic in the extreme. He felt like hanging up ("Have you ever seen such hard-heartedness in a woman just informed of her husband's death?") and rested his finger on the button, but instead heard himself say, "Don't you at least want to know how it happened?" This was followed by a spate of whistles, coughs, and gurgles on the line: a sparrow shat on the wire, he thought, or one of those goddam blackbirds is playing tricks, while at the same time the sharp and bony woman responded with something that he couldn't understand but that encouraged him to insist, "Are you sure you don't want to know?" And then he heard her say quite clearly, "No doubt the police will be coming by, I'll have plenty of time to find out all the details"—

and that's when I realized she didn't like him, they'd probably hurt each other too much over the years, having reached the point where they hated each other in the slow and sullen fire of couples, in the resentment that comes from broken hopes, in the disappointment over what could have been and wasn't— "The police will no doubt come by and give me a complete rundown of what happened, but at any rate I'm not at all surprised, because for some time now nothing can surprise me where he's concerned," and I recalled the tubby fellow with glasses, looking a bit ridiculous in his denim overalls as he sat in the restaurant at the inn, politely requesting the menu, choosing wines, fish, meat, dessert, smiling the sad smile of a photograph, squishing bread into little balls with his fat, stubby fingers, or leafing through magazines in the lobby, his legs crossed, talking in a labored English with the foreign guests. "Do you have children?" I asked, and the voice broke into an ugly cackle, as if a denture were doing somersaults on a xylophone, if you know what I mean. "No, you can rest easy," she said, "there are no unfortunate orphans for the reporters, no children with troubled eyes hugging their mother under a headline reading UNIVERSITY PROFESSOR COMMITS SUICIDE TURNING BACK ON THREE INFANTS; there's nothing special, it's a run-of-the-mill tragedy without scandal, don't worry." And once more her ironic, bristly, heartless cackle, and I said, "Aren't you coming back? Don't you want to be with your husband?" And she replied curtly, "We decided to separate on Sunday, and besides, we never had a real wedding." Who would have dreamed, I thought, a respectable-looking professor writing plain as day *Married with* on the registration card; how disgraceful, how shameful, how unthinkable. "I don't know why I'm telling all this to you. I guess deep down I am a little shocked by the news," she said. Shocked my ass, you little bitch, women are never shocked by anything. "You can't imagine," I said, "how many sea gulls are gathered around him; they ate his flesh down to the bone, even his hair, and around his knees you can see hard white things." There was another pause, an absolute silence this time, a deep place without words where we both fit, a crevice like the ones horses jump over in films, and her voice—almost pleasant-sounding—emerged from a sort of pitch-black tunnel. "Birds?" she asked, "the birds from when he was little?" And I thought, She must be delirious; the death of her husband must have touched her after all; she tries not to show it, but now and then it comes through, in a gesture, a tone of voice, a frown. I pressed my mouth against the Bakelite funnel, "What's this about birds, ma'am?" but I heard only her breathing over the phone, a strange wind that advanced and receded. At that moment the manager and a uniformed guardsman burst in all a-bustle. "Get off the phone immediately, we've got to call the fire department," ordered the guardsman. "I hope this unfortunate event doesn't reflect on the inn's reputation," sighed the manager. "Don't worry, ma'am, a week from now it'll all be forgotten," the guardsman replied. "Yes, but did you notice how the sea gulls are acting?" asked the manager. "So what is it with the birds?" I shouted into the receiver. "They'll calm down too," we were assured by the guardsman, who was fat, short, gray-haired, and reminded me of someone at a costume party dressed up as a cop. The breathing in my ear grew faint, more distant. "Hang up the phone, dammit," the fat guardsman said in a louder voice. "I'm not playing cowboys and Indians." The calendar model grew in size until her pink presence occupied the entire cubicle and a huge breast, looking air-inflated, pressed against my chest, while hundreds of swift wings fluttered against the glass, the inn was drowning in pigeons. "They'll calm down too," the guardsman reassured us. "I worked for twenty years with quail, so I know all about the memory of our feathered friends." In the window loomed the lagoon, the linen clouds, the threat of rain that kept stalling. "Get in your car," I said, "the firemen will be here in no time flat." "Who are you prattling to?" the manager demanded suspiciously. "Don't think I won't deduct the call from your paycheck." And before she pulled the peg out by the wire I heard, "The birds of the farm, the blackbirds, the robins, the sparrows," and then nothing except the whine of the interrupted phone call, the calendar model embracing me, the guardsman leaning forward, and dialing Aveiro, and the pine trees, which were slowly sliding far away from me, swallowed by a diaphanous sheet of mist. And that was all he said. Read, ratified, and signed.

———————

HE ENTERED THE ROOM carrying a tray with breakfast (bread in a wicker basket, packets of butter, teacups, little chrome pots, things that rattled and clinked), and he smelled the clammy, lukewarm, unpleasant smell of sleep, the perspiration in the sheets, the jumbled covers, the fog on the panes. Hanging on the inside of the door, a cardboard rectangle with a hole that fit over the knob warned DO NOT DISTURB in huge threatening letters.

"Good morning," he said, holding the tray in his hands and looking around at the room's ruthlessly sunlit walls and contents, the ugly furniture, the printed envelopes on top of a small desk, the plastic ashtrays, a wastepaper basket in a corner, the veranda, the lagoon with ducks poised on its surface, rocking gently from side to side, and you blindly groping for your glasses, your nose and lips still swollen with sleep. The collar of her nightgown resembled a garland of lace daisies draped around her narrow shoulders and flattened chest. Her jaw mumbled the night's final, confused message, wrapped in incomprehensible shadows of syllables. He looked but couldn't find a place to set the tray, so he pulled a chair to the edge of the bed, using his foot as a hook: the green color of the seat offended him like an unjust insult, and only then did he realize that when he went out he'd forgotten to turn off the bathroom light, now barely showing, defeated by the increasing intensity of morning. A boat sailed in a cloth frame between the two cream-wood headboards. Your hand finally stumbled on your glasses, which you put on like a piece of clothing; your eyelashes shrank and, while you checked the time on your watch, your face became lively and alert: you must be trying to figure out what we're doing here, he thought.

"Aveiro, what a creepy place," frowned his horrified cousin as her needles moved ferociously, knitting the endless sweater. "I stopped by there years ago on my way to Oporto, because everyone insisted that I had to see the Vouga River: a dreadful town that reeks of rotting fish. Take Lisbon from me and you've taken everything."

"It's the Montijo of the north," Carlos said with contempt. "Sludge, rubbish, and humidity. Anyone who likes the Montijo's seaweed, the way he does, is sick in the head."

"He'd cross the Tagus River in the afternoon when he didn't have classes," the musical sister stated while rotating the piano stool, "and he'd sit by himself on the jetty and gaze at the water. He could stay there for hours, uttering not a word, petting the stray dogs that came up to him. I went with him once but threw up on the ferry the whole trip."

He turned off the pallid bathroom light, which languished on the carpet, and came back to find her sugaring her tea with the still boneless movements of one who's just woken up: so much hair on your arms, Marilia; how was I ever able to make love with you?

"Bread or a roll?" she asked with her efficient, practical, annoying professor's voice: Godardesque decadence, the renewal of American film, the café in the park near the university, with grass and swans behind your hair. Will I be able to explain that I want out of the relationship ("A roll"), that I don't like you anymore, that I want to start over on my own

("Just butter") and in another place, with less books, less exhibitions, less German film series, less bearded friends with dogmatic opinions, less culture? He gazed at her and thought, We already look so old in the morning: crumpled, yellowed, worn out, with wrinkles that suddenly show up on our faces. He thought, How the hell was it four years ago? And the taste of the bread, the butter, and the milk that trickled from the little metal pitcher was not the same as in Lisbon. Your body had assumed the sheets' fragrance, with an artificial, muffled freshness, moving like a caterpillar under the covers. The woman touched him on the face with two indifferent fingers: even your fingers have grown old, Marilia.

"You're cold as ice," she said.

Your tenderness doesn't move me, your caresses don't excite me: he felt so far away from you, so far from everything, hovering, solitary, in a sort of interior desert, as if there were no one around him, as if he were truly and eternally alone.

"It's February," he answered. "It's cold outside."

The pines, the other trees, the sand, the river, the many-bladed wind of winter shaving the mist; and everything probably blue in June, in the month of my birthday, heat, the inn at full occupancy, Belgian families, holiday leisure.

"It's cold outside," he repeated, annoyed, thinking, When are these caresses going to end? "From the look of the clouds, it's never going to rain again: the ocean will become a desert of sand, Marilia, like the moon, like the head of the queen of hearts, or like my mother's." (I have to phone the clinic and talk to her.)

"Like the head of your ex-wife, if you'll allow me," Marilia substituted with a sarcastic smile. "You thought Tucha was a genius when the poor thing couldn't distinguish between the *Mona Lisa* and the pictures on a merry-go-round."

But I felt at ease with her, with the kids, with the apartment on Palmeira Street. I didn't want to leave for anything in the world, I even missed the kitchen tiles. That's where I screwed up, he thinks, letting myself be weaned away, because I had a modicum of happiness there: we'd listen to records at night, talk about trivia, you in the rocking chair, me on the floor with a forgotten book lying at my side; when we were quiet we'd hear the breathing of the boys in bed. But there was always, even then, my guilty conscience, the Party accusing me like an open, throbbing wound, my cowardly remorse, the price I paid for living with you. The gray-haired woman who scratched her head with a pencil beneath a poster of a man clenching a raised fist next to a factory full of belching smoke-stacks pronounced in separated syllables:

"Incurably bourgeois."

He opened a circular packet of jelly like the ones served on airplanes, tasted it, and put it aside: too sweet, provokes spasms in my glottis—my throat contracts, I can no longer breathe, the furniture waves and twirls in a muddled dance, the floor disappears like water down a drain. Marilia chewed with the serenity of a Walt Disney cow, and he thought, If I keep this up much longer, I'm bound to despise you. He picked up the phone to ask for the clinic where his mother was, but changed his mind. The room extended onto a small veranda with two chairs, a white wooden table, and a cement and iron balustrade; perhaps at the end of a spring afternoon one could sit there with drink in hand, observing the giant shifting shadows of twilight, the sun's orange descent into the sea. His sisters played cards in the living room, their backs to the sunsets, while his father, on the other side of the room, tirelessly deciphered the hidden meanings in the newspaper, extracting and inserting various eyeglasses from his pockets. Tucha, kneeling on the rug, changed the diapers of the youn-ger boy, who lay on the sofa kicking his legs in the air. He thinks, surprised, Babies have ten toes and toenails and hair like us. He thinks, If Marilia got pregnant again, what would happen? The diapers, the bottles, the feverish excitement of the first few days, and then the sleepless nights spent placating the tiny, infinitely hungry mouth. His grandmother's piano was carried down the stairs while the irascible old woman beat her cane against the handrail on the landing, and soon it was her turn, the coffin carried down the stairs in jerks, the men in black, the house suddenly quiet, uninhabited by her cries and complaints. A few days later they divvied up what remained of the furniture, the dishes, the pictures, and the musty suitcases of clothes, and the rooms, now larger, resounded with the echoes of my footsteps, my cough, and my asthma whistling off the walls. They also took the curtains, so that the buildings opposite moved in on me, peering curiously: I never believed they could overpower you, Grandma, despite your diminutive size, your brittle, squirrelly bones, and the bed they tied you to in hopes of subduing your wind. If Marilia got pregnant, would I have the guts to leave her?

"Hurry up!" shouted his father, clapping his hands outside where the trailers were, "The show begins in half an hour."

The woman got up, removed her lace nightgown (the fuzz on her pubis, he thought, bury my hand, my nose, my penis, neighing, into that dark and deep, curly, endless triangle), and walked naked to the bathroom with her huge peasant feet, spaces between her toes, almost pink, like a child's. I shook the manes and muscles of my flanks (the sweat of my loins gleamed) and trotted toward the window: his hard testicles rippled against his belly's tendons, his cock slowly emerged from its sheath, like the revolting trunk of an elephant. A drool of sorts shone on his lips and nose, his hoofs quivered on the rug: I can't make love to you because I'm about to call it quits with you, we're going to leave Aveiro like two strangers. A new flock of ducks descended on the lagoon in a prudent ellipse, the tarnished reflection of the boats trembled. A steaming cylinder dropped from his anus, hitting the ground softly. He turned halfway around, knocking into the furniture heedlessly (a bottle of water jumped up from its saucer in fright), the room being too cramped for his long brown torso; one of his horseshoes bashed into the metallic heater mounted on the wall, breaking two or three parallel slats; the breakfast tray slid off the chair with a crash; I like the sagging cheeks of your bottom, I like your thighs, I like your sloping shoulders, the circumflex accent of your collar bones; hot vapor was emerging from the bathroom in tenuous, whitish billows, reflected by the mirror on the closet opposite; you had drawn the plastic curtain and put a transparent cap on your head; I could make out your figure, bent over and soaping your legs; I'm going to go in from behind, rip apart your vulva, turn your kidneys out onto the bathtub enamel; he raised himself on his hind legs in a furious snort.

"What's this?" the woman asked with sponge in hand: "Have you flipped out or what?"

In so much wetness it was hard to distinguish her body, her eyes beady with fear under the shower cap, her flaccid breasts with their dark nipples. His tail brushed against the door, his nostrils inhaled acidly, his neck shook wildly from side to side:

"Get back," the woman demanded. "What the hell's gotten into you?"

She set down the soap and tried to protect herself with the laughable shield of the sponge (What are sponges made of, an intrigued whisper inside him asked, sea creatures, synthetic products?); he tore the curtain with his snout and his enormous teeth while she took refuge in the corner with the faucets, looking surprised, worried, and almost pleased; water dripped off her damp pubic hair; I supported my hoofs against the wall tiles, scraping the glazed clay with the iron, half-moons of mud, half-moons of shit; I must have stepped in my own turds just now; another cylinder, smaller than before, tumbled out of his anus to produce a dull thud on the yellow rubber mat with holes; and right as he impaled her, in a single thrust and with all his body's raging force, he saw the hazy image of a horse in the mirror, with a panache of flowers on top its head, just like in the circus.

"Alley-oop," his father shouted while cracking the whip, "alley-oop!" And he jumped hurdles with unswerving obedience, turned in a circle, reared up on his hind legs, and returned.

He fastened his zipper, embarrassed, and returned to the room to change his soaked shirt. His tennis shoes made a strange, tonguelike sound on the ground. Marilia, wrapped in a towel, with the shower cap hanging on the nape of her neck and a few locks slanting across her forehead, followed behind him, dripping and bewildered:

"What did you take?" she asked. "What's with you today?"

And there was a repugnant gratitude, a desperate hope in her voice. How dumb of me to fuck you, he thinks; we should have been talking, dividing up the pictures and Roland Barthes books in a civilized fashion, preparing a cordial parting so as to remain friends: how do people do it? He put on a polka-dot shirt and sat in the green chair next to the window, not looking at her but feeling her every movement behind him: her arms twisting like a contortionist's around her back to fasten her bra, her hair hurriedly combed with a wire brush, an unexpected line of mascara on her eyelids. Outside the day swelled like a pregnant belly, its veins branching out in the dense sky, behind the clouds, into bushes heavy with rain. The mist transformed Aveiro into a confused splotch in which the vertical brush strokes of smokestacks could barely be differentiated: we could go there to eat and talk. Maybe she'll arrive on her own at the conclusion that it would be better for both of us if we split up. Maybe she'll bring up the idea herself and all I'll have to do is agree, without sounding too enthusiastic, saying yes, you're right, we'll try it out for a few months, get in touch now and then, talk about it, and see where things stand. Marilia took a small bottle from her purse and perfumed her neck and ears with uncharacteristically feminine gestures that alarmed me; he thought, Now she's all happy, she's been without it for months, fantasizing, racking her brain, and now zap, her doubts have vanished. He hung his clothes on the bedposts to dry and looked at the scraggly pine trees that bordered the highway: you've got to overcome your fear, coward, and tell her how you feel.

"How about lunch in Aveiro?" he proposed.

His cousin, seated before the television, undid a row of stitches and started over:

"His mother died two days after he did, and fortunately she never found out a thing. They gave her yet another injection in the chest, and hooked her up to yet another machine, what a nightmare. Poor woman, she weighed about fifty pounds—a sack of bones without a soul."

"The cancer of his first wife and the suicide of his only son profoundly disturbed my husband," reported the tall, elegant redhead, shaking a multitude of bracelets that jangled metallically. (Repeated plastic surgery had transformed her face into a smooth, taut, expressionless mask of plaster youthfulness.) "Perhaps that explains why he's unable to have relations with me; he takes his sleeping pill, pecks me on the cheek, turns his back to me, and snores. I'm forever telling him he should go to the doctor, but he says it's nothing, just the pressures of his work, headaches, the usual excuses. The truth is that he feels old, too old to get it up anymore. He spends the evening nodding at the VCR with the newspaper on his knees; the film ends and he sits there like a log before the blank screen, his chin against his chest, and his bald crown on display."

"Aveiro might be fun," she accepted with a conspiratorial smile, and for an instant her black pubic triangle, her sagging tits, her naked body drenched with water and slick with soap vividly reappeared in my mind. "When you stop and think about it, we hardly ever visit anything."

You forgot all about the conference and she was grateful; she was surprised, almost happy that he'd stepped into the bathtub with his clothes on, reaching his blind hands forward in spite of the shower, in spite of the slippery enamel, in spite of the water; you were happy that my mouth touched your chest, that my tongue licked your neck, that my finger ran slowly back and forth across your clitoris. "You've gone completely nuts," and your voice was affectionate for a change and consented; you opened your thighs wider to facilitate my index finger's left-right repetitions; the steam fogged my glasses and you stopped existing though you unbuttoned my shirt and unfastened my belt and yanked down my pants and underpants; the shower water ran down my knees and ankles, soaking my socks; I planted my palms on the wall and leaned into you as you fondled my asshole, my balls, my groin, my cock, and you inserted my desire, "Wait a second, go slow," into your body's depths; the plastic shower cap rubbed my face; your throat produced a rhythmic moan as my buttocks advanced and retreated, your fingernails digging into my back, your teeth into my arm; the steaming water kept falling from the ceiling over our passion of engaged rocking chairs; we inched our way down along the wall until we were squatting next to the drain; you pulled me out of your vagina and slithered around to my navel. "Let me drink it, let me feel your milk on my tongue," and the blood in my penis suddenly converged in a kind of vertigo, it arched, it pulsed, it gleamed, exploded once, twice, three times, a piston shooting me out of myself with savage energy, and then I slowly began to empty myself, to go soft, to lose the metallic and elastic texture of my muscles; you pushed away my knees, stretched out, and panted, face down in the tub, oblivious to me, far away, twisted up like a dress that's removed, while I stumbled toward the room with the daffy, waddling gait of a penguin. I wiped my glasses on the bedspread, the hazy universe came into focus, and instead of my mother's tall redheaded friend crossing her

107

elegant legs in the armchair (the smell of her perfume, the smell of her stockings, the smell of her clothes) my grandmother appeared, brandishing her cane and shouting, "Put me in the piano, you little whores," from her bed, where she was sitting up, all riled, her hair all disheveled, with the IV dripping, dripping, into her arm.

They walked down to the lobby, where the monstrous pink-and-green plants were growing in their tank of algae (How many guests have been devoured, he wondered, methodically chewed up by the enormous jaws?), and lay the key on the counter, behind which the creature with the gigantic eyelashes calculated her endless sums with a tarantulan languor, verifying each subtotal with the pensive point of her pencil. At one end of the lobby, next to a poster for Albufeira ("Sunset in August"), a half-open door led to a prehistoric switchboard, a termite-ridden desk, and a bundle of papers skewered by a nail and oscillating to the sound of an agonizing ring. A truck parked out front was unloading cratefuls of soft drinks, the pine trees and the water rustled in the mist: nothing here mirrors anything, he thought, except this sad and strange sky, full of cloudy staircases, the wind's restlessness, the birds' invisible (brown?) wings. The car refused to start, the frozen battery scraped the bottom of the engine like a piece of wire in a can; the vehicle smelled of cold tobacco and of tanning leather.

"It feels to me as if this weather's never going to change," he said as he turned the key again, stepped on the accelerator, and pulled out the choke, "as if we're going to live forever under this bell jar, waiting for God knows what. The back of my neck is sore from the humidity. My thoughts and my hands feel like they've changed places. I don't know where I begin or end."

Somnolent trucks labored along the highway, pursued by irate, open-jawed dogs; a black-and-purple bird tumbled sluggishly through the pine trees; the car began to hiccup along the gravel drive—it's obvious that this weather will never change, clouds and more clouds, clouds on top of clouds—they reached the asphalt, picking up speed as they proceeded to Aveiro. During lunch I'll inform you that I want us to separate for a few months, that I need to think; we'll stay friends, visit each other; I'll help you if you need anything, trees slipping vertically past, along with sporadic, miserable villages. The musical sister lifted her fingers from the piano and told the class:

"First the triangles. No tambourines until I give the signal."

My high school choir director, he thought, stuttered, wore glasses, screwed his face up in weird ways, and was given to irrational fits of anger: he'd smack us in the middle of a puff on his cigarette, whose tip of ashes never once fell, and at the annual recital—when the gymnasium was packed with impressed parents and the fierce vigilance of the principal in the first row, all of which dissolved with the backs of the other chairs into the web of shadows—he'd stand before us with baton in hand and a pleading expression on his face, his forehead glistening with nervous sweat. My father always went abroad when it was time for another dissonant performance; he never saw me in the honeycomb of heads that made up the choir, brightly lit by a rusty spotlight, singing rhapsodies of folk songs in corny arrangements. The director would wave his sleeves in a state of extreme tension, blowing on a pitch pipe before each song. The car engine was now running with purring obedience; there was a sign on the right side, *Aveiro*; there were more houses, then buildings, stores, cross streets, a square, and at every corner a trace of the river's smell, sullen and stubborn beneath the lumpy sky. We stopped at a small square next to a gas station where a hunchback with grimy overalls and a sewer rat's nose was squatting on a canvas stool, waiting for customers. The mist stuck its uncomfortable hand into the spaces between my jacket's buttons. Two Indian priests wearing cassocks walked past without looking at them; the choir director wiped his arm across his forehead, spun around on his lustrous shoes, and bowed with emotion to the spotlight, grateful for the applause. He thinks, My mother detested the high school, which she claimed was swarming with Communists and naked prostitutes that taught French, and maybe that explains why my dissipated life didn't surprise her. But I imagine she crosses herself, Marilia, whenever she remembers you; the choir director designated us with a gesture as wide as it was vague, and the audience clapped harder; you avoided talking about me to your friends, pretending ignorance if they asked you anything; she was mortified that her son's father-in-law was a national guardsman. All right, we'll separate, she said, I understand perfectly. It's not worth making a big scene over. We walked over narrow, winding, deserted streets; Without fail I'm going to talk to you during lunch; the tall redhead, wearing dangling earrings, waved at him periodically from a second floor balcony; Maybe my father could no longer get it up, and she laughed in bed, wrapping her naked body around the chauffeur's blue uniform with silver buttons; I wonder if Mom suspects. Marilia took my arm on the pretext of some uneven steps—like a couple, he thinks, a confirmed couple; why is it you don't have the guts to clarify things, explain what's what, are you afraid that she likes you? What you're really afraid of is being all alone; a sheer veil of teeny drops would come with the wind, graze his face, and go, then come, and go; they chose a small restaurant next to the lagoon and its muddy water, with a lone customer who used his fork's teeth to spear a fish's boiled eye—white, bugging, round, blind—chewing it with the elastic mouth of a toad; the waiter handed them the menus. I'll bet you're going to order whole squid—and all of a sudden, by her gestures and her glance, he realized, She still likes me, and this morning convinced her that the specter of divorce has been eliminated; now she's calm, serene, secure, and in love. Jesus what a pain. He ordered whole squid for her, grilled sliced pork for himself, and white wine; the waiter placed a paper tablecloth between us, and I looked out at the turbid still water (there weren't as many sea gulls on this side), rife with floating chaff, pieces of wood, a basket, assorted debris, unidentifiable objects, boats with their oars resting inside, the diffuse pitch of the brume, and perhaps—far in the distance—the sea; the embalmed face of the waiter came into focus (his tiny eyes, his eyebrows), and his mouth, surrounded by concentric wrinkles, approached me:

"We're out of sliced pork. It's marked with an X on the menu, didn't you notice?"

I knew I'd never write my dissertation on Sidonio Pais, the ideas were stuck, I couldn't get them out: notes, outlines, torn pages, disjointed and dead paragraphs: either I never had any talent or I lost it with my baby teeth; perhaps all I have is a kind of cleverness, a formal agility for grasping things on the surface, without depth, like this river's opaque water, paralyzed by an inexplicable indecision. He thinks, How I hate squid; I'm repulsed by the legs, the suckers, the inky sauce, the pallid and fibrous meat.

"Squid, how vulgar," the ghost of his mother disdainfully ruled. "Order a steak, at least."

"A steak, well-done," the waiter yelled to an invisible kitchen, where no doubt a fat woman struggled in a filthy confusion of pots, aided by a flat-chested girl with imploring eyes.

"She'd order squid in restaurants," said the oldest sister with a grimace. "Does that give you an idea of the sort of person she was?"

"I'll bet that the sauce dripped down her chin and that she used toothpicks afterward," Carlos added. "And no doubt she spit olive pits onto the blade of her knife."

"She wasn't completely stupid," said the obstetrician, "but there are things tied to your chromosomes that take generations to be refined and perfected. Good taste, for example.

111

Propriety. Good manners. If you're not born with them, there's absolutely nothing you can do."

The salt and pepper shakers, the shoddy utensils, the chipped plates: I'm never going to write anything; I'll never do anything worthwhile. A squatting silhouette was fishing on a wooden jetty: Uncle Francisco, he thought, but the gestures were different, the figure's posture not the same. Francisco's wife, ageless and resigned, would spend her weekends in bed with an ice bag on her head ("You've no idea how much a migraine aches, child"), waiting for her husband to return, smelling of salt and fish stew, with a basket of nauseating, minuscule fish. He lit a cigarette and the waiter hurried over to provide him with a cracked ashtray made of black plastic. He thinks, It's time for me to start talking. So he inched his elbows forward on the paper tablecloth, carefully pushed the fork with his index finger until it was parallel to the knife, coughed discreetly as before a significant speech, and at that moment a pair of sea gulls landed on the jetty next to the fellow with the fishing pole and for no reason at all began to caw.

WITNESS HILARIO A., divorced, forty-two years old, waiter at the inn of Aveiro and resident of same. He took the oath and under questioning testified: That together with the aforementioned Vitor P., identified on page seventy-two of these proceedings, he was responsible for the restaurant and room service, both men sharing a room in the attic, next to the quarters of the manager, whose hot shower they were entitled to use once a week, while she personally observed how long the blue flower of gas remained lit in the enamel aperture of the hot water heater, because three minutes is ample time for a man to lather up and rinse off. He further stated that the room

112

was located directly above that occupied by the victim Rui S. and his presumed wife. And due to structural deficiencies, he could hear every sound, no matter how slight, proceeding from the floor below, including the creaking of the bedsprings, burps, intestinal rumbles, splashing in the toilet bowl, and noises of affection. According to the deponent, the victim Rui S. and his presumed wife were characterized by an intriguing silence, which he attributes to the fact that the woman was unattractive; my coworker told me that she was so masculine she even had a beard. "Did you notice the whiskers growing on her chin? I'll bet she shaves them every morning and has more hair on her chest than I do." And I replied, "I don't doubt it, considering you pluck yours every time you go to Lisbon to dance in one of those transvestite nightclubs." And he said, "I've worked in two of them and believe me, those people are the happiest in the world, with their false eyelashes, lacquered blond hair, and rich perverts in big cars waiting for them at the exit, kissing them on the lips, grabbing their muscular legs, and slipping twenties into their shiny black purses. Hell, if I had the money, I'd go to one of those clinics in Morocco to change myself into a woman—plastic tits and all—so that you wouldn't even recognize me; you'd look at me and get such a hard-on it'd stick out like a car antenna and stiff as a brick; you'd give three months' wages for twenty minutes of ecstasy; if you want, just pretend I'm a girl and we'll start here and now." He'd sometimes hook up with certain solitary, shy guests, withdrawn like eels, the fastidious sort who use a wet fingertip to pick crumbs off the tablecloth as if plucking a harp, middle-aged gentlemen who are overly nice, overly careful, overly cheery; he'd go to their rooms in the middle of the night with a gleeful smile and shoes in hand, returning at dawn, yellow with insomnia, to stretch out on the bed and stare at the ceiling, thinking; and whenever he stayed in number seven I'd hear their conversations, their tickling, their trembling, along with oaths, promises, declarations, and pathetic coos. But according to the deponent, the victim Rui S. and his presumed wife displayed the intriguing, absolute silence of disenchanted or bored couples, each leafing through his or her magazine on his or her bed in tranquil hatred, in serene misery, in patient rage. They said little during their meals: they ordered their food and wine, then looked out the window at the lagoon, whose water seemed to be flowing against the current on account of the rains still not falling— my father wrote me from the country, "Son, I'm afraid next year we won't have anything to feed the cows." The gleam in their eyeglasses disguised the emptiness in both their faces. I wrote back, "Stick the cows' horns up the Minister's ass for not having built the dam he promised before the last election." And then one afternoon my coworker came into the pantry all excited, "Come and take a look, handsome, there's a dead body and the police out there," and through the window I saw a group of people in raincoats, the gray sky, the trees, and February's clouds surging on the horizon, sculpted from some sort of rock, hollowed out of the basalt, and tumbled by the wind, with the fingerprints of the houses and pine trees impressed on their thick, colorless skin, like footprints on the beach at dawn. A photographer was taking pictures, hunters with shotguns aroused the alarmed curiosity of the birds, the manager provided explanations to a man taking notes on a memo pad. I went out with my apron still on, my sleeves rolled up, and my right hand holding onto the neck of the chicken I'd been plucking over a zinc pail, and as I ran, the creature's stiff feet swung back and forth and its round body beat against my thigh like a herniated testicle; it's not every day you see a dead body, but they'd already covered it with a piece of canvas and all you could see was a vague lump that could have been a corpse or any number of large oblong objects; the odor of sludge drowned out the human smells and voices; I went up closer with my chicken in hand, and the man taking notes lost interest in the manager, who looked at him poutily, and asked me, "You there in the apron, do you work in the inn too?" Then he asked me about the guests in room seven, how they acted, what they talked about, what they ate and didn't eat, if they went out a lot or a little—"Son," wrote my father, "we don't have anything to feed the cows"—if they received visitors or made phone calls, if I'd noticed anything strange in their behavior, and then he asked about the woman, tall or short, blond or brunette, nice or nasty, her looks, her clothes, her manners. I think the guy must have had asthma because he breathed like a fish, purple and tense, his mouth wide open, pronouncing the letters while his pen wrote them down; a burgundy splotch covered part of his neck and left cheek, giving him a hybrid, lunar redneck look. The sea gulls cheeped behind him in restless, feverish circles; the firemen's stretcher carried the body to the ambulance, which had a red light on top that twirled and emitted an alternately loud and soft howl as it sped down the highway; a stain was left in the sand; a couple of men with shovels covered it over and insulted the birds, calling them sons of bitches under their breath; the photographer put his camera in his shoulder bag and everyone, including the hunters with shotguns, came to the bar at the inn to have a brandy on the house. It's bad for business if this makes many headlines, guests stay away, it scares off the tourists, the travel agencies cancel their contracts, we're counting on Americans to come in the summer so we can get dollars, you know how it is, so they guzzled one brandy after another, discreetly, the manager filling their glasses above the blue line; their ears gradually reddened, infantile giggles began to punctuate their stupid severity, a fat inspector tried to whisper something to the manager while grabbing at her sadly withered buttocks, with the useless cloth of her dress offering little protection. They ate dinner noisily at one enormously

115

long table, leaving God knows how many empty bottles, stains, crusts of bread, leftover vegetables, and cigarette stubs in saucers; a fellow who hadn't bothered to take off his coat was snoring, fast asleep in his slice of melon; the irate cook spat into each dish of pudding before putting it on our serving trays; my coworker whirled from policeman to policeman with the aerial movements of a ballerina; the photographer stood up to make a speech, but his legs gave way, he crashed back to his seat and gave up, the troubled air of his gaze drifted into a blurry coma, and he ended up distractedly murmuring an irrational sentence about Japanese watches and lace panties. "Anything to make these morons content," the manager confided to me between her teeth, but in spite of all this the news, as you know, hit the newspapers like a bomb the next day, with the front pages covered with grotesque photos, and it took us hours to clean up all the crap they strewed around the inn. One of them fell headlong into the plant pond, knocked over a bunch of flowerpots, broke thirteen porcelain frogs, and just lay there, stretched out in the water, looking up at his companions proud as a walrus, his drenched mustache quivering like a veil over his mouth. They finally left at dawn, when an indigo line lightly traced the city's hazy profile. The sound of the car engines shot through my head like a burning wire; I walked out to the sand, shivering from the cold that seemed to proceed from the tall and glaring pine trees, from the night that shrank in on itself like the skin under the lids of insomniac eyes, giving way to a tremulous, milk-colored light, so that my surroundings began to come into focus; I could see the anchored boats, the trees, the pearly surface of the beach, and the first flock of ducks arriving from downstream to settle onto the lagoon. The rear lights of the cars blinked uncertainly on the highway. Soon it will be day, I thought, and the clouds approached and withdrew with lazy indifference; I heard coughing behind me, and there was the cook, her face drawn with fatigue, staring at the spot where the body had lain, the grass, the prints of many feet, and, above all else, the absolute mineral silence of the dawn, and the sea gulls still sleeping, still absent, in some place or other God knows where.

———————

HE THINKS, It figures that you said nothing of what you'd planned during lunch; it figures that you sat there silently the whole time, staring out at the afternoon, at the glassed-over lagoon, squeezing the yellow plastic mustard barrel over a cast-iron steak that came with a fried egg and greasy, half-raw French fries. Now and then a fisherman or two walked in and ordered a coffee at the counter, and (he thinks) it was as if they dragged the smells of fish and seaweed behind them, as if the odor of wood from the rotting pier came in on their oilcloth caps or in their rubber boots. He thinks, And the elation in your eyes, Marilia, gradually dissipated, your gestures became sluggish, meditative, your eyebrows more serious, knitted together, your shoulders narrower, tense under the eternal wool poncho that resembled an insect's cuirass. He thinks, We spent the afternoon strolling around Aveiro in silence, and from the streets, the houses, and the small squares, there arose a humid, lukewarm fragrance, an animal breath of something living that the February cold was slowly killing: we ended up sitting on a bench, looking at the buildings; without touching each other, without talking, without smiling, we sat on the bench, hands in our pockets, mulling over igneous, contradictory thoughts.

"Where in the world did you unearth this girl?" his father demanded.

"What did he say the gal's name is, Jorge?" asked his mother, looking at her husband as her sharpened red nails reached into a tortoiseshell cigarette case.

You'd gone to the bathroom ("Where can I wash my hands?"), led down the hall by my musical sister, who sniffed for light switches with her myopic snout, while the rest of us stayed in the living room—seated in a circle next to a table laden with whiskeys and cheese hors d'oeuvres shaped like cocoons or pieces of bamboo—my parents, my other two sisters, and my brothers-in-law, all their stern eyes glaring at me in a silent rage, with the furniture, the paintings, the books in the glass-doored bookcase, the Chinese vases, and the color photos of the grandchildren, all glaring at me in a silent rage made of resentment and contempt. We'd been living together on Azedo Gneco Street for some months at the time, surrounded by posters, dust, and wobbly furniture, and my initial enthusiasm and admiration were waning fast. He thinks, That's when I began to feel that I'd never be able to be seriously in love, that I'd never be seriously interested in anyone.

"Marilia," his mother repeated, chewing on her syllables as if weighing the name with her tongue. Behind her the clock on the wall, which was decorated with oriental motifs, got louder and quieter like a distant, wavering echo. "Marilia—how ludicrous."

He thinks, It must have been four or five o'clock when we got up from the bench to drop anchor in a dark café on the corner of an almost treeless square. The neon tube on the ceiling conferred a melancholy unreality on the chairs and on the worm-eaten counter. A tall and blind young man, holding an incised cane between his knees, seemed to be scrutinizing a future of catastrophes with his white, statuelike eyes. Periodically his hands would tremble, and on one occasion he exhumed a large red handkerchief from his pocket and hawked loudly into it. His father struggled with the lid of the square ice bucket (He never really understood how to open that thing, he thought) and reached into the cold cubes, stuck one to another, with his thick, authoritarian fingers.

"Your stupidest mistake," he declared, "was to separate from Tucha."

"At least she knew who she was," added his oldest sister, who was crunching on a cheese stick like a cartoon rabbit chomping its carrot: her long face lit up with a cruelty that surprised him.

I think, Again the stiff solemnity of this house, the rooms wrapped in shadows, even in the daytime, frightening with their invented ghosts, the weight of the folds in the drapes, the grave, heavy, pontifical atmosphere, the critical brows of the grandparents on the wall, piano music from far away. In the enormous kitchen the elderly maids put on their glasses to see better; they wavered between addressing him as Young man or Professor; the seamstress—hands joined together and tears in her eyes—gazed at him as at a sacred church statue. He thinks, Old old Deolinda. He thinks, How long has it been since you've been back home? A year, two years? But the smells were familiar, the branch of the bougainvillea still grazed the window, his brothers-in-law sat ever more at their ease in the plump, black leather armchairs. Perhaps in the storage room there was still the wicker chest with the masks and robes of ancient carnivals, lace cloths that would evaporate at the touch of a finger, long, frilled skirts from a bygone era. The obstetrician studied the empty depths of his glass while Carlos, with a bartender's flourish, broke the seal on a new bottle.

"Tucha didn't remarry," his mother observed accusingly. "She lives by herself with the boys and behaves the way she should: she doesn't go out at night, and she doesn't have affairs. Whereas you had to hop straight into this mess."

He ordered two beers and watched the bubbles rise along the side of the glass, made iridescent by the neon tube that cast the antiseptic pale light of a barbershop. The blind man spat loudly into the handkerchief, and through the open door a small white bitch, with teats touching the ground, could be seen scampering on the square, avidly pursued by a pack of exalted mutts. A busload of people rolled past without stop-

119

ping, and he distinguished the driver's sharp profile as if it were pasted on the window, a dark silhouette, an erectly sitting cutout without features, and other silhouettes just as still, black, abstract. I'm incapable of talking to you, he thinks; I'd never be able to bear your disappointment, your anger, your cigarette burning with uncommon fury, and your mouth of cavities opening wide to hurl ironic insults: "You miserable little bourgeois shit, go stick your doubts up your ass."

"Just answer me this," his mother insisted as she carefully flicked her ashes into the ashtray. "Do you think your children are happy? That's all I want to know. Do you think your children are really happy? Have you by any chance consulted a psychiatrist?"

He thinks, The youngest is afraid to ride in the boat at the park. Could that be synonymous with anguish, a symptom of neurosis, the sign of some problem, of something serious? In the dark café of Aveiro he tries to remember what his children are like, but the picture eludes him just when he's sure he's going to capture it, and he's left with a fleeting glimpse of two children's faces on the shore of the pond, amidst swans, grass, cars, and the terrace restaurant with painted metal tables where he sometimes went in the summer to feel the smell of June in his nose, dazed by the oily film on the water. He thinks, What really rankles you is that I never gave you a child, while the woman lifts the glass to her mouth and a driblet of beer foam hangs hideously from her chin like drool from a wagon-pulling mule.

"Aren't you cold?" Marilia asked with a seemingly stagnant, sibilant hatred.

He thinks, It's impossible that you don't know what's going on in my mind, you were always smarter than me. Everything was easier, less tedious, with Tucha. I'll bet you're perfectly aware of my doubts, my fear, the lacerating paralysis I feel inside. It was twilight in Aveiro; some of the shop signs were already blinking; soon the rows of streetlamps would light up, neighborhood by neighborhood, the filaments of the bulbs vacillating at first, then gaining force until swollen with light, suspended from their metal question marks, and the Vouga River would sink into the darkness like a gigantic submerged swamp.

"You could have spared us this disgrace," his mother said, almost in a whisper, since Marilia, piloted by his sister, should have been returning from the bathroom by then, and it was hard to hear the sound of her clogs on the hallway carpet.

His father stood up from his armchair (the springs emitted a relieved sigh like a burp from a monk), examined his gray hairs in a gilt-framed mirror, straightened the knot in his tie, and stroked his cheek with an indignant thumb.

"What gets my goat is the politics," he undertoned while cautiously peering at the hallway door. (I thought, When I was little they talked in French.) "Marrying a Communist and to top it off she doesn't have an iota of respect for the law."

"Everyone knows that the Communists are atheists," added Carlos with his legs crossed, smiling with satisfaction at his own silk socks. "I read in a book by a National Security officer that they hook up and break up like bunny rabbits."

He thinks, You bastard, I never liked you; I never liked your stupid self-confidence, your categorical statements, your pompous and arrogant masculinity. He was two years ahead of me in high school, and everyone knew him on account of the punch he once landed, I can't remember why, on the Physics lab assistant, a rachitic individual who played clarinet in an amateur band. He thinks, You knocked out five of his teeth with your punch—at the end of the semester your parents switched you to a rural Catholic school for future boxing champions. People looked at you from afar with respectful caution. The clarinet-playing lab assistant, who could no longer blow, switched to bass drum; your parents paid for him to get his jaw fixed; the fellow dropped out of sight and returned a few weeks later with shiny new incisors that threatened to fall out of his gums whenever he talked, producing a rain of spittle. Marilia sat on the floor with her legs crossed, sucking on the orange slice from her vodka: my mother's face twisted to the right in a frown, and it suddenly occurred to me just how threadbare your slacks were, how raveled your sweater. His musical sister occupied a chair at some distance, serenely leafing through some notebook or other, indifferent to the family. He thinks, A piece of sheet music? Verses? I know that you wrote verses, I once ran across your name on the cover of an anthology being remaindered at a book fair, weird poems with isolated words, or in the form of a star; if they found out at home, they'd have fainted. Or maybe not, maybe they'd gotten used to your homeliness, your daffiness, your perpetual alienation from everything. And perhaps you, the ugly duckling, were in fact the one genuine Communist of the family. But you lived with Mom and Dad, hardly went out at night, and never disturbed their peace with anything outlandish.

"A beer for the road," he said to Marilia, "and then we can leave. I'm getting chilly too, I left my coat at the inn."

The lights were turned on outside; groups of men wearing canvas shoes and cement-speckled slacks came in for their nightly aperitif of red wine before supper and settled into the café's proud, heavy, stiff-backed chairs, which stood beneath engraved hunting scenes and paintings of the English countryside. The blind man raised his hand to order a shot and his fingers hovered like insect antennae, as if to measure the nothingness. A low rumble of conversation meandered through the room, confounded with the dignified digestive ticking of the clock with a Chinese cover. The ageless woman who waited on the counter filled the glasses of his brothers-in-law, and he noticed her stout, cylindrical, ankleless legs, her cloth slippers, and the tiny, obedient dog that sniffed at her varicose veins.

"My tonic, Dona Almerinda," the blind man ordered in a voice without echo or inflection, searching with his vacant eyes for the long and transparent bottle that must be (he thinks) a kind of moonlight in his darkness.

"One more beer," I said. "And some nuts, please."

My father leaned toward you with an urbane smile on his plastic aging-actor's face:

"So what is it you teach at the university?"

Dona Almerinda weaved among the men with glass in hand, and I thought, It's not that he wants to make conversation, he just wants to make fun of you in front of the others. He thinks, What sordid, venomous telescopes their smiles are. His oldest sister's mouth, half open, suggested a nauseating carnivorous mollusk. Carlos gave a light to his mother-in-law and to an aged workman who leaned toward him with a cupped hand before his lips; then he lit himself a cigarette and put the gold lighter in his jacket's breast pocket. He thinks, The porcelain lamps, the chests of silver, the absence of dust. He thinks of the card tables set up in the sitting room, of the whispers, the squeals, the cackling laughs of his mother's friends, of the overflowing ashtrays, of the smoke that hovered motionless near the ceiling. The redhead, lying on the sofa, pulled on her black stockings and smiled at him slowly: her chest softly rose and fell, filling the air with her body's shrewd perfume.

"The French Revolution?" marveled his father, smoothing his hair with his hands. "And why not the Portuguese Revolution, if I may ask? There was a revolution in Portugal, wasn't there? A Communist revolution, I believe."

"This is the last one," I guaranteed with an apologetic gesture. "Beer hits the spot today."

The men in canvas shoes were eating codfish fritters, pumpkin seeds, and dinky shellfish whose meager contents they sucked out before spitting the shells on the floor in a placid indifference. The cold from outside and the warmth of their breath formed a strange mixture in which floated the occasional fragments of voices, the light from the television, which was on a shelf in the corner, and burps that sounded like tires going flat. There were probably no more fishermen on the jetty, and gazing out the window he foresaw an immense and speechless night. The beer's bitter taste made my bones stiff, thick, heavy, unable to fly, and he thought, No longer am I a bird; I'm anchored in the slime and sludge of Aveiro with its blighted boats, reduced to wood skeletons, devoured by the mussels and squid. He thought, I don't feel like getting up, like moving so much as my little finger, like feeling the rush of blood in my limbs, the troubled gallop of my veins. The obstetrician pensively scratched a pimple on his forehead while my oldest sister unfurled an idiotic, ironic expression, watched over by the workmen's blank stares.

"Why not study the Communist revolution of April '74?" his father stubbornly pursued, patting his hair against his temples with increasing fury. "Why not teach your students how to destroy a country with childish games and general disorder, how to let your overseas territories go all to hell, how to end up with Russia's lackeys baying in the National Assembly?"

He thinks, Green with rage, green with sincere indignation. He thinks, Outraged because of unions, because of strikes, because for a while they ruffled his smooth-running business. And his mother who complained how hard it was to get maids? Or to get a gardener to come and take care of the yard?

"Dona Almerinda," the blind man called with his chin sticking out toward no one. "Bring me a hard-boiled egg and two glasses of white wine."

From the other end of the room the musical sister said, "Oh Dad," but the old man had launched into an impassioned speech about our civilizing work in Africa, centuries of ingenuity, sweat and blood freely given to a band of filthy blacks, about the inevitable decline of a prosperous country set on a

124

downward course to sure ruin, while my mother underscored the most significant passages by hotly murmuring:

"It's a veritable disgrace."

The bulbs in the streetlamps, which he glimpsed through the door, were now floating weightless, fixed in the night; windows began lighting up here and there, also hanging in the darkness, faintly veiled by the mist from the river. The workmen gradually gave way to the first drunks, frantically slow, attracted to the neon ceiling light like large tattered moths. One of them leaned his arm on Carlos's armchair and their two heads, one dirty and one clean, one coarse and one smooth, confronted each other at opposite ends of the table with drinks, with irony, and without affection. Marilia extracted a Portuguese cigarette from a glass-bead purse that hung around her neck from a string and proceeded to light it, no one in the room having offered her the lighter. The glass door of the dining room suddenly glowed, and he could see the maid, a young blonde who walked with difficulty in her high heels, setting the table: sterling silverware, crystal glasses, the opalescent sheen of the china. There were ponderous reproductions of the old masters on the walls, liquid eyes of half-naked saints that poisoned the soufflé in his teenage years, and the bell in the shape of a hoop-skirted farm girl, used by his mother to issue peremptory orders. He thinks, Twenty-some-odd years of long drawn-out meals, arrogant haranguing, and tiresome lessons on teaching dogs good manners.

"Were any of your companies nationalized?" Marilia calmly asked my father. "Did the Communist demons make you work as a porter? It's an easy job, you know, my uncle was a porter at a bank."

I sipped on the beer and glanced at you out of the corner of my eye: quiet, rigid, and tense, staring at the door with brave and defeated eyes. You'll endure this till the end; you'll keep your composure in this hell. He thinks, If only I weren't so fucking weak, if only I could raise myself to your level. You reached for a peanut from the plastic plate, opened the gray-brown shell with your teeth, and tossed it to the floor with a flick of contempt, prompting the astonished indignation of my sisters. He thinks, Like it or not I'm still attached to these velvet drapes, to this heavy furniture, to these people who don't understand that something has changed, and changed irrevocably, so that they're going to drown in their Persian rugs, clinging to the cardboard pomp of the superiority they've lost.

"If you'd like to work in my office as a typist I might be able to find you something, provided you're competent and presentable," his father answered with rancid rage glowing between his eyes and mouth. "You might even get elected union representative if that suits your fancy: you see, we've got the situation back under control, and the Communists in check— for fifty years we kept the weeds from getting a foothold, so we know how to deal with them."

He took two or three decisive steps on the carpet, took another look at his hair in the mirror, approached the redhead on the sofa who languidly beckoned with a twinkling array of humongous rings (her long earrings bounced like lustrous pendants against her long neck), and embraced her, pedaling his shiny shoes in the air. His trousers bunched up in corrugations and revealed his gray socks and a hairless, octopus-colored section of leg. The silhouette of the maid twirled in the dining room, distributing the napkins (He thinks, You were never accorded the honor of a napkin ring), while the moans of the old man became rapid and anguished. He thinks, Should I help him to unfasten his belt, to pull down his antiquated underwear with buttons? And he remembered the fort at Caxias, watching the political prisoners being released on television, the arms waving from atop the army trucks, the envy he felt because of not being a hero, not owning a uniform, a gun, not having freed anyone. He remembered May Day, the singing, the shouting, the people in the streets: for once we were pure, he thinks. Even I was pure; before and afterward I was a schmuck but not on that day. His parents embarked for Brazil the next week, returning two years later with a vindictive smile. Carlos shut down one of the factories, the protests ended, his father hired a band of thugs with clubs to keep workers from meeting together; his obstetrician brother-in-law ran for deputy on the ticket of an extremely Christian party; and Tucha went to demonstrations, waving a flag and vociferating against socialism with her friends.

"If I was a union representative," Marilia asked, fiddling with her hideous elephant-skin bracelet, "would you sic your mastiffs on me?"

He thinks, That unbearable dinner, the roast beef I couldn't get down, my mother extracting Valiums from her pill box, my father's annoyingly condescending laugh:

"For God's sake, child, we have more civilized methods for resolving labor disputes: a dismissal with just cause, for example."

He thinks, How long did that torment last? The soup could never be finished, it got higher and higher in the bowl; the grains of rice multiplied on his plate; the wine tasted like sulfuric acid; the spaghetti balled up in his mouth, unchewable. "We've got to get going, the last bus is at eleven-thirty." And their cars were outside, lined up along the sidewalk, displaying the huge chromed teeth of their grills. He thinks, The porch light, the gate, the pruned boxwoods, and the affectionate, distraught face of his sister the music teacher saying good-bye in the foyer:

"It didn't go very well, did it?"

Dona Almerinda served the blind man and ensconced herself behind the bar to deal with the drunks, made gruff and demanding by the wine.

"I've seen the miserable life that the Russians have to endure," his father stated. "The only pastime they're allowed is visiting Lenin's mummy. People actually line up for the gruesome spectacle."

"Those poor people," sighed his mother, who was helping herself to dessert.

He thinks, My favorite dessert, the Bavarian cream of my childhood, when the leftover portion placed in the refrigerator, turning hard, was eaten with furtive fingers when the cook wasn't looking. He thinks, She made it for me, she must have made it for me; perhaps she still harbored a hope that I hadn't gone completely astray, because I am her son after all, aren't I? There's always something that remains that you can cling to. His musical sister stood at the gate among the bougainvilleas and wild roses waving farewell as we walked down the street toward the bus stop. We didn't have the two-door yet; we didn't have enough for the down payment; we managed to save only a paltry sum each month. "Maybe in April, Marilia, maybe in July," the car salesman smiled, twirling around and bowing before one model after another, overly exuberant, overly helpful; reflected, multiplied, and deformed in the mirrors, in the windshields, in the metallic surfaces, and in the convex sheen of new paint, he lifted up hoods, explained engines, proudly revealed the spaciousness of the trunk, frowned at your poncho, wary and effusive; I signed the check standing up, bent over a desk full of papers. "Can we take it now?" Marilia asked. The salesman became serious; he was very sorry but no, tomorrow or the next day; the paperwork had to be done; a final inspection of the car had to be made; he gave me a friendly slap on the back. "You understand, we don't want you to be dissatisfied later and give us bad publicity." He held the check with two fingers and with a meaningful look handed it to a busy-looking girl leafing through a stack of bills with her right thumb; he promised to provide them with free floor mats to make up for the inconvenience while the girl phoned the bank to verify the check; they distinctly heard the girl repeating the check number; they'd taken a seat in a corner next to a low table covered with magazines; the girl nodded yes. "Let's go to the garage," said the salesman. "Maybe our service department has managed to do a miracle," he winked, slowly sliding into an obnoxious familiarity; we walked down into a narrow garage where men in spotless overalls ran lazy cloths over polished, gleaming surfaces; a bald guy—dressed like the others and reading the newspaper inside a glass cage—had a discussion with the salesman (who pointed at us with his chin), gave a curt order to one of his men, and coughingly led us through a group of parked station wagons to a beige automobile, which the sales- man slapped admiringly several times. "Here's your hot rod, you lucky dogs." They signed more papers while the overalled employees reparked the surrounding station wagons; the runny nose handed us the keys with consummate indifference; we took our places in the front seat, side by side, as on a throne. I tried out the gear shift, the pedals, the blinker ("Ev- erything okay?" asked the salesman in a bored hurry). Look- ing up the ramp they could see a bit of the street, people walking quickly in the sunlight, the upper half of a bus; they could hear the usual city sounds. He adjusted the rearview mirror thinking, You're mine, looked triumphantly at Mar- ilia, switched on the ignition, put it in first gear, released the hand brake, let out the clutch too fast, and the car stammered, jerked forward four times, and crashed in a loud clang of denting, twisting, tearing sheet metal against a corner of the wall. He opened the door in a daze and the salesman—getting up from the ground (Did I hit him too?), his tie flung across his back, his jacket falling from one shoulder—glared at him, wild with rage, his gloss of amiability irreparably cracked, and growled "You lousy son of a bitch" from the side of his mouth while the overalled men, utterly stunned, approached the crunched car slowly, as if it were an undetonated bomb.

The television suddenly flooded the café with the chords of

a rousing march, and a fluorescent face announced the next day's programs, now and then displaying its uneven teeth, from which a cone of blue light seemed to emanate, projecting pale shifting diamonds onto the floor.

"Your father's an asshole," she remarked abruptly and with unexpected vehemence, leaning against the bus stop in the tepid, familiar night of Lapa, his parents' neighborhood. He thinks, Four years younger back then; Christ, it was ages ago. If you knew how ashamed, uneasy, and torn I felt, you'd have dumped me like that, presenting your self-criticism at the next Party meeting: "I confess I got interested in a bourgeois man; I confess that in these last few months I neglected the working class."

"Not only your father," she added in a wrathful torrent, "but also your mother, your sisters, your brothers-in-law, the whole shitload. First-class assholes." She wore an engraved silver ring on the middle finger of her left hand, her lower lip quivered in humiliation, embarrassment, fury. Had you been to Morocco to camp around with a flock of dirty and bearded friends with backpacks and no money, trying to sell junk jewelry as solemnly as if you'd made a pact signed in blood? We know so little of each other, Marilia. I never asked about your old boyfriends and yet I can picture them behind your eyes when your mind is elsewhere: pale and skinny guys who went to repertory films, spent summers discussing Stendhal at conferences, and were more important to you than I am; guys who worked for the radio or newspapers and who confided their verbose confessions to you over suppers eaten in taverns or over beers in the bars where the Left hung out, getting drunk while plotting grandiose and unlikely projects, a cultural review, a collective book, a unified resistance movement. The plastic plate full of peanut shells repulses him, the dismayed and insistent voices repulse him, the night outside that seems to throb to the rhythm of the river repulses him, and your tense body with its narrow shoulders, waiting, repulses and frightens him. He thinks, Time to leave, get in the car, go back to the inn, down the now dark and threatening highway that cuts through the pines, His family no doubt stayed up after they left to give vent to their mean and outraged indignation, his mother playing the martyr, emitting resigned sighs in between cigarettes.

"Your father got so upset he had to take a tranquilizer for his blood pressure."

He thinks, My father's blood pressure was the center of the family's worries and concerns, the point toward which we all anxiously converged, terrified at the prospect of a heart attack. "Today it was 170." "Today it was 140." A nurse from the clinic came in the afternoon to monitor the rising and falling mercury column in the blood-pressure contraption; he would squeeze a black rubber lemon and listen through the stethoscope while his father, right sleeve rolled up, kept his eyes closed in anguish. Only at those times did I see something of your body besides your face and hands; at those times I saw your hairy forearm—the color of a frog's belly—constricted at the elbow by the contraption's cummerbund; at those times I saw your flesh's vulnerability. The nurse gathered the instruments into a bag and received the envelope from my mother in the foyer. "Thank you, Valdemar, see you tomorrow." And as respectful compliments trailed after him through the yard, you, Dad, sat by yourself among the bookshelves of the study, the gray hairs at your temples slightly disheveled, pathetically opening and closing your hand. For your birthday my brothers-in-law gave you a Japanese miracle that measured blood pressure all by itself; a coin of sorts was placed in one's palm, a button was pressed that produced a high-pitched beep, and luminous digits appeared in a little window; it could be carried in one's pocket, taken to the office, or stored in the glove compartment so as to check during red lights if pressure was up or down; and he would draw charts, figure averages, and debate with the doctors; he knew about all the appropri-

131

ate drugs, all the diets, all the hazards; he talked for hours and hours—beaming with enthusiasm—about strokes and heart attacks and offered to take anybody and everybody's blood pressure; he called each of his employees into his office, told them to take off their coats and unbutton their cuffs, applied the marvel of oriental technical know-how, wrote down the pressure on a slip of paper, and handed it over. "Here take this along the next time you go in for a checkup; don't forget to show it to the doctor; you can tell him I was the one who measured it." Sometimes he'd call home in the middle of the afternoon to announce gleefully, "I went down from 180 to 170." He'd test his blood's momentum in the middle of meetings, interviews, and dinners; on one occasion he made two ministers and deputies reluctantly and incredulously roll up their sleeves while the soup got cold on the table. "You go ahead, Fernanda, we'll be right there." She reported that even during movie intermissions he'd go to the bathroom to press the button before the astonishment of the zippers and return to his seat either cheerful or sullen, depending on the result; he'd stand at the urinal, his legs spread apart, and instead of peeing, click! No, he wasn't off his rocker, the family explained, it's just that he got enthusiastic about things; there was his electric train phase, for instance, when he inundated a sitting room with tracks, signals, and miniature stations; fuses blew left and right; he had his sons-in-law pilot locals and expresses and lost his temper when they goofed; he got everyone upset, until one fine day he suddenly lost interest and went back to television and the newspaper; he offered the heap of paraphernalia that sparked frightful short circuits (we'd sit still in the darkness, waiting) to the indigent people of the parish, a passenger car to this one, a freight car to that one, a wayside station to that unfortunate family, so poor, what a pity, "Now I hope you can make good use of it and Happy New Year." There was the summer of roller skates; he'd skate to work on the sidewalk while the chauffeur trailed along in the Jaguar ten reverent feet behind; he had cement laid around the entrance to the factory where Grandfather's terrifying bust occupied a granite pedestal; and in the morning the workers were given an hour off on the condition that they skate clockwise around the main building; he himself gave lessons to beginners or pirouetted in front of the stumbling board of directors while patting down the hair on his temples; he promoted employees on the basis of how they did their figure eights; one fellow rose from attendant to section chief because he could clear three kitchen stools without losing his balance; another jumped from clerk to sales director after setting a new time record for skating from the parking lot to the cafeteria; and as part of the application process, job seekers began to be subjected to a slalom through a forest of empty beer bottles, which he himself supervised, armed with a stopwatch. After he gave up on skates we went through the horrendous cactus phase; we all carried Mercurochrome and a pair of tweezers in our pockets to extract the treacherous needles that dug into our skin; every room in the house seemed to be invaded by perfidious hedgehogs whose bristles would pierce through the sofa cushions and into our bottoms. Next came the celebrated period with baby crocodiles in the bathroom, crawling minerally across the tiles, opening their scaly jaws like scissors, replete with foot-long baby teeth; one of them tumbled down the stairs and latched onto the leg of the maid who was serving lunch; we began hearing, "Ay ay ay ay ay ay," while croquettes and rice and hollandaise sauce spilled all over the obstetrician's new blue-striped suit; to be on the safe side, I began peeing in the garden until the potted geraniums smelled like ammonia. "What's with the flowers?" my dumbfounded mother wondered. "Don't you find their fragrance rather odd?" Visitors kept their distance from the buffets with vases; my mother's canasta friends would ask her to open the windows, even in winter. "I'm having hot flashes, you know how it is." Not to mention his bizarre collection of shrunken Jivaro heads that opened their jaws in the middle of the night, releasing the stench of addled eggs, or his obsession with his false teeth, which seemed to grind their plastic molars all by themselves on sleepless nights; he'd go right up to people on the street and ask, "Mind if I have a look at your plate?"; they'd gape at him in astonishment and head in the opposite direction. And probably his passion for birds only lasted for a brief spell of my childhood, and I'm the one who's blown it all out of proportion. I remember books and print albums covered with dust and forgotten in an old wooden chest in the attic; robins, sparrows, parakeets, cockatoos, and sea gulls, and a stuffed owl gaping at us from a tree branch with the unblinking eyelids of insomnia; "Your father's an asshole, your mother's an asshole, your sisters and your brothers-in-law are first-class assholes"; the blind man nodded off to sleep, snoring through the thick reeds of his lips. "He probably doesn't have anywhere to go," said Marilia, pointing at him. "He probably doesn't know what to make of his miserable life," and I thought, You no doubt imagine I want the apartment for myself, that I'll foist you back on your parents; one of the drunks was crawling on the littered floor, inciting Dona Almerinda's dog to bark; his purple gums swelled and shrank; "Ruff ruff ruff" barked the drunk while sliding in the sawdust and nut shells; Dona Almerinda nudged him with her slipper and the guy lost his balance, grabbing onto the legs of a crony in a postman's uniform, and they both crashed to the floor with the exaggerated hullabaloo of clowns. You think I want the apartment for myself, but in fact I'm the one who's going to leave; during this last beer I've hit on a new vocation, that of minstrel; I'll buy an accordion to play from town to town; I'll take the blind man along, and we'll be happy; his father—much younger than now—sat him on the edge of the well, his still unwrinkled face smiled affectionately; "Your father got so riled up he had to take a tranquilizer for his blood pressure"; the shadow of the fig tree cast a sort of luminous veil on his forehead while men in vests skated behind him, the birds rose diagonally in flight, toward the forest, in a confusion of somersaults. "Do you still want me to explain the birds?" asked the old man, laughing as he patted the white hairs of his temples. I'll buy a newspaper, he thought, and put a red X next to the rooms for rent, in run-down neighborhoods, or with a private bath but outside town, or with kitchen privileges near the train station, or a studio in Alfama; we'll split up the prints and the books; I'll rent a van to move them; and when I begin to feel really lonely, the spines lined up on the shelf will probably bring gusts of nostalgia; the black-and-white past will take on color; I'll remember your body in bed, your idiosyncrasies, your per-fume, your daily habits, the bus to the university, and the barbecued chicken with potato chips for Sunday dinner; I'll probably start liking you as soon as I've lost you; they ended up eating horrid pork livers in the deserted café; Dona Al-merinda closed the cash register behind the counter, wetting the tip of the pencil on her tongue; "You're all a bunch of assholes," she said, bursting out in tears; the bus came into view, jostling on its gigantic wheels; he squeezed her shoulders with his arm and she shook him off with rage, "Let go of me go to hell let go of me"; he paid the driver for two tickets and Marilia glued her nose against the window, observing the buildings and streets that paraded by with an attention they didn't deserve; and she looked minute and fragile and desper-ate beneath her red poncho. "You're no longer interested in birds," I accused my father. "All you worry about are num-bers, bonds, businesses, stocks, notaries, and the like; go up-stairs to the attic and see how the albums are all rotting, how we're all rotting." We ate a third of the pork livers, drank a coffee that was half grounds, and left the café to hunt for the car in the pitch black of the square, where two drunks wal-lowed on a bench outside and slept one against the other, apathetically, like elderly lovers. "Come over here so I can take your blood pressure," his father ordered, and he reluctantly approached the imposing machine; the old man's polished baldness twinkled under the overhead light; the backs of his hands were full of the brown freckles of his sixty years and his fingers trembled. You'd no longer be capable of holding someone on your lap, he thinks, you no longer care about the farm, you don't care about anything except factories and heart attacks; Marilia walked into the apartment, took off her poncho, kicked off her clogs, threw herself on top of the bed with her back turned toward me; I broke one of my shoelaces and tossed the piece that hung in my hand toward a corner, and said, "Just relax, for Christ's sake, we won't go back there; I didn't choose the family I have, but anyway that's it, I promise"; the coldness and humidity had crystallized into a myriad of brittle needles on the trees of the square; it would never rain again, and Aveiro would drift eternally in the mist like a rudderless ship, with its dead-end alleys, out-of-the-way cafés, dreary bank branches, and empty squares; inside a lit-up pharmacy a young man in a white smock was wrapping up some medicines, and the odor of the syrups mingled with that of pain and the ebb tide; they found the car parked up against a sycamore as if held to the trunk by an invisible halter; the bells of some church rang an infinity of slow measured chimes, the sound resonating medievally, in concentric circles, through the saturated atmosphere. "140 over 80," his father informed him. "Remember that thirty is a critical age; you should start laying off the salt." The dark eyes examined him with clinical objectivity, devoid of compassion. My other shoe's lace held on by a thread, I sullenly brushed my teeth. "Relax!" I yelled from the ceramic tiles. "I won't ever inflict those assholes on you again." "I'm still interested in the birds, Dad, I still want to understand them better." "You've no idea how he mortified us," sighed his mother. "He brought over an absolute slob of a girl." He switched on the engine, turned on the headlights, and took off for the inn. Pines and more pines, the tattered night fog forming solid volumes that quickly disintegrated. "And she lashed out at us with that Communist propaganda against God." The pork livers churned uncomfortably in his stomach, full of needles and sharp edges and tiny jets of acid. I stretched my lips to view my molars in the mirror and found my face staring back at me, bewildered and lunar; this is what I am now, this strange shell, these wrinkles. "I don't give a damn about them and I'll never set foot there again, I swear." And his voice reverberated against the tiles, the porcelain, and the snake of the shower head; I peeked through the door and you were still lying in the same position. "The birds," his father murmured with an intrigued look, "what's this with the birds?" You probably fell asleep in your clothes, and I'll have to shake you awake, help you take off your sweater and slacks, then pull your underpants off your dead legs as you moan and protest in your sleep. "Stop it, lay off. I'll get up in a minute." The lagoon resembled a huge, diaphanous, lifeless puddle shining in the darkness. "I hope he doesn't have the gall to return to my in-laws' house," the obstetrician remarked to a concerned friend at the club. "Teresa came away from there fit to be tied, she had to take two Nembutals to get to sleep." "Are you asleep?" he asked the unmoving silhouette cautiously while taking several timid steps across the linoleum; one of your shoulders stood out sharply against the shadeless window; trees and more trees on the highway going back to the inn, trees hulking in the darkness, trees tangled up in branches and fog. "We're going around the lagoon, Marilia; soon we'll hit the bridge." Soon we'll hit the pachydermic inn. The alcoholic vertigo slowly wore off, giving way to an unforgiving emptiness. A cat galloped across the roadway in front of them. "The birds," murmured his father with a perplexed look, "what's this with the birds?" And meanwhile the birds flew out from the fig tree, the chestnut tree, and the surrounding trunks in a single huge wave that proceeded toward the forest. I parked the car on the gravel alongside the cars of the foreign couples, and not the slightest sound could be heard from the water, not even a current, not even a ripple—a total and horizontal, crepe-colored silence—and far away the lights of Aveiro, refracted in the fog. "Are you asleep?" he repeated while creeping closer, bending forward in hope of catching her eye. "Don't be angry, I already told you that we won't go back there." They had to ring the bell to be let in by the bellhop, whose eyelids were deep red with fatigue; the plants in the lobby swelled and puffed the anxious breath of flowers; your clogs echoed on the stairs ahead of my embarrassed soles. "Birds?" asked his confounded mother, "what's this nonsense about birds?" They opened the door, groped for the light switch in the minuscule entryway, and the darkness dissolved into beds, nightstands, an armchair, our suitcases atop a wooden stand. "So the guy hasn't a shred of common sense, fine and dandy, let him screw himself," the obstetrician said while finishing off his glass of dry port, "but is it asking too much for him to behave with a modicum of decency?" He kept tiptoeing toward the supine body; his mouth smacked of the grade-school freshness of toothpaste; the hair over his ears was wet from washing his face; they hung their coats on hangers; we started to undress; I felt nauseated from the pork livers, the sauce, and the beers; my throat burned from a bitter reflux; I lay down in my underwear, pulled the covers over my head because the light was hurting me, heard your bare feet coming and going across the floor, a glass filling up with water, a burp of sorts, and then the creaking springs of your bed, the fidgeting of your legs in search of a place to curl up for the night. "The birds," said his father, his incredulous face of the present peering over the newspaper, "I don't remember anything about birds." A piece of moon, fluid and transparent, peeked out from the clouds and then vanished, swallowed by the throat of darkness. "It was when we spent holidays at the farm years ago," he explained from underneath the sheets to the old man who stared at him without comprehending. "Next to the well, remember? And Mother would wait for us in the living room when it was soup time. There was that smell of summer at the end of the day, the smell of earth, of ripe apples, of the restless herbs at twilight." The owl flew across the barn wall; Dona Almerinda finished verifying the cash receipts, put the slips in a drawer, and announced, "Closing time." The garbage truck rattled down below while orange-suspendered men tossed the crap of Azedo Gneco Street inside it, the sad crap of our neighborhood, the leftover food, the scraps of paper, the chicken bones, the empty cans, the inert rag of my dead body. "At the farm?" asked his baffled father, opening and closing the tortoiseshell frames of his glasses. "What happened at the farm?" I'm going to puke, he thinks; why the devil did I take a chance on the slop they serve at taverns? His musical sister was crucifying Debussy in the distance. A strange torpor was draining his body; I'm falling asleep, he thinks; and as he dove into a sludgy lake full of familiar silhouettes he could still make out his father's frowning, troubled forehead; now I was right next to you; I pulled on your shoulder: "I swear to God that I'm through with the family; I'm through with their house in Lapa; we'll never again so much as go inside the gate"; and in the hazy light of Lisbon, in the foggy light of Aveiro, your eyes were as tragically devoid of expression as the plaster eyes of the lately departed.

SATURDAY

He got up twice during the night, sweating and shaking, to barf half-digested pork livers all over the toilet bowl, and he was so dizzy, so pale, so queasy he thought, terrified, I'm going to die, while the woman turned from one side to the other because the light, my footsteps, and the sounds of my puking throat must have been an unpleasant invasion in your sleep, like the ring of an alarm clock, which sits on the nightstand, practically touching one's cheek, and in the morning buries itself like a dagger inside one's ear. It was probably five or six o'clock; his soul was pouring out of his puckered mouth in gelatinous pieces; and I ended up sitting in my underwear in the green chair next to the window, looking through the metal slats of the blind at the dying lagoon night, striated by threads of a dim light that seemed to proceed from the webs of the pine tree shadows or from the turbid basaltic layers of cloud. In my mind I pictured my stomach as a whitish, heartburn-afflicted octopus that expanded and contracted inside my belly as its acid tentacles slithered through my veins toward my hands and feet. I must have had a fever, because I felt the kind of chill that comes with the flu, in spite of the sweater I was wearing: the hair on my legs poked straight out of my goose pimples; my testicles disappeared in the red forest of my pubis. The running faucet of the sink or bidet spurted out its wrath behind me, in the reverberating tile cubicle where I'd emptied myself out, like the afternoon I went to the midwife with you, full of embarrassment, to eliminate the fish that was beginning to get big inside your uterus. Now as you calmly sleep, unaffected by the beer and pork livers, and I can make out the shape of your body under the bedspread in Aveiro's grungy dawn, now as I'm about to die of indigestion, of colitis, or of a last and definitive burst in my intestines, now as my gums taste of rancid sauce and rotten peanuts, and on waking up you'll probably find me leaning over the bathtub, staring with a vitreous frown at my own distorted reflection, now I remember the afternoon when we stepped off the bus and walked to the midwife's, and I felt so afraid, so guilty, so sorry. There was no discussion, there was hardly even any mention of it; you'd told me when we first started living together, "I don't want any kids," and I never dared to ask why, for fear you might change your mind: the two I had by Tucha and a couple more by you would have been an impossible brood for me, an impossible expense, an impossible worry, four children yelping on all sides, changing, growing up. There was a room at our apartment full of boxes and newspapers; it was dark, dank, and dusty, and I sometimes thought, We'll put her crib in here. I always thought *her*, never *his*, and I'd already invented the sound of her voice, her laugh, the way she'd cry, her hair color, her name, her round bottom. I thought, We'll put

142

her crib in here, and I never said a word to you. I'd listen to her inaudible giggles during supper and smile inside myself or behind the instant soup. You announced, "I don't want any kids," knowing that I knew that you said it because of me, because of my stupid dread at the thought of producing a toothpick-chewing guardsman's grandson, because I wasn't able to shake off my father, my mother, and the East India tureen in which they'd cradled me. So that when you explained, "It's been two months since my last period; I know of someone at Flores Square who handles these things," I kept reading the same uninteresting magazine, in the canvas chair, under the horribly gaudy chrome lamp you'd unearthed at some junk shop one afternoon, triumphantly installing it in the midst of the other rubbish that decorated our living room. And if at that moment I'd said, "No, Marilia," if I'd said, "Marilia, let's have the baby," would that have changed anything between us? A sudden whirl of vomit surged in his stomach and he stumbled to the lighted bathroom, his agonizing hands covering his mouth: I'm going to die. They passed an antique shop full of leg-short chairs, cracked dishes held together by metal clamps, and nineteenth-century furniture drowning in the shadows; they passed a tavern and ulcerous old houses on which the October sun beat down without mercy, revealing the flaws and fissures of the façades and the scab-colored rust of the gates. We avoided each other's eyes, he thinks while seated on the toilet panting, while invisible hands cruelly wrung his intestines and a shot of air escaped from his anus. We looked at the numbers on the buildings; we stopped before the five-and-ten store windows; we leaned over to read the headlines on the piles of newspapers stacked on the ground and watched over by plump, aproned women jingling change under their skirts. He thinks, Is that what the midwife will be like—a woman with a bun and dubious fingernails, who talks in a harsh, sandpaper voice? He thinks, Of course I felt guilty, of course I felt distressed, I wished I'd continued on my own, in rented rooms, without complications, without fears, without dramas. The pangs came and went, Marilia coughed from her bed, I listened to her body turn over under the sheets, and sigh, and groan.

"Fortunately he didn't leave any other children," Carlos said with a chuckle of relief, cutting the tip of his cigar with a strange sort of scissor. "Tucha gave us enough headaches as it was over the inheritance."

A building like any other, next to a garage where a man hammered at a bumper on a grease-blackened workbench. The entrance door was open. "It's on the third floor," Marilia said, and they went up an inordinately steep and decrepit wooden staircase, illumined by a faint, stew-colored light, which the doormat-tongues seemed to lap up with the lazy appetite of oxen. Marilia pressed the brass doorbell: a hollow sound tumbled through what he imagined to be an infinite cavern, corridors and corridors at the end of which, in a room full of pails of bandages and surgical instruments, an old woman in a bloodstained apron would plunge her arms, up to her elbows, between your open thighs.

"Are you sure it's here?" I murmured, apprehensively noting the silence of the apartments, the rotting and splintered wood, and a gigantic spiderweb hanging from the panes of the skylight above. As if someone inside had heard me, a peephole was uncovered and an eye appeared, staring into my eyes with rancorous suspicion.

"Of course we managed to hush her up with some shares of stock, but it was at our expense that she went to live in Switzerland," Carlos added from within an oily cloud of smoke. "Just imagine if a second broad started claiming a slice of the inheritance, threatening us with attorneys, judges, and courts."

"What do you want?" demanded the eye without ceremony. Underneath the door, next to the rug, he could see the tip of a slipper and a chicken-thin ankle. He thinks, Why don't

144

we get out of here? He thinks, But I don't want kids. Seated on the toilet at the Aveiro inn, pressing his hands against his stomach, he thinks, I felt so helpless, so worthless, so ashamed of myself.

"I have an appointment," Marilia explained in a faint voice. "I talked to you on Monday, and you said to come today at eleven, and not to eat anything beforehand."

The eye shifted from me to you, slid down your body to look at your abdomen, then turned abruptly, sternly, in my direction.

"She can come in, and you can wait down below. There are plenty of milk bars around the square."

He thinks, This hag's going to kill you on account of me, and he squeezes his pocket linings to dry his damp hands. The door opens, and Marilia goes in; he spots a buffet with a mirror in the foyer, a coatrack with a man's raincoat, a bare-foot and bare-bottomed girl brandishing a spoon, before the lock clicks shut with an orgasmic sigh, and he's left standing alone on the landing, stupidly immobile, his head resounding from the anguished pounding of his blood. I turn off the bathroom light after wiping my mouth with a towel. I sit on the edge of your bed, gently running my hand over the sheets that cover your sleeping body. The nighttime clouds slowly dissolve in a blaring silence; the lagoon water draws nearer through the blinds; your head changes position; and it's dawn. Carlos placed his cigar stub in the huge ashtray and rubbed his double chin with the contented tips of his fingers.

"Now that the Communist threat has blown over we can peacefully pursue, thanks to cheap labor, my father-in-law's game plan. The Japanese and the Americans are just wild about our product line."

On the square the leaves of the trees seemed to be varnished with light, cars and people moved like wind-up toys, and the store windows possessed the unreality of watercolors. He sat on a bench that faced the building and fixed his pupils on the third-floor curtain. If anything goes wrong, I'll call the police, I'll turn in the midwife, I'll complain to my obstetrician brother-in-law. Perhaps I can stir up my father's powerful indignation.

"An abortion when I was with him?" asked the frowzy, gray-haired woman, scratching her head with a pencil. "It's possible. I don't really remember, it's been years."

"He came by the school to borrow some money from me," the musical sister reported while wiping her glasses with a handkerchief. "I was leaving and found him leaning against a lamppost, bright red with embarrassment. He didn't know how to begin. He babbled that Marilia was pregnant, he needed two hundred dollars, and he couldn't talk to anyone about it but me. And I had the feeling, you see, that everyone in the snack bar—the help, my fellow teachers and the students—could hear us."

An elderly woman with dyed hair and a dog on her lap sat down next to him, and the animal, a horrid white creature with a blue leash, immediately began to growl in his direction, displaying its tiny, sharp, fishlike teeth. He prudently slid to the far edge of the bench, and the old woman studied him with hatred.

"I need two hundred dollars," he told his sister, looking at his lemon tea, at the curved peel floating in its own steaming pee. "Marilia got pregnant, and I thought you might be able to help me out."

He thinks, That scuzzy snack bar full of people from the school, her colleagues, who acknowledged her from afar with knowing looks—how nice for the poor dear, in spite of being homely and wearing glasses, she snagged a boyfriend. And he imagined the gossip the next day, the whispers, the allusions, the jokes. His sister drank mineral water, blinked, didn't say anything, and finally fished through her handbag in search of her checkbook, placing a multitude of objects on the table top: agendas, eyeglass cases, key rings loaded with keys, photographs, ballpoint pens. He put the paper rectangle in his pocket and left her sitting in the snack bar with her glass full of bubbles, her apprehension, her generosity. He thinks, I never paid you back that money; it never occurred to me that I owed it to you.

"No, I really don't remember," said the gray-haired woman, grabbing hold of a jam-packed book bag. "Is it that important?"

He got up from the bed, returned to the bathroom, and scrutinized his face in the mirror: pale, limp, disfigured, shapeless, as if reflected by a distorting glass. An abulic tuft stuck to his sweaty forehead; his nearly transparent ear lobes drooped down his neck like drops of stearin. The old woman and the dog seemed to be growling in unison now, united by the same driving rage, and the animal exposed its colorless gums in an accusing grimace: you're killing her. He thinks, At this very moment the slipper-shod midwife is chucking pieces of cotton drenched with dark liquid into a corner of the room; the waddling child with the spoon is tripping on the metal legs of the operating table. He thinks, And you? Lying there with your eyes closed, in a mild stupor from the gas mask? Or lucid and frowning, eyes riveted to the ceiling, recriminating me in silence? He tries to visualize what's happening, but the images shuffle, and he loses the picture, then tries again. The old woman and the dog snarl louder and louder. What's going on behind the innocent curtains of the third floor? They resemble each other, they're going to break out barking at the same time. His sister finishes her mineral water and waves across the snack bar at the bearded gym teacher, who responds with a quick, disinterested smile. He arrives at Azedo Gneco Street with the check and announces to Marilia, who's lying on the floor pasting clippings into an album:

"I got the dough."

He thinks, Not even "Hi," not even "How are you feeling," just "I got the dough," in a cold, hasty, conspiratorial voice.

He thinks, An alliance of two laughable criminals for the sake of a naughty little deed. Neither of us wants children, I because I've already got a couple, you for obscure reasons, the Party, the proletariat, whatever, but in fact for both of us the real reason is we don't believe in each other. It all boils down to that: we don't believe in each other.

"A third-floor flat on Flores Square?" repeated the gray-haired woman, rummaging through the clutter of her memory. "Yes, I went there two or three times, a creepy place, a frightful midwife, but I don't remember if any of the fetuses were his."

"He rushed out of the snack bar," his sister said, her fingertips holding onto the check as onto a photo that still hadn't dried. "In thirty years I swear I've never seen him so discombobulated."

He lit a cigarette without moving his gaze from the window, and the fiercely barking white doggy coughed and choked. The old woman addressed him with hissing impatience:

"Do you mind smoking elsewhere? My dog's asthmatic."

"I've never performed a single abortion," avowed the eye whose hair had been bunned by a redheaded beautician. "Can you prove otherwise?"

He circled the iron fence that enclosed the square, drying his palms on the linings of his pockets under a sun that bruised the rich fruits and vegetables in crates in front of grocery stores, and he kept his increasingly nervous eye on the curtains, feeling the smell of May's trees in his nose. He thought, Marilia's shaking with pain, tied down by straps to an iron table while women clean her vagina with gauze pads, and here I am, safe and sound, useless and pathetic, dying to urinate like at exam time. He passed by the bench on which he'd been sitting, and the old woman with the dog recoiled; and he leaned over the sink, impelled by an uncontrollable geyser of vomit that bubbled up out of his bowels and inundated the porcelain cavity with a sort of greenish mucus that crawled slow as snot toward the drain. With teary eyes and a dripping nose he raised his head back up and at that moment saw her, saw you: extremely pale, wearing your sunglasses, leaning against the doorjamb, and turning your chin left and right in search of me. Her purse hung wide-open on her arm and a tail of her crumpled blouse stuck out of her skirt. He thinks, How transparent your nails are; you'll faint for sure unless I get you straight home.

"No, by all means, come in and have a look," the eye insisted. "We'll see right here and now if you can prove your affirmations."

"I'm weak, get a taxi," Marilia answered, supporting herself on his arm as on an uncomfortable crutch. Her features, drawn and ashen, evoked an ID photo taken in one of those square booths that eject a strip of four damp shots through a metal slot: four identical and fuzzy faces resembling us at our ugliest. Above, on the third floor, none of the curtains moved. A young girl dressed in black entered the building, and he automatically thought, Another victim. The old woman was now trying to get her dog to urinate against a tree whose roots were pushing up the stones of the surrounding walkway; she lifted up one of its hind paws with her wedding-ring hand in a scene of repugnant tenderness, as if she were applying a catheter tube to her husband. Two or three occupied taxis passed by, answering no with a finger to his frantic wave, until finally a decrepit Mercedes driven by a fat man with pockmarks pulled over to the curb in a shivering fit.

He blew his nose into a piece of toilet paper, flushed the toilet for the twentieth or thirtieth time that night, and began to breathe more slowly: his agony, his nausea, and his regurgitations ebbed away from him like the ocean at low tide, and an immense fatigue climbed up his legs and stomach to open its lazy wings on his chest. The clock on the nightstand read exactly seven. The morning wind ruffled the water outside, and the clouds grazed the tops of the pine trees with their thick veil of lusterless, bleachlike drops. I pulled the cord that closed the blinds and got into bed to try and sleep.

"When I miss him a lot," his sister said, "the first thing that comes to mind is that time he asked for the money and looked so upset, the unlucky soul. Believe it or not, I think that of all the people I've ever met he was the least prepared for life."

In the taxi I put my arm around your shoulders and fondled your ear lobe, that strange piece of inert flesh. You'd been wearing the same earrings since you were little, a tiny blue stone hugging each ear. "My godmother gave them to me, I can't get them off anymore." Tucha, on the other hand, possessed a veritable arsenal of variously colored earrings and long pendants that swung around her neck when she moved her head, producing a light, tinny jingle. He thinks, How her clothes, her lipstick, her shoes, and her makeup excited me, and how indifferent, estranged, and disinterested Marilia leaves me. He played with her ear lobe and then her nose and chin while the taxi hobbled from red light to red light, on its last legs, taking them home. They were passed on the right by a cripple piloting a complicated tricycle, and the cabdriver rolled down his window with what remained of the handle so as to lean out and launch a rain of insults. He thinks, We're never going to get to Azedo Gneco Street. Our neighborhood's running away from us. But the buildings began to look familiar, he recognized the streets, the corner, the police station—we're almost there. The apoplectic cabdriver turned his head all the way around:

"Did you see that motherfucker?"

"I never had any reason to complain," noted the gray-haired woman as she put the pencil in her bag. "No infection, no unusual hemorrhaging, no particular problems. Do you want the address?"

"If I got pregnant," declared the musical sister, "I wouldn't be able to sit still until I had the baby. My family has mostly girls, and perhaps my baby would be the boy everyone's been wanting."

He paid the fat man, who was raving against cripples and door handles, opened the door to their building, bent over with key in hand like a whiting fish with its tail in its mouth ("Why in God's name do they put the locks so low?"), pushed the elevator button, and when the elevator arrived, it contained a drunk in tatters, slumped on the floor and snoring.

"It must be an angel," Marilia suggested with a stoic smile, "and the top button leads straight to heaven. This guy came down by mistake and is condemned to spending the night on park benches."

"Everyone knows you don't need a passport from Azedo Gneco Street to get to heaven," he said, thinking, You make a beeline for bed, and I'll call up my brother-in-law: who knows what complications could develop from this.

The mannequin, the wagon wheel, the tiny hallway, the bedroom: the mattress on top of a straw mat, the sheets in their usual jumble, books, papers, magazines, the fishless aquarium, the desk covered with rocks and shells, jars of marbles, and the rest of the junk you're forever surrounding yourself with. You stretched out on the bed without removing your shoes: you aged twenty years this morning. I went to the kitchen to get a glass of water and you said no, shaking your head, without speaking. Seated on the precarious arm of a stuffed chair in the living room, he dialed the hospital. "The doctor still isn't in. The doctor just left. Maybe he's delivering, can you hold for a minute? He's in a meeting. May I tell him who's calling?" And after an interminable wait, his voice came on the other end of the line, "Hello?"

"I realized what was up immediately," claimed the obstetrician, removing his rubber gloves. "I prescribed an antibiotic

151

and lots of rest, that's about all one can do in these cases."

"We just got back from an appointment with a midwife," he stammered, "and Marilia's bleeding pretty badly."

I heard other voices on the line; maybe someone was listening to our conversation; maybe my brother-in-law would babble the news to my sister, and my sister would tell the rest of the family; no way she'd let an opportunity like that slip by: "Mom, guess what Jaime told me! If Dad ever finds out, he'll never speak to him again."

"An abortion?" inquired the obstetrician in a professional tone that revealed a trace of perverse glee.

"Excuse me," the eye imposed, "but I'm the one who insists you come in and have a look for yourself. It's a very serious matter to throw around accusations against honest people."

"No, don't be ridiculous," he answered after an anxious pause. (I've already screwed myself.) "It's one of those routine exams women have, you know how it is."

"I could drink a tea if you bring it to me," Marilia said in a discolored voice.

"Why didn't you go to the doctor?" the brother-in-law inquired with satanic insistence, entangled by a faint whirl of words in the background.

He could locate neither the sugar nor the teacups in the kitchen chaos. The sink faucet dripped against the dirty dishes, crusty with the remains of an antediluvian dinner; the stove was covered with ancient rust and crud: how long since someone cleaned this crap? he wondered in annoyance. How long has the garbage been accumulating, along with the stacks of magazines in the closet and the open cans of food that smell rancid? He wanted to light the stove to heat the water, but the wooden matches broke monotonously, one after another, and he threw the box on the floor, furiously.

"It's hard to get an appointment," he lied, "and there's a midwife right here in the neighborhood."

You were probably listening to me from the bedroom, Marilia, and no doubt could tell how annoyed I was: what were you thinking? A caged canary hopped and jeered in the window of the building opposite. A man in an undershirt, his collar bones protruding, observed the sultry lack of animation down below, Azedo Gneco Street snoring at lunchtime, drowsing Mexicanly. In the washtub on the balcony a few pieces of clothing floated in some filmy suds. He found a tea bag mixed in among the packs of spaghetti and suspended it in the aluminum coffeepot. It was hard to move around in the kitchen; he hated the plethora of plants that kept multiplying in glass jars on the shelves; he hated the stench of rotten food swimming on the surface of the tiles like an anemone cadaver.

"For me to give you the right advice you'll have to tell me exactly what happened," insisted his brother-in-law, unctuous and honey-tongued like the foxes in fables. The telephone went into periodic fits of clicking and clacking: this phone system is an absolute disgrace.

"This is my room. This is my little boy's room. Here's the toilet, and the living room," itemized the eye, ironically indicating each room with the exaggerated gestures of a tour guide. "Maybe you think I do abortions in the kid's crib?"

The drain was stopped up, and he ransacked the cupboard under the stove for the plunger. One afternoon, years ago, one of his sisters (which?) had chased him around the yard brandishing this unlikely weapon because I'd tried to look under her skirt at the strange mystery of a woman's smooth pubis; and as we ran we heard the panicky shouts of our mother from upstairs: "The flower beds! Don't do this to me!"

Lying on the mattress and trying to sleep in the morning of Aveiro, its brightness shimmering in the blinds, he thinks, You always said *me*, didn't you, Mother? Everything around you had to do with you: "It made me sick." "He kept me waiting up till two in the morning." "She looked like a blimp to me the other night." "He died on me when I least expected it." The universe obediently revolved around the now-skeletal axis of your body, prostrate in the clinic, where even time seems paralyzed in the hexagonal clocks of the corridor. He advanced with the pot, teacup, saucer, sugar bowl, and teaspoon trembling precariously on the wicker tray; and seeing your eyes closed, your skin taut and bluish under your eyelids, and your hands like glass birds on the sheets, I thought for a second that you were dead. But your chest slowly rose and fell, and from time to time your mouth seemed to twist into a pastry swirl as if you were getting ready to proclaim a definitive revelation to the posters on the walls: "Proletarians of the World, Unite!" "Everlasting Glory to the Working Class." But there was the sun on the windowsill, the white-painted balconies at the back, a sad and homey discomfort that impregnated the room with a moribund air, and the sweetness of a modest eternity in the silence of the furniture. Necklaces of various hues hung from a corner of the dresser mirror, along with yellow and brown strings of beads, and an old rosary that had belonged to he didn't know whom—he'd felt it would be indiscreet to ask. I felt like a foolish and pathetic scoundrel as I stood there holding onto the woven tray handles, forming a right angle with your wide body, shrouded in your woolen poncho.

"Give her an ice bag," the obstetrician advised. "That always helps to stop a hemorrhage. And if you like, I'll pass by there tomorrow morning before I go to the maternity ward. No, it's no trouble, it's on my way."

He finally set the tray on the floor (some of the tea spilled onto the saucer) and squatted on a low sheepskin stool that you probably found in some junk shop or bought from one of those roadside vendors who shake their precious goods at passing vehicles. I turned one way and the other but couldn't fall asleep, because the reflections of the water—enlarged by the concave metal of the blinds—formed strange and luminous shapes on the inside of my eyelids, because images and words and sounds marched through my head in a dizzy cadence, because the plants in the lobby were devouring my feet and chewing my legs with their soft acid teeth. He poured two spoonfuls of sugar into the cup and extended it toward Marilia, who strained to raise her head up from the pillow (one of her neck's veins throbbed), and just then the doorbell rang, a curt, dry, imperious ring.

"It's not worth the bother, thanks," he blurted out. "By Tuesday she'll be fine."

He opened the door without looking through the peephole and found the drunk from the elevator standing on the doormat, smiling the prodigious, harmonium smile of apparitions. His tattered clothing occasionally shook around his body in a whirl of feathers; his long nose resembled a curious beak. He smelled awful, of dirt, liquor, and unidentified refuse, and he appeared to be on the verge of puking up glaucous globs of red wine. Marilia's flat voice reached him from the bedroom:

"Who is it?"

"For crying out loud, it's no trouble at all," swore his brother-in-law, "and this way I'll get to have a look at your place. It's a shame—don't you think?—how little we visit each other."

He thinks, The story of Teresa's visit went all around the family, whetting everyone's appetite for scorn: come one, come all, and take a peek into the life of a failed Communist, a bourgeois revolutionary: uproarious giggling over the doilies, the Spanish dolls, the polka-dot curtains, and the photo of your father in uniform, staring with his huge round hillbilly eyes.

"What do you want?" he asked the drunk, whose scabby lips widened in an elastic, brotherly grin. "I don't have any money."

By way of response, the drunk opened his arms to embrace him with such impetuous enthusiasm that he nearly fell backward onto the marble landing: the tall clown and the short clown, he mused on seeing the fellow's gigantic shoes, in a circus without an audience, lit by a flickering ceiling lamp. With great effort the drunk pulled a grimy booklet that had lost its cover from his pocket.

Victoriously waving the filthy pages, he drawled, "Dear brother, for just fifty cents you can have Eternal Life. Who can't spare fifty cents to save their soul?"

A long and thin cicatrix crossed his left cheek. The lining of his jacket showed through the tears in the fabric: neither a Gypsy nor a smuggler nor—as far as he could tell—a Jehovah's Witness, but a mercenary for the Salvation Army.

"Thanks a lot," he excused himself, "but Marilia has her own doctor, we'll see him on Tuesday. I just wanted to calm her down, you know."

"A large hemorrhage, are you sure?" the gray-haired woman asked. "No, that doesn't ring a bell, everything always went smooth as silk."

"And what if I'm not interested in Eternal Life?" I argued. "What if I'm fed up with all this shit?"

The drunk slapped his dismayed hands against his trouser legs with such force that two clouds of dust lifted up in the air. A piece of dried mud fell from his shirt like a scab:

"Hell, my friend," he promised with a tragic face. "The first express train available to the gnashing of teeth."

"Rui," Marilia called from the bedroom.

He thinks, Will you be able to manage the tea by yourself? And he imagines thin fingers with white nails groping feebly for the teacup, her mouth open like a waiting bird's. The evening wind whipped the grass around the well. The house's diamond-shaped shadow devoured the tiled pond and its plastic fish, the forgotten lawn chairs, and his musician sister's tricycle, fallen on its side like a dead animal, its stiff wheel-paws suspended in the air. From the chicken coop, with its smell of straw mixed with turds, came an edgeless quiet of

156

slumbering eggs. The trees nearest to them murmured like harps, and his father pointed toward the woods, whose dense and bluish hue was shifting:

"They've gone to sleep."

In the living room there was a book with drawings of naked, winged men, of falcons with human torsos, of bizarre, mythlike hybrids of people and birds: and if Mom rose up right now, above the table, he thinks, and began to fly like a nervous parakeet over the soup bowls? He'd never actually been to the woods, since they were too far away, on someone else's property, fenced off by barbed wire in some parts and by a stone wall topped with glass shards in others, so he'd lean against a power-line post and stare in fascination, imagining strange feathered beings, cheeping and hopping in the secret thickness of the trees.

"Hell, dear brother, the fires of hell," swore the drunk as he tried to kneel on the doormat. His pockets bulged like saddlebags with stale bread. The thin hair on the crown of his head was held in place by dandruff and grease. "Now Eternal Life, hot damn"—grandiose swirling gesture summing up the indescribable pleasures of paradise—"is another story. How about a quarter, pal?"

"They've gone to sleep," his father repeated. "We won't see any more of them until tomorrow morning."

"Get lost," I beseeched the drunk. "My old lady's sick."

"Ten cents," the other proposed. "One measly dime in exchange for everlasting happiness. Come on, you sinner, don't be such a tightwad."

With his eyes closed he saw the bizarre birds of the drawing book rise in flight from the Vouga River, heading toward his window, then away, then back again. Their enormous wing quills shed a powdery mist; bits of bread kept falling from his pockets, and his waxy eyelids squinted at me. Gases ran through my intestines like rats in an attic; a flask of acid dripped drop by drop inside my stomach; a tooth in the back

157

of my mouth began aching. He searched his pockets for a coin and the eager drunk stepped closer, his appetite whetted. The brother-in-law's voice became resentful:

"I get the distinct impression you don't want me in your house. I hope you have the good sense not to set foot in mine."

"He called up to ask a favor of Jaime and then had the nerve to insult him," complained the oldest sister, with a fashion magazine on her lap. "Needless to say, we cut ties then and there."

"As you can see," the slippers declared, "your accusations are preposterous. I only work in the maternity ward. My children give me plenty to do here at home."

"Five cents," implored the drunk, his limp fingers trying to grab onto the lapels of his lost brother. "Five cents and we'll drop it."

"My family is a bit on the conservative side," whispered the musical sister as if her parents might overhear. "If I ever told them about the check, they'd probably have a heart attack."

The tenant in the apartment directly below, an energetic judo instructor who consistently scorned the elevator, climbing the stairs two at a time with a gym bag over his shoulder, came out onto the landing to talk with his daughter, and the presence of that imposingly friendly athlete, who always greeted the neighbors with muscular good cheer, injected him with the necessary courage to confront the drunk's sluggish tenacity.

"I don't have one red cent," he declared toward the stairs in hopes that the superman would hear and that his salvational X-ray glance would pierce the staircase. "Now beat it—I already told you that my wife is sick."

The beggar, still kneeling on the doormat and staring at him with pitiful, wax-coated eyes, tried to stand up on his unsteady ankles, but one of his shoes slipped on the marble. He lost his balance, his booklet's unbound pages scattered across the ground, and desperate to keep from falling he grabbed onto his, onto my ("What is this? What is this?" I screeched in alarm), trousers.

"It's nothing," said Marilia's distant, grating voice. "It's just that if you don't eat your breakfast it's going to get cold."

She was standing next to my bed in her nightgown, wiggling her hips, and her face gradually appeared from beneath her mop of uncombed hair. Outside the window, the sea gulls alighted on the water in large geometric groups, wrapped in a halo of grayish luminosity. The furniture reassumed its humble brown and green condition. A small boat sailed downstream.

"I spent the night throwing up," he complained. "The pork livers we had at that café didn't agree with me."

His limbs seemed to be missing their bones; an unpleasant caramel sweat made his back stick to the sheet as to a candy wrapper. He sat up against his pillow and looked loathingly at the bread basket: croissants, biscuits, sweet rolls, and regular rolls, with nipples like those on striptease dancers. And inside him—obsessive, merciless, bitter, and inexorable—the stammering speech about separating that he knew he'd never deliver. He drank a sip of coffee, pushed the cup away with the back of his hand, and turned his head toward the lagoon (How my head hurts, he thought, How my blood stumbles through the veins of my ears): the dark and ethereal veil of clouds was moving closer. In a few days it would begin to rain.

———————

DEATH OF RUI S., RESEARCHER AND LECTURER AT THE COLLEGE OF LIBERAL ARTS IN LISBON. Rui S., whom we had the honor of including among our contributors since the very first number of the College of Liberal Arts' *Journal of History*, died suddenly in Aveiro on the tenth of this month. He was thirty-three years old. Born into a family of considerable renown in the financial world, he attended high school in Lisbon, distinguishing himself early on for his personal candor, his keen intelligence, and his extraordinary culture. From this period date his first writings (faithfully preserved by friendly hands), consisting of stories and poems, which were printed in a student paper he helped to direct. In these early texts, we can already detect the intense inner turmoil that would never leave him, being largely responsible (according to the testimony of those close to him) for his unremittingly hapless existence. Shortly after graduation, he enrolled as a history major in the College of Liberal Arts, thereby breaking—brusquely, it would seem—with a family tradition that produced brilliant economists and managers, so as to dedicate himself to the research of certain lesser-known aspects of our centuries-old national history, striving to link social and psychological points of view, on the theory that the causes of historical phenomena could be learned through a careful examination of the intimate and hidden profile of their interpreters. An outstanding paradigm of this approach is found in his undergraduate thesis, "Dom Antonio I, Story of a Collective Suicide" (xeroxed edition of twenty copies, undated), and in brief essays published in this journal: "The Latent Homosexuality of Dom Miguel" (1968), "Maria da Fonte and the Class Struggle" (1969), and "Popular Resistance During the French Invasions" (1971), which earned him some bitter medicine from the repressive and cruel system of censorship then in force. During the same period, he exercised a courageous political role (distributing pamphlets and photocopying announcements) as representative of the Recreation Division of the Liberal Arts Student Association, a post he would eventually relinquish over fundamental differences concerning the right course to be followed by the student resistance movement in the long fascist night we sorrowfully traversed. After graduating, he was admitted as a lecturer to the college (where he'd already served as teaching assistant for Modern History II), and it was then that he more fully developed, through a scrupulous analysis of economic factors (he had an unusually keen grasp of Marxist theory, in relation to which he always maintained an honest critical distance), his personal historical concepts, particularly concerning the First Republic, of which he was a passionate exegete. He successively published "Psychological Profile of Manuel de Arriaga" (in *History*, no. 3, 1974), "Teofilo Braga and the Socialist Doctrine" (in *Journal of Ideas*, no. 12, first series, 1976), "The Casino Conferences at the Founding of the Republic" (inset from *Historical Moment*, 1976), "The Evolution of the Concept of Monarchy in the Work of Ramalho Ortigão" (in *History*, no. 10, 1978), *Introduction to the Study of the Carbonari Movement* (author's edition, 96 pages, 1978), "Antonio José de Almeida— Itinerary of a Life" (in *Journal of History*, no. 17, 1979), *The Sociopolitical Roots of Regicide* (author's edition, 57 pages, 1980), "From the Franco Dictatorship to the Constitutional Republic" (in *Journal of Ideas*, no. 1, second series, 1980), but he didn't complete his still-untitled doctoral dissertation, which examines the Sidonio Pais administration, excerpts from which we hope to publish in the near future, provided we secure the authorization of the departed's widow or her representative(s). Under the pseudonym Alberto Júdice and in self-subsidized editions, he concurrently published two short, dense volumes of poetry—*Return of Prometheus* (1976) and *Love's Interregnum* (1979)—whose decisive critical success unfortunately failed to find a response in the ever-capricious reading public, as well as a short story collection, *Interrupted Journey* (1977), published in a limited edition that, in accordance with the author's express wishes, was not commercially distributed, but which we know received hearty acclaim from illustrious writers such as Fernando Namora, Vergílio Ferreira, José Cardoso Pires, and Agustina Bessa Luís. In his capacity as an instructor, Rui S. compensated for a certain difficulty in the area of verbal expression (common to brilliant minds) through his unusual affability, human warmth, erudition, and mastery of the material on which he expounded, characteristics that quickly endeared him to his students, as is evident, for example, from the affectionate nickname— Michelin Tire—they conferred on him by virtue of his good-naturedly rounded physique. Though of a shy and retiring temperament, the late professor was always ready to meet with students—whether in the college corridors, in the library, or in his cozy home—to discuss the more controversial points of the syllabus—as established by the College Board of Directors—for each course he administered. Lacking material ambitions, he led an extremely simple—one might even say austere—life, which would seem to reflect his personal Leftist ideology, though he was unaffiliated with any party, during a certain period of his brief existence he was known to be a fervent adherent of dialectical materialism, a position he subsequently called into question in an article published in our journal under the title "Democracy and Socialism: A Confusion to Be Avoided," which the Most Reverend Archbishop of Braga did us the honor of citing in an Easter homily. The writer of these modest lines, editor-in-chief of the *Journal of History* and treasurer of the Lisbon Chapter of Catholic University Action, nurtured a fond admiration for Rui S. and had the privilege, on several occasions, to engage him in discussions on the social doctrine of the Church and the content of the latest papal encyclicals. The deceased instructor always displayed a lucid understanding and, if I may dare to say so, a tacit adhesion (albeit never translated into actual words) to Christian personalism and its virtualities as the only means of being in the world of man today—struggling by peaceful means to limit the tremendous economic and social injustices of modern civilization. I lived on Sampaio Pina Street not far from his apartment, and now and then, if his light was on, I'd ring from down below, the door would open with a clack, I'd take the elevator, and upstairs I'd find his vacant eyeglasses, his nervous hands, the smile that always seemed to be begging its own pardon, the books scattered about at random, the tin toys, and the permanent confusion of newspapers. We'd sit down to talk in faded beach chairs next to an old, disconnected heater—and with a rich family like his I never understood that environment of listless squalor, the cracked coffee cups, the torn rugs, the junk-shop furniture whose legs were propped up by wooden wedges or folded cardboard. Where did he ever dig up so much foul-smelling rubbish? I wondered. The flush mechanism on the toilet, for example, was bent and rusted to where it would no longer work; the sink drain was consistently stopped up; an ancient radio that sat on the floor in a corner would emit coughs and whistles; the posters— drably depicting political figures, caricatures, and steel workers raising their muscular fists—stuck up on the walls had yellowed with age. Was he an ashamed Communist? a closet hobo? the child gone astray that millionaires need as an example for their other children not to follow? The guy would clean his glasses by slowly wiping them with his shirttail; it seemed that his blind orbs had turned inward, like caged birds; he'd offer me an awful brandy in a tiny glass whose dust he'd first blow out as if blowing out birthday candles. "How about a drink? How about wetting your whistle a little?" His infantile grin would hover in the living room like the late presence of someone departed; he'd articulate occasional sentences and absentmindedly trail off—oblivious to me—into an interior labyrinth that was presumably replete with the sad garbage and wormy books that obstructed the apartment. "One of these days I'll bring a cricket to cheer up your palace," I once promised him, "a cricket, a chameleon, a canary, or some other bird," and when I mentioned birds he looked at me in astonishment without uttering a word; he cracked his knuckles and stood up. "Wouldn't you like to have, say, a parrot?" I insisted. "A goldfinch, a parakeet, one of those beasties that go cawacawacawa?" And he remained speechless, his nose pressed against the lace curtains in the window.

In the morning in our neighborhood there weren't even any pigeons, just old ladies on their way home with plastic sacks full of groceries, just ugly, weather-beaten buildings, just a hopeless melancholy in the air. I thought, If at least the river could be seen from the window, if at least a snippet of it could enliven the living room ... And then too, he lived with that vulgar, aggressive, disheveled woman who put out cigarette after cigarette in the wooden ashtray, banged pots and pans around in the kitchen, and treated her husband, it seemed to me, with amenities devoid of affection—and the fool didn't even realize that she didn't like him, that she disdained him, that she was ready to dump him for the first zealous, bearded Communist who came along, because as for her, my God, there could be no doubt that she wanted the barefoot long-hairs in power; she also taught at the university, but the only ones who attended her classes were atheists and fanatics, sinister sorts with yellow eyes, conniving in the corners in the name of the proletariat—and sometimes, if we were talking and drinking coffee on the canvas chairs, the broad would quietly appear in the doorway with a sardonic smile, or she'd crumple up my words and toss them into the wastebasket with a definitive argument, "It's that simple, pal, all your mumbo jumbo doesn't hold one drop of water," and he'd observe her with his neutral, opaque eyes, devoid of feeling and enthusiasm, hands resting on his knees, his fat body there as if waiting (for what?), his fossil smile there as if waiting (for what?), his nose sniffing as if waiting (for what?), and I thought, You can't possibly not see that she doesn't like you, that she's playing with you, that she's indifferent, that she despises you, that she wouldn't give two cents for you, dead or alive. She'd leave the room, shuffling her ironic clogs down the hallway. "How's the brandy?" he'd ask to fill the silence. "My doctor made me lay off alcohol because of a bout with hepatitis I had way back, he made me lay off fats, emotions, exercise, and Portuguese stew, he made me lay off all of life's pleasures except for being here with you to discourse on history, on Philip I, on Philip II, on Philip III, on 1640, on 1908, on all this learned crap I loathe." But what did he in fact want? What did he desire? What did he feel?, I kept asking myself, my stomach burning and my eyes sulfuric with tears from the indescribable rotgut that he always foisted on me in that microscopic glass after carefully blowing out the dust. "I've got a birdhouse on my balcony," I informed him while noting his unpolished shoes, furrowed by wrinkles from so much use. "Why don't you get one to amuse yourself?" For a second his face loosened up and became animated, his cheeks quivered, his nostrils puffed with interest; "I like birds," he said in a strange and infantile, faraway voice, the voice of a child searching in the darkness for the ear that listens. "I like birds, though they were never explained to me; my father got bored with them ages ago, he collects baby crocodiles in the pool." You've been swilling down shots on the sly, I thought, and now you give me this about crocodiles in pools. "One of them almost bit off my sister's leg," he continued while contemplating the toes of his shoes. "She dove in and came back out with an alligator hanging onto her thigh; you've no idea how many teeth those critters have, white, tiny, and triangular, and sharp as knives." "Who wants tea?" boomed the shrew from the kitchen, her howl amplified by the pots and tiles; all of the pigeons disappeared from the room in a noiseless flutter. I shook my head no. "I do, dear," he vociferated in a limp, discouraged, spineless shout. "I do, dear," I repeated inside myself—my God, you've turned into a castrated pussycat. "If it's only for you then it's not worth the trouble," yelled the voice. "Let's wait till more people are interested." And lickety-split I heard the clogs clump toward the bedroom and the door slam shut. She locked herself in her cage to sleep, I thought, and to let me know that it's late; she probably sleeps on a pile of straw, and on top, her own dung and the steer or donkey bones that were thrown through the bars from a safe distance, twenty-five cents to visit on Sundays, children and servicemen free—the Communist Beast of the American Circus, the Revolutionary Amazon, Engels's Granddaughter, scratching her armpits in the cage. I got up, he got up, we both got up, we stood for a moment amid the rubbish of the living room; I had to walk like a stork to avoid stepping on papers or cardboard boxes or mounds of books; I had to walk as if jumping awkwardly from stone to stone, until we reached the miniature foyer. "Think about the pigeons," I advised on parting. "Maybe you'll find out the explanation on your own." And as I descended in the elevator he just stood there, still, on the dimly lit landing, wiping his glasses with his shirttail, his hair in a mess, and his eyes dazed, as if he'd just woken up, while the Communist Beast was waiting for him in the dark of the bedroom, moving her claws in the smelly straw of the sheets. The ill-starred historian is survived by the widow, and by two sons, minors, from his first marriage. The *Journal of History*, written by the students of the College of Liberal Arts, offers its heartfelt condolences to the distinguished members of the mourning family.

HE SAT ON THE PLASTIC AUREOLE of the toilet and shut the door; the steam from Marilia's shower still blinded the mirror, so that my face was a hazy and whitish shape, like the imprecise oval of the moon when there's fog, or like the blob of the city, he thinks, far away on the other side of the Vouga River, fractured by layer on layer of mist, kicking its legs in the gray and unlimited space of the distance. He thinks, Shave, shower, brush, while you wait for me, stretched out on the bed with a detective novel on your chest, the title in huge letters, a gaudy cover, a man and a woman with big tits shamelessly kissing each other. He turned on the faucet and a jet of transparent glass, closed in by a flowered curtain, shot out from

166

above, next to the ceiling, shattering against the rubber mat and forming a puddle that spread throughout the tub: when I was a kid my mother would monitor my baths, scrubbing me with a round sponge, passing her quick and neutral hand, weighed down by rings, over my goose-pimpled testicles. "Wash behind your ears; wash your neck good; wash your belly button. Don't forget to wash your bottom after you do a b.m." His heartburn was almost completely gone; his stomachache had shrunk to a trivial, bearable, long-distance sensation: once more in good health and without excuses, once more with an infinitely long day to face. The razor blade was dull; the shaving cream refused to adhere to his chin; the menthol in the toothpaste made his tongue smart; and seated on the plastic aureole of the toilet, he dried his body's curly dark hairs with the sandpapery towel, using circular motions that gradually expanded, like the concentric ripples of a well when a stone falls onto the water's smooth surface. Wrapped up in the faded bath towel, he found you, I found you: not lying in bed, not reading, but with your nose pressed against the window and your hands folded behind your back like a stern policeman, indifferently observing the morning wetness.

"I don't know. I never knew her very well," said the musical sister in her empty classroom, with tambourines, triangles, drums, castanets, and wooden fifes lined up on the desks and illumined by a greenish light from the windows. "She was rather tight-lipped; we hardly ever talked, and after my brother passed away I never saw her again. Sometimes I run across her name in the newspaper, she does reviews of history books. I heard they gave her a devil of a time at the university for belonging to the Party. But as for my brother's death, I don't for a minute think she's to blame."

"The servants of Moscow," Carlos pompously proclaimed, "are the ones responsible for the miserable state we've sunken to: unions, strikes, Commie priests, demonstrations, the whole shebang. Fortunately, the Association of Industrialists is acting as watchdog: the Portuguese people have no desire to be a satellite of the Russians."

Exactly like that, Marilia: completely dressed, your back toward me, and planted in your clogs (did I ever see you wear any other kind of shoe?) as you examined the fog with the hollow eyes of an admiral, of a stuffed mammal, of a museum wildcat. Lately you had often assumed that posture, absorbed, distracted, alien, examining Azedo Gneco Street four floors below, with its dull buildings and dilapidated serenity, and I could never guess what you were thinking, what was going on in your head—what projects, memories, regrets, and joys assailed and abandoned you like an ocean tide: like right now, he thinks, away from home and before this lagoon, your body framed by the milky light from the window, as if you were an old photograph.

"Let's go have lunch somewhere," she said suddenly. "I need to talk to you."

You turned to me and for the first time in all these years I almost found you attractive, almost without defects, almost pretty: it wasn't Godard, nor American cinema, nor the new novel, nor the months you spent in prison before the '74 Revolution, nor your knowledge of abstract expressionism, nor your ordeal with the secret police, all in contrast to my disgraceful ignorance; it was just you, your outline against the water surface, your dry, caustic, and courageous eyes, the straight line of your head, your large rustic hands held motionless against your skirt, resembling the wrinkled feet of birds.

The gray-haired woman finished organizing her book bag, closed it with the key, and stood up:

"You know what I feel like doing on days like these?" she said with an unpleasant smile that revealed the poor state of her teeth. "Writing poetry instead of being militant. But don't breathe a word to anyone; it's a secret."

I tucked my shirt into my pants, pulled my sweater over my

head, and zipped up my plaid jacket, which in a way represented my commitment to a political uniform, my dubious, hesitant adhesion to the working class: LECTURER FROM THE COLLEGE OF LIBERAL ARTS DRESSES LIKE A PLUMBER. Was this enough? Could I in this way be at peace with myself? Would this enable me to placate the persistent little demon of my guilt over what I should have been and wasn't?

"Writing poems," insisted the gray-haired woman with her hand on the door handle. "Really, I'm serious. I could spend entire afternoons watching the ocean at Boca do Inferno beach, sitting in sidewalk cafés, talking with foreigners, visiting museums, and letting the revolution happen by itself. It has to happen, you know, one way or another."

"But, Mom," he argued, "in Italy there are plenty of Communists who go to Mass."

"Italy isn't Portugal," cut in his youngest sister, stirring the coffee with her precious gestures. "And the Pope has already said what needs to be said on the subject, so don't try to feed us a bunch of Marxist hogwash."

He thinks, Erect, stubborn, determined, staring at me in our room at the Aveiro inn—as when you challenged my family the time we ate at my parents', and I was at a loss, divided, fainthearted, with my insides lacerated by a thousand cruel swords, among the gleaming dishes and the soft light from the lamps, weightless, as if drifting.

"Let's have lunch out somewhere, I need to talk to you."

How long has it been since we've talked, Marilia? How many months have we lived side by side in a stagnant speechlessness? He thinks, It's wake up, get out of bed, eat, go to work, come home, eat, work, sleep—and if we passed each other in the corridors at the university, we didn't even trade glances; we were like two strangers, without so much as an invisible thread joining us. He thinks, Whenever someone said, "Your wife . . .", I'd freeze, dumb with horror and astonishment: that ugly and horridly dressed creature—five years

169

my senior, planted in her hideous masculine shoes, plastering the walls with posters proclaiming strikes, followed by a group of obstinate and submissive students fanatically in favor of a rigid socialism—is my wife? He thinks, If Tucha's parents saw you with me, if Tucha saw you with me, if my children saw you with me, they'd imagine I'd married the concierge; they'd turn their heads away; they'd perform complicated gymnastics to avoid talking to me. He thinks, The monkey of the bourgeoisie is still on your back, still oppresses you, still dominates you. He thinks, Why can't I let the shell of things matter less to me than the core? Why is it that appearances, for Christ's sake, worry me so much?

"Did you, for instance, read what the Archbishop of Braga had to say about this matter?" the obstetrician asked with a smirk of triumph on his face. "Why don't you inform yourself about things before throwing out the first lie that pops into your mind?"

You didn't defend me, Marilia, you didn't say a word; your nose—speckled with blackheads—turned slowly from one to another with the indifference of a mechanical radar. The gravel around the inn had been watered down, and as they walked over it their shoes produced the sound of grinding jaws. The river seemed to know neither floods nor droughts: the same narrow neck of sand, the same anemic grass, the same height of brothy water, while behind the inn there was the damp, murmuring, incessant restlessness of the pine trees. The car made a little hop onto the highway and began gliding toward Aveiro. A tiny green light flashed on and off on the dashboard: we're going to run out of gas, he thought. The elderly man presiding over the meeting, installed at the head of the table with a pad of paper and a ballpoint in front of him, raised his arm and the chattering died down:

"The comrade has asked permission for her husband to attend the cell meetings as an observer."

If the engine stalls, he thinks, we'll be forever lost in the middle of the pine forest, beneath the translucent cardboard sky, aging inside the car like the ancient mummies that bite their own mouths with their huge, discolored, gumless teeth.

"Well?" he asked, inside the taxi, practically without moving his lips. A bloated vein throbbed in his forehead.

"I wasn't in any pain; it was no big deal," Marilia said. "Don't worry about it. I think I was lucky. I didn't even bleed much. When we get home I'll lie down for a few hours and be fine."

A teenager with an acne-inflamed face stared at the elderly man while raising his hand high like a student in class. An expression simulating adult seriousness crumpled his features.

"Comrade Tino has the floor," the man announced, striking the table with his ballpoint.

They passed two bicyclers bent over their handlebars in fetal postures, pedaling slowly with the leisure of humanists. The judo neighbor, in a white kimono, crossed the roadway in four swift somersaults, disappearing in the silhouette of the eucalyptus trees, and he was surprised to hear himself affirm, "I like you," as his fingers blindly sought Marilia's hand on the thin knees at his side. The houses swelled as they rolled into close view, crashed against the car windows, and retreated, immobile and insignificant, in the rectangular mirror.

"The comrade's husband," proffered the teenager energetically, "is my professor at the university. His petit bourgeois teaching is reformist, and his personal convictions without substance. He generally transmits the opinions of reactionary historians. To accept him as an observer"—his acne flaring, his lips trembling—"would amount to introducing a Social-Democrat mole into the cell, with no useful trade-off for the working class."

"Let's start again from the beginning," the musical sister asked the unruly class. (A couple of little boys were desperately slugging it out in the back.) "Three-four time. Tambourines watch your rhythm, please."

171

More houses, more eucalyptuses, trees he didn't know, and villas built by returned emigrants, with lots of verandas, lots of bright tiles, lots of wrought iron, and lots of porcelain frogs in the yards.

"There," Marilia said.

A roadside restaurant next to a gas station, soft-drink ads pasted on the door and the windows, an old, red-lettered bullfight poster that was coming unglued and fluttered some. Rotted boats were crumbling in the sand, and there was one in which a rusty anchor pointed its three black points at no one. The students began to sing, accompanied by pipes and drums, and little by little the voices acquired body and conviction. Comrade Tino suddenly shut up, apparently in the middle of a sentence, as if an electrical mechanism had broken in his throat, although his acne pimples kept burning with indignation, or rage, or militant zeal, or impassioned love for the working class, and the elderly man now uttered incomprehensible sentences. He had a red flag on his shoulder; a few people jotted down notes; a mulatto at the far end of the table raised his hand. I like you, I like your poncho, your clogs, your unshapely naked body lying flat on the sheets; I'm used to the odor of your sweat, to your irony, to your biting dry wit, to the taste of your soft tongue in my mouth; I'm used to the scar from where they removed your appendix, to the scar on your knee, to the scar on your heel; I want to go back to the Sundays at your parents' house and their obsequious solicitude; let's try it again, Marilia, with our right foot forward, buying tickets for the Belgian film festival; I'll sit through every one of Delvaux's dull films out of love for you; I'll convert to dialectical materialism; I'll hold up posters in demonstrations, "a product of the affluent bourgeoisie," the mulatto droned, "and a backslider: our proletarians give us enough trouble as it is when it comes to party discipline. I'll abide by the decision of my comrades, of course, but I'm

172

convinced of that." They got out of the car and the water's breath wrapped us in its cadaverous halo; try what again? With our right foot forward to where? It smelled of gasoline, oil, and engine fumes. How I miss Azedo Gneco Street, he suddenly thought. I even miss the disorder and the dust. They pushed on the door, entered, and the clatter of dishes and trays, the sounds of the voices and the clinking of the utensils tumbled toward them in a hubbub. They sat next to a bunch of taciturn truck drivers drinking a final nip, their elbows propped on the paper tablecloth piled with the remains of their meal.

I'VE GOT A TOOTHACHE; it's one of the molars that my dentist still hasn't gotten to in my visits, every three months, when he leans over my mouth with a dental mirror in one hand and the drill in the other, disseminating a sweet, asexual perfume of disinfectant and cologne. The receptionist usually looks after my puppy, tying its leash to a chair leg; maybe she walks it in the streets of Lausanne, some of which I can make out beyond the blinding round lamp and the window: a square, a few houses, and the excessively clean, naked, antiseptic world of snow, the ice-crystal fruits of the trees, the milky skin of the pedestrians, the spotless fabric of the words of silence, the inordinate whiteness of death, pain itself. Pain itself. I'm seated in the dentist's chair, shiny and sharp tools entering and leaving my mouth, searching, pulling, and pressing; something (a hook?) pierces my jawbone and ramifies in my head like a vibrating tree; a groaning wail rises in my throat. I lean over the little basin and spit out globules of blood that a jet of water hurriedly sends down the drain, while the nurse— her back to me—prepares something I can't see in a glass dish. I lower my eyelids, and two light-galvanized curtains throb

173

before my pupils: hazy forms approach and withdraw, Lausanne disappears, and I'm no longer forty-seven; my tensed muscles relax, I open my eyes, and I'm back in Lisbon, in the attic apartment that my first husband's father set us up in; the kids are sleeping in bunk beds in the back room. I fish a Brazilian record out of the cabinet. I pull it from its cellophane wrapper with three fingers and turn around on my knees toward Rui's round face and I say, "I want to break up."

"*Crachez*," orders the dentist.

Another glob of blood, dragging with it a tiny hard piece (of bone?) the color of porcelain, the color of lead. I again lean my head back, opening my mouth wide and closing the purple-red curtains of my eyelids. "I want to break up with you," I announce. I'd already met Franco; he was going back to Switzerland, to Geneva: "Why don't you come with me?"— his gray hair, the suave smile of a bartender or ski instructor, the ring of African silver, his way of holding his glass, of drinking, of talking, and Rui, stock-still in the middle of the living room, would look at me awkwardly, dumbfounded, without understanding. Franco had visited us two or three times; he was great company, talkative, interested in history; Rui—sunken into the sofa—would listen with his huge and nearsighted, sad moose eyes, occasionally mumbling "*Je suis bien de votre avis*." We'd meet in the apartment of a girlfriend who was on an assignment in London; Franco would lay his cigarette in the ashtray on the nightstand and bend over me; his broad chest with its tickling hairs began to rise and fall gently; he stuck his hand in my vagina, sniffed it, made me lick the marine dampness of his palm while traveling around my breasts with his tongue. "I'll join you in Geneva as soon as the divorce is settled," I decided. "I like your tanned skin, your wrinkles, your sinewy biceps," his tongue slid up my neck to the summit of my chin. "*Aide-moi*," he asked as he pulled my arm around. "I'll go to Geneva, to the Congo, to the North

174

Pole, wherever you want me to go. I love you." I found the leather pouch of his testicles, the plump cherries hidden inside, and then at last his massive root, a swollen tube of flesh with a soft and rounded head that I guided past a series of membranes into my inside. I bent my knees, opened my legs wider, and began to moan softly.

"Crachez à nouveau."

The dentist was about my age and wore frameless glasses and rubber gloves. He had a permanently serious face, speckled on the cheeks and forehead with a multitude of freckles, and a little parrot nose—with tufts of red hair hanging out the nostrils—that advanced and retreated before my gaping mouth. Five months later when I arrived in Geneva with the kids and called up Franco, it turned out that the phone number belonged to a grocery store, whose proprietor informed me that Franco had gone to Boston to work as the deputy director of some multinational firm: he never answered my letters. I ran into him by chance a few years later, in a restaurant here, accompanied by his entire family like a United States president, old and skinny and worn out, consulting the menu with the help of two different pairs of glasses, flanked by his wife, an aged and squalid creature whose ridiculously low-cut dress revealed her protruding ribs. The nurse handed the dentist some pincers, and he buried them in my gum with a single swift jab: the pain increased, spreading an unexpected length, toward my ear and my nape before vacillating, retreating, and slowly dying like a candle burning out. The smocks untied the napkin from around my neck and obsequiously stepped back. I got up from the chair ("Where can I comb my hair?"); the dog barked in the hall on hearing my footsteps; his trembling muzzle tried to hide in my chest. And by the time I reached the street the anesthetized side of my face had begun to revive, like years ago, after Rui smacked me (with open palm, in a rash, nervous, desperate swipe) for announcing, "I

175

don't like you; I want to split up," and the record I'd been holding rolled around the carpet until it banged into the couch; one of the children began to cry in the back; the crying got worse, and Nuno appeared in his pajamas, a tiny figure standing in the doorway and hugging his pillow, staring at us with wide-eyed surprise.

———————

HE THINKS, Would it still be possible to sail in those boats? In the sand, large blue flies were preying on an indistinct shape: a dead fish, leftover food, an oil-blackened cadaver washed up by the water, covered with slaver and seaweed. On the other side of the windows, the billowing clouds kept swelling and spreading, swallowing the large paper sheet of sky inch by inch. Next to the gas station a turkey, tied by a string to a stake, rubbed its hoop skirt of feathers in the dust and shook its double chin like a businessman.

"I don't feel like lunch," Marilia said. "Order me a fish cake and a coffee."

The food was passed to the waiter through a square opening in the wall tiles, and he could see the smoke and windows of the kitchen, the darkened walls, dubious dishcloths hanging from nails, and the fat arms of a woman stirring food. I'm not hungry either, he thought. The men were eating vegetable soup with bread and drinking wine by the glass, and they wiped their chins and foreheads with their coat sleeves.

"Two coffees and a fish cake," he said to the waiter who skipped among the tables carrying a stack of plates and silverware. A calendar advertising batteries hung directly over his head. Rows of bottles occupied the green-painted shelves. Behind a Formica counter, a man with a harelip and a tired air served shot glasses of brandy. Someone deposited two coffees, packets of sugar, and a plastic plate with a fish cake on their table. Marilia plunged her spoon into the foaming black

176

liquid; her face resembled that of someone on the edge of a swimming pool, hesitating before jumping in, testing the water with a foot.

"I think we should go back to Lisbon," she mumbled. His father, seated at the desk in his study, applied a careful drop on the head of the butterflies, and as soon as the creatures stopped shaking he riveted them onto a sheet of pasteboard with a pin. His baldness shone under the red-shaded lamp, and a cozy lukewarmness, brown and gold, emanated from the leather-bound encyclopedias.

"Now that all comrades have had the chance to speak, it's time to vote," the elderly man announced, using his hands to quiet everyone down. "Whoever is in favor of granting observer status will raise his hand," he decided, conspicuously crossing his own.

The emphatically bad coffee wouldn't dissolve the sugar, instead leaving a grainy paste on his tongue. He drank it in one shot, tilting back in his chair, while his father placed the sheet of pasteboard into a box with numbered drawers and names in Latin written on labels above the metal handles.

"Listen, our relationship's not doing very well," Marilia blurted out. "When you get down to it, it's probably never done very well. I've been mulling it over and I think we should take a little break until we get a better grip on what's happening."

"Do you think this is cruel?" asked his father as he ironically raised his stiff and prickly white eyebrows. "On the contrary, son, this way they won't transmogrify."

He'd lost his happy, youthful, enthusiastic smile and the exuberance of the farm, where they'd go every July in a big car full of suitcases and maids. The farm manager's wife would have the windows wide open for them, the furniture dusted, the floor waxed, and yellow flowers in the vases. The bedrooms upstairs smelled pleasantly of fresh wood and resin; the afternoon wind brought the warm fragrance of the orchard.

My father, wearing old trousers and a scruffy sweater, would walk through the chestnut trees with his hands in his pockets, haloed with light, while my sisters rode their bikes on the pavement outside the garage, their hair flying free, and the chrome handlebars shimmering. A vast blue peace, a sensation of eternity, would descend on the profile of the mountains in the distance.

"What?" he said so loudly that various other diners turned around in alarm, and Marilia herself recoiled a bit in her chair. "What?" he repeated in a murmur.

But now he'd turned into an elderly man, with his skull's bones showing through his skin, his hands covered by the brown spots of old age, the protruding and vulnerable tendons of his neck squeezed as in a bundle by the collar of his shirt. Armed with a pipette and special tiny glasses attached to his regular ones, he sought the insects' heads with a transparent drop that trembled: an old man, he thinks, an old man reduced to an old man's hobbies, ensconced among his useless dictionaries and encyclopedias. Only three people, including Marilia, raised their arms, and one of them, sitting at your left, ended up lowering it slowly, like a shriveling tentacle.

"Separate from each other until we get a better grip on what's happening," she replied in the same unloving, unhating voice she'd just used, holding onto the fish cake with an infinite disgust. "Who knows? We may even reach the conclusion that we can't live without each other."

"Contrary to what you may think," his father informed him, "they don't suffer a bit. A rattle or two, a spasm in the wings (which we secure with the pincers so that none of their coloring is lost), and that's it." His eyelashes stirred behind the double glasses like the legs of a centipede, and it was easier to distinguish the sanguineous striations of his eyelids. "And this liquid"—and he pointed to the brown bottle at his side—"acts not only as a lethal agent but as an embalming fluid: the body is preserved intact, almost forever, like the Egyptian mummies, understand? There are perfect specimens over three hundred years old: they belonged to some duke or other, I saw them in a museum in London."

"Abstentions," ordered the presiding officer, unbudging, with a sheen of implacable satisfaction on his face.

He ordered another coffee and a fish cake for himself, to try to alleviate the alarmed emptiness of his stomach. "No, I'll have a hard-boiled egg instead." In the sand a skinny kid with his slacks rolled up to his knees, followed by a droopy-headed mutt, pushed his small boat toward the tin-colored mire.

"And a bottle of mineral water, please." The waiter bustled in and out of the tables, shaking his head yes without looking at anyone. His temples throbbing quickly, his hands with nothing to grab onto: I like you, insisted a stupid, broken, false voice inside him, and a slight burp escaped from his mouth.

"No abstentions," the presiding officer called out, looking straight at the guy who had raised his arm and then lowered it and who now returned a submissive, intimidated glance. "All comrades against the proposal, please show your hands."

Sometimes, Dad, you'd sit under the trellis vines to talk with the blind man who had worked as a steward for Grandfather and who lived in a little cottage on the edge of the farm, next to the dividing stone wall that bristled with bottle shards, and in those moments an emerald shadow, embroidered with gold, draped your gestures like priestly vestments. As the blind man listened to you, he scratched his ear with his monstrous, double-nailed thumb, which he'd passed on to his son, who manned a machine in the tomato paste factory and showed up now and then on an infernal-sounding motorbike, wearing a huge helmet that made him look like a monstrous beetle. Seated under the trellis vines you'd spend whole afternoons talking to the blind man or smoking in silence, both of you still, side by side on the stone bench, while the emerald shadow shifted its angle, the branches of the trees in the orchard became harder, and the house, covered with climbing plants, stood out in metal-sharp contrast against the pale sky. Perhaps the blind man, who walked unaided and without stumbling along the farm paths, cautiously feeling his way with a cane, could have explained the birds, opening and closing his mouth with its one tooth, crooked and decayed in his meager gums; perhaps his felt-cloth sea gull's voice could have told me about the woods' commotion when the birds return, about the night's cold that hovers over the ground, piping in the grass, and about the feathers that finally rest quiet in the thick of the branches. The presiding officer verified the vote count without changing his expression.

"Confirmed," he announced. "Two in favor, no abstentions, nineteen against. The comrade's husband, by majority decision, cannot attend the cell group meetings."

"You were never very interested in this, but let me show you my collection," his father proposed, going over to a large cabinet full of shallow drawers that was sandwiched between two bookshelves, near the table with cigars and liquor. "Five hundred and twenty-seven different specimens isn't bad, huh? Did you know I could sell these for a pretty penny to a natural history museum?"

Questions that were in fact affirmations, he thinks, with your authoritarian cough, jealous to affirm your power: my sisters inherited something of your arrogance, of your dogmatic certainty that you constitute the center, the axis, the motor force of the world. Only the music-loving sister resembled me, shy and withdrawn, lacking self-confidence, always searching for something irreparably lost. His father pulled on one of the fishhook drawer handles and showed him a glass case with twelve crucified insects mounted in order of size on small cardboard rectangles.

"What do you think?" he asked proudly.

"We'll separate as soon as we get to Lisbon," Marilia clarified, stirring the sugary paste at the bottom of her cup. "I'll leave the apartment and live with my folks for a while. It's easier for me, because you might have a hard time finding a place to crash."

"Comrade, do you wish to contest the result?" the presiding officer inquired, leaning forward with ominous amiability. "Anything that seemed undemocratic to you, that struck you as irregular in the debate or in the voting?"

I would perch in the round window of the attic, full of dismantled beds and wobbly chairs, so as to get a better view of the woods' shifting silhouette, the swift figures of the night's first owls, horizontal in the lavender transparence that separated the apple trees from the orchard, and I'd see the blind man below, pruning a rose bush with a slow and accurate upward motion that exactly matched an experienced, unending caress: if I could touch you like that, if I could only fondle you like that, my fingers transformed into the panting of kisses, perfume of sighs, a light breathing in your hair, then you'd stay with me always, you'd never leave, you'd say to hell with your parents' place in Olivais, near the hydroplane of Cape Ruivo, among the smoke-belching oil refineries.

"Live alone in our apartment," he asked, "to watch the garbage pile up? I told you in the car just now that I like you. I thought I didn't like you but I do."

The waiter set the boiled egg on the paper tablecloth and disappeared carrying aluminum platters dripping with greasy sauce. Another bird, he thought, a poor aproned bird dazed by customer requests, by shouts, by the multitude of stubbly, obscenely chewing cheeks and by the cook's orders through the opening in the wall tiles. The skinny kid pushed the boat into the water, threw the dog in like an inert bundle, hopped in himself with the grace of a grasshopper, put the ropes in the bottom, and began vigorously rowing, pulling away in jerks along the smooth surface of water without reflections. He cracked the egg's shell by tapping it against the edge of the table and removed it with his fingers as if peeling an orange,

181

then he extracted the translucent, white membrane that lined it inside like a rubbery film, that stuck to his hands with the insistence of glue. He sprinkled on salt and pepper and apathetically chewed the soft substance, while outside a second boat was shoving off from the sand toward Aveiro, this time manned by two small men with sullen faces, resembling an irate couple of sparrows. The truckers in the restaurant talked in cheeps, in croaks, and in short, hoarse clucks, or else moved up and down the bar like parrots on perches. Marilia looked at him, her tiny round cockatoo eyes jeering and mocking from under her head's flamboyant feathers.

"Who says you have to live all alone in the apartment? Why do you always have to dramatize everything?" you ask while pecking at the egg with the help of your curved yellow claws. "You're not a cripple, as far as I know. You can easily find someone; there's a slew of available women out there."

"Are you calling the internal democracy of the cell into question, comrade?" the presiding officer sternly inquired. "Are you aware, comrade, how serious an accusation you're making?"

"He was never a member of the Party. He never belonged to any party whatsoever," guaranteed the musical sister as she took a sip of orangeade. (The swans glided back and forth in the park pond.) "Poor Rui, I can't picture him with flags or banners or getting militant about anything. He was an individualist, don't you see?, a loner, a bourgeois like everyone in our family. He lived in an imaginary time, in a dead time, outside of space, in an unreal past of silver tea services and chitchatting maids."

The restaurant was now completely full of birds, and even the man who ran the gas pump outside started hopping about like a lame sparrow as he checked the tires of a cement truck. The birds' cries formed a kind of shrill chorus that deafened and frightened him; a mechanic suddenly rose up, batting his sleeves as if to take off in flight toward the ceiling. The boiled egg tasted like birdseed; he wiped his fingers on his trousers and leaned back in his chair like an old hen fidgeting on its roost.

"You need a definite place," Marilia said in a parakeet voice. "If you go from one rented room to another, you'll get superdepressed, I know how you are. Like one of those sick pigeons installed on the feet of statues, you know what I mean?" Her face, red and blue and tilted forward, contemplated him with the same neutral objectivity she used when critiquing the films of Kubrick. "You'll be better off in our apartment than in a rented room with kitchen privileges, don't you think?"

Cramped rooms, closets with wire hangers, windows looking onto gloomy inner patios or quadrangles or miserable alleys covered with trash and filth, beds with stained cotton bedspreads, rusty sinks, deaf and grumpy landladies, clothes sporadically washed at laundries. He thinks, In one of the places I lived there was a paralytic in the room next door who groaned all night so that I couldn't study; he didn't quiet down until the early morning light finally managed to pierce the dusty and grimy windows. He eventually died and the black-draped coffin was lugged down the stairs like my grandmother's, carried by two or three indifferent men. He thinks, Our rooms were separated by a flimsy partition covered with flowered paper, and I never met him, never so much as saw his face. There was also a former opera singer, who always wore a white carnation in his threadbare lapel and who hid from everybody at the end of the month, in hopes they'd forget he hadn't paid the rent and probably never would be able to pay it. One night I found him begging for change from the people in the café where he went to read the paper: with a dignified air he went from table to table, bashfully proud, as if he were doing them a favor. He lived in the attic, whose walls he'd coated with posters of himself when he was younger and had eyes that shined like hair cream.

"I sang at São Carlos Theater," he informed me pompously, while showing me a stack of handbills. "Baritone. No, no, here, read it for yourself." He pointed with his nodulous, gout-afflicted finger. "Amilcar Esperança, see my name? It's plain as day, right there, Amilcar Esperança."

He removed the rubber bands from a mildewed portfolio and exhibited old news clippings.

"Do you want to read what the critics wrote?" he asked with a gleam in his eyes. "What the press proclaimed about me? Wait a second, no kidding. Look here: IN AMILCAR ESPERANÇA PORTUGAL FINALLY HAS A BARITONE. Not bad, huh?"

"Comrade," questioned the presiding officer with ice-cold rage, "are you by any chance insinuating that I influenced the vote? Are you sure you're fully aware of what you're suggesting?"

"My folks need me; I'm all they have," Marilia said, flicking her plastic lighter on and off, ostensibly fascinated by its flame. "With her high blood pressure, my mother's bound to have an attack one of these days, and someone needs to be there to help out. They can hardly read or write; how are they supposed to cope?"

"I came this close to singing in a recital on the other side of the border, in Badajoz," revealed Sr. Esperança, tossing back his thick hair with a sharp toss of his head. "As the star of the program, my good sir."

"Don't leave me," I murmured, and I immediately remembered the conversation with Tucha years before, the shattered bibelots, my rage, my bitterness, my final resignation: stumbling down the stairs with my suitcase, flagging down a cab, getting off at a basement room on Luciano Cordeiro Street, with a dilapidated couch, an improvised wardrobe made of crates and a printed-cotton curtain, a shadeless lamp on the floor, and the landlord, stiffly formal, coughing out the catarrh of his cigarettes behind him:

"As you can see, it's a fabulous room."

He thinks, No way I can live on my own; he thinks, Maybe I can still patch things up; he thinks, We can stay in Aveiro three or four more days, glue back the pieces—us—and start over. I reached my hand across the paper tablecloth to grab onto yours ("I love you"), but the lighter disappeared from under my palm, taking refuge in your lap, staunchly extinguished: for Christ's sake, you mean I can't so much as touch you anymore?

"Here's the washbasin," explained the catarrh cougher, "and there's a shower stall at the end of the hall: Wednesdays and Saturdays, when consumption is down, at fifty cents a wash. Soap and towels are of course your own responsibility."

"I performed in the Coliseum with an international circus troupe," confided Sr. Esperança, caressing my elbow with his nostalgic phalanxes. "I came in after the magician, to do an act with the clowns. They slapped away at each other while I, dressed in a striped T-shirt and suspenders, intoned an aria from *Tosca*, oblivious to them, until they chased me out of the ring with a broom. It was a roaring success; unfortunately they never repeated it. That's when I became pals with the dwarf who comes on Sundays to play checkers with me; he was the one who threw a cake in my face."

"I propose that the comrade be suspended immediately," said the presiding officer, hissing with anger, "for calling the proletarian solidarity of the cell into question on merely sentimental and therefore bourgeois grounds. Let me just add, comrades, that here we have blatant proof of capitalism's pernicious influence."

The dwarf, whose skin was the color of crumpled cellophane and whose tie was always impeccably knotted, would arrive after lunch, walking like a marionette in his patent-leather shoes and smoking a cigarette in a plastic holder. After rubbing together his teeny hands, which were attached to arms that could barely reach to his nostrils, he'd plop into a chair, dangling his legs before the checkerboard. He made a living as a restaurant porter, the patrons getting a kick out of a misshapen homunculus disguised as a barrel-organ monkey opening the entrance door with a shriek of jumbled words.

"Artists get no respect in this country," Sr. Esperança explained in a tone of bitter contempt, aligning the red and black disks for the next round and immediately pushing forward the pajama button that substituted for a lost checker. "Look at how we're treated, for example."

"It's my turn to start," yelped the offended dwarf.

Sr. Esperança hastily pulled back the button and turned around the board so as to play with the black pieces.

"Sorry about that, Santos. I was talking to the professor and got distracted. You know how riled up I get over the injustices in the world. I get downright hysterical, yes sir, hysterical."

A hint of sunlight fell briefly on the paper tablecloth, descended outside along the lagoon, and disappeared: a despondent luminosity surrounded the dull faces, the bottles on the shelves, the walls plastered with sad ocher, and a framed saint he couldn't make out well, in spite of his glasses.

"I'll take my clothes," Marilia proposed, "half a dozen books if that many, and that's all I'll need. You wanted to come to Aveiro so we could talk about this, right? This being the first time we've gone on a trip in four years, there had to be a reason. Or am I off base? Be frank with me; I don't like to play games."

His father closed the top drawer and opened another one lower down, full of large specimens whose wings resembled painters' palettes.

"South American," he said. "From Bolivia. I had them shipped here direct by plane."

"Poor poor Santos," Sr. Esperança exclaimed, giving the dwarf a slap on his already alarmed shoulder, "that move is going to be your death."

"Excuse me, comrade," shouted the presiding officer to the

teenager with burning acne, "but you'll have an opportunity to present your Trotskyist points of view at some future date, unless of course you have the good sense to reflect carefully in the meantime. I call for an immediate vote on my proposal, forgoing all potentially divisive remarks."

"Get yourself a cleaning woman," Marilia advised, "and you'll see how quickly you adjust. If you like, I'll pop by every now and then to give you a hand. Men are so helpless on their own, don't you think? Anyway, there's no doubt in my mind that you had something like this up your sleeve."

"I voted against observer status," yelled the combustive teenager (Do you go to bed with him?), "but I must state my opposition to the methodology employed. I charge our comrade chairman with abusing authority, and I hereby give warning that this incident will be reported in writing to the Party's ranking authorities."

Early in the morning I'd look out the window and see my father under the grapevines talking to the blind man, or looking at the rose bushes, or giving instructions to the farm manager, and he was relaxed, without a necktie, seated on my oldest sister's bike, his trousers secured by clothespins. My mother would be reading a magazine out in the yard, seated in a canvas lawn chair next to the fish pond, which was covered with large, lusterless leaves and which was replenished by a stoneware lad's endless stream of urine. There are bound to be some photographs from those days, Marilia, not at the farmhouse, which was sold to developers when Lisbon began booming, but at the house in Lapa, in some chest or other in the attic, in envelopes or in mildewed albums, photos of smiling people in groups, looking at us with eyes from the past, the color of dried tobacco.

"Yes, the idea did cross my mind," I admitted, crumbling the eggshell between my fingers, "but these few days gave me time to think things over. The fact is that I don't know what I'd do without you."

"You fell into my trap," the dwarf squealed jubilantly, hopping up and down in his seat. On his left hand he wore a ring with a black stone, wrapped with tape to make it conform to the lizard dimensions of his bones. "Now just watch how I respond to your move."

"This creature here is extremely rare," his father said, looking at a dark insect with spellbound admiration. "You'd faint if I told you how much I paid."

"When we were kids," recalled the musical sister, "he and our father got along well. There were three girls, you see, and he wanted a son, a man he could talk to, a man he could hand the business over to. But Rui didn't turn out right; he never wanted anything to do with the firm, so my brothers-in-law kept working their way up, and now they control everything."

Trying to maintain his composure, he asked the waiter for another coffee, but a gnawing anxiety kept growing inside him, making his hands sweat and his blood gallop faster. Outside, the gas pump attendant was filling the tank for a truck driver perched high in his cabin, with a dead cigarette stub stuck to his lower lip, while on the other side of the road, the shoulders of the pine trees shivered from fever, hulking, dark, and dense. A part of the night is always hidden in the trees, he thinks, a solid fraction of shadow that no sun can penetrate, the nucleus of darkness that the birds inhabit in the afternoon. A motorboat ruffled the flat sheet of water, leaving behind it an inert trail of foam that drifted toward the shore in a succession of smaller, ever-smaller waves, and hundreds of sea gulls, impelled by the force of the undulations, rocked right and left in the distance, in the middle of the lagoon, where their heads and necks could hardly be distinguished.

———————

SOMETIMES ON SUNDAYS, when Santos was here, he'd come by to watch us play a game or two. He'd knock on the door, ask if

188

he could come in, and sit on that crate over there, because as you can see I don't even have proper furniture, just a few pieces lent to me out of charity and a box full of pictures and news clippings of my musical career, which I'll show you in a minute, if for no other reason than to give you an idea of the utter disregard for artists in this country: if your newspaper would be so kind as to attend to this matter you might be able to get something—a pension, a retirement income, a modest stipend—for one who carried the name of his country ... unfortunately I can't say abroad, as circumstances always prevented me from accepting the numerous invitations I received, for example, from Badajoz, that's right, on the other side of the border, who—as I was saying—carried the name of his country all over the country, singing for Broom and Company, the famous clown troupe, which had the honor of closing the Grand International Ibero-American Circus Extravaganza. I sang an aria from *Carmen*, dressed up as a bullfighter, with a rubber ball for a nose, and accompanied by a saxophone and a concertina, until Broom came out and twisted his ear and he shut up, and then Whisk, who was Broom's brother, sneaked up from behind in his old shoes full of holes and twisted his other ear and he started back up. The opera was a huge success in the provinces; the only problem was that Broom paid me poorly and never on time; there were days that in order to eat I had to borrow a few bucks from the dwarf, who had his own comedy routine with his dwarf wife and three dwarf kids—they'd kick and slap each other until the audience would be dying of laughter—maybe you remember the Hungarian Gnomes, which was their artistic pseudonym; they pretended to be Hungarians, an Asiatic people, and they even spoke an invented language that no one understood, but they were as Portuguese as you or I, or even more so as they were born in Oporto. Santos's father worked as a stonemason's helper in Miramar; he was a strapping fellow who looked upon his son contemptuously, as the runt of the

189

litter; his brothers are probably still there in the hardware store they ran, all dark and rusty and trembling from the pounding of hammers. Santos's wife finally got fed up with slapstick and being Hungarian, so she dumped him for a bank teller, a skinny guy who had a fetish for dwarves and hid ladies' black underwear in a drawer at the branch where he worked. Santos stayed on in the circus but gave up Hungary to become a Colombian; they'd tie him to a target and shoot arrows or hurl knives without ever hitting him, and in the intermission he helped the guys who stretched the ropes for the acrobats or put up the protective fencing for the troupe's only lion, a decrepit, centenary creature that looked—no kidding—like a camel-hair overcoat with tattered lining found in the trash and that yawned the whole time a trainer with gold braid, a make-believe pistol, and a whip tried to convince him to perforate a circle of tissue paper or to climb onto a platform and stand on his hind legs. The fact is I could no longer depend on Santos for steak sandwiches and fries; he started hitting the bottle so that it was him asking me for money. The one who saved me was Mme Simone, the bird trainer, who always smelled of birdseed and bird droppings; she closed the first half of the show with her pigeons and turtledoves pulling tiny plastic wagons and pushing miniature tin handcarts with their breasts, all in silence, poetic, beautiful. Mme Simone had platinum-blond hair and extremely plump shoulders, exposed by her long, low-cut dress; she commanded the birds with a wand, every now and then turning her mascara-caked eyes to the audience; in the trailer she wore a Japanese satin robe, on the back of which a dragon stuck its tongue out as blue and green flames shot from its gaping mouth; she had an image of St. Philomena with an oil wick and a picture of Errol Flynn, remember him?, in a frame with porcelain roses: Errol's mustache smiled at St. Philomena with such shameless audacity that it seemed he might (forgive me, Lord) come out of the roses to fondle her breast if she'd let him. Mme Simone would make me croquettes, stews, and soufflés, all carefully prepared and served; she'd put an oil-cloth with yellow and purple diamonds on the table, a bottle of white wine, and two rolls; she'd wind up the gramophone, play a tango, and settle into the couch to watch me eat; she must have been fifty-five or sixty but the massive amount of makeup she wore submerged her wrinkles in its uniform paste, until she smiled, when zigzag cracks would open up as on old building façades. I chewed on the croquettes, dazed by her perfume like a fly hit by spray. Mme Simone would cross her legs, her robe would open at her thighs, and a gigantic chunk of flesh would appear to my terrified astonishment; she swung her slipper—decorated with a huge powder puff—on the tip of her toe or else leaned forward to talk to me, and I'd get a glimpse of the two hanging worlds of her breasts. At that time I must have been, let me think, thirty-three or thirty-four; I parted my hair in the middle, wore a polka-dot bow tie, and considered myself the Portuguese Tito Gobi. I was forever expecting a letter from La Scala inviting me to sing with Stefanini before an astounded audience of critics in tails. I imagined the entire front page of the next day's *Diário de Notícias* taken up with AMILCAR ESPERANÇA MAKES ITALY BEND ITS MUSICAL KNEE AND IS RECEIVED BY THE POPE. Mme Simone's croquettes, moistened by wine-rich saliva, slid softly and smoothly down the hatch; a stray turtledove or two would flutter by my head with the heavy flight of heartburn-afflicted angels, disappearing into the curtains in a flapping whirl. There was constant cooing from the cages stacked up in a corner, loose feathers wafted inside the trailer, landing on the rug, on my shoulders, on my plate, on the trainer's long, platinum-blond hair, which fell down her back in scintillating waves; the sprawling farm of her thigh grew larger with every swing of her slipper; her eyelashes blinked slowly in my direction, covered by microscopic palettes of glitter; her lips pursed into a miniature hat crown, and I thought, Any minute now her face is going to burst into a thousand pieces like a jigsaw puzzle. I thought, How many hundreds of crisscrossing wrinkles will appear under this cement surface? Mme Simone got up to make me some coffee, and her robe produced a sound like rustling rolling papers at the same time it scented the air with her drugstore perfume; she lit the paraffin stove with a dexterous match and a blue corolla blazed furiously on the metal stem. "Strong or weak?" she asked in a voice that swooned to my grateful stupefaction. "In between," I whispered in panic, hunting in my pockets for a cigarette. She filled two cups and placed them on a tray advertising tacky furniture and then set down a tin sugar bowl out of whose white powder a spoon handle protruded; she arranged everything on the chair next to the floral-patterned couch, sat back down, displaying the thick, elephant wrinkliness of her knees, and then proposed in a carnivorous voice, "Amilcar, wouldn't you rather have coffee in the parlor?" I downed the white wine that was left in the glass, first of all because there are lots of hungry people in the world, and second because it helps me with the high notes, and believe me, dear sir, my sense of artistic duty has always come before everything else—either you're a professional or you're not, and if you are it implies a continual sacrifice, a total commitment, the giving of yourself, a sacred mission. The pigeons and turtledoves stirred in their wire cages; I buttoned my coat and walked urbanely toward the flora, genteelly installing myself on one end, tapping a cigarette against my thumbnail; through the trailer window I could see the tattered circus tent and a bit of the cage where the centenarian lion nodded in the perpetual slumber of a retired civil servant, on the verge of a coma. I could hear Broom arguing with his brother as usual; they were bachelors and slept together, and over time they'd acquired the acrimonious habits of married couples. I stopped tapping the cigarette on my nail, lifted it to my mouth, and the flame from a lighter surged unexpectedly before my nose; the cement cracked with an interminable smile full of teeth like yellow seeds, the perfume was choking me, the platinum hair was blinding me, the blackened eyes were swallowing me, her dress's V neck abruptly deepened when she leaned forward, and inside I could make out lavender lace and tulle flowers, a slipper freed itself from her foot and fell next to my shoes, Mme Simone's scarlet nails caressed her own double chin with voluptuous languor, the many stones of her swollen rings flashed. "Kiss me, Amilcar," she ordered in a sigh, opening her fat arms, which exuded a confused mist of deodorant and armpit. A dove cooed behind the curtains; the gramophone began a fiery two-step; the tray slid to the floor in a clatter; Broom called Whisk a lying piece of shit; and I found myself exploring the voluminous mysteries of the Japanese robe, with the platinum waves brushing my face, and a benevolent vampire sucking my neck and saying, "Amilcar." We got married in Almeirim, with Santos in a tuxedo as our witness, grave and concentrated and microscopic. I can still see him signing his name, with his tongue hanging out, next to the X that the clerk had penciled in the margin so that no one could make a mistake. "Sign there." The next week I moved into her trailer and helped feed corn to the pigeons and rehearse new routines with the beaks, for instance, getting them to stick their heads out of a birdhouse all at the same time, or to fly around with the Portuguese and French flags in their beaks because Mme Simone had a great-great-grandfather from Marseille, and forty years previous she'd harbored a tumultuous passion for a trapeze artist from Nice who cheated on her with a contortionist from Lisbon, leaving as an inheritance a daughter my age who taught primary school way the hell north in Mirandela, the most nearsighted and pimply creature I've ever met; the lenses in her glasses were thicker than portholes and the way she talked you'd think she were explaining that one plus one equals two to a class of mongoloid orangutans with tooth trouble, scabies, and hepatitis. Simone when she mentioned her daughter had always said, "If the circus passes through Mirandela, you'll meet Hortensia and can be her stepfather; the poor girl doesn't even remember Charles," so the day came, and while our colleagues set up the tent on a vacant lot, we looked for her house, and the people in the streets kept turning around to stare at us. It was a miserable second-floor apartment on a miserable lane with miserable funeral parlors on either end ready to miserably bury Mirandela hook, line, and sinker. We went up a spiral of stairs worn down like old bones and at the top there was her door, the doormat, and the metal button of the doorbell; your tight-fitting scarlet dress inflamed the murkiness, a sixty-year-old woman with a good girdle is still a woman, yes sir; the hinges turned, and the skinny and ugly schoolteacher appeared on the threshold. "Hortensia I got married with this gentleman here," and the face of her daughter doubled into two of shock; the perplexed points of her eyes blinked behind her glasses. In a dining room full of decrepit furniture propped up by pieces of cardboard we drank some port in little blue glasses, and past the polka-dot curtains I could see the lane, homesteads with chicken coops, and lots of rooftops. Deeply stirred by the reunion, Simone retouched her makeup—hat-crown mouth, lips, eyebrows, cheeks—in a little round mirror with Esther Williams's picture on the back side. "I want my two darlings to become friends." The schoolteacher glared at me with infinite disapproval. We left at eight because the show was going to begin and because the turtledoves were dying of hunger in their cages; so after an afternoon of accusatory silences, hostile interludes, and the exaggerated tenderness of my wife, with the neck of a bottle in one hand and her long gold cigarette holder in the other, we reached the trailer as a small line was forming in front of the ticket booth, drowned in the loudspeaker music and in the voice of Broom announcing the performers, while a spotlight focused on the cage of the feeble lion surrounded by a group of admiring onlookers, with the animal occasionally opening its empty jaws out of drowsy resignation. Mme Simone talked to the pigeons in affectionate little squeals; Broom's grandson rapped on the window that it was time to take the birds into the ring; an employee who helped with the bookkeeping carried the cages into the wings; she changed out of her red dress into a long, black one with ruffles that swayed like boughs, and between the two toilettes appeared her pale flabby meat chunks, her sagging buttocks, her varicose veins, her stomach's uncontrolled curves, her bunions—and I think it was when I followed her legs down to her bunions and observed her scaly, gristly, scrunched toes in the round mirror with colored lights that I was using to comb my hair that I decided, No way; I felt a sudden disgust inside, a blind and profound nausea, an urge to vomit. I wasn't to go on until the second half, so I had time to pack my bags, though in my haste or nervousness I forgot my socks. I caught the nine-ten mail train to Lisbon and thus cut short the most promising singing career of my day—anyone with the least bit of objectivity who's attended my performances will confirm my words. Simone died a few months later from a cerebral concussion when the large trapeze fell on top of her; the company disbanded; Broom came to Lisbon and got a job as a public urinal attendant downtown but was fired for filching disinfectant powder; the lion was sold to a returned emigrant who had it stuffed to place in his foyer; and I found this room and worked for a few years in nightclubs in the zone, singing light-rock sambas with the lead vocalist of Jorge and His Rhythm Demons, all of us dressed in white shoes, striped coats, and straw hats; it was in Woodpecker Bar that I met up again with Santos, who was in charge of checking coats and furnishing American cigarettes to the ladies; life doesn't always work out like we expect, does it?, and the only thing we can do is accept it. The dwarf and I play a few rounds on Sundays or go down to the park with the bandstand to reminisce about the circus; have you noticed how in his old age he looks like a newborn baby, red and wrinkly, full of funny faces and jerky movements, a baby dressed as a man, with a hat on his head and a tie clip? We set up the checkerboard next to the window so that we can see a bit of the city, cars, pedestrians, a church, statues, these high-rises they have now; Santos brings a pint of brandy to stoke the soul's flame, and sometimes—and I think this information is what interests you—the professor would come to my room, knock on the door, ask if he could come in, extremely polite, well mannered, a little depressed; he'd pull up that crate and watch our games in silence, without drinking, or he'd study the posters on the wall, pictures of me with wide trousers, a Tyrolean cap, and a false mustache, or of Mme Simone in a whirlwind of pigeons, smiling and much younger than when I knew her, and one afternoon he asked me, "Why so many pigeons?"; and I explained, "That's my late wife, who trained turtledoves," and the professor was quiet, studying the birds, examining their beaks, their eyes, their wings, the fine mesh of their feet, the white, gray, and bluish quills of their wings, which flitted through the room for an instant in an anguished farandole over the head of the dwarf, of me, and of the professor, who regarded them in a stupor, his chubby cheeks trembling with that melancholy friar's smile he had, don't you remember how he smiled like one of those clay monk figures on which you pull a string and a penis (pardon my French) pops out from his cassock? The dwarf told him what the birds could do with the little tin carts and the miniature swings and the guy was hanging on every word. Finally he said, "Maybe Mme Simone could have explained the birds to me. I've been trying to figure them out for thirty years," and then he added, "Maybe I will have a tad of brandy after all." He sipped from the mug, turned purple, and started coughing. He's got a health problem, I thought, and at that precise moment I was absolutely certain I heard feathers rustle and birds coo—I don't know if they were in the ceiling, in the closet, in the quilt, or where, but the murmur spread from wall to wall until the entire room had transformed into a huge, vibrating, unbearable hive of sounds, and slowly the professor sat up straight in his chair, finally dissolving with open wings—a kind of ridiculous, nearsighted seraphim that coughed—into the faded blue of the poster.

ONE BY ONE the boats began returning to the narrow neck of beach in the gray afternoon, and the big trucks stopped making the highway shake as in scenes from old films, so the gas station attendant walked into the restaurant to talk with the fish cake waiter, their two heads leaning close together at the age-warped bar, like a pair of plotting lovers. He thinks, We've spent the whole frigging weekend traipsing from one raunchy café to another, seated in hard, uncomfortable chairs, watching the succession of rain-pregnant days, gray and thick and heavy, looking at the sea gulls and the ducks gliding over the lake with the mechanical inertia of toys, hearing the wind in the flute of the pines, smelling the rotten seaweed and the withering, bloodless reeds on the shore; and just like that, "I think we should end it, I'm going back to my folks, You can keep the apartment, If you like I'll come and give you a hand once in a while," in short, everything I was planning to tell her before I discovered that I really do like her, that I'd miss you, damn it, that I wouldn't know how to get along on my own, without you, the same speech, the same words, almost the same coldly cordial tone of voice, and me brandishing a hard-boiled egg, with salt and pepper falling off onto my wrist, converted into the pathetic, surprised dummy. He thinks, Soon we'll go back to the inn without saying a word the whole way (what's there to say now?), so far from each other that if by chance we should touch, we won't touch, as far and estranged as I was from Tucha, Marília, when I pressed the elevator button on the landing, alone with my suitcase while she politely waited at the door, as if I were a visitor, he thinks, with a vague smile of harsh pity on her face, her hand on the doorknob, the kids peering from behind, their curiosity piqued. "Where's Daddy going to?" asked the littlest one and the blood in my veins froze. Tucha answered, "I'll tell you in a minute." The tenant from the fifth floor on the right was downstairs checking his mailbox: our usual neutral, how's it going, our friendly indifference. He thinks, What would happen if I hugged him and started crying?; and he confronts the old, familiar, opaque street. He set the egg down on his plate, wiped his fingers on a napkin taken from a plastic holder, placed his elbows on the table, and tried to present a natural, nonchalant air as thousands of invisible needles jabbed stubbornly, incessantly, sadistically at his viscera.

"You don't like me anymore?" he asked in a diminutive voice whose hesitancy betrayed him.

"You've never killed a butterfly?" asked his incredulous father approaching a net-covered box with something fluttering inside. "The only thing that's tricky, son, is to keep from damaging their wings."

The men pulled their boats onto the beach with their backs to us and disappeared under the restaurant's wooden veranda with coils of rope hanging from their shoulders: where did they go? he wonders. Where will they go now? Variously shaded, overlaying gray patches meandered in the lagoon; the sky resembled an inordinately large, concave face without features, propped up by the dark tops of the pines.

"If there's one thing we can't allow, comrade," warned the presiding officer in a disturbingly serious voice, "it's personal feelings taking precedence over the tremendous collective fight we're engaged in for the final victory of socialism."

"It's not exactly a matter of liking or not liking," Marilia said, using a cigarette butt to trace a pensive swirl in the ashtray's ashes. "You always frame questions in emotional terms that simplify and trivialize. It's a matter of me feeling that right now, for a variety of reasons, we should proceed in this way. Things aren't going very well between us, maybe they never did, I don't know. Different class origins, different upbringings, different cultures, different objectives. For four years now I've been virtually cut off from the Party on account of our relationship, and I think it's time to get active again. I've felt awful where the Party's concerned; I hate to leave things hanging."

"Do you want to sell cheap editions of Marx on the street as if you were hawking pulp magazines?" I asked spitefully.

"You have to use extreme care when grabbing hold of them," explained his father, whose delicate, careful fingers roved inside the box with the slow, slippery motions of sea-weed. "There are special gloves and pincers, but I prefer to do it this way."

"He stopped going to the house," said the oldest sister, "so that I hardly saw him anymore. Hardly ever again, in fact."

The presiding officer leaned forward and grabbed onto the edge of the table with such force that his joints turned white:

"The working class admits no weakness, comrades," he thundered. "The dictatorship of the proletariat tolerates no vacillation."

The neighbor from the fifth floor continued to look at his mail in the entryway, which the concierge had dotted with famished-looking potted plants; I waved a mechanical arm at the taxis, and Tucha put our kids to bed upstairs with the sterile efficiency of a nurse. He thinks, They realize that something out of the ordinary happened but they don't dare ask what—they put on their pajamas, brush their teeth, and crawl into bed. He thinks, How I miss their little toothbrushes, while the ducks lift up from the water and trace a large hyperbola heading toward the town. He thinks, Their color-ful clothes on the chair, their tiny shoes; he thinks, Their breathing when they sleep; he thinks, How was I able to let all that go?

"If they tell me to sell Marx in the street, I'll sell Marx in the street," Marilia declared, pulling a lighter out of her eternally idiotic purse made of beads. "But why in God's name is it so hard for you to accept that you're not the center of the world, that there are other things a lot more important than you?"

"Like the oppressed," he said. "I know the spiel by heart." (And the needles pricked and pricked, an infinite anguish.)

The gas station attendant retreated to his glass box, replete with cans of oil and stacks of bills: soon he'll close, I thought, hop onto his motorbike, and hiccup down the highway, shaking on the asphalt with a clatter like rattling cans. His father's hand finally emerged from the box, and he was holding between two fingers a pair of vibrating wings with a minuscule body that violently batted its legs and antennae.

"That concludes the first part of the operation," he said, sighing with relief. "Now watch how I proceed."

"Naturally I heard about Rui every now and then," said the oldest sister, shrugging her shoulders. "That he still taught at the university, that he was writing a subversive dissertation, that he couldn't work up the guts to split from that uncouth creature he'd married. It's a small world, you know, plus I had two friends who decided to study history for kicks and they would always run into him there."

"Comrades," declared the presiding officer while releasing the edge of the table, "in the future under no circumstances will I permit petit bourgeois deviations in the cell, deviations for which I've been largely to blame in the past. As the one in charge, I'm prepared to present my self-criticism here and now, and in the name of international socialism I demand that the rest of you do likewise."

He thinks, Never again the squint-eyed concierge watering the emaciated plants at the entrance, never again the cheerful plumber who came like clockwork once a week to unstop the same sink with the same fishhook-shaped wire, never again Tucha railing at the cleaning lady every time a dish got broken, never again Pedro in the morning, holding onto his pillow and asking in silence with his round eyes if he could climb into our bed. From the boats' ancient hulls, with the paint all peeled, there oozed an oily water like soup, and the grays of the river slowly changed color.

"However hard it is for you to believe, you are not the center of the world," Marilia insisted with a lit cigarette forgotten in her inanimate hand, "and you're old enough to know that by now. You're a human being like the rest, with the same importance as everyone else."

He thinks, No aggressiveness, no irony, no hate, no trying to impose her ideas through her usual complex network of syllogisms that inevitably strangled my capacity to respond. Almost tenderly, he thinks, kindheartedly, as if talking to a child that's a bit dim-witted, a bit dense. He thinks, What do you feel for me right now? Pity? Suppressed indignation? Resigned grief? Total and absolute indifference? And yet her face was the same: asymmetric, ugly, and implacably serene. My father flattened the butterfly's wings onto a sheet of paper, secured the tips with tiny pins, and moved his eyes, searching for the small bottle of lethal liquid.

"A beer," I ordered with a raised finger from the waiter who had perched on top of a stool to turn on the television that almost touched the ceiling. Far above us the ducks flew by in a triangle, toward the gusty pine forest, toward the full and broad sea: were there bald escarpments in the north, places to land, places to sleep, hollows in the sand full of anxious chicks? The gas station attendant put a padlock on the glass cubicle, spent a while fastening the buckle on his dented helmet, started up the rusty old motorbike by pushing a pedal with his tennis shoe, and took off in a cloud of fumes in the direction of the ducks. A taxi finally stopped, Azedo Gneco Street gave way to other labyrinthine streets, street vendors, a cinema, the snack bar where he played pool during high school. An epileptic lying flat on the sidewalk and foaming blood in sudden fits was being observed with an entomological interest by a pair of old ladies with shopping bags in their arms.

"I propose that this unpleasant incident," said the presiding officer with a sour smile, "be immediately and completely forgotten in the name of cell unity." (The voice strove in vain to acquire the sweetness it didn't possess.) "Let's not allow even the slightest divergence, comrades, to come between us."

And the sea gulls, he thought, when will the sea gulls go away? Or those small, white, long-tailed birds hopping in the sand—when will they go? When will the lagoon be free of the birds, becoming smooth and flat like a stomach, slowly rising until it touches the night? His oldest sister picked up the telephone receiver with a languid gesture:

"They had my brother for one of their classes but didn't understand squat of the bizarre theories he expounded. They got bored stiff and quit after six months—they missed playing bridge. We're about to head over to the club to play a few rounds."

He thinks, What's become of the concierge? What's become of the bureaucrat on the fifth floor who was always sad, plodding, slow, full of bows, good manners, beg your pardons, if you pleases?

"Your father went away," Tucha explained. "From now on it'll be just the three of us at home."

"Just a smidgen, applied very carefully on the head," his father said. A blue drop trembled on the rim of the bottle, finally breaking loose and landing on the insect: its trunk vibrated for a second, its legs shook spasmodically, its wings threatened to tear away from the pins. His father tilted his head sideways, whistling softly as he waited.

"More than anything else, I'm your friend," Marilia said, taking a sip from my beer and smiling at me with a white

202

mustache around her mouth. "That may not mean a lot to you, but I'm really and truly your friend."

The liquid's bitter taste, the darkening tonalities of afternoon like the pupils of eyes falling asleep, the waiter once more perched on the stool, fiddling with the television's column of buttons in search of an elusive image. And the wind outside, blowing the wilted plants around in the flowerbeds.

"On Sunday," announced Tucha cheerfully, leaning against the boys' bunk beds, "Daddy will pick you up and take you to the zoo, where you can visit the monkey village, eat peanuts, and give ten cents to make the elephant ring the bell. Won't that be fun?"

He thinks, The felt dolls in their room, the pictures of bears and cats on the wall, the Spiderman hanging by a string from a high-rise, the blue furniture with those dumb-looking flowers, the permanent disorder of their wicker toy basket. The surrounding night of Lapa, he thinks, tame and friendly, almost intimate, the tranquillity of familiar streets, of familiar smells, of the silence.

"Long live the working class," yelled the presiding officer, standing next to the red flag in the corner and raising a clenched fist into the air. "Long live the fight to liberate oppressed peoples everywhere."

"Hello?" droned his oldest sister into the phone, winding the kinky cord around her thumb. "No, I'll be there in a minute. I was just about to hop in the car. The tournament begins at five-thirty, right?"

"My relationship with you was like a time-out in my life," Marilia explained, wiping her mouth on her sleeve. "I discovered that marriage isn't for me, you see; there are other things that mean a lot more to me."

Only after he was seated behind the wheel did he remember to unlock the other door. The restaurant waiter was craning his neck behind the counter, raptly watching the TV's invisible images.

"There," said his father, securing the immobile insect with his fingertips and transferring it to a sheet of crinkly pasteboard. "Definitively dead. That's not so hard, is it?"

As he began to pull out, passing by the square glass cage, he turned on the headlights, for it had gotten dark. It had gotten so dark that he couldn't make out the asthmatic presence of the waves nearby.

SUNDAY

THE LAGOON WORKED ITSELF into his sleep the way two voices mix together: at first it was just the motionless, soulless pool of water, the furred neck of sand, the pine trees splintered in the fog, the far-flung boats and the city in the distance, hazy like the eyes of the blind, but then the sea gulls and ducks and all the other birds of the Vouga invaded his legs and arms, devoured his rotten-plum testicles, ripped out the lining of his stomach with their claws, perched on his shoulders and back, pecked at the confused dream with which he wrestled (his mother roosted on an enormous egg containing him and his sisters while she played cards with her friends), and when the first flock flew cawing into his head, he awoke with the sensation that castaways were adrift in the foam of his bones, and he recognized a taste

as of seaweed in his mouth, which had opened with a soundless scream. The bed sheets floated slowly toward the veranda,
scattered algae danced on the pillow, and a transparent fish,
blinking its fins, escaped from between his thighs and vanished into the dresser among his shirts and underpants. Marilia snored softly and he was moved by her hamsterish
breathing, he was moved by her fingers, which hung outside
the blanket, periodically reaching and withdrawing in sluggish vegetable spasms: so many years watching you sleep
when my pill wore off and I'd wake up with anxiety in the
dark; I'd turn on the light and the serenity of your figure
stretched out at my side irritated me like an unjust fate; so
many years slowly detesting you from the stony depths of
insomnia, gleefully thinking of your thin neck's fragility, of
the scissors in the sewing box to cut your wrists, of squeezing
your neck with the pillowcase.

"No, I never suspected that she didn't like him," said his incredulous father, searching for cigars in his vest pocket. "For
Christ's sake, what more could a hick girl like that want?"

I'd wake up, grope for the button on the lamp (the streetlights from down below underlined the blinds with a colorless
softness), and think, It must be 3 or 4 A.M., because it's always
around now that I rise to the surface of myself, to the surface
of the sheets, with the crying of my children echoing in my ears
and Tucha—ugly, uncombed, threatening, gargantuan—
pointing her gigantic finger toward the street, "Get out of
here, I don't want you anymore." In the refrigerator, whose
contents from a distance resembled those of a woman's handbag, he would find ice water that tasted like iron; his bare feet
would curl up on the cold kitchen tiles; the electric clock over
the door read two-thirty; and he'd end up sitting on the sofa in
the living room, neither smoking nor reading nor thinking of
anything, just staring with wide-open eyes at the geometric
shadow of the bookcase. Some time ago his doctor had prescribed a pill whose effect lasted until five or six, drowning his

dreams in a jumbled mass of which he could remember only disconnected episodes, and he got in the habit of not getting up, of feeling the day grow in the visceral sounds of the building, in whose bowels tumbled dishes, flush tanks, knives and forks, the elevator's dull whistle, and the shrill, forever-arguing voices of the neighbors. Like now, here in Aveiro, he thought, in the inn room saturated with the humidity imposed by the lagoon and the sea gulls, listening to the footsteps of the elderly English guests proceeding down the hall like deep-sea divers while your rising and falling chest, besides forcing your ribs together and apart like a folding fan, also seemed to be like an ocean tide controlling the waving of the furniture, the ticking of my blood, and the rippling of the walls.

"If you don't light them with wooden matches, the taste just isn't the same," his father explained, displaying his cigar with the smile of a magazine ad: a still-handsome man, well dressed and with graying temples, ensconced in his leather chair in a cozy corner of the library. He stretched his cheeks while exhaling a puff of smoke and examined the ashen tip with a grave look. "Please understand that from the start I had as little to do with their relationship as possible."

"It took a long time for me to get up the courage to talk to him honestly. I hate ambiguous situations," said the frowzy woman, brushing dandruff off her coat with the back of her hand. "Not really for lack of courage, you understand, but because of his fragility. Until finally I took the opportunity of a weekend trip and broke the news to him. That of course had nothing to do with what happened afterward; nobody dies anymore over a breakup."

The cousin from the clinic entered the ring, growling inside a cage, her cheeks covered with long Santa Claus whiskers.

"The bearded woman, ladies and gentlemen, just arrived from Colombia for this occasion," shouted the Indian doctor to the rapt family in the stands. "She will rip through three phone directories all at once, thanks to the amazing strength of her muscles. Given the natural danger of her jungle temperament, we ask that the distinguished audience not come too close."

Your watch on the Formica nightstand read six-thirty; the flocks of sea gulls circled unceasingly over the surface of the lagoon. A shapeless shadow grew, approached, and suddenly came into focus in my head: we're separating. Marilia's breathing fanned the furniture in a kind of rage, the ceiling seemed ready to fall on our heads in dusty chunks of plaster, panes of glass were clinking somewhere, the air in the pipes sighed and the sound echoed for a long while in the silence, vibrating like a violin: we're separating we're separating we're separating we're separating, repeated the caws of the birds with mocking irony; a dog barked ferociously under the window (We're separating); the pine trees waved at one another with their long dark arms in which the crouching night hid (We're separating); a chilly breath in the tops of the eucalyptus trees whispered its meaningless secret: we're separating. Sr. Esperança, with painted eyebrows and large red suspenders, adjusted the microphone while the dwarf, standing on a chair behind him, tried out the clarinet, its sexy sound swirling around him like a tenuous smoke ring.

"He never came again for checkers on Sunday; later on we happened to read in the paper what happened," he said in the zinc voice of the Last Judgment, distorted by the loudspeaker funnels. "In his memory I'll sing for you all the popular two-step 'Te Quiero España.' "

"What an idiotic thing to do," smiled his father with a weary wave of the hand that made the class ring on his little finger flicker. "As far as I know it's the first time anyone in the family ever killed himself over such a trifle."

"He didn't seem particularly shaken up when we talked about it," said the frowzy woman, walking down the steps of the university toward the bus stop, her book bag dragging behind her like a sulky child. "He didn't react, didn't say

208

anything, just looked at me with his usual vacant look. As if it were all the same to him, you know what I mean?"

"He was a certifiable neurotic," declared the obstetrician, hanging his white coat up in the hospital locker and removing his vest from a wire hanger. "And neurotics, you understand, take emotional upheavals with considerable calm. If he killed himself—and note that I consider suicide a mere hypothesis—but if he killed himself, as I was saying, it was undoubtedly for some other motive."

Now I'm completely awake, he thought, lying on a bed in this horrid, stupid inn as it gradually emerges from the Vouga River, there remaining only a slight tremor of water on the surface of the mirrors and the outline of a sea gull in the blinds, hovering over the lagoon like a huge and weightless bird of cardboard. I'm completely awake in the deafening roar of my head, submerged in the morning's plaster silence, and I resemble the excavated skull of an old old animal with eyes full of fog and teeth that rattle in horseshoe jaws, with your ancient presence at my side, snoring like a deformed crocodile in the sheets. Six-thirty, six-thirty-five, six-forty, six-forty-two: a slanting orange light finally breaks through the brume and approaches the shore in a halo of countless suspended particles of mist, in whose bilge appear the birds as rudderless, aimless ships, reduced to the thin outline of their bones, x-rayed against the opaque sheet of sky. He propped his back against the headboard, ran his fingers through the thin, almost transparent hair on his crown, and closed his eyes: he immediately found himself on the street and Tucha upstairs, closing the door, distractedly patting the kids, calling a friend on the phone ("I finally got rid of him, can you believe it?"), talking with snickers and whispers, her legs crossed on the floor pillows: Goddam bitch, you screwed my life. All that time to get you to go out with me, all that time to get you to marry me: "I don't know, let me think about it, it's awfully soon." Your younger sisters made fun of me in the hallway the first time I had dinner at your house; your father gave me a limp hand-shake without bothering to hoist his butt out of his chair; he just kept watching the news through the bottom half of his glasses:

"How's it going?"

Tucha's mother ordered the soup to be served with an imperceptible wink: on the wall between the curtained windows hung a nineteenth-century English landscape, its green colors thick and majestic:

"A bit of a lazybones for my taste, and spineless," she said, her neck's tendons showing through her wrinkled skin. "He had no class, no flair, if you know what I mean; it was obvious from the start that he wasn't up to my daughter's level."

One of Tucha's sisters, wearing slippers and a glittery pair of leotards, climbed onto a yellow-and-white platform and slowly bent backward till her head touched her calves:

"Fat people are disgusting," she articulated with difficulty through a forced smile, her teeth clenched. "The guy's paunch always made me feel like puking."

Marilia, he thought, what will I do now? I'd never realized just how important you are to me: I always thought you were too strong, too practical, too decisive next to my constant hesitations, my fear, my stupid panic over everything, my perpetual question, What next? It wasn't only Marx, American cinema, avant-garde theater, stubby fingernails, your bad taste in clothes, and your father's walking around his house in an undershirt with thousands of his chest's hairs poking through the cotton: there was security in your disorder, domestic tranquillity in the dust of the furniture, the certainty of your presence in the dandruff flakes on your hairbrush, the sensation that you protected me from shirts being badly washed by the laundry lady, from running out of milk, from having to see a psychiatrist, from loneliness, and from flu, there was the hope you'd save me from missing Tucha and my kids, and from the constant, inquisitive acrimony of my fam-

210

ily, from the questions, the sidelong glances, the feigned surprise, the frowns. He got up to drink some water because his mouth tasted bitter, and on the other side of the curtain he saw the usual landscape, anchored like a boat: the same eucalyptus trees and pines, the same road with hardly a car, the same cold and clammy fog.

"After he left home I never really knew what his life was like," explained the musical sister, awkwardly and unattractively dressed in an evening gown and moving her arms and hands like a windlass under the high wire, where the gym teacher performed complicated exercises. "A confirmed bohemian, I'd say, always on a tight budget."

"Not enough dough, not enough dough," cried the obstetrician from the shadows, daubing Carlos's face with a foam-covered toilet brush, while his other hand secured a gigantic wooden razor. "Some people just love to wallow in the mire."

"My sons-in-law were forever calling my attention to his inability to manage himself, and they showed me time and again how foolhardy it would be to give him a position of rank in the firm," his father said, shaking his head with sad resignation while at the same time pulling a bunch of paper geraniums from his coat pocket with the agility of a magician. "The fact is that he was a quirky guy with quirky interests and absurd notions. Like this, for example: shortly before he died, he came and asked me to explain the birds, as if the birds could be explained. I didn't know what the hell he was getting at. You don't understand the birds, do you?"

He stood up amidst a burst of applause (part of the family had jumped to their feet in the wooden stands, cheering him on wildly, their hands clapping in a unanimous frenzy, their mouths opening and closing to call out his name, syllable by syllable) and headed toward the bathroom, followed by a cone of light from a projector, with his clown-suit pajamas dancing comically around his waist. His black-painted eyelids, reddened nose, and unshaven beard provoked general hilarity in the audience: a fat uncle at the back, his mouth wrenched wide open, clapped his palms against his knees, bent over with laughter. After he'd spread the Palmolive cream over his cheeks, the spotlight changed to purple, his face suddenly resembled a hemorrhoid ready to burst, and a tremendous cackle broke out in the stands, underscored by a whine of trombones from the orchestra. Alien, ridiculous, and bungling, he saw himself in the mirror wiping his face with the towel and thought, For how many years now, day after day, have I repeated this corny act? Why don't I just quit the circus or why doesn't the circus simply fire me? he thought as his father's voice, a bit muffled, came through the wall tiles, announcing the next performer to a tumult of clapping and shouting from the eager audience.

"Like so," murmured the old man, brandishing the bottle he used on butterflies, "a single drop on the head is enough." And he tilted it so as to apply his lethal drop through a pipette into his wife's pallid nostrils. "Notice," he said, "how quickly they die: a split second, one or two spasms, and that's it." He turned on the bathtub faucets, sat on the edge, and let the water fill to the overflow drain, occasionally testing the temperature with a fingertip. The plumbing fixtures, ceramicware, and glassware in the minuscule room slowly fogged up, the ceiling light withdrew far overhead, drifting in a steamy brume until it was no more than a distant moon, dim and opalescent. He unbuttoned his pajama top, displaying a rounded, amorphous body that draped over his bones in soft wide folds, there was the hirsute rose of his pubis and his convergent, cross-eyed knees that irately chided one another: the dwarf, wearing epaulets, solemnly bowed and pointed at me with his huge glove:

"Ladies and gentlemen, girls and boys, distinguished audience, we're about to reach the high point of our show here today," he cried while swiftly somersaulting around the ring. "The Grand Monumental Garibaldi Circus offers you live and untelevised the unique act of suicide by its main performer. The management urges heart patients, pregnant women, the clinically depressed, and sensitive people in general to leave the hall so as to preclude unpleasant emotional incidents. As you can see with your own eyes, the unforgettable Rui S. is about to take his very last bath."

He lay down in the tub, leaning back against the enamel, closed his eyes, and let his slack limbs rise lazily in the water like floating hair. Even his head—dazed by insomnia and the steam—bobbed lightly as his father pinned his mother to a sheet of cardboard with something (a name in Latin?) written at the bottom. He thought, What drawer of the cabinet is he going to stick her in? And he began to lather himself (neck, armpits, stomach), using one of the sample-sized soaps wrapped in silver-and-green paper, to chase away his sleep. His father bent almost to the ground and placed the cardboard sheet in the cabinet for specimens that were less rare or in poor condition and from which a viscous odor sometimes emanated. His embarrassed face rose up to apologize:

"I still hadn't perfected my technique. I ruined a bunch of insects using the wrong liquids: it's unbelievable how much ignorance ends up costing us."

He shaved in the bathtub, grabbing on to his chin and cheeks at random, and when he got out of the water, wrapped in the bed-sheet toga and with his bald forehead crowned by wet strands, just like the Roman senators in movies, he realized he was being watched by the entire company, festively dressed in exuberant feathers and velvet capes, silently bunched together behind the curtain at the side of the stage. The musical sister, half-hidden by the squarely muscular silhouette of the gym teacher, wiped her tears with a discreet handkerchief, a streak of mascara ran down toward her mouth, the curls of her hairdo were gradually uncoiling into her usual dull bangs. The Indian doctor, with a long needle poking all the way through his skinny fakir's chest, was filling out the death certificate, which he had propped on one of his skeletal knees. The band (three or four cousins with funereally thin hair, who were installed on a platform next to stage) started to play a cadaverous tango, horribly out of tune, and he began to dry himself in time with the drums as his diffuse torso reappeared in the mirror, from bottom to top, rusty and pale like a mermaid's fiancé: with this moribund face all I need is a hook in my mouth, he thought, all I need is to have been just reeled in. He thought, When we get to Lisbon will you grab your suitcase and run or will you stay in our apartment for a few more days, already distant, alien, foreign, staring at the dinnertime potatoes with apathetic concentration? Will I toss out your photographs or put them in the chest; will I act furious, sad, resigned; will I weigh anchor like a miniature ship inside a liquor bottle; will I fill the lecture halls with my ethanol breath? Will I look you up later, Marilia, with tears in my eyes, pleading like an abandoned pup for you to come back to me? Will I get off the bus in your parents' neighborhood to wait for you by the mailbox, my life in a shambles, carpeting the sidewalk with my impatient cigarette butts? Or will I wander into a tempestuous relationship with a fickle, sardonic, adolescent student who will drag me every night by the leash of her insistent demands to smoky bars full of girls with dirty hair, sandals, and long flowered skirts, accompanied by guys with knapsacks and unquestionable genius who annually enter poetry contests with notebooks of viciously splintered verses? His youngest sister, wearing a lot of makeup, a petticoat, and white gloves that came up to her elbows, rode a unicycle and twirled her arms in the air, tracing two elegant arabesques with her wrists:

"We're all here, we're all here," she purred in her pouty doll's voice. "We couldn't miss his death, could we?"

"I ruined a lot of insects in the past, there's no denying it," lamented his father, pleated by vexed wrinkles, "but now I never flub up. Do you want to see?"

He began methodically opening the cabinet drawers, and pinned onto cardboard sheets I saw the birds of my childhood, the ones that at twilight would fly up from the fig tree by the well and head toward the woods, their wings now crucified and their watery eyes wide with terror.

"Shall we cut into their stomachs?" his father proposed with a conspiratorial smile, reaching toward the silver letter-opener. "If we rip open their tummies and look inside, maybe you'll discover this explanation of the birds you've been going on about."

He put on clean underpants (the audience applauded this hygienic detail), the socks and shirt he'd worn the day before (there was a disapproving whistle or two), his bombazine trousers (I almost never wear them, he thought, what possessed me to put them in my suitcase?), and the jacket that was part of the Communist uniform; then he stood still for a minute in the middle of the room, watching you sleep and wondering, Why? Something irreparable had broken the night before, like a tired old motor that conks out, and suddenly he felt completely abandoned and extremely alone in the Aveiro morning, which was still rippling its colorless shadow in the mirrors. A filtered light fell slantwise across the furniture, across your poncho hanging from the chair like a snake's shed skin, across a heel, poking out of the sheets, suspended in the nothingness like the foot of a hung man. He thinks, The first time I saw you naked was in the apartment of a friend of yours on the western edge of Lisbon; you invited me to go there so we could talk in peace about Orson Welles. "No one's ever shot a film like *Citizen Kane*; remember the scene of his old age?" I preferred the Italians, Fellini, Visconti, which you dogmatically classified as decadent art. The apartment was a fifth-floor walk-up that looked out over a road with streetcars, scrawny trees, old and uninteresting houses, ramshackle sheds, and the metallic sounds of garages. He thinks, We talked for hours sitting on stuffed chairs covered with pearl-colored plastic, surrounded by walls bearing unsightly art reproductions, by curtains and ceilings browned from smoke, and by the utter impersonality of the metal ashtrays and modular furniture, each of us with a glass of tutti-frutti punch in hand, stubbornly serious, our feet resting squarely on the striped, folded blanket that served as a rug. There were some accounting books on a bottom shelf, old magazines, a porcelain piggy bank "Souvenir of the Algarve," and pipes that periodically belched a turbulence of gases behind them. In the bathroom the incredibly filthy tub with its torn shower curtain and the fetid, stopped-up toilet with sanitary napkins and toilet paper bobbing in a foam of urine made him nauseous, and he preferred to wash his hands in the bidet rather than in the sink full of blond hairs and dried splinters of soap. Even the mirror was brown with fly excrement and smashed insect guts, and the two or three bottles of perfume inside a white cabinet were coated with dust and mildew. They made love quickly and uncomfortably in a small room on a couch whose springs kept escaping from under their bodies, and then, as they lay on their backs smoking a cigarette, depositing the ashes in the outer cellophane wrapper, and picking through Brazilian newspapers from the pile of yellowed papers under the bed, they heard the key in the door, covered themselves with the printed cotton bedspread, and almost immediately the briefcase-clasping friend flew in, her flounces bouncing up and down; she tossed the briefcase into a corner, plopped down on the floor, leaned against a cabinet with glass doors in which folders and magazines were stacked up at random, and proceeded to bitch about her high school students (She was the kind of person, he thought, who breaks toothpicks into little bits in restaurants), to wipe her eyeglasses with her shirttail, and to remove bits of dried egg off the bedspread with her fingernail, overcome by a sudden, inexplicable urge to clean up.

"She was flustered, poor thing; she didn't know what to

do," Marilia chided him in the bus afterward, "and you, with your dummy face and quiet as a tomb, didn't help matters."

Between sips of tutti-frutti punch ("This is the only thing I drink, sorry I can't offer you anything else"), from scraps of conversation and occasional dialogue, I figured out that the friend taught mathematics in a town across the river, that she'd lived for a few years with a Brazilian studying medicine, that she belonged to a revolutionary organization, and that she didn't like to take baths: a goatish perspiration gradually mixed with their own in a braid of intensely unpleasant odors as a sheet of sunlight climbed like a slug up the wall, divided in two by the corner of the cabinet. As soon as the friend stood up, making her dishwater-blond hair bounce around her neck, he seized his underpants off the floor, put them on, and kneeled to look under the bed for his socks.

"You should have thanked her for letting us use her place," Marilia continued in a controlled voice, after a furious silence, "instead of practically dragging me away naked." (He saw her reflection in the window against the waning afternoon: two ranting Marilias, he thought.) "After this episode there's no way I can ever go back there."

But I felt uncomfortable, humid, humiliated, naked before that overly talkative, overly chummy woman, constantly dropping names of people I didn't know, laughing with you over old private jokes, recalling a mutual Paleolithic that excluded me. And I was irritated by your lack of reserve with her, your shoulders exposed, your bosom hanging out over the bedspread, your navel popping into view, the edge of your pubic forest. I pulled up my trousers while you two talked, buttoned my shirt, tied my shoelaces any old way, and leaned conspicuously against the door, waiting for you, but instead of noticing me you were eager to keep up the ardent dialogue, with your breasts shaking from enthusiasm and your hand clutching onto the empty glass of tutti-frutti, oblivious to me, setting up get-togethers, visits to exhibitions, a night at the house of an old painter boyfriend, where every chair stained my trousers seat with paint and where a solitary old lady with a purple streak in her hair levitated in a corner, utterly alienated, sniffing cocaine through a thousand-escudo note:

"My mother," introduced the painter with shoulder-length hair and a singsong voice, twirling about like a ballet dancer as he distributed white wine to groups of bearded adherents and irreversibly loyal girls wrapped in the sweet and sluggish smoke of hashish.

"Didn't you realize that she was as embarrassed as we were and needed a little conversation to relax?" Marilia asked in the same pointed and accusing tone, which was echoed by her reflection in the window: building façades, stores, street corners, and people bunched around a newsstand flowed past behind her. "But since you don't like any of my friends you didn't understand boo of what was going on."

He leaned forward in the seat on the bus and also saw himself in the window: a hazy face with two dark holes instead of eyes and moving shadows on his cheeks and chin. He furtively opened and closed his fingers, and his image imitated him simultaneously: no doubt about it, he thought, it's me. It's me and probably with the same dorky, comatose expression I wore as I wandered through the painter's studio, tripping over absurd canvases (one black stroke, two black strokes, three black strokes, always the same, on a white or yellow or green background), over twisted feet with overgrown toenails and Franciscan sandals, over tennis shoes, over intellectual agrarian reform boots with tire-rubber soles, and over the extended body of the purple old lady, whose necklaces swung left and right as she rabidly kissed a beardless kid with an elephant-skin bracelet around his ankle, both of them rolling across a straw mat from Morocco. If these are the boyfriends you had before me, then they must be the ones you'll have after me, he thought, with his hand on the doorknob, observing your slumber in the Aveiro morning, with the sky unfolding into more and more clouds, like the sections of a fan being opened from the horizontal surface of the lagoon, which mirrored the flattened silhouette of the city lightly sketched on the silk. Poets with scurvied gums, dubious film-makers with definite opinions, jazz critics barking at one another's shins with mellifluous ferocity, ill-defined persons with Indian scarves around their necks, all rummaging desperately through their pockets for a cigarette, as if looking for a saving bottle of oxygen. And beneath us the Lisbon night, he thinks, the piles of cans swept up by the street cleaners, the polar streetlights—like stationary stars—projecting blue ovals onto the building walls, the neon light of a TV shop piercing the darkness next to a police station.

"We're all here, we're all here," the youngest sister repeated, pedaling up a spiral ramp. "Except for Mother, of course," she added in her doll's murmur.

His father continued to show him drawer after drawer of crucified fowl, the birds of his childhood hanging inert, stomach-side up in their skies of labeled cardboard, pulling their feet against their thin shivering bellies; and while he closed the door softly, so as not to wake Marilia, and went down to the ground floor of the inn, pursued by the projector cone and by the band's funereal music, he cast a glance at the multitude of familiar faces of performers observing him, crowded together behind the curtain, disguised by makeup, false noses, wigs, and feathers; and in fact he couldn't find his mother among the confused tangle of cousins, acquaintances, high school classmates, and old friends that he ran into occasionally, now fatter and balder, grave and preoccupied. He thought, They've probably phoned for me a million times from the clinic; Dad probably cut short his business trip, grudgingly, to rush back to Lisbon and to her room, patting down his hair, and he'd talked to the doctor in whispers in the hallway, opening and closing the frames of his glasses, until at last he'd sat down alone in one of the stiff, gold-nailed chairs in the lobby, extremely ill at ease, gazing at an old magazine with a notary's neutral eyes.

"Tucha I could leave or take," his mother's voice boomed into the microphone, making the tent's supporting poles vibrate. "But this Marilia, God help us, I'd rather her name weren't even mentioned."

The thick sensitive hands of the farm manager, lightly poised on the knees of his trousers, twitched like antennae. His wrinkled nostrils gently sniffed the air:

"We're going to have a good year, young man."

We're going to have a good year, young man, he thinks down at breakfast, disgustedly examining the usual wicker basket of bread, the pats of butter, the metallic containers with coffee and milk, and the plastic fruits in a porcelain dish. An anemic thread of water ran from a waterfall built into the wall and tumbled from shell to shell, ingloriously disappearing into a kind of bidet drain. The waiter, wearing a vest, carrying a towel over his forearm, dozed against a buffet full of glasses and stacked plates. Outside the windows the day was the same as ever, swelled with the pus of the rain, and the customary sea gulls danced in the distance, in a darker, ink-colored patch of lagoon. A cuckoo bird swam clumsily through the mist among the pines.

"The final meal of the ill-starred historian," the dwarf announced with a sarcastic somersault to the amused giggles of the audience. Sr. Esperança placed checkers on the board for a new game, and as soon as a black piece was jumped, it was substituted for the pajama button:

"Whose turn is it to start off?" he asked, uncertain, scratching his head. A young, tuxedoed man on a poster, to whom he bore a remote resemblance, bent a shoulder forward and smiled too amiably. A diagonal stripe in a corner announced in red AMILCAR ESPERANÇA, THE ROMANTIC VOICE OF NORTH-EAST LISBON.

He thinks, Why is it I don't see my mother eating breakfast

at one of the tables in this empty dining room, with an open book next to her coffee cup and a forgotten slice of toast in her hand, inches from her mouth, waiting for an international phone call that will never come, waiting for Dad to say cheerfully and tenderly, "Hi, love, I'm returning earlier than planned from Italy; how about us spending the weekend at the beach?" He drank a sip of coffee and looked at the water, at the ever-drier bushes and trees on the shore, and at the humidity that coated the veranda with its anxious animal breath. The coffee burned his tongue so that for a moment he stopped feeling the painful sore on the inside of his cheek, which he couldn't help but constantly suck. The audience, leaning forward in their seats, watched in rapt attention as he thought, without fear, without alarm, What will it be like when we get back to Lisbon this afternoon? Do I help you pack your bags? Do I put up no argument? Do I call a taxi and wait with you in the living room, quiet and tense, for the sound of the motor down below and the hesitant honk? Do we part on the landing with a resentful kiss, seething with hatred? Do I go back in, shut the door, and remark with melancholy that all of the dust, all the old magazines, all the useless books, and all of the trash belongs to me alone? How do I work the washing machine that we bought secondhand from the squint-eyed pawnbroker, limping around his dark shop full of the shipwrecked remains of people's misfortunes? If the bell rings down below, do I answer it; do I ask who it is, my torso bent like a jackknife over the landing rail? The audience applauded his domestic doubts as he wiped his chin on his napkin, pushed back his chair, and stood up. In the windows the fog was unraveling like a frayed garment while the boats, facing the opposite direction on the sliver of sand near the inn, were taking on faded colors, like faces waking up from long comas. Melted streaks of sunlight wandered aimlessly among the clouds, and the horizon was deserted, forsaken by the birds and the dogs.

"Me explain the birds to him, imagine how absurd," his

father said with a resigned grimace. "As if I, a simple business-man, could turn into a biologist just like that."

On his way out he brushed the table where his mother should have been and took a large, serrated knife from the buffet with the plates and glasses while the dwarf, suddenly lit by a violent lavender spotlight, bawled out:

"Ladies and gentlemen, boys and girls, distinguished audience, please be so kind as to take a moment and observe the terrible suicide weapon: there's no trick, no sleight of hand, no gimmick: as you can see, we're dealing with authentic and genuine stainless steel of Portuguese manufacture, the very same instrument that won Lisbon back from the Moors, that spread the Faith and the Empire, that went around the world, and that currently pushes rice onto our forks and helps us extract fish bones at restaurants with incomparable grace."

And in a theatrically interrogative tone, the kind used to stimulate viewer curiosity at the end of an episode, he asked:

"Just how will the inventive Rui S. use it?"

They weren't butterflies, he thinks, they were goldfinches and greenfinches and sparrows and blackbirds and robins and hoopoes crucified on the cardboard; it was the birds from the fig tree, the birds from the well, the birds from the woods that he collected in the cabinet in his study, in its dozens of drawers, proposing to me in a conspiratorial whisper that overpowered my ear with his cloying old man's breath in spite of his colognes and deodorants and sprays:

"Shall we rip open their tummies to see what's inside?"

"To cut his wrists, his carotids, his throat, or to perform hara-kiri?" the dwarf asked stentorianly while girls with high heels, tiaras, and frozen, red-lipped smiles marched around the sand, wiggling their bottoms and carrying signs that read CUT HIS WRISTS, CUT HIS CAROTIDS, CUT HIS THROAT, PERFORM HARA-KIRI. "Ladies and gentlemen," the dwarf bellowed solemnly, "the management, eager to oblige the select group of spectators assembled here, will distribute mystery envelopes full of valuable prizes to those who correctly guess the method of suicide chosen by the unfortunate history professor. This has been made possible through the generous collaboration of Donald's Condoms, Donald's the number one enemy of population growth; of Mrs. Penelope's Stockings, *penelopize* your legs and feel the difference in your husband's fond look; and of Iron Hand Gymnasium, conveniently located near the oil refinery—Iron Hand, because in less than a year it will make you the envy of every man on the beach and the passionate target of the opposite sex."

He put the knife in his coat pocket without being seen by the sleepy-eyed waiter and left the dining room. His body was tense, his back was sweating, his shirt stuck to his shoulder blades; an elderly woman in a box seat hurriedly buried her face in her hands. And there was the reception desk, he thinks, the key board, the illustrated postcards in their rotating wire rack, the telephone, the VISIT AVEIRO brochures, the huge, round, earthenware ashtray imprinted with the inn's initials, the nasty clerk—her glasses held by a chain round her neck—completing some chart or other on graph paper in an illegible hand. He thinks, And under the spiral staircase there were the plants in the pond with their dark, almost obscenely green leaves, shiny on one side and dull on the other, their tendrils similar to gelatinous tentacles, the mossy stones, the porcelain frogs: I once succeeded in dragging Tucha to the plant conservatory after hours of forceful botanical arguments ("I can't believe you've never been there; there are some beautiful ferns designed by Chanel and imported directly from Paris; surely you've seen photos of them in *Vogue*"), we sat on a wooden bench under a horrendously smelly shrub, and I was just about to fondle your breasts, grasp your thighs, and kiss you when suddenly—after a class field trip piloted by a decent-looking teacher passed by, followed closely by two guys with mustaches and dark glasses, smoking cigarettes and grumbling madrigals—what I'd thought was a miniature eucalyptus transformed into a short, fat, uniformed guard, who approached us in a torrent of hatred:

"What kind of shameless behavior is this?" he croaked.

Tucha, who had turned pale, smoothed down her skirt, straightened her blouse, and brushed back her hair with her flustered hand, while I shrank back against the slats in the bench, speechless with fright, opening and closing my cheekless, gumless, toothless, tongueless mouth, reduced to a useless cavern of terror. The guard glared at us, boiling with fury, as a new group of kids came around the bend of the walkway.

"And get that paw off of her, you animal," ordered the scarlet-shaded guard. "Either you respect authority willingly or I'll make you respect it with a good swift kick."

I'd completely forgotten the sinful thumb I'd applied to the root of your hips, softly rubbing your pubis up and down; I'd completely forgotten my knee pressing into yours, our calves one against the other, our silly heads too close to each other. I was sweaty with panic and yet the man was shorter than me, weaker, and much much older, easy to intimidate with the threat of a slap or the omnipotent ghost of my father. He thinks, Was it then, Tucha, in the face of my cowardice, my inability to fight, that you began to despise me? He nervously scooted to the other end of the bench; a branch grazed his ear, and the guard's belly, covered with huge silver buttons, approached his nose. It was a small, flaccid, vulnerable belly: but even so I was helpless, he thinks. I kept shrinking and turning whiter, blood pounding through my temples, while the other guy perceived my fear and grew in confidence and self-importance:

"And now, you scoundrels? How about a little fine? How about a little time in the clink to cure you of horny outbursts in public?"

He thinks, A dinky bald head, minuscule stupid eyes, a match in the twisted corner of his mouth, dancing to the

224

rhythm of his words, a sniveling nose, radiating with importance, swollen like an ailing penis. His lips contemptuously began moving again, spraying spit all the while:

"Three days in confinement will cure horniness in a hurry."

Tucha had opened her purse and was searching for a hanky to dry her eyes. He thinks, How old were we then? Twenty-two, twenty-three? He contemplated the plants in the lobby for a minute, slimy like mucous membranes, disgustingly carnivorous, and then leaned against the wire cypress that held illustrated postcards until the nasty clerk with glasses finished her chart and stared at him with a crease of irritation on her forehead. The guard stuck his fingers in his holster belt and gently rocked his round, unmuscular body. A pencil point protruded from his pocket.

"Identity cards," he demanded, through tight lips, in a voice oozing with threats. "Your identity cards and your work papers."

"Could you figure up our bill, please?" I asked pleasantly. "We're going back to Lisbon today."

Our car was the only car out front, parked on the gravel with the grill pressed against a bed of geraniums as if it were grazing them, as if it were a gigantic metal mammal with opaque, slumbering headlights for eyes; and then there was the sand, the sticky and foggy morning, the shoulders of the trees shrugging in the silence, and the sky and the lagoon reflecting each other like facing mirrors. The guard's ears twitched as he read; he took a step backward, indecisive: his tone of voice became worriedly respectful:

"This paper means that you're a doctor professor?" he asked, pushing his cap down the back of his head and crumpling it nervously.

"The ill-omened young man," the dwarf sighed pompously while he used a bombastic index finger to point me out to the family in the stands, "is going to leave the inn for his very last

225

stroll. Ladies and gentlemen, we're about to reach the high point, the acme, the culmination, the climax of our unforgettable spectacle. Maestro, Ravel's *Bolero*, please!"

The four or five sorry band members changed rhythm at the behest of a skinny fellow wearing a toupee and tie, who directed them with a broom wielded in broad, vehement gestures that made his shirt sleeves—already too short—crawl farther up his arms, exposing his white, incredibly long-fingered gloves; and in the distance the ducks and sea gulls of the Vouga River were lightly oscillating over the water, immemorially motionless, waiting for what? The desk clerk regarded him perfunctorily while thumbing, without looking, through a stack of rectangular cards bearing microscopic numbers:

"The room has to be vacated by twelve o'clock sharp," she informed in her harsh way.

What a withered woman, he thinks, what a withered body, what a withered, rancorous, haggard turd. He thinks, The heartburn she must have, and the carbonized bowels, roiling inside with sulfuric fury. The band members had variously colored noses, floured cheeks, coconut hats, striped sweaters, and thick charcoaled eyebrows.

"That's right, he's a professor," Tucha said. "He teaches at the university." And her voice, tarnished with corrosive hatred, seemed to mollify the guard, emptying him of the authority of his loud accusations, diminishing the aggressive importance of his uniform, turning him into an insignificant, provincial, and submissive being, ready to offer profuse apologies. That was when I decided to marry you, he thought, that was when I admired you for the first time: your large eyes, your disdainful mouth, the panic you forced yourself to swallow, converting it into the inflexible attitude of a ruling mistress. He thinks, The way you handled maids, plumbers, supermarket help, and seamstresses, the superiority that was so obviously and unquestionably yours from the day you were

226

born, the cough you got from your viscount grandfather, the drawling and imperative snobbery from your mother, who gave orders to her children over the backgammon table. He thinks, That was when I decided to marry you, so you could protect me from others, prevent conservatory guards from threatening me with the law, so you could do the things I was incapable of doing, however simple they seemed to you. The effusive dwarf returned to the microphone:

"One more piece of good news, ladies and gentlemen," he announced jubilantly, while a drumroll silenced the band. "Our mystery envelopes—to be awarded to those who correctly guess the form of suicide, whether cutting of the wrists, carotids, or throat, hara-kiri, puncturing of the lungs, or a well-aimed stab in the heart—have just been enhanced thanks to a generous donation from Ejacula Cream, guaranteed to increase penis size by one full inch. Do you suffer from problems of size? Are you too embarrassed to use public urinals? Does your wife complain of sexual dissatisfaction, so often the root problem in marital misunderstandings that can lead to painful separations and divorces? Are you, in short, distressed by the unimpressive length of your sexual organ? Apply Ejacula in the morning and at night to achieve the majestic dimensions you aspire to. Ejacula, the cream that, according to the latest statistics from the Arizona State Institute of Pleasure, Phillips, Phillips, and Phillips, has established the Portuguese at the very top of the nonsocialist world in areas concerning erectile capacity and the volume of cavernous bodies. Ejacula, the only medication of its kind with no disagreeable side effects, no rash, eczema, disfigurement, or pain. And now, after this wonderful news, once again Ravel's *Bolero*. Maestro, if you please!"

The man with a tuxedo and a head of jute hair raised his broom, the accordion player signaled with his chin to the clarinet and the electric guitar, and the music started back up at a lugubrious pace picked up measure by measure; the nasty desk clerk turned her back on him conspicuously, to examine a file, flaunting her supreme disinterest in him; I hesitated a second, feeling disoriented, then used my knee to push against the glass door, which swung open noiselessly, its hinges putting up only a minimal, oiled resistance, and went outside into the morning cold, which was musty with a hovering and oppressive humidity, as if thousands of transparent particles of cotton danced suffocatingly in the air. The guard sheepishly handed back the ID cards:

"Forgive me, Doctor Professor, but I thought that you and your wife were one of those perverted couples that come here to feel each other up in public. We have strict orders not to allow monkey business, because there are a lot of kids, a lot of school groups that come through, you understand, Professor, and I have to keep close tabs or I could lose my job: I had no way of knowing that you were a person of rank, sir."

The strip of sand, the shit-colored water, the shivering distress of the eucalyptus trees, unknown birds flitting through the branches, the putrid and cancerous sludge—like curdled milk—along the shore, and beyond all that the ducks, now planing in the direction of the town. Could you figure up our bill, please? We're going back to Lisbon today: long roads, open country, occasional villages, the uncomfortable, compact silence imposing itself over the sound of the motor, feeling like a sort of stomach cramp. I want to separate from you, separate from you, separate from you, repeated the gentle gray waves that lapped the shore, breaking against the anchored boats. And on Sunday I'll fetch my kids, take them to the gardens of the Gulbenkian Museum, stretch out on the grass under a willow tree with my eyes closed while they play ball, or talk, or fight, or fall, or cry. He thinks, I never cared for them that much. I never paid them much attention; they were always fuzzy, undefined, an embarrassment in my life— two strange beings that I had to feed, dress, entertain, and vaccinate; and sometimes from my bed I'd hear their wailing nightmares that shook the whole house awake and kept me from getting my rest, from forgetting myself, from sinking into the swampy depths of sleep. The knife handle pressed against his ribs, the tip of the blade pricked his waist: standing on the gravel at the entrance to the inn, he listened to the tarantulan sound of the audience, their sporadic coughs, the shuffling of feet, conversations, whispers, laughs here and there; he tried in vain to distinguish the faces that the darkness made anonymous, and he could barely make out the set of spotlights, raining an excessive and unpitying luminosity onto him. Next to the curtain where the performers entered, his sisters elbowed one another anxiously, encouraging him with hand signals, and the musical sister—her face a paste of makeup and tears—smiled at him. I can't flub this, he thought; I have to make this a good performance. The inoffensive little guard escorted them to the conservatory exit, dissolving in apologies:

"For the love of God, Doctor Professor, please don't report me to the management. I get irritated over the stupidest things; it's a real problem; in fact I just began a treatment for my nerves at the Health Service."

He desperately searched his pockets and pulled out a medicine bottle with cotton under the lid:

"The doctor prescribed these tranquilizers; he said they're the strongest that exist; he ordered me to cut out booze, cigarettes, and coffee. And even so I lost my head with you people." And his beaten dog's eyes looked at them pleadingly.

Tucha straightened up, and I thought, You're going to pay, buddy, because when she smiles like that there's nothing you can do but swallow hard and say a prayer:

"Write your name and number on a slip of paper. My father's a deputy in the national assembly, and I'm sure he'll want to speak to your superiors. He's rather proud of his daughters and becomes highly upset when they're not properly respected. And it just so happens your impudence goes beyond all acceptable limits."

The now microscopic guard pathetically began to kneel in his shabby trousers. His thinning eyelashes trembled:

"Have a little pity on me, ma'am, 'cause if I lose this job I'm cooked for life. I've got five mouths to feed. My wife can't work on account of her high blood pressure; she's forever swelling up on me, and her stumpy legs won't support her; she lies in bed like a log for days at a time; I have to pay someone to look after the kids." (He imagined a brood of runny-nosed, large-eyed children poking through the mud in an outlying shantytown.) "We don't even have enough money for a decent house; we live in a borrowed shack; my oldest daughter's sick; if I get fired, I don't know what I'll do." His chunky fingers shook spasmodically, his lower lip looked ready to break out in sobs, and a scarlet boil on his forehead threatened to explode.

I have to make this a good performance at least, he thought, and not disappoint the spectators, not frustrate my sisters' anxious expectations. "Here we go!" he yelled with a bow to the audience as he walked from the gravel to the inn's strip of sand, covered with seaweed, refuse, broken baskets, and moldy pieces of wood. My clownish patched jacket and baggy trousers fluttered in the wind. Tucha's smile broadened and sparkled with perverse pleasure:

"You should have thought of that earlier if you're so worried about your family."—(Her sharp implacable tone shredded the guard's insides, his thick blood flowing onto the pavement, to be instantly sucked up by a row of famished shrubs.)—"All I'm interested in is your name and number: clods like you shouldn't be working here."

He looked up at the façade of the inn, which from his new perspective seemed to be leaning, as if ready to tumble down all at once on top of me, and as with the midwife's apartment he tried to figure out which veranda was theirs in the long row of equal verandas, all with the blinds down, with the same chair and the same table up against the railing in the same rusty neglect: this one? that one? the next one? A spirited ovation immediately exploded from the stands as the dwarf struggled to stay afloat in the turbulent river of applause while he shouted:

"Let's hear it for the last longing look at the window of the beloved lady—a gaze worthy of Romeo, a veritable glance of Abelard. Notice the performer's magnificent control, his stupendous gestural execution, the way his arm hesitates, ready to lift up in a dramatic wave of farewell, even giving the illusion of rising an inch or two, but finally remaining rigid at his side, in the desperate, inert melancholy of the impotent. Allow me to point out that this brief but extremely difficult theatrical sketch was brought to you exclusively by Pop'n'Crackle Explosive Vaginal Cones, just insert one, dear ladies, and five minutes later your husband, lover, or boyfriend will get a festive reception, an impressive fireworks display of silver sparkles, rising from your thighs in a glittery fountain and culminating in a detonation equivalent to five hundred grams of trinitrotoluene, enough to propel your bed in a whirl of scorched sheets and twisted brass to the refrigerator in the kitchen. Remember, ladies: Pop'n'Crackle Explosive Vaginal Cones convert love into a new adventure, transforming the monotony of your sexual relations into historic occasions that none of your neighbors will ever forget."

"Have a heart, lady, have a heart," begged the green and millimetrical guard while groping in his uniform's breast pocket for a pencil stub and a piece of crumpled paper, both of which dropped onto the ground along with a rabbit's foot and a plastic fig wrapped up in the cord of his whistle. His face alternately swelled and shrank in terror like the mouth of a fish, and his teeny eyes blinked, stark white with anguish. The microbe agonized at the conservatory entrance in a puddle of sweat mixed with his eye wax, bad breath, and body odor, and Tucha regarded him sardonically from top to bottom, cruelly triumphant.

The rusted foundations of the inn were buried in the sand, forming a kind of shed that contained piles of oars, anchors, and water-ravaged ropes, boat wreckage, heaps of ashes, and large trash containers against a brick wall. An old man dressed in tails (a murmur ran through the stands when the spotlight shone on him, exaggerating his jacket's tatters) used a branch to fan the embers of a little stove in the gray morning, and now and again the coals would light up, as if tiny bulbs illumined them from inside, like thick orange crystals. In which circus did we work together? I wondered. Through which rural towns did we travel in ramshackle trailers pulled by decrepit American cars, with our loony seals, our wilted-skinned elephants, our pups dressed as melancholy Spanish ladies, our absurd hippos, and our terrifying bats? In which miserable restaurants full of mustard stains and long-legged flies did we eat stew while looking out the dirty window at the insects of summer? What stupid sketch did we do together on nights when no one but a fireman and three bored privates came to the show? My father leaned forward in his chair until our noses touched:

"We have to open their tummies to see how they work," he insisted, handing me the paper knife. "Are you sure you don't want to try?"

Could he be the old man crouching under the inn in the immense silence of the lagoon and the trees? he wondered. Could it be him with the manicured nails and the alpaca evening jacket, and its patches, its ridiculous width, and its pockets full of rubber squeeze bulbs for producing false jets of tears which were simply never noticed by the executives and the secretaries? The hobo pulled a dead sparrow from a sack, impaled it with a sharp stick and began roasting it—feathers and all—over the clay stove. The smell of burning flesh spread like a stain. The guard grabbed Tucha's wrist and shook it in desperation:

"By the bones of my sister who's in the grave," he wailed, "I swear I had no intention of being disrespectful."

Sr. Esperança, wearing a carnation in his lapel, stepped up to the microphone, raised it a bit, tested the sound by tapping it with the curved tip of his index finger, and proclaimed:

"I approve of the suicide as a harsh but deserved punishment, because he never gave me the slightest help paying my rent. It's only because of Donald's Condoms, the number one enemy of population growth, that I reached an understanding with the landlady this past month."

He pulled a full glass of wine from his pocket and lifted it in the air toward the audience:

"As a nationally and internationally famous baritone, as a man who's proud to be one, and as a distinguished gentleman, I propose a toast to Donald's Condoms, made in Portugal, lubricated with palm and olive oil and tear-resistant, available with or without a crown of hair and in four colors—red, indigo, sepia, or turquoise—as well as in dignified black, especially recommended for recent widows, colonels in the reserve, and chaste librarians. I'd also like to take this opportunity to warn you against the danger of accepting imitations: when buying Donald's Condoms at your local pharmacy or drugstore, make sure that the unmistakable duck is duly stamped on the padded tip. With Donald, in small, medium, and large, you're sure of having a safe relationship, as Dr. Nelson de Jesus, Junior, the illustrious founder of Donald Sexological Industries and honorary life president of its board of directors, recently pointed out to newspaper and television reporters as he left the Vatican palace in Rome, after being received in a private audience by His Holiness the Pope, who expressed paternal jubilation and warm support for his noble enterprise, dispensing as it does with the accursed and sinful pill, and who graciously accepted a solid-gold condom to alleviate the stark austerity of his office desk. Dr. Nelson de Jesus, Junior, also took the occasion to offer members of the Curia a super-deluxe variety of Donald's Condoms, in cardinal scarlet, with a small crosier imprinted on the base, in recognition of which he was named a Knight of the Holy Sepulcher and Guardian of the Christian Faith. Choose Donald's, the Catholic condom."

A motorboat pursued by a crown of famished sea gulls slid past the inn downstream, the coughs from its engine disturbing the mild restlessness of the eucalyptus trees. Dona Sara reclasped the brooch with the picture of the deceased that fastened the top of her dress, turning red with a modesty inappropriate to her six hundred years:

"Here's the room," she said in a sigh from beyond the grave. "The first six months have to be paid in advance."

Embarrassed, I began to pull Tucha by her dress sleeve, but she shook herself loose, her elbow jabbing my stomach, so that the stewed lamb I had for lunch rose to my mouth with a sting of garlic and hot sauce. She was circled by a phosphorescent nimbus of vengeance; even the strands of her hair seemed hardened and electrified by the sadistic taste of victory, and the tip of her tongue appeared between her lips exuberantly. He thinks, My God how beautiful you were that afternoon.

"Get out of my sight, you slob," she hissed while pointing to the plant-lined walkways, the white-framed panes, and the graveled distance with its humid and woolly shrubs. "Get out of my sight before I change my mind."

Dona Sara wrapped the money in her handkerchief, turned around, and shuffled toward the door, dragging her spindly legs forward with effort. As her hand grasped the doorknob she gazed back at him with a sour expression:

"I meant to tell you that I don't allow visitors here."

"What a first-class, bitch your ex was," Marilia said as the interminable ashen tip of her cigarette fell into smithereens on her lap. From the apartment overhead someone (a male voice) shouted unintelligible phrases out the window. "If you two were in the wrong, what did you expect the poor guy to do?"

If Tucha's a first-class bitch, then am I any less of one? he thinks, while the audience clapped for Donald's Condoms and the old hobo defeathered the sparrow cracklings before lovingly placing them between two halves of a roll:

"Have a bite?" his father asked.

"Regardless of what time of day it is, is that clear?" Dona Sara repeated, once more readjusting the brooch with her skeletal and stark-white fingers, agitated by an incessant distress. (You must have high blood pressure, I thought, and diabetes, and uremia, and Parkinson's.) "Positively no visitors."

Her slippers shuffled down the hall and out of hearing, while phlegmatic gargles intoned an aria in the attic. Marilia brushed the ashes off her skirt with a biography of Antonioni, and I thought, If I'm a first-class bitch, then why for crying out loud are you here with me?

"Every time there's a dispute you act more apathetic than a porcelain ox," Tucha reproached him while quickly walking out of the park to the subway station. "The other night in the disco you would have gotten creamed if it weren't for my brother."

The hobo, still chewing, got up to urinate against a post, nonchalantly flicking his cock up and down when he'd finished: but after she got to know him Dona Sara forgot about her rule; she invited him to have tea in a hexagonal room crammed with Chinese chests and heavy old furniture; an invisible clock periodically chimed the infinite hours; she'd offer him stale cookies, parsimoniously lifting the lid of a shoe box; and when Marilia stopped by to drop off some books, she insisted on meeting her, and they spent an eternity with teacup in hand, sunken into the hugely uncomfortable, springless sofas, refusing crackers and listening to Dona Sara discourse about happier days, while her mummy fingers stroked the brown photo of her husband, Porfírio Alves, who had retired from the Telephone Company, and was run over by a bus on Infante Santo Avenue ages ago. Little by little he got to know the other boarders: a middle-aged black man, extremely correct and polite, who worked for the Development Bank and was, for obscure reasons, a great fan of the Covilhã Soccer Club; a merchant marine pilot who gave his wife a good thrashing every time he returned from a voyage, "As a matter of principle," he told me solemnly one day at the bus stop, although horrified me couldn't figure out what principle he was referring to; Senhor Esperança, world-class baritone and habitué of the courtyard; a pair of spinster twins who had been salesclerks at Grandela Department Store, were always together, wore identical heraldic rings, and had tea with us on Tuesdays in sepulchral silence, tirelessly turning out crocheted doilies with symmetrical hand movements; and Father Mendonça, who sucked on menthol drops in an effort to quit smoking, filling the air around him with a drugstore freshness, and led a strangled life in his celluloid collar, always referring to God as a tyrannical, overly demanding boss. I began to feel at home, he thinks, and I moved to Azedo Gneco Street against the advice of the merchant marine pilot, who the night before had broken his wife's left arm, as a matter of principle, and goaded me, "Beat her some more!", tugging at my coat collar in a raging and tormented, brotherly entreaty.

"How unbearably bourgeois your ex must have been," Marilia said, using a biography of Visconti to brush a new cylinder of ashes off her skirt while I timidly passed her the bronze cat ashtray, remembering my nighttime asthma attacks in that indescribably dusty depository; night after night I was wide awake, sitting up in bed, wheezing, while the stars stuck to the window in a suspended harmony, and the neighborhood pressed in from all sides with its drab little shops and withered buildings. Marilia took off her shoes and began to scratch her bunions pensively:

"How long were you able to put up with it?"

The old man finished eating the roll and remained stupidly still in the shed's square shadow, watching the dying embers in the stove turn more and more pallid, bidding farewell to the dying sparks. A brown liquid thread dripped slowly from the corner of his mouth as his little finger picked between his teeth like an avid corkscrew. The drunken youth hesitated: the intermittent lights of the discotheque alternately illumined and darkened his face, his disheveled hair, and his torn shirt with missing buttons. Two peacemakers held him by the arms, pulling him toward the bar.

"If you bother him anymore," warned Tucha's brother heroically, still on his feet, straightening the slightly twisted knot of his tie, "I'll make mush out of your face."

You had no one, Marilia: your mother once made a vague mention of a much older half-brother who'd immigrated to Canada, a guy who looked like you, his hands on his belt, in a framed photo that sat on the television, with a presumably foreign wife at his side and a whining, openmouthed child between them. The spotlight shone once more on the bird-eating hobo, who had dropped his pants and, balancing on wide open legs next to the stove, defecated an interminably long carnival streamer to the general laughter of the audience. His yellow hair vibrated a thousand-wire antennae, and his humongously fat false buttocks, made of cloth, shook in ridiculous tremors. From somewhere in the darkness the voice of his youngest sister rippled into the microphone:

"This amusing sketch was offered to you by the stockings and pantyhose of Mrs. Penelope, *penelopize* and feel the difference in your husband's fond look, the fabric that transforms your legs into genuine moments of seduction. Light and soft to the touch, rich in subtle shades, and available in black net with dots or in a simple flesh-colored variety, Penelope stockings represent the guarantee of a great romance. Imbued with a gentle aroma of lilies and wildflowers that will withstand repeated washings, and accompanied by a set of red garters decorated with beautiful tulle roses, the stockings and pantyhose of Mrs. Penelope—*penelopize* and feel the difference in your husband's fond look—are especially recommended for first dates, visits to bachelor or widower uncles, responses to personal ads, and for women who've resigned themselves to spinsterhood and take refuge in the Blessed Sacrament on display at the Monument to the Martyrs or in weekend box-lunch excursions to the Batalha Monastery and the Coach and Buggy Museum. Penelope, the stocking that brings out the feminine in you, Penelope, the cure for bashfulness, the assurance of an irresistible attraction, the look that will make you envied, admired, and desired. *Penelopize* and feel the difference in your husband's fond look."

He began to walk upstream along the shore, grinding the sand as if stepping on sandpaper or bits of glass. A cold wind blew up his trouser legs, down his shirt collar, and between his buttons. The waves of water, folding and refolding in thick leather pleats, seemed to smoke like lye; "bourgeois bastards," said Marilia; "capitalist bastards," said Marilia. "I don't know how you put up with it for so long." And in the distance he saw Aveiro, blurry and gray against the gray sky and gray water, trembling in the nakedness of morning. I have to at least make this a good performance, he thought, the knife jabbing against the flab of his thigh with every step; I have to at least not let the impresario down.

"It's almost time for the finale of his act, and the performer has not committed the least technical flaw," cried the dwarf, with a note of relief in his voice, to the flagging audience. "This magnificent apotheosis, sure to impress each and every one of you, was achieved only once before, in London, in 1936, by the glorious and unforgettable Aristotle Szadagadanis, the Greek circus star."

The breeze changed direction and the ducks dispersed, some of them moving farther down the lagoon, beating the air with their disconcerted wings as the fine feathers on their necks bristled in a kind of anger or alarm. I should phone the clinic, he thinks, I should try to find out what's happening.

"Do you want to marry me?" he asked Tucha as they walked down the subway stairs covered with fruit skins, papers, trash, and the gelatinous lacquer of spittle. The square cement mouth—with walls covered by the remains of posters and messages written in inflamed chalk—swallowed them like jostling carts entering the Haunted House, and in the dim interior, lit by long neon tubes, they confronted the usual hurried and anxious multitude.

"Me? Marry you?" exclaimed Marilia, laughing, sitting on her friend's bed completely naked. It was summer, he thinks; you wore blue plastic sandals and had temporarily left off wearing the poncho; your amused tits quivered and your body was suspended like that of Chinese gods in the dusty luminosity of twilight. He thinks, Your large ankles, your farm girl hands, the guttural and masculine cackles that ran down your trunk, spreading through your buttocks and making your lower back shake. "Me, marry you?" she repeated, stupefied. "Wasn't one disastrous attempt enough for you?"

Neither one took me seriously, he thought while kicking a rusty can he'd dug out of the sand with the tip of his shoe; neither one of them believed me. He'd pursued Tucha for two years, forever insisting, calling her up, inviting her out, writing long, impassioned, corny letters, two years of swearing his eternal devotion until the married man with whom she had carried on a nerve-racking affair finally immigrated to Rio de Janeiro without so much as a parting word, and Tucha, enraged, said yes, her face glassy with tears, her eye makeup transformed into a pair of pathetically imploring splotches. A few months later he walked slowly down the aisle in a tuxedo, arm in arm with a white and fluffy, seemingly gaseous form, while the ridiculously feathered heads of their aunts craned from the pews on both sides to get a better look and the church threatened to drown in the heavy waves of the organ's triumphal march.

"Marry you, imagine," Marilia murmured pensively, shaking her head no as she searched for her pack of cigarettes in the mound of crumpled clothes on the floor. "That's the last thing on earth I would ever have expected out of you. What I want to know is if you're just bourgeois, or crazy, or both."

And again, like the first time, months of stubborn insistence, months of a resigned and unrelenting siege, of affectionate glances that elicited no response, of excessive doting, of dramatic and exaggerated pleas. He knew a handful of the people she'd been involved with, never very seriously, a couple of squalid university colleagues, off-the-wall Party comrades, a gray-bearded sculptor who was notably unclean, wore sandals, and had the air of someone who might walk on water in a tunic, distributing abstract miracles to the regulars of the Fine Arts Society: and why not me, he thinks; what do these guys have that I don't; why don't women take me seriously; why don't they look at me with bugging eyes, crazy with desire? One time when I was in the waiting room of the endocrinologist, I read an article in a Brazilian magazine entitled "The Erotic Charm of Fat Men," with mulatto women in bikinis and high-heeled slippers voluptuously pawing spherical men who resembled peeled hard-boiled eggs: the text extolled the seductive merits of a double chin, the orgiastic coziness of immense bellies, the joy of entwining one's legs around a pair of elephantine ankles; it quoted personal testimonials in italics and transcribed the fiery verses of romantic poetesses driven wild by flab to the heights of enraptured sonnets; and I thought, Why bother to diet? Why bother to lose weight? Why take the doctor's pills to become elegant like an exclamation point? I'm going to put on a few more pounds, and then a bevy of blondes in low-cut evening dresses, beautiful and all made-up, like the actresses on bubble gum wrappers, will no doubt start flitting all around me fascinated. But

Marilia, he thinks, probably married me because of her parents (So who's the bourgeois?), who were threatening to die of grief if you kept living with a man in mortal sin. They cried during the entire ceremony, noisily blowing their noses with feeling at every phrase spoken by the justice of the peace, and afterward the four of us went to a café for a snack, your mother eternally dripping emotions over her lemon tea as your father, in a red-and-yellow tie, with his shirt collar unbuttoned, drank beer after beer in a heartfelt silence. We ate cream puffs, rock-hard pastries, and toast so dry it could have passed for slices of pumice stone. At the surrounding tables solitary gentlemen and ladies with little dogs in their laps sipped on soft drinks with funereal solemnity, and the waiters called out customer orders to a cubicle in which some entity or another presumably existed to dispense the filled pastries and bottles of orange drink. They said good-bye on the sidewalk in front of the café, with more sniffling, more tears, and more sobs muffled in handkerchiefs; we walked a block down to get the bus to Azedo Gneco Street and, turning around, I saw the old couple trotting together toward the streetcar stop, she trying to keep pace with her much taller husband, and they never looked so aged and vulnerable and pitiful as on that afternoon. As soon as we arrived you shut yourself in the bathroom for a good long while, and when you came out, you carefully avoided looking at me: your eyelids were swollen and your nose was red; you sat on the floor and leafed through a book, and when I tried to kiss you, you pushed me away with all your might as if you hated me, and I decided to write the magazine I'd seen in the endocrinologist's office to let them know that "The Erotic Charm of Fat Men" was pure bullshit. Fortunately things got better, no doubt for the same apparent nonreason that the sky clears; we had dinner at a Chinese restaurant full of bustling Orientals and paper lanterns imprinted with a St. Anthony from Shanghai; my clumsiness with the chopsticks made you laugh, and on the way

241

home, excited by the sweet and sour pork, I kept thinking about making love to you, but, nevertheless, yet, however, the elevator went on the blink between floors; the alarm wouldn't sound; we beat our fists on the grates until four in the morning, and at last the man from the first floor appeared in purple pajamas, followed by his nightgowned wife, who phoned a brother-in-law who was handy with machinery; the guy showed up in a bathrobe that was soon coated with grease; he screwed and unscrewed part after part while the entire building, in their slippers, looked on sympathetically, encouraging and consoling us. One lady gave us some chocolate liqueur to drink through a straw, and another prayed the rosary for us, kneeling on her doormat with her eyes closed; at 7 A.M. the firemen arrived in a brouhaha of sirens, ambulances, silly helmets, ropes, hoses, and ladders; the handy guy in the bathrobe, black from head to foot, was tenaciously hammering in the depths of the basement; the firemen—commanded by a leisurely fellow wearing long johns that stuck out of his trousers and three medals that looked like bottle caps on his chest—broke through the metal slats of the doors with a blowtorch, scorching my only decent jacket with an infernal heat (our hair burned like the legs of insects); and we were almost free when someone outside turned on the hose, which rose up from the ground in an uncontrollable erection, spraying straight at the praying woman, who tumbled down the stairs and broke a collarbone; the drenched tenants fled screaming from the jet of water; the medal-bearing fire chief snarled, "Who turned on the goddam water?" before the nozzle hit him smack in the face, propelling him backward into the apartment of the chocolate liqueur lady, where he slammed into the china cabinet in the foyer, toppling a porcelain hobo that looked just like President Manuel de Arriaga without the tails; an enormous mirror in a worm-infested carved frame fell onto his helmet and shattered; the landlord starting pulling out his hair, crying, "Oh my God, my darling building," and then the torrent of people and water that was rushing down the steps submerged all of him but a single waving, shipwrecked arm in the pool on the ground floor, where the water was so deep you couldn't touch bottom and where the potted plants had been recycled into a wilted forest of corals; and when the hose finally went limp and died, lying back down in innocent, concentric spirals of canvas, there were people lying everywhere in swooning wetness, and we walked up the remaining flight of stairs like cautious storks so as not to step on the gurgling victims; we signed a petition to the nuncio demanding the immediate canonization of the rosary zealot; the fire chief—revived by shots of chocolate liqueur, whose owner generously passed out glasses to the whole department—blew on a whistle that nobody heard; the pandemonium of vehicles on the street increased; we closed the door, undressed, brushed our teeth, wound up the alarm clock, turned off the light, and listened through the fluid vapors of sleep, past the howls, moans, sirens, and drops of water falling in the darkness, to the tenacious hammering of the handy brother-in-law, who continued his obstinate mole's labor in his well, impassive as a termite.

"Marry you?" asked Tucha and Marilia indignantly in stereo.

"Ladies and gentlemen, girls and boys, distinguished guests whose presence and enthusiasm honor us here tonight," cried the dwarf while signaling with a raised sleeve for Ravel's *Bolero* to stop. "We have the privilege of presenting to you The Wives. A round of applause for The Wives, if you please."

The orchestra drum let loose with a lugubrious roll and a spotlight switched on, illuminating the ceiling of the circus tent (a star could be seen through a rip in the canvas), a gently swinging trapeze bar, and, standing on the bar in slippers and sequined bathing suits, Marilia and Tucha, who waved to the

243

audience as chalk dust fell from their palms. The maestro gyrated the broom handle in an authoritarian ellipse, the drum halted with one final boom, and the spectators tilted their heads back to contemplate the aerial performers, while he trudged along the sand with his hands in his pockets and his nose pointing down in the turbid morning dampness.

"We didn't want to get married," they said in unison. "Matrimony was no more than an unfortunate mistake on our part."

"Our children, too," added Tucha, whose spherical buttocks twitched under her clothing. "We had them by natural childbirth, but he never breathed with the right rhythm, so it threw off my contractions, and the doctor said I was lucky they weren't born as mongoloids. Can you imagine two kids at home with their tongues hanging out, drooling and grunting things no one understands? I'd put them straight into an institution."

"At first," Marilia said, "I thought he was a redeemable bourgeois, a potential socialist, one who might through reading and the example of others be converted to the glorious ideology of the working class. I regarded living with him as part of my militant duty, until in a cell meeting my comrades scientifically demonstrated the contrary: that there was no changing his hardened capitalism, his atrocious elitism, and his absolute egotism. Naturally I made an immediate self-criticism before my fellow Party members."

"My psychiatrist," said Tucha, "explained to me that Rui was afflicted with sadomasochism in its severest form, which is why he wanted to have abnormal children. Only by separating was I able to resolve my Oedipus complex non-neurotically: were it up to him, I'd have stayed in the oral phase forever."

"It's fair to say that he forced me, by his omission, to have an abortion," Marilia charged. "When I said I didn't want

244

children, it was merely a way to test the waters. He always replied that two children were enough for him, that he didn't want any more complications. His blood carried the self-centeredness intrinsic to the ruling classes."

"He never once served me breakfast in bed," Tucha complained. "He'd lay sprawled out on the sheets like a frog on a board, his mouth open and waiting. And if there was a skin on the heated milk he wouldn't drink it."

"He thought that wives existed for the sole purpose of serving him," Marilia completed. "With me he always gobbled up the hot toast on top, leaving me the cold slices."

"I would fillet his fish," Tucha said, "and even so, if he came across a single bone or piece of skin, right away he'd start bitching. Fortunately the children didn't inherit his table manners."

"He wouldn't even eat chicken," Marilia said, "just hamburger and rice with tomato sauce. Years and years of hamburger and rice with tomato sauce would make anyone go batty."

"Instead of rolling up the toothpaste tube," Tucha said, "he gave a random squeeze and squirted out half the tube onto his brush. It's a wonder it didn't plug the drain."

"Whenever he took a leak," said Marilia, "he always left a spray of drops on the toilet seat, so that before I could sit down on it I had to wipe it with toilet paper."

"He never went with me to the supermarket," stated Tucha, hanging from the bar of the trapeze by her knees while Marilia, hands joined to Tucha's, swung in the emptiness. "And when I say supermarket that also means the butcher, the baker, the tailor, the toy store, and so on. I was the one who took the car in to get the oil changed."

"He thought that everyone existed as a function of him," Marilia affirmed, flipping over herself in a complex maneuver that the orchestra emphasized by speeding up the rhythm, and the audience applauded loudly. (In the ring, illuminated by a smaller spotlight, the dwarf moved forward and backward with open arms, as if prepared to catch her should she fall.) "He required constant availability, unlimited affection, and unconditional adoration, and who can put up with that for very long?"

"He didn't even fold up his sweaters," said Tucha resentfully, "every morning I had to decide what clothes he'd wear, because if it was left up to him, the result was frightful. At one point I was convinced he was color blind."

"He remained a reactionary of the worst stripe," Marilia said as she slid down a rope into the ring, where she raised her hands and turned both ways to thank the crowd for its enthusiasm, which the dwarf encouraged, obliging her to skip to the center of the ring. "The cancer of capitalism infected him from top to bottom, the ghost of religion shackled him, and the class struggle was a source of continual panic. It's a good thing that the Party saved me from getting infected, always showing me the right line of action."

"Only after separating from him was I able to be happy," Tucha said, sliding down the rope in turn, and the dwarf pushed her toward Marilia, who looked at her with a wide conspiratorial smile on her carmine lips. A bunch of ex-boyfriends, overcome with admiration, leaned over the railing of their box to give the acrobats a vigorous ovation, and as he stared at the eucalyptus trees of Aveiro, almost white in the fog, their boughs at the top seeming to dissolve in the clouds, he thought without melancholy, Already I feel so far away from all this. And the knife handle, pressing against his armpit, hampered his movements like a cyst.

"All the birds from the farm are here," his father revealed, piling on the carpet the sheets of cardboard holding crucified birds, with beady gelatinous eyes and black-and-red feet. The hair on his temples had begun to break loose from his hair cream, and a liberated strand danced in the cavity of his ear.

The designer desk lamp lit up only the bottom half of his face, leaving his critical and scrutinizing eyes in the shadows.

"So shall I open up their tummies and explain them to you?" he asked while he reached for another cigar in the silver case.

As the morning distended and grew, he felt as if his body were moving in the dim light of an attic, in a glass egg, in a kind of pus crystal that altered sounds, regrouped the trees, divided the wind, and bore the dull odor of the lagoon, reminiscent of the putrid smell of a cadaver: Tucha and Marilia ran offstage as the spotlight followed them; the box with the ex-boyfriends quieted down; a magpie squawked in the brush; in the clinic they were tying a handkerchief around his mother's jaw; the sky seemed to be formed of steps of water that shaded the lagoon, copying one another in an endless succession; with knit eyebrows his father examined a butterfly that gradually turned into a goldfinch whose eyes stared in terror, and he turned around to look at the inn. Have you woken up yet? Are you taking your shower now? He thought he heard a car motor on the highway—The English couple, arriving guests, you? The sound of a motor. With this weather who is going to hole up in this Noah's ark piloted by the nasty woman at the reception desk? "Maestro, Ravel's *Bolero*, if you please," the gnome ordered in his ridiculously imperative, bitonal squeak, getting dressed, eating breakfast, lighting a cigarette while seated on the bed, with a wrinkle on your forehead; the conductor waved his broom forcefully, and the dreadful band recommenced with a clap of the cymbals; Carlos—with galloons on his shirt, tall boots, and perfectly parted hair—cracked his whip to send away the last plumed horse, propped his left foot on the splintered edge of the age-worn stage, displaying the shiny point of his spur, turned to the stands with his usual defiant, self-confident, insupportable look, and there once more was the obnoxious dumb smirk from dinners at his parents', the sarcastic anti-Communist jokes that weren't funny, the legs crossed with a lordly air in the leather armchair, and the eternal urine on the rocks in his hand:

"How are things in the Party, comrade?" he asked, bending forward to help himself to the appetizer of cheese that some-one in the audience offered him and that he wolfed down with the impassive voracity of a chameleon. I hate your toreador spangles, I thought. I hate your cologne, your silk ties, the monogram on your shirt. I hate your subservient liveliness when you talk with my father, the shameless way you stare at women's thighs, leaning toward them to murmur phrases out of the disdainful corner of your mouth.

"Mom," whimpered his youngest sister, in tears, "someone called up to tell me that Carlos is involved with Filipa, that friend of mine from high school."

Carlos plopped down on the sofa and lolled between his wife and a Gypsy-like woman of roughly the same age, with-out letting go of his whip, which snaked along the carpet, twisting around a carved wood table to disappear into the dark mouth of the entrance hall. The spotlight focused on him revealed a thin streak of sweat next to his hairline, and his upper lip also shone, surrounded by the dark growth of his beard:

"I'm here with you today," he announced in the dull and crumpled tone that made his words exasperatingly irksome, "at the gracious invitation of the Iron Fist Gymnasium, the only gym in Portugal where specialized instructors have the know-how to transform your body—no matter how stunted or scrawny or anemic or hunchbacked—into an impressive statue of bulging muscles that will make you the preferred object of female glances and the envy of your friends at the beach this summer. Try out Iron Fist Gymnasium and become fearsome, sought after, respected, and adored, thanks to your biceps' sheer bulk and power. Would you like to improve your professional status, to form new relationships, to be regularly invited for drinks, receptions, and birthday parties, to occupy positions of high social rank, to seduce that lady you've been unsuccessfully pursuing for years, instead of taking your chances on the personal ads and meeting in dubious cafés with infinitely pathetic, middle-aged women who stir the sugar of their solitude in the bottom of their teacups, accompanied by a Harold Robbins novel? Iron Fist Gymnasium—directed by specialized instructors, including the formidable Jacinto da Conceição Augusto, Mister Muscle of Iberia in 1959 and currently the consort of a Swedish princess—will give you the joy of living and the ability to open beer bottles with a flick of your pinky or to knock down steel doors with the casual shove of an elbow. With classes in directed, corrective, rhythmic, applied, and maintenance gymnastics, with a Finnish sauna, specially equipped rooms for fencing, boxing, racquetball, and karate, massages administered by the expert hands of Julio "Goldfinger," a section devoted to Turkish baths and Scottish showers, and the Iron Fist Vitamin-Plus Restaurant, reserved exclusively for members and serving twenty-three different and complementary pills, lozenges, and capsules, as well as intramuscular, intravenous, and oral ampoules, syrups, aerosols, wafers, suspensions, electric and insulin shocks, ointments, tonics, and suppositories, Iron Fist Gymnasium constitutes a ground-breaking innovation, providing the Portuguese population with the opportunity for good health, well-being, and the figure and tendons you deserve, and eliminating the specter of physical, mental, or psychosomatic illness, high blood pressure, heart attacks, varicocele, microcephaly, macrocephaly, syphilis, gonorrhea, typhoid and Malta fever, eczema, strabismus, baldness, goiter, rheumatism, headaches, earaches, sore throats, exophthalmos, convulsive, preconvulsive, and nonconvulsive coughing, constipation, sprains, ingrown nails, hemorrhoids, corns, anxiety, pain, schizophrenia, fractured femurs, insomnia, alcoholism, blackheads, drug addiction, scurvy, and suicide attempts or the contemplation thereof." (The spotlight changed color, turning lettuce green while Ravel's *Bolero* relentlessly carried on its march, pushed along like a turkey by the maestro's frenetic broom.) "And speaking of suicide, ladies and gentlemen, and referring specifically to the sketch being performed by my brother-in-law at this very moment"—(A hundred or so feet ahead, he thought, and I'll see the sea gulls up close, the ones that float on the water and the ones that scratch their backs with their beaks while perched on the cork buoys that mark off the lagoon)—"and with respect to the liberating or crazy or desperate or perhaps simply harebrained act that will be attempted by this fat individual in a few moments"—(seen from the window he was now no more than a tiny shadow walking obstinately through the sand in the gray morning, an insignificant figure disappearing into the distance, into the confusion of pine trees and fog, like a hero at the end of a film, a speck that flickered, seemed to grow, and then vanished)—"and it is my strictly personal opinion, my hunch, my guess, my private conviction, ladies and gentlemen"—(he confided something into the ear of the Gypsy-like girl, who broke out laughing and pulled on his ear in amused reprehension)—"that he will fail ingloriously in his exploit, or projected exploit, just as he's failed in every area of life."

"A scratch on his wrist at the most," opined the olive-skinned girl, jangling the bracelets on her wrist. "A Band-Aid or two and he'll be fine, you'll see."

"Carlos is absolutely right," agreed the youngest sister, glaring with hatred at her rival. "If Dad had been foolish enough to put him into the firm, it would have been a complete fiasco."

"This Filipa gal is nothing to get excited about," answered her mother. "Let out the leash a little and he'll get bored in no time."

"It's obvious he's going to fail," Carlos repeated while

stroking the girl's knee with a lethargic thumb. "In thirty-three years he's never managed to do anything right."

"Just look at his marriages," declared the voice of the obstetrician from the middle of the stands, brought into view by a roving spotlight that let darkness fall back on successive rows of spectators, some of whom hurriedly waved on the chance there was a hidden camera. "Just look at his history of screw-ups."

"How about a few more goldfinches?" his father suggested cheerfully while continuing to open up cabinet drawers and tossing sheets of pasteboard full of dead birds onto the floor. "Goldfinches, greenfinches, nightingales, hoopoes, robins, blackbirds, canaries," he rattled off, "any bird you want."

What screw-ups? he wondered, sitting in the sand amidst the scrub, peering at the dense, syrupy, still water of the Vouga. Separating from Tucha? Marilia's abortion? Not working for the firm like my father wanted? Not accepting—out of pride? out of principle? (what principle?), out of a mere childish need to rebel?—so much as a nominal position on the board of directors? What screw-ups? he wondered, intrigued, rummaging through the sudden, disturbing, vast emptiness of his memory as far back as the arm of recollection could reach.

The coldness shaved the bushes and the branches of the pine trees; it made the eucalyptuses shiver and the water surface ruffle like a thinking forehead. A truck occasionally roared down the highway that he couldn't see, and the sound would slowly diminish as it went toward the town, pursued by the fury of dogs.

He wonders, What screw-ups?—and the blind man from the farm suddenly appears ("Brought to you by Pop'n'Crackle Vaginal Cones"), walking under the trellis and searching with his cane for the stone bench where he usually sits at the end of the day, his face dappled by the filtered green of the tree leaves and by the shadows and splotches of light that the sun dis-

251

perses and reunites, as if perpetually disassembling and reassembling a pointless puzzle ("Let's hear it for the special effects crew," the dwarf bellowed, and the crowd clapped hard), until the tip of the cane brushed against the limestone, and he hesitantly extended his hand toward the smooth surface, bent his knees, and sat down, making himself comfortable: his dark glasses, round and threatening, regarded the entire farm in silent attention. The August wind brought him the sweet smell of the orchard, while the blades of grass in the flower beds celloed.

"Remember—Iron Fist Gymnasium," Carlos shouted as his thumb disappeared under Filipa's skirt, forming a bulge that crawled toward her crotch.

Lying in the sand, his head propped up on a bent elbow, he saw the clouds way overhead journeying toward the sea, looking almost solid in their rubbery thickness, stretching and contracting like the cigarette smoke of the spectators next to the rows of yellow circus lights: the February cold hardened his face as if wrapping it in an uncomfortable clay paste. He listened to the breathing of the trees, the scattered quacking of ducks, a wood pigeon that traversed the eucalyptus trees; he watched the tide's lazy descent, receding inch by inch down the sand with its debris, its seaweed, its swollen cat cadavers; he imagined Marilia packing her suitcase in the inn, grabbing her clothes out of the drawers, and tossing them in unfolded, using her hand to sweep combs, tubes, and toothbrushes into a threadbare sack, leaving the empty hangers to swing on the aluminum rod, and then, without any warning or gesture or change of expression, the blind man said, "Is that you, sport?" And I thought, How did he make it to Aveiro; how the devil did he discover me here? Did you stumble your way through the bushes and reeds until you recognized my smell the way old dogs distinguish their masters? He thinks, I don't even know if you're still alive; it's been ages since I asked my parents about you; it's been ages since anyone's gone down to the farm on holiday; by now moss must be growing on the furniture, on the tablecloths, on the curtains, on the iodine-colored smiles of the photographs, and the attic with its unsteady floor must have been invaded by vines, by ivy, by the carnivorous hunger of termites; in all likelihood the house has sunk irrevocably into the past like one of those crumbling boats tied to the boulders in the Tagus River; dahlias and narcissuses are probably growing in the tureens; a strange flora of lichens is thriving in the pillowcases, in the bedspread, in the towels, in the mildew of the sheets; Marilia pulled on the straps of the suitcases; she's about to call the desk to have a bellhop carry them down or else she'll try to drag them down herself, hampered by her poncho, and a maid will help out; she'll pay the bill, call a taxi to take her to the train station, and explain to the nasty woman, "My husband will follow me in the car." How many days will the car stay there before anyone touches it? he wondered as a gull's cheep pierced his head from ear to ear ("Just like a needle," the dwarf informed the audience, "a very fine, incandescent, painful needle") and the wind whipped the eucalyptus trees furiously; his hand inadvertently touched the knife handle (a murmur swept through the boxes, spreading to the precarious slats of the balcony), he hesitated, drew back, and the carpet in the study was now completely covered by birds with gaping beaks, stiffened legs, and motionless beady eyes, which he and his father, standing side by side, observed with rapt attention.

"Is that you, sport?" the blind man asked again in his parrot voice.

"Screw-up after screw-up after screw-up," came the doctor's voice from far away. "Hundreds of screw-ups have their price."

He heard a rustling to his left, and without looking he knew that the blind man had sat down next to him, his dark glasses turned toward the water, reflecting in their lenses a tiny, tremulously drifting ship. How's my mother? he wondered;

what's happened the last few days in the clinic? How many horrid striped sweaters has my cousin knitted since Thursday, counting the stitches with pursed lips?

The abandoned farmhouse, the abandoned well, and the abandoned fig trees dripping their pinkish and useless milk to the ground, the forest fluttering blue in the background during the long, heavy, scarlet afternoons of summer, full of mute, unmoving birds that wait for night on the tree-branch staffs, like soundless thirty-second notes, a solitary lawn chair, its colors fading, as lonely on the patio as the rusty gate, the house's sad rooms, the lighter-colored rectangles left by paint-ings on the now empty walls, a sewing machine covered with dust in a nook, a leaning broom behind a dirty curtain. He went from room to room almost without touching the floor ("A round of applause for the set designers and the produc-tion staff," the dwarf demanded), as if in the sifted and unreal light of dreams, observing old objects from the past, now paler, stranger, and smaller, charged with some hidden mean-ing that he couldn't grasp, that he'd never grasp, wide-open wardrobes with the livid remains of hanging clothes, faded watercolors, moth-eaten drapes falling off their rings, beds without mattresses reduced to skeletons of slats, circles of chairs full of murmuring ghosts, of invisible mouths convers-ing in low tones, of heads gravely bowing to one another in a confusion of secrets; he descended to the ground floor with the subtlety of perfume and walked through the glass-walled pantry and between huge pots of withered plants waving their long necks over clay rims, through the dining room where time had stopped dead in the immemorially broken clocks. "Let out the leash," his mother said to his youngest sister, "and this Filipa rigmarole will come to a quick halt," the storage room with its pile of bicycles covered with spiderwebs, mouse droppings, and refuse, the kitchen with the marble-topped table in the middle, the aluminum sink by the window, the chipped refrigerator, the now burnerless stoves, the wall tiles fractured with cracks in which the daisies of absence proliferated, and then he went outside into the neglected yard, where the lawn mower leaned against the wall and the dried-up cement ponds were coated with a whitish powdery filth. Stretched out in the sand about two hundred yards away from the inn, amidst the increasing cries of the gulls (I won't open my eyes, he thought. I won't look at them until I reach the well and my father carries me piggyback back to the house), he heard the sound of his shoes crunching the unraked dry leaves that were piling ever deeper on the patio, and then the gravel of the walkways crushed by his heels, and then the hard, dull drumhead of the soil, the roots dissolving into carbon, the elastic blades of grass that stretched and contracted like fingers, feebly protesting against each of his steps. He thought, It's going to rain, the way it's raining tonight as I write the end of my book, lying next to you in the gigantic quiet of our bedroom, with one leg across your legs and the soft sigh of your sleep breathing with the slow rhythm of the words; he thought, It's going to rain, the way it's raining on the paper, the way it's raining on the bed, the way it's raining on our entwined thighs, the way your child is raining in your womb, calling me with the transparent, Martian voice of anemones; he thought, Soon I'll lay down my pad and pen on the nightstand, and I'll cuddle up next to you and turn out the light; your round arm will embrace my neck, and my penis will grow next to your isosceles pubis, passionately, as the clouds of Aveiro grow, opening their wings in the basaltic morning sky, as the untended grass on the farm grows, as my fingers grow across your breasts, your back, and the full, round flesh of your bottom, as your saliva grows on my tongue, and our feet cross and uncross faster, ever faster. "Is that you, sport?" asked the blind man while his cane explored the sand all around him with antennalike agility; Carlos explored the inside of Filipa's skirt, staring at her intently, with the tragic look of the men on old postcards with long, dark eyelashes and hair parted in the middle; he heard the motor of Marilia's taxi rumbling on its way to the inn; the smell of the water came closer, panting from fatigue; behind a bush he made out the fig tree that had stood by the well, now stripped of all its leaves and life, dry and ashen, reduced to the knotty, goutish joints of branches; he saw the outline of the well, the rusty pulley, the old bucket; Filipa unbuttoned her blouse, freeing the leather tips of her breasts, the knot of skin in her navel, and the smooth, flat board of her tummy, raised at her waist by the bones of her pelvis; Carlos licked her flanks, squeezed her tits, groped for his zipper with his free hand (The hand with the heraldic ring, he thought, so absurdly massive and pretentious); Ravel's *Bolero* turned soft and conspiratorial; Sr. Esperança, now elegantly dressed in a tuxedo, grasped the microphone gracefully, pulling it toward his mouth, and pointed at the half-naked couple that tumbled off the sofa and onto the carpet before an indifferent family:

"This erotic sketch, on a par with the best houses of Paris, London, New York, and Manila, was performed by talented national stars whose only training was in the circus, and was brought to you by a product purely our own, purely Portuguese, the latest marvel of national science, developed by a research team in Coimbra: Ejacula Cream—by popular demand, now also available in a spray—the medication that will increase the size of your organ by one full inch in just two weeks' time; it's easy to use: just apply twice daily, in the morning when you wake up and at night before going to bed, at the very same times you brush your teeth, that is, and, in fact, you can use the same brush and the same quantity of product—a tad will do—for both types of treatment. You may rightly ask: How was this miracle achieved? How was this heretofore unthinkable wonder accomplished? How is it that in the comfort and privacy of my own home I can finally realize the secret desire of my life? How can this extraordinary, fantastic enlargement of my penis occur? The man responsible—director of the Independent Scholar Institute of Coimbra, a knight in the Order of Christ and the Public Good, Secretary of the Agricultural Society, Honorary Member of the EUCC (European Union for Christian Coitus), and officer of the ISVVS (Iberian Society of Vulvo-Vaginal Studies)—has now made public his marvelous secret: the purple lichen of the Mondego River, an extremely rare fungus found on the banks of this poetic waterway, not far from its mouth, and gathered only in the early morning on Fat Tuesday and Ash Wednesday. After being carefully pulverized, kneaded, acidified, dehydrated, freeze-dried, atomized, concentrated, and combined with a virgin girl's menstrual fluid, a child's snot, a whale's sperm, and the sweat from a sock, this lichen confers the hardness of steel to your pubic muscles, increases testicle size to an average volume of 57.3 cubic centimeters, and brings in its wake, with its apocalyptic, I repeat, apocalyptic results, the exalted, frenetic, overwhelmed, and obedient surrender of women. With Ejacula, my dear friend, you'll transport an authentic tank trailer in your pants."

Carlos, in his underpants, pulled a tube from his coat pocket and held it up like a bullfighter, to thundering applause, while the Gypsy-like girl, seated on the ground, reached a pleading hand toward the Ejacula Cream.

"Even if he begged me on his knees for a divorce," the youngest sister told their mother while carefully wiping her face with a tissue so as not to ruin her eye makeup, "I would never so much as discuss it on account of the girls: I don't want them to end up like Rui's kids."

"Ladies and gentlemen, girls and boys, illustrious guests, distinguished audience," the dwarf shouted with tragic twists in his voice as the spotlights crisscrossed the dome of the tent and Ravel's *Bolero* fiercely pursued its implacable march, pushed along by the broom-wielding maestro, whose toupee was slowly slipping down the nape of his neck, uncovering his perspiring baldness with its several strands of white hair flut-

257

tering at random, "we have the honor of announcing that the remarkable Rui S. will proceed, in just a few short moments, to the historic consummation of his courageous act. For the first time in Portugal, in a strictly untelevised performance brought to you by our gracious sponsors, a performer will sacrifice himself before your eyes, thereby providing you with a few moments of pleasant distraction from your daily concerns, headaches, and anxieties."

The taxi returned, going in the other direction, toward Aveiro, and the sputtering sound of the motor seemed to be entangled in the morning humidity like the groans of a castaway washed ashore and wrapped up with the questions, exclamations, hypotheses, and sighs of curious onlookers. He thought, How many hours before you reach Lisbon? He thought, What will your parents say when you walk through the door? He imagined her mother's tears and questions, her father's perplexed, bovine silence, the three of them eating dinner while the TV newscaster looks up from his reading to stare at them with the moribund eyes of Our Lord of the Passion; he imagined the retired uncle—who always showed up after meals to sit at the far end of the table and drink his widower's brandy in small sips—appearing on the threshold, confused, loosening his tie with a finger ("What happened; what's going on; whose suitcases are those?"), hesitating before entering, before sitting down, before talking, before pulling the deck of cards from his pocket to play his everlasting solitaire, wetting a thumb with the tip of his tongue to deal the cards out onto the table.

"To be a ticket collector for the streetcars," he stated proudly, standing up straight, almost on tiptoe in his little suede shoes, "was a big responsibility in my day."

In spite of the relentlessly blinding spotlight (perhaps a ray of sun had penetrated the fog to graze his face with its sad and dusty light), he could distinguish him—insignificant, humble, shy, caught by surprise in his huge overcoat full of buckles and playing cards—swaying next to the more modest circus employees, the ones that set up the fences for the tiger act, put the net in place for the trapeze artists, and rolled out the splintered red-and-white platforms for the lions; and he thought, Funny how I always got along with you, old fellow; he thought, One Sunday when you were sick I visited you at your house, a minuscule entrance, toy-sized rooms with a few pieces of furniture, covered by newspapers, blankets, or sheets, a narrow stairway that led upstairs to you, pale, gaunt, and unshaven, in a collapsed Tom Thumb bed, with the nightstand full of bottles of syrup, which hid the picture of a scowling, solemn, ugly woman rolling her bugging eyes around the room. The sound of a broken toilet assailed us incessantly and made the Michelin wall calendar tremble on its tack. Grime speckled the window curtains, behind which emerged the neighboring buildings, wavy and unfocused, as if a mysterious wind were blowing against façades made of paper. There was an old magazine lying open on the bed, a badly nicked sofa in one corner, its back protected by a diamond-shaped doily yellowed with age, and an anti-insect strip tied to the ceiling light by a string. I sat on the edge of the mattress (What skinny hands you've got, Uncle, I thought; what fragile, lizardlike wrists—how is it you can get this body to stand up?), and an indefinable house odor—a composite of many hard-to-distinguish odors—hovered in the room and invaded his nostrils nauseatingly; the old man's bones stretched the skin of his face so that it resembled the countenance of the dead, pointy and taut as if listening to inaudible sounds of shadows; he pulled a thermometer out of his armpit, held it up to his nose to decipher the silvery column, announced "One hundred and four" in his weak crow's voice, and the screeching sea gulls came closer and closer; he heard their swiftly beating wings; he smelled their feathers' salty aroma; and an image of the ocean would now and then loom behind his eyelids. "To be a ticket collector for the streetcars," mumbled the widower, "is a complicated task, you know." He found himself next to the well, under the fig tree, with the unfocused forest oscillating in the distance; the maestro's fallen mop of hair splattered like a jellyfish on the platform, his broom whirled in a desperate frenzy, the musicians raged like flames around their crazed instruments, and the blind man's cane touched his knee. "Is that you, sport?" the parrot voice inquired, dissolving into the wet mass of the lagoon morning; he peered inside the well, leaning over its crumbling rim, and saw no water at the bottom, only a spot of mud gleaming among tufts of grass and pieces of rock; his father appeared on his left, smelling of cologne and deodorant, and pointing to the carpet of brush, rotten fruits, pebbles, and dried turds that covered the ground, he asked, "Did you notice the birds?" As he grabbed the handle of the knife he noticed that his mother, his sisters, Filipa, Carlos, the obstetrician, Marilia, Sr. Esperança, the blind man, and the widower uncle were all pinned to the sheets of pasteboard, their arms spread wide and their eyes beady with fear; now and again the dry eucalyptus leaves blew a secret, multiple, indistinct set of phrases in his direction; he saw the nasty desk clerk from the inn, his university colleagues, his mocking students, the midwife's suspicious frown. "Silence, please," the dwarf howled, to no avail; the audience pushed and shoved to get a better look; the spotlights were all on and whirling helter-skelter around the ring, the stands, the balcony, the ceiling, highlighting and forgetting countless objects and faces, trapeze bars, cables, ropes, poles, and beams; his father smoothed his hair against his temples and handed him the paper knife. "I'm going to help you grasp the birds," he said. "I'm going to help you understand them." The cloth horse-suit worn by two cousins started galloping home; he saw himself on a cardboard sheet, labeled and numbered, the fuzz on his breast, his beak, his claws, his eyes wide with terror, the unfurled wings of his arms; I leaned over myself, curious, and the sea gulls began their shrill scream in the walls of my skull, the eucalyptuses swayed, the first flock of sparrows flew up in disorder, out of the orchard and into the woods. "Cut this one's tummy," my father instructed, pointing with his finger. "Cut this one's tummy so that I can explain it to you." He still opened his eyes, still tried, with all his might, to get up from the sand, to rise in the saturated air and join himself to the sea gulls that circled around his supine body, but the knife, the needle, the knife pinned him down to his sheet of paper, and as his eyes began emptying and his ears stopped hearing the audience's wild clapping, he was able to make out, beyond the resplendent circus lights, on the far side of the lagoon, the outline of the city, which slowly shrank until it had vanished completely in the colorless fog of the morning.